Aimellina Daughter of Oomara stood on the side and watched, her hands curled into fists. The rhythm of the drums pounded through her body like a fever. Dancers leaped and spun in front of her, their ebony braids flying. They were her friends, her age mates. Now they were all to ride to glory.

All except her.

"The *enaree* made a prophecy the night you were born," Aimellina's mother had said when she forbade her to ride with the others. "The *enaree* said you would live, but die young and far from your own tent."

Aimellina went to find the *enaree* in his tent. Her heart beat unaccountably fast as she waited for his permission to enter.

"I knew that some day you would come to me, Aimellina." The *enaree* gestured her to sit. "You are grown into a fine strong archer, just as I foresaw."

"Ar-Dethien-Gelon marches on Azkhantia with his army and my mother has forbidden me to ride in our defense!" Aimellina burst out. "All because she fears your prophecy. Surely in all your knowledge, with all your powers, you can give me something that will set my mother's heart at ease."

For a long moment, the *enaree* sat silent. Finally he said, "And that is all you wish? Your mother's blessing, not the protection of your own life?"

Aimellina's heart shivered. Then, like all brash young things, she shook it off with a proud toss of her head. "I want to ride, to fight, to serve my people. To win glory. The rest is in the hands of the gods."

SWORD AND SORCERESS XIII

AN ANTHOLOGY
OF HEROIC FANTASY

Edited by
Marion Zimmer Bradley

DAW BOOKS, INC.
DONALD A. WOLLHEIM, FOUNDER
375 Hudson Street, New York, NY 10014

ELIZABETH R. WOLLHEIM
SHEILA E. GILBERT
PUBLISHERS

CONTENTS

Contents

INTRODUCTION

Now that there have been thirteen of these collections, I have more trouble in choosing a final lineup. Many of my writers are now working on their own writing or even editing; Mercedes Lackey, Diana L. Paxson, Jennifer Roberson, and many others are now—after thirteen years—well established as writers on their own. Some of them still send me something every year, but many are now too busy with their own work to write for me. I've been doing editing long enough that a sale either to *Sword and Sorceress* or *Marion Zimmer Bradley's Fantasy Magazine* can, as many people now know, serve as a stepping stone to a career. And that's probably what some of you want. Note: if you want to send me a story, *first* send a #10 SASE (Self-Addressed Stamped Envelope) to me at PO Box 72, Berkeley CA 94701. Do *not* submit anything to me until you have read my guidelines.

In some ways an editor is like a fifth grade teacher. The rest of the class goes ahead into sixth grade. The editor doesn't; she does the same job over and over.

By now I get so many good stories that I could select my writers on their previous record—but that way I'd never discover any new writers. (This year I turned down a story by my own secretary, who has been in every Darkover anthology, five volumes of *Sword and Sorceress,* and both volumes of *The Best Of Marion Zimmer Bradley's Fantasy Magazine.* She even agreed with my decision and is still speaking to me.) And new writers are my justification for reading the whole sorry slush pile all the way through every year.

See you next year, I hope.

PATIENCE

by Jo Clayton

I chose Jo Clayton's *Patience* to begin the collection because not only did I find it powerful and well-written, but it also embodied what seems to be one of the "themes" this year: the shapeshifter, and the dream quest. The stories in this collection that are based around these themes—and I'm not saying *all* of them are—mostly use only one or the other, but Jo managed to use both and pull it off quite nicely at the same time.

Jo Clayton began as a farmer's daughter, born out of Depression and Dustbowl, reared on a sandhill farm near the San Andreas fault. That's my generation, too. I too came from a barren New England farm to become an editor and writer.

Jo was a teacher in Los Angeles and New Orleans urban schools, then took up the writing life, which she calls "quite as precarious as living perched on a major fault." At present she has sold 32 books and 22 short stories and is working on a trilogy for Tor books.

Patience squatted by the trail and inspected the hoof marks cut deep into the drying mud. She was a small fierce woman who was misnamed in the womb by a mother eternally hopeful and eternally disappointed by life. Mule—as in stubborn as—would have been a better name, though even her stubbornness was wearing thin on this long and frustrating trek.

Two years ago the man who rode that horse had killed her father and her brothers, had snuffed their lives as casually as another would blow out candles, had burned her homeplace to the ground and ridden off without a backward look. She didn't know why he did this, though she supposed her father had tried to cheat him in some way. She'd long ago resigned herself to the idea that her father was not a nice man and her brothers were very much like him. Nonetheless they had a right to their lives and they *were* her only blood kin. She'd been following the killer for most of those two years, painstakingly tracking him through half a dozen changes in his mounts, slowed over and over again by the bad luck he'd strewn behind him like caltrops to catch her feet. Last night's rainstorm was just another irritation to add to a long list. A long, long list.

"Maybe our luck is changing, Henry."

The mule whuffed when he heard his name.

"Could have missed this trail easy enough, but here it is, like he wrote an invitation summoning us."

He'd come along this track after the storm, when the mud had gone to gel but before it was too dry to yield such deep, clear impressions. Eight hours ahead of her. At least. She grunted her weary body back onto her feet and walked round to the mule's side.

"Henry old son, if he wriggles free again, I am going to stand there and scream for one full hour." She pulled the tether loose and hauled herself into the saddle. "We've got some daylight left. Might as well try to shave away some of that lead." She tapped his side and the mule started walking. He was a tall, lanky creature, uglier than an inquisitor's soul, with a movement that looked like nothing on earth, but was surprisingly comfortable; he could keep going for hours at a stretch and he thrived on thorns and browse and the occasional mouthful of grass. Patience adored him. Most other creatures, especially the human kind, she eyed with antipathy and distrust, but Henry she simply loved.

She was short and plump with long black hair she wore in twin braids. She had a fondness for beads carved from wood and stone—carved them herself, using the small, precise motions of her fingers as a kind of meditation. She wore a number of those strings about her neck along with a round silver mirror on a leather thong.

That was her skrying mirror. Once and only once she'd used it to search for the killer. He'd looked back at her, black eyes filled with contempt and threat. A moment later a mountain fell on her, or at least a part of it. The slide spooked Henry into running at a speed he'd never achieved before.

After they won clear of the bounding boulders and flying branches, both she and Henry nearly drowned fording a stream that cut across the killer's trail. Then Henry threw a shoe. She had to spend a week finding a farrier to get the shoe replaced, and it cost her coin she didn't have to spare. Then the supper she ate at an inn turned on her; she spent three days spewing and emerged from the ordeal weak and shaky as an octogenarian with palsy.

The whole two years had been like that, but she was still on his trail and no matter what happened or didn't, she wouldn't quit. Even if he finally set up an ambush and managed to kill her, her ghost would haunt him till he was the sorriest man alive.

The path led out of the foothills and onto the flat grassland beyond where it joined a road that followed the curves of a river. There was one last recognizable track in the dried mud on the shoulder, but the road itself was alkali dirt where all marks blew away in a fine dust that got on everything, powdered her hair, made a mud mask of her face and whitened the leaves of the high hedges that marched along both sides of the road.

Henry hated the dust. He snuffled and snorted, shook his head, and whickered a protest every few strides.

She passed a gap in the lefthand hedge and a moment later heard the sound of hooves behind her. When she looked back, she saw three men on shaggy buckskins coming along the road. She touched her prayerbeads and kept her ears pricked for any change in the sounds they made.

She didn't know this country or these people, but Kemook had taught her how to shape her wariness of strangers into a pattern of controlled caution. "Ek'che'ro'a ko'in'ta," she whispered under her breath, the words of her teacher's hometongue slipping softly from her throat, the cascade of the clicks like the clacking of a ratchet that wound up the summoning spell.

From the time she followed Sister Kemook out of her mother's sickroom and pestered the Okua into taking her as apprentice, it seemed easier to use Okuat to make spells and the songs she needed to guide her prowling of the Dream Lands—and somehow more apt, as if her own ordinary speech hadn't enough connection to such Places.

"Ek'che'ro'a ko'in'ta, aTu'lik. Na'ko'inga a, sa'ahti'ga," she whispered to her Guide and her Guest. *Fly before me, King Loon. O White Bear, be a cloak to me with your strength and your wisdom.*

The men didn't try to catch up with her or speak to her, just rode along as if they were simply on the road by chance—which she didn't believe for one moment.

When she turned a curve in the road, three more men sat their mounts, waiting for her.

She brought Henry to a stop and waited for someone to say or do something. White Bear was heavy on her shoulders, his claws pricking her and King Loon soared overhead, the cries that brought madness waiting in his long black throat. If they took her for an easy target, well, let them discover their mistake.

One of the men kneed his horse forward, stopping when his mount was nose to nose with Henry. He was a wiry ancient with skin burnt dark by the sun, his face shaped by much squinting against the wind into a mask of wrinkles. "You know the Dream Road," he said. He was a man accustomed to undisputed authority and when she didn't answer the implied question, he raised his voice and shouted the words at her.

Annoyed, she let King Loon loose one of his lesser cries as the only answer she'd make to demands.

The cry echoed over the land and even the leaves of the thorn hedges shuddered as the sound touched them. The men went white and shaking, the horses began plunging and trying to run.

When the angry old man had sorted out the confusion, Patience said mildly, "If you have something to say to me, say it, then get out of my way."

13

His mouth went tight and his eyes mean, but there was too much need in him to let him give reign to his temper. "Yesterday a man came to my house. He set his hand on my grandson and the soul went out of the boy as if he'd tumped him on the head. He looked at me, and he said, 'there's a Dream Walker following me. Catch her, and she'll get this soul back from where I sent it.' Is it you he was talking about?"

I am going to scream, she thought. *He's done it to me again.* With a whispered chant and a thank-blessing, she dismissed White Bear and King Loon. "Might be," she said aloud. "Take me to the boy."

Patience knew what had been done as soon as she got a good look at the boy, but she wasn't about to announce her discovery. The ignorant expected a show from the Walkers of the Dream Lands, having no idea of the simplicity of knowing and no understanding of the years of sweat and pain it took to achieve that simplicity. *Make it look hard,* Sister Kemook said. *Make them work and pay good coin for what they want. Then they'll respect you for all the wrong reasons, and they'll believe what you tell them.*

She turned to the old man. "I want a bowl of water that has been fresh lifted from your well. Have one of your women fetch it, not a man. And I will need seven candles that have not been burned before and a handful of your best flour. And after I've finished the looking, I want a pot of tea and some bread and cheese. I'll be hungry."

He wanted to chew her up and spit her out, but he simply swung around and stalked from the room.

* * *

Chanting one of Sister Kemook's meditation songs, Patience set the basin with the water on the barely moving chest of the unconscious boy, used the flour to write glyphs on the floor, set the candles in the knotted, tangled wordsigns, and lit the wicks. Shifting the chant to her deepest notes, she began an intricate stomp dance about the bed, shaking strings of prayerbeads so they clicked rhythmically in time to the scuff of her bare feet.

When at last she bent over the basin, she pressed her lips together in anger at the cold black eyes looking back at her. Laughing at her. Saying without words he thought she was a hoaxer with no more power than a spent match. She flicked the water with her fingertips to dismiss the image, then she straightened and stepped beyond the circle of candles to stand facing the old man.

"What is the boy's name? I don't ask his truename, only his use name."

"Angven."

"This is not his usual sleeping room."

"No. I brought him here so his mother could tend him without exposing herself to men's eyes."

"He sleeps by himself?"

"Yes."

"His door can be barred?"

"Yes."

"While I'm eating, have him taken there, wash his body, and put him into a clean white shirt. I have seen where his soul is and I will call it back, but this is a hard and dangerous thing. Once I am inside that room, put a guard on the door and let no one in. If I am not out within three days, that means your grandson and I are dead. If I am disturbed, it could mean that our

15

souls will be forever exiled and our bodies will certainly die and rot. Do you hear me?"

"Yes."

"Do you understand what I'm saying?"

"Yes."

"Then bring me my food and let the rest be done."

Patience walked around the small room, drawing in lungfuls of the air, sniffing at the assorted odors that were part of the body's exuviae. She shook the shutters to make sure they were firmly shut, pushed a wad of kerchief into the latchstring's hole, then she crossed to the boy.

Angven lay with his hands crossed above his heart, his eyes closed, his breathing shallow and very slow. She touched a finger to the center of his forehead, clicked her tongue. He was winding down toward death, the thread connecting body to soul drawing finer and finer. Sometime in the night it could break, and then the breathing would stop altogether.

"But we're not going to let that happen, are we." She bent down and licked his face, slowly, thoughtfully, lips, eyelids, cheeks and brow. Tasting him. When she was done, she straightened, said, "There. I know you, boy."

After she stripped off her clothing, folded everything neatly, and set the boots she'd carried here beside the pile, she undid her braids and combed out her hair until there was not a knot in all that silky black length. Then she settled herself on the oval braided rug, crossed her short legs, and rested her hands palm up on her knees, a string of her carved prayerbeads hooked over her thumbs. The food she'd eaten and the thick, sweet tea were heavy in her stomach. Ordinarily she would have fasted before a spirit journey, but she was too depleted by the long chase to take a chance on her body burning itself out.

She dipped and twisted her thumbs. The cool smooth wood of the beads slipped over her hands, the beads clicking softly as they moved. Her breathing slowed. She watched it, in out in out, and felt the burn behind the navel.

Felt the heat expanding through her.

Felt the taste of the boy strong on her tongue, the smell of him in her nostrils.

Then she floated in a place of no-sound, no-light, no-sensation.

The darkness grayed and she saw a silver thread fine as spidersilk.

She drifted along this line until it passed out of the place of nothing and into a black and white and gray world with a silver bowl of a sky, lit by a huge full moon.

The thread turned invisible, but she felt its presence like a smell, the boy's smell, and she followed it until she came to a bow-legged shoat rooting in the mud of a riverbank.

When he saw her, the young boar squealed a threat and rocked back and forth on his stubby legs, swinging his long snout with the two curved tusks. The tusks were small yet, but they could still rip and tear the substance of her spirit body.

In the shadow of black leaves and silver gray trunks, she squatted, motionless and nonthreatening, on a patch of short black grass and pondered what she saw.

The shoat went back to shoving his snout through the mud and eating the tubers and roots he dug up. He was much at home here and seemed to have forgotten that he was the soul of a boy. "You aren't going to want to go back, are you," she murmured. "Well, when I have your Name, the choice will be mine, not yours."

She rose from her tussock of grass, waded into the clear water of the steam, and began collecting the shiniest of the pebbles that layered its bed. The water was ice melt, but though her flesh body back in the boy's bedroom would be shuddering from the cold, her soul body did not feel it. It was one of the dangers in visiting these worlds where lost souls walked that she could bring her flesh body near to death and not even know it.

The shoat lifted his head now and then to watch her as she went in and out of the water, making piles of the pebbles as she collected them. He was curious about what she was doing, but not yet worried by it.

When she decided she had a sufficiency, she smoothed a patch of the mud and began pressing the shiny pebbles into it, spelling out Angven in Dream runes. It didn't matter that the boy couldn't read them, his soul would know what they were.

The name completed, she straightened and sat on her heels contemplating him, whisper-singing the charm that would draw the Name to her.

A pebble stirred.

Clicking faintly it rolled down the pile and settled on the mud. One by one, the remaining pebbles rolled and settled, writing a new name, the Name of Angven's soul.

She looked at it when it was done and wasn't surprised to see the runes B A Y D, for that word in Dreamspeak meant Boar. It was sometimes true that the shape of the soul matched its Name—only sometimes, though, and guessing was as much a peril here as exhausting the body.

She took a pebble from each word and held them in her fisted left hand, shook them so they clacked against each other, building a rhythm that caught the ears of the shoat. When she saw the little squinty eyes staring at her, she began to chant, "Angven Bayd Angven Bayd." Over and over she sang the words, fitting the syllables into the clicks and clacks.

Step by step she drew the shoat to her. Shaking his head, pawing at the mud, squealing with fear and reluctance, step by step he came until he stood before her.

She put her hand on his snout, fitting her fingers between the curve of his tusks. "Bayd," she said and smiled as his eyes glazed over and his head bent to her. He was tamed and would answer to her for the rest of his life should she desire that.

She bent over him and began smelling him and touching him with her tongue until she tasted a faint, bitter tang between his ears. She rubbed her face against the spot, sniffed the smell deep inside her, licked and licked at the place until she'd got all trace of it off the little boar.

Leaving the shoat sleep-spelled on the mud, she stood and opened her mouth wide, letting the tip of her tongue quiver between her lips. The tang of the killer was faint but there, riding the breeze that flowed past her face. She nodded with satisfaction. *If I can't turn your little trap back on you, Killer, may Kemook switch my tail with fine birch rods.*

There was the faintest of sounds, felt rather than heard, and a sudden intensification of the killer stench.

She flung herself to her left, falling to her knees

with one arm curved over her head, the other stretched out as far as she could reach. The spell net settled over her head and one shoulder, held off her face by the curled arm. She scrambled to her feet, swung her free arm around, and caught hold of the net's tether, a silver filament no thicker than a hair, hanging in a wide curve from the silver sky.

"O'ko'mi'chuk!" she cried and her soul-form was heavy as the world itself, her arm unyielding and strong as steel. She jerked hard at the tether.

And felt a give. She'd pulled him off balance.

She hauled on the tether once again and his soul popped through into the Dream Land. For the smallest of instants she saw a bloodbat fluttering against the silver sky like a fragment of burnt paper caught by the wind. It was gone before she got more than a fleeting glimpse, the charred scrap exploding into a black jaguar leaping at her, eyes a hot yellow shocking in this achromatic land.

His claws raked the arm she whipped down to protect her throat, but her soul stuff was too dense to wound and when his body slammed into her, he rebounded from her heaviness. She had time to call the White Bear into her before the jaguar found his feet and came at her again, his furious yowl echoing across the Land.

Her Guest ripped away the net as if it were rotten thread and a swipe of his powerful forearm sent the spirit cat tumbling end over end.

The jaguar landed hard and crouched on the mud, shaking his head, the color leached from his eyes until they were so pale a gray he looked blind. As Patience and the White Bear took a step toward him, he snarled and started to fade.

Patience flowed out of her Guest. "No, you don't. Not again. Symuddu! Stay!" She was taking a chance in a place where a wrong choice could kill, hoping that first fleeting shape as the killer's soul tumbled into the Dream Land had betrayed his Name. Bloodbat. Symuddu in Dream Speak. "Symuddu, by your Name I nail you here."

She relaxed as he grew solid again. The guess was good. Drawing a tether line from herself, she spun a noose in the end, flicked it out, and dropped it over his head.

His tail switched back and forth and as he sucked strength from his flesh body, yellow bled back into his eyes. His spirit body grew thicker and more massive as he pumped himself up so he could use the strength he was summoning to break the tether and fight the Name-bond, attack her once again, and turn his fumble into victory.

She laughed at him. "O Symuddu, you've been slippery prey, but you're a fool withall. Betraying your Name like that. T'k, when I was just a yearling apprentice, my teacher would have whomped my behind if I'd done something so silly."

He snarled as she walked to him, but the rage went out of his eyes as she set a hand on his brow. "Mine, Symuddu."

He sank down, his head resting on her feet.

"Yes. You're mine now and you're going to pay for killing my kin." She grimaced. "Before I try figuring out how—and not with your life, little man, that's too easy—there's a bit of business to be finished. On your feet and walk beside me over to that pigbaby. That's it. Nice kitty." She felt his anger and laughed aloud, then got her arm around the shoat and lifted him onto her hip.

Once the boysoul's split hooves left the gray mud, he was light as smoke and as hard to hold onto, but she managed. She wound Symuddu's tether about her free wrist as an extra precaution and chanted herself back to Angven's bedroom.

When she woke from her seeker trance, a lanky, naked man lay on the rug beside her and a pig-shaped shimmer hung over the body of the sleeping boy. "Well!" she said to the shimmer. "Get you home. Now!"

There was a squeal of protest that did not sound here but in the Dream Land, then the pigshape melted into the boy's body.

As Angven's eyes opened, Patience dropped the prayerbeads around her neck, got to her feet, and without hurry put on her leather trousers, then shrugged herself into her shirt. After she'd pulled on her boots, she looked down at the naked man, raised her brows, then snapped her fingers.

A large black mastiff got to his feet and stood tongue out and panting, waiting for her to tell him what to do.

Angven was sitting up on the bed, his mouth hanging open as he watched all this. She walked over to him.

His eyes widened and he flinched away as she reached out to touch him.

"Don't be more of an idiot than you have to. I'm not going to hurt you." She flattened her hand across his brow, nodded with satisfaction. "Home and whole. Good enough. Stick out your tongue."

She touched it with the tip of her forefinger. "You won't speak of anything you've seen. If you try, the words will clog in your throat. You can put your tongue away and shut your mouth now. That's the boy. Get off the bed and stand up. You'll follow me out, then you'll tell your grandfather that you're feeling good, though you had strange dreams."

She left the house on Henry the mule with a supply of flour and jerked meat in her saddlebags and five pieces of silver in her pouch. The black mastiff ran at her stirrup, outwardly docile, inwardly plotting escape and revenge. She knew that and it amused her for a while. When she was once more on the alkali road and heading back home, though, her amusement trickled away in a sigh, and she put her mind to the serious business of deciding what his punishment was going to be.

SUN DANCER

by Leslie Ann Miller

Leslie Ann Miller lives in Stillwater, Oklahoma where she works as Safety Training Coordinator for Oklahoma State University. She lives in a small house with an ornery calico manx, walls of bookshelves, a collection of medieval weapons, and trumpet vines creeping in through the window from the overgrown rose garden beyond. In this romantic-sounding place, she created this unusually intense and vivid story.

"Stand up straight!" the trader growled, rattling the chain around Althea's neck and poking her in the ribs with his scimitar. The blade cut the skin on her bony ribs, but she did not flinch from the pain, nor did she look at the crowd of faces leering up at her naked body. He did not care that he damaged his merchandise. Nobody would buy her, she knew. Nobody wanted a half-starved slave girl scarred as badly as she was scarred, punished by her former owner for no other reason than he delighted in her pain. Nobody would waste their precious gold on a scrawny, sick desert daughter who was unfit for work. Nobody

24

would buy her, and so she would be killed, slaughtered on the seller's block like a goat, not worth the effort to keep alive.

But the thought of dying did not frighten Althea anymore. She would welcome Death with open arms and go happily to rejoin her family, butchered by enemies nearly four years ago.

"Two silver." The sound of a woman's voice from the back of the crowd made Althea's heart stop.

"Two silver?" the trader repeated incredulously. "For this piece of filth?" He kicked Althea in the back of the knees for emphasis, and she collapsed onto the oily, bloodstained platform. "You are an emissary from the North, and therefore I tell you this: you waste your money. You will be lucky if this trash still lives in three days' time. Better to bid on one more healthy." He gestured at the line of slaves waiting to be auctioned with the rest of her former master's estate. They were not so scarred, not so thin and sickly. They were not from the desert, and therefore they had not been hated by their master.

"Two silver," the woman repeated angrily.

"Two silver, then," the trader growled, yanking Althea back to her feet by the chain around her neck. Her feet slipped on the slick surface, and the trader cursed as she fell again. "Desert scum," he hissed and kicked her in the ribs, shoving her forward with his booted foot.

The crowd stepped back, surprised and amused, as her body toppled from the five-foot platform into the dust at the feet of her new owner who had pushed through to the front.

"Can you stand?" the woman asked in a thick accent, kneeling beside her.

Althea did not answer. She was past caring, past thinking. Past all things but feeling pain and hunger. Those two she could no longer dance from her mind.

The woman was tall and long-boned with short-cropped, sandy hair. She was dressed like a man in boots, trousers, and mail armor. She even carried a short, straight sword which swung from her red leather belt. She swore under her breath and picked Althea up with strong, wiry arms. She shouldered her as she might a sack of grain and shoved the amused crowd aside as she carried her purchase forward to the overseer of the auction. She shoved two silver coins at the man, who grinned.

"Beware lest she cast a desert spell on you, Emissary. You know the power of the desert devils. She is of their stock." He spat to the side and made the sign to ward off evil.

"Somehow," the woman said acidly before Althea fainted, "I don't think she'll be much of a threat to me."

The unbearable smell of food drew Althea back to the misery of consciousness. But this time her head was lifted and warm broth spooned into her mouth. She thought she must be dreaming ... food, liquid, given to her freely. Perhaps ... perhaps she was dead, but she could not open her eyes for the weight of her eyelids. If she were in the Hall of Dancers, she would dance, and so in her mind she danced the Dance of Sunlight and Joy. The taste of the food was delightful on her tongue, and her stomach no longer ached with the rest of her body.

* * *

The distant music of desert pipes roused her from the darkness. Without opening her eyes, she lay in silent wonder ... wonder, because she was neither too hot nor too cold, neither hungry nor thirsty. Her skin felt clean, and she was certain she was lying on something soft. Even the pain of old bruises seemed muted and dull. She must be dead, why else would she hear the music of her people? And then her eyes flew open, and with the light, the music fled.

"Good morning," her new master said, looking up from where she was sitting cross-legged, packing a saddlebag which was beside her on the floor. "Very timely of you to wake up," she smiled. "We were just talking about you."

Althea's dazed eyes drifted to the large, hulking man standing in the doorway to the small room. She'd never seen a man like him before. He was big as a mountain, with a bushy, brown-red beard and piercing green eyes. He, too, was dressed like a warrior, but the sword he wore strapped to his shoulder was straight and longer than any sword she'd seen before, nearly as tall as herself, she guessed.

Her master followed her gaze and grinned. "Smile, Trent, you brute. You'll scare her to death glowering like that."

The man smiled on command, revealing a mouth full of clean white teeth. "All smiles aside, Elintina," he said in a deep, booming voice, "we must leave, and quickly. We must reach the coast before Rasharis catches wind of us. We have tarried here too long already."

"I know," her master said, turning back to Althea. "Listen, Trent and I are going home ... back north ... far away from here. They said you're from the desert, and we'd just be taking you farther from your home. We've managed to heal the slave brand on your forehead so it just looks like an ordinary scar now. If I gave you some gold or silver, do you think you could get back to your people on your own?"

Althea stared at her, and knew she stared, and knew that she would be beaten for staring, but could not help herself. She thought, surely the woman did not mean what she said, surely she misunderstood because of the strange accent. It was not possible that she could say what she thought she said.

"Perhaps she does not understand the common tongue," the man suggested.

"Maybe her brain has been addled by abuse," her master said, then sighed heavily. "What do I do, Trent?"

"You bought her," he said. "It would be cruel to leave her here by herself, as helpless as she is. When you offer help, you take responsibility for the consequences, just as I did with you so many years ago."

Her master smiled. "I hope she will not be as troublesome to me as I was to you."

"You were never troublesome, little page. Just . . . entertaining, sometimes."

Her master made a snorting noise, like a horse, and groped in the leather pouch attached to her red belt, pulling out a handful of coins. "Here," she said. "I offer you a choice. You're free to go and take this money to help you on your way, or you can come with Trent and me. I can't guarantee your safety if you come with us, and it won't be an easy journey. But we'll make sure you get food to eat and, with any luck, water to drink. Do you understand what I'm saying?"

Althea did, but thought she must not. Surely they

knew that they could not release her? She was a slave, now and forever. It was a crime to remove the slave brand. They could be severely punished for doing such a thing, and she would be killed. Even if they turned her loose, and she weren't caught immediately, what would she do in a city where all her kind were hated and feared? Her sand-colored eyes and dark brown skin told any who saw her who and what she was, and she was far too weak to Dance her way to freedom. Even if she could escape the city, she was not sure she could find her people. They drifted the sands at random, avoiding all contact with outsiders. And if she did by chance find them? Her family was all dead, murdered, and she was too old to continue training as a Dancer. Plus, her father's enemies were undoubtedly still alive. If she returned, they'd make sure she did not live for long. No, her people were lost to her, now and forever.

Freedom offered nothing to her but uncertainty and probable death. Despite the beatings, humiliation, and pain, she'd never tried to escape her old master for that reason. And so long as she could Dance in her mind, nothing they did to her body would matter. She closed her eyes and ignored the outstretched coins.

"Well," her master said slowly, "I guess you'll come with us, then."

They traveled northeast through sparse grasslands. She shared her master's horse, an unthinkable thing, but caused, no doubt, by the necessity of speed. Althea reveled in the sun on her face and arms, and almost wished she had not been given the large white tunic to wear. She felt her strength returning with every minute of delicious sunshine. She'd spent most of the past four years locked in her former master's palace. They knew the children of the desert drew their life from the sun and therefore kept her from it.

"She stares at the sun unblinking," the man called Trent remarked.

"Perhaps that is one reason why the Estari fear her people so much."

"That and other things, I'd guess."

"Do you honestly believe those stories about desert curses and disappearing castles?"

Trent shrugged. "I can Speak to the stones . . . why not? There is more between the realm of Gods and this Earth than you and I will ever understand, little page."

Her master chuckled. "That is certainly true. The auctioneer told me to beware of her, like she would be some threat. Gods above, it's not like she has the strength to stand, much less hurt me somehow, all skin and bones that she is. My armor weighs more than she does."

"Mistress Serenia was a tiny woman, and yet she went to face the horror of Three Crossings," Trent said. "Her Voice could call down a mountain. Size is irrelevant to power, Elintina."

"Are you saying I should be afraid?"

"I'm saying you should be cautious with all unknowns. You know nothing about this girl. When she regains her strength, who knows what she could do to you?"

"Trent! Lord's piss and Lady's tears! She's just a child! All I have to do is look at her and she flinches."

Althea could feel Trent's piercing green gaze upon her as she stared up at the sun, filling her mind with light after so many years of darkness.

"She has strength or she would have died before

now," he said. "And for whatever reasons, the Estari fear her people. It would be foolish to dismiss their fears without consideration. Rasharis, as I recall, has the same skin and queer eyes. And he is someone I fear with good reason."

Althea ignored their talk. Let them believe what they would about her. She knew she was no threat to them. How could she be? She was a slave . . . a slave, but in her mind she spun with the sun in the wide blue sky, and forgot about the northern barbarians who discussed her as they might a stranger's horse.

"You know," her master said to her one night as they sat beneath the stars, "I would like to call you by your name. Name?" She pointed at her chest. "My name is Elintina. Elintina." She pointed at Althea. "Your name is?"

Althea looked at her bare feet as she sat cross-legged on the sandy ground. Slaves were given names by their masters, and besides, she would never tell her real name. Names had power, and she would not give anyone that power over herself.

"Still don't understand, eh?" her master sighed, and stretched out her long legs, her knee-high black boots flattening a clump of sandgrass.

"I think she understands," Trent said. "She just chooses not to speak."

"Maybe she cannot. She hasn't made a noise yet. Not even when that slaver cut her side with his sword and kicked her off the platform."

"Hmmmm. Could be. But she certainly isn't addled. She understands what we're saying well enough, don't you, girl?"

Althea continued looking at her dirty toes. Let them

think what they would. She would obey their commands to avoid a beating, but so far they had not told her to do anything. Of course, she was still too weak to do much. Her master still had to help hold her on the horse, and she knew they were saving her punishment for when she was stronger.

"Look at me, girl," he said, and Althea obeyed his command though he was not her master. She feared him for his size. She looked at him, but forced herself not to see him. Instead, she saw the pattern of the Star Dance in her mind, and danced it in the black sky behind his head. "No," he said. "Look at me, not through me. Look at my eyes."

Reluctantly, she let go the dance, and forced herself to meet his sharp green stare.

"Good," he said. "Now, see the truth in my eyes when I tell you these words. We mean you no harm. We will not hurt you. You are free to leave if you so desire. We hold no slaves. Indeed, our God forbids us from doing so."

He said the words, and his eyes flickered not. Althea heard his spoken words. But she also heard his unspoken: We mean you no harm, unless you disobey. We will not hurt you, so long as you work well. You are free to leave, because we know you will not. Our God forbids us from holding slaves, but you will be one to us anyway, because you have no choice. There was no reason for them to have helped her live if they stood to gain nothing from her, and all she had to offer was her body and her labor. Those, they could have. But they would never touch her soul, no matter how often they ordered her to look into their foreign eyes.

He shook his head. "Still don't believe me, eh?" He

glanced at his companion. "She's a tougher nut to crack than you were, little page."

Her master grinned. "I didn't believe you either, until you saved my life from those bandits outside Lonport." She ruffled Althea's hair, and Althea winced at the contact. Her master did not seem to notice for she continued talking, undisturbed, speaking to her directly. "Trent saved my sister and me from the squares of Lonport. I wasn't a slave, but I was a half-starved canal brat, and none too trusting of strangers ... or anyone for that matter. He saved me, and I eventually learned to trust him. Maybe someday you'll learn to trust me, too. I hope so, anyway ..." she trailed off, looking at Althea with a frown.

Althea stared at her feet. Foreigners. Barbarians. She tried hard not to think of the stories of the icy, wet north that the older dancers used to tell to frighten the younger girls. Perhaps their God forbid slavery. But the stories often spoke of human sacrifice. Perhaps that was what they wanted her for: a living sacrifice to one of their hideous Gods. No. She would not think of that. It didn't matter anyway. She stared at her feet and danced a spinning pattern in her mind.

The cat had been following them all day, and Althea became alarmed when Trent and her master began looking for a place to camp that evening. She was certain they were unaware of being hunted. If so, they would not have been looking for trees and rocks to provide shelter, shelter that would hide the approach of the cat when it attacked that night. Althea knew the cat smelled the blood of Trent's horse which had cut its leg that morning, and if it were like the great desert cats, it had no fear of humans. Their mere presence would not frighten it away. The northerners would undoubtedly kill the cat, and Althea could not bear the thought of that.

"You should not stop here," she said awkwardly when they finally found a spot to their satisfaction and Trent prepared to dismount. She had learned the language at her former master's palace, but she had not been allowed to use it often. Only rarely had she been allowed to speak at all.

He froze, staring at her though she avoided looking at him, then his face broke into a grin. "So you can speak after all." He looked around. "Why should we not stop here? This is the best campsite we've found in days!"

Althea swallowed, fearing she would anger them. If they thought she was lying, they would beat her. "There is cat which follows us," she said. "It will use the rocks to hide its approach. It will attack tonight if we stay."

"A cat?" her master repeated. "I haven't seen any cat. How do you know?"

Althea didn't answer. How could she explain if the northerners were so blind?

Trent stroked his beard thoughtfully. "Well, if she saw fit to give us warning, perhaps we should take heed. As I recall, there is a small river up ahead. Would the cat follow us across the river?"

Althea looked at her thin fingers tangled in the horse's mane, and shook her head almost imperceptibly.

"Very well," he said, "We'll go on. And thank you for the warning."

Althea shuddered, disturbed because he sounded so sincere.

* * *

Twenty horsemen waited on the plain between them and what the northerners called "the ship anchored in the harbor." Althea had never seen the sea before, but her attention was drawn first to the banner flapping in the wind above the horsemen. The Estari called them "sand pirates." They were outlaws of her own people, traitors and murderers banished from the Halls of Sand. She'd been sold to such pirates by her father's enemies, and they in turn had sold her to the slavers.

"We can't get to the ship," her master said, her voice tight. "Not even tonight. There'll be moon, and there's no cover at all."

"I wasn't anticipating Rasharis beating us here when I made arrangements," Trent said, glancing at Althea. "The delay in the city cost us dearly."

"I'm sorry, Trent," her master said, shoulders slumping. "What would you have done in my place?"

Althea felt both sets of eyes on her.

"Probably the same thing," he finally sighed. "I'm sorry. I shouldn't keep questioning your action."

"The captain can see Rasharis there. Surely he'll realize we can't reach the ship and do something."

"What can he do but wait? If he sails up coast, Rasharis will follow. If he leaves, we are left stranded."

"They could help us fight," her master suggested.

"They were not commissioned to fight Southern Swords," Trent said firmly, running thick fingers through his beard.

"And I don't suppose they'll do so out of the goodness of their hearts, either, eh?"

"Not likely."

"You know, Trent, I really don't know why I keep

following you all the time. It never fails that we wind up in a situation like this. It's a miracle I've survived to reach adulthood."

The big man chuckled. "You follow me because the Lord directs you to, little page. And I pay you well enough, do I not? Besides, you know I need you to keep me out of trouble."

"Ha," said her master without humor. "I drag you into it far more often than not."

"Ha," he repeated. "If you knew what I was like before you tried to pinch my pouch that day ... Well, never mind. We shall have to come up with some ploy to get out of this. Even with my Voice and your natural abilities at sneaking, we shall have a hard time of it tonight, I fear."

"Could you Call the wind to cause a sandstorm?" her master asked thoughtfully.

"Mmmmmm. My voice is better suited to commanding earth and stone," Trent said. "Even if I could summon enough wind for a sandstorm, it might force the captain to pull up anchor and leave the harbor to escape the blowing sand. No, we'll wait for tonight. My Voice is strong enough to stop any weak-willed warriors, and our two swords will have to be worth the rest."

"Those are Rasharis' men, Trent, do you honestly think any of them are weak willed?"

The big man smiled. "Desperation will improve my strength. We will manage, fear not. The Lord and Lady will provide."

Overhead a hawk cried out in the stillness of the sky, and Althea cowered, knowing that it was seeing for the one they called Rasharis. It would not miss them lying against the sandy bank of the hill, looking down at the plain. Rasharis would know they were here, and would know exactly what they did and where they were when darkness fell. Her master and Trent would be slaughtered, and she would be captured again . . . the nightmare relived, only this time she would know that even her worst fears were not so horrible as reality.

Were they anyone but sons of the desert, it would be easy for Althea to dance a pattern to grab the rays of sun to blind them, or shift the light reflected off the sand and grass to mask their presence. But her unpracticed dancing might have little or no effect on her own people. It had been so long since she had danced outside her mind, she did not know if she yet had the strength or skill to succeed.

And if she were successful, what then? She stared at the "ship" floating on the blue expanse of water . . . so much water. She had never dreamed there was so much water in the world, endless miles of it stretching to the very horizon. It was terrifying, the sight of it. And if her master succeeded in getting to the ship, would she not be taken aboard as well? To sail across that undulating expanse of horror to a land so foreign that she could not even picture it in her mind? The stories said that water fell from the sky in the northern lands, and the sun was often hidden. How could she leave her sun and sands behind?

The answer, of course, was simple. She could leave them behind because they held nothing for her but death. She did not know that her new master would be any kinder than her old, but was it not better to opt for the choice which still had possibility for a life less cruel? Certainly, she had not been beaten in nearly seven days. She was fed and given water that she did not even need. And if she were to be sacrificed to some demon God in some foreign temple, they did not, at least, seem determined to make her suffer for it in advance.

Rasharis knew they were there, so she had nothing to lose by starting the dance. It would be easy enough to find out if it would work. And if it did not, at least Trent and her master would not continue under the incorrect assumption that Rasharis did not know that they were there.

She started with her hands, weaving the delicate patterns to capture the sun's light.

"What are you doing?" her master demanded.

Althea ignored her, rolling onto her back so she could expand the flowing designs with her arms. It felt good, so good, to finally let her body meld with the forms she'd practiced in her mind for so many years. Every fiber of her being radiated with energy, light and joy as she soaked up the sun's energy.

"Uh ... Trent! Is she supposed to be glowing like that?!" her master stammered, scooting away from her.

Trent was pushing himself away as well. "I don't know, little page. Perhaps we should try to stop her?"

Suddenly they froze.

"Where'd she go?" her master asked.

"I don't know!"

"Gods above, I don't like this!"

"We'd best get back to the horses," Trent said urgently.

"Wait," Althea breathed, spinning to her feet. She knew her voice would sound like the wind through the grass, but they had to stay closer for her to encompass them with her dance. Her mother could dance an entire hall invisible, then shift it across miles of dunes and sand. But she was not so skilled as her mother, nor so strong, though she felt more certain in her patterns than she had before, perhaps. "Stay with me," she said.

"Did you hear that?!" Trent demanded.

"Aye!" her master said. "She said, 'Stay with me.' But we can't see you!"

Althea glanced toward the pirates as she danced upon the hilltop. They did not seem to see her, either, and her heart soared upward. It was working! "Stand up!" she said as she wove a circle around them, weightless so that her feet left no marks upon the sand, spinning beams of sunlight from her fingers to mask their presence. Spinning.

"I think not!" Trent said, and his voice dripped with a resonance of power.

Was this what they meant by the Voice, Althea wondered? But quickly she refocused her mind on the design she was spinning. Total concentration was necessary to maintain the illusion. It was distracting even to speak.

"Are you threatening us, girl?" Trent asked, and his Voice still hummed with energy.

"Do you wish to get to the water's edge?" Althea asked, her soul singing with power and energy. Her feet completed the pattern of the circle, then started on a new. Overhead, the hawk cried out, noticing their sudden disappearance. Rasharis would be looking for a dancer now, but Althea was confident that he would not find her, nor the ones she circled. She felt strong in the sunlight, stronger than she had as a young girl. She could dance on sunbeams now, so bright and vivid!

Her master stood up, looking down at the raiders with trepidation. "Come on, Trent," she said, drawing her sword. "What have we to lose?"

Trent sighed, climbing heavily to his feet and drew his own huge sword. "Very well, little page, and a glorious day it shall be."

Althea reached up and grabbed a sunbeam, pulling them toward the water. Trent and Elintina followed, towed in a web of brilliance invisible to their own eyes. In a searing blink of an eye they raced across the plain to the water's edge, Althea letting go at the last moment before they plunged into the sea itself. Her hand burned with fire and her mind exploded in agony as the pattern shattered. She collapsed to her knees on the sandy beach, drained, exhausted, and empty.

"What happened?" Trent demanded, blinking like a desert owl caught in daylight.

"Gods above, we're on the beach!" her master said. "Hey ho! Are you all right?" She knelt beside Althea, putting a hand on her shoulder.

For once, Althea did not flinch at the touch, but at that moment, shouts went up from the pirates, and her master stood back up.

"Uh-oh," Trent said. "I think we've been spotted."

"Out of your armor," her master said, standing back up. "We'll swim for it."

"Ha!" Trent said, turning toward the harbor. He cupped his hands. "Yo there! *Lonport Maid!* It is I, Trent Axbreaker," he bellowed, and his Voice carried such power that it hit Althea like a slap, stinging. She had no doubt that it would carry across the water to the ship. "Send a boat to meet us!" he shouted, and Althea saw men scurry on the ship. Trent unbuckled his sword belt and shrugged out of his heavy mail shirt.

The earth rumbled with the sound of approaching horses.

Althea stared at the water in horror. Had her master said "swim?"

Her master had already shrugged out of her mail. She looked at Althea. "I don't suppose you know how to swim?"

Althea swallowed and shook her head.

"Well, don't panic. Any canal brat worth her salt can swim for two, and I won't have a bit of trouble helping you as long as you don't struggle. Understand? No struggling!" She took two steps toward the water. "Come on!" she waved.

When it became apparent that Althea was not going to move for all the sun's gold, her master swept her up into her arms. "Here we go," she said, wading out into the water, Althea clinging to her neck in abject terror. She cried out in fear as her master turned around and plunged backward into the water, supporting Althea with her own body, holding her tightly against her chest.

Althea's senses were filled with cold and wet. Her mind screamed in blind panic at the terror of the water closing over her body. Her master kicked against the waves, and Althea closed her eyes, trying to grasp the pattern of a dance, any dance, it did not matter, anything to keep her from going mad with fear!

"WATER! WAVES FLOW TOWARD THE SHIP!" Trent Commanded as he splashed beside them, and Althea felt a surge of power as a wave lifted up and washed them forward with incredible speed.

"Weeeeee!" her master laughed, and Althea wondered how it could be that she sounded happy. "We'll be out of bowshot before Rasharis reaches the beach!"

"That . . . was . . . the general idea," Trent gurgled,

his head bobbing up and down as he struggled to ride the wave with his massive body.

In minutes they reached the small boat sent out for them from the ship. Strong hands grabbed Althea's shoulders and pulled her up and over the sides, helping her collapse in a puddle at the bottom of the boat. She lay there, unable to move, shaking uncontrollably. Soon her master was pulled inside, then Trent. They babbled in excited voices while Althea shivered, her mind too numb with cold and shock to translate what they were saying. Her seeking eyes found the sun, and she desperately clung to its warmth.

Somebody was shaking her shoulder. A face blocked the sun.

"Hey, are you all right?" her master asked, her wet hair dripping water down her face. "You can move now. It's all right, we escaped."

Althea tried to move her hand and found she could. She struggled to sit up. The other men in the boat watched her curiously, and she avoided their eyes. Her master helped her settle numbly on one of the wooden benches in the gently rocking boat.

Her master noticed her shivering. "I think she's cold," she said, and Althea did not think the concern in her voice was feigned.

"Och!" one of the other men spat. "A good dunking in water this warm never hurt anyone. It be warm as bath water this far south."

"She's from the desert," her master said. "She's probably not used to being wet." She took Althea's hand. "We'll get you dry and warm as soon as we get to the ship," she said. "I promise." She smiled and squeezed her hand. "Thank you for helping us."

Althea stared at her hand in her master's and thought perhaps, just perhaps, that she had made the right decision. She nodded, barely, and looked up at the sun, her heart and mind dancing with something she'd not had in many long years: hope.

SPIDER'S OFFER
by Charles M. Saplak

Charles Saplak has published fantasy, science fiction and horror stories in many markets, including *Year's Best Horror Stories, Cthulhu's Heirs, Tomorrow,* the British magazine *Beyond,* and many other places.

Biographies like this make me wonder wistfully, "Why haven't I encountered him before?" But maybe this will make up for lost time. He currently lives in the small town of Radford, Virginia, with his wife Karen and daughter Charlene. He credits Charlene with leading him toward the field of fantasy fiction.

D usk settled over the battlefield on the evening of the first day of what was to be the final battle for the Kingdom of the recently deceased Therault the Just.

Princess Dehaev limped past the soldiers who sat slumped around meager fires, past the sullen prisoners whose hands and feet were tied, past the bodies of the dead, both those who had been laid out in ceremonial poses ready to be burned or transported back to their family tombs, and those who lay sprawled, open-mouthed and dull-eyed where they had fallen.

Deathsmell hung over everything.

Dehaev tasted her own blood, sour and like rusted metal in her mouth.

From everywhere came the groans and sobs of the wounded. From the enemy camp across the vale came distant screams.

Daheav's chest ached with a dull grinding, telling her what she tried to ignore; that the hammer blow from the infantryman she'd engaged in the vale earlier had surely broken some ribs. She would probably die, but not quickly.

Chaikev, her page, ran to greet her and offer her a shoulder to lean on as she made her way to her tent.

"Your lieutenants are waiting, my Princess," Chaikev said. The young girl looked up at Dehaev with tearful brown eyes, although she tried to make her voice brave and steady.

"They may not have to wait long," Dehaev said, grimacing. The page either didn't understand the grim joke or else had the discipline not to acknowledge it.

Just outside the tent Dehaev gently pushed Chaikev away and took a deep breath. She forced herself to straighten up, grinding her back teeth together so as not to call out in pain from her ribs.

"That will be all for now, Chaikev. Lay out some bread and water in case I wish to eat later, then eat some for yourself." The page nodded, then hurried away.

As Dehaev limped into the tent, her three lieutenants stood simultaneously. She waved an arm at them telling them to sit. As the three complied, Dehaev noticed that her stepcousin Corrandin, a woman five years younger than she—did so slowly and in apparent great pain.

The three lieutenants—Corrandin the True-Hearted, Caerghal the Apelike, and Maastracht the Well-Traveled, Widely-Liked, and Deeply-Learned—took places around a small board which had been recently painted to look like the unnamed vale on which the battle was being waged. Placed on the board were numerous wooden pieces.

Dehaev took the spot her lieutenants left open for her around the board.

Caerghal rubbed his dirty face with a knobby hand which contained dried blood under the nails. "We've completed the muster of the troops, and our spotters and sappers have reported back on Jhalyn's forces. That's the size of it, right there."

He tapped the mapboard. The wooden pieces each bore inscribed symbols which represented types of forces—a phalanx of lancers, a rank of longbowmen, a platoon of swordsmen. One by one Caerghal flicked pieces off the board until a little less than half of each side's forces were off the vale.

"Any ideas on how to dispose our troops tomorrow?" Dehaev asked.

Maastracht shook his head. "We have no choice. It has to be a defensive disposition. Jhalyn is as clever an opponent as any we've ever faced. If we try to make a decisive attack, we'll leave ourselves open. And she has the daring and her troops the discipline to spot any advantage and pounce on it."

"I have an idea," Corrandin announced, her face grim.

"What is it?" Princess Dehaev asked.

"You're the rightful monarch of Therault now. Take

a patrol of handpicked soldiers. Leave for the city of Therault. Wait for reinforcements. Even if we fail to stop Jhalyn, you'll still be alive."

Dehaev held her tongue, then nodded, searching Corrandin's eyes. "Wouldn't Jhalyn send patrols after me as soon as she realized that I was running away?"

"I could wear your armor, Princess. We are of the same build, with the same straw-colored hair. I would fight to the death. It might take her days to realize that you've left."

Yes, you would fight to the death, stepcousin, Dehaev thought.

"I won't say that I haven't thought of running," Dehaev said so that all three lieutenants could hear. "Still, there would be problems. There would be a more than even chance that Jhalyn would discover the ruse and find me and kill me before I got back to Therault. And if I ran, how could I expect my soldiers to fight on? Of course they would, but would they deserve to win a battle fought in my name if I turned tail and ran? Furthermore, why should the people of Therault stand up for me if Jhalyn marched on the city? There will be many who feel that her claim to Therault's throne is stronger than mine already. Wouldn't many people of the kingdom prefer to have a monarch who is willing to fight, instead of one who ran from battle?"

Dehaev shook her head sadly. "No, my friend, we can only . . ."

Chaikev burst through the tent flap.

"Some respect, page!" Lieutenant Caerghal snarled.

"Princess D–De–Dehaev!" the page panted, her face speckled crimson like a dead leaf, her eyes wide in the lamplight.

"What is it, Chaikev? Spit it out," Dehaev said.
"Some of your troops are killing the prisoners!"

Dehaev strode forth, ignoring the ache in her ribs, knocking troops out of her way as she moved. Eventually she shouldered past the last back, and stood in the center of the crowd.

A hammerman and two swordsmen stood within a pile of bloody corpses. Each of them was painted with fresh red blood and bits of freshly spattered brain. Lined up before them were a rank of prisoners. All were bound hand and foot. All knelt. Some were hunched over, crying, or shaking, or perhaps muttering supplications in strange tongues to whatever gods they worshiped.

A few held up their heads, ready to curse or spit at their executioners. A man with the prominent nose and dark skin of Mag-Kavone, with the drooping mustache and shaped beard that those warriors wore, knelt before the three. The hammerman had the bloody fingers of one hand tangled in the man's hair, and held his hammer in the other.

Dehaev, in spite of herself, looked deeply into the man's eyes. She saw neither hatred nor entreaty there, but rather a kind of dogged hope against all odds. With his head in his executioner's hands, with his own hands tied, he still felt hope.

"Who ordered this?" Dehaev asked.

One of the swordsmen turned to face Dehaev. "*They* ordered it," he said, his face crimson beneath the dirt and blood, his lips trembling, his shoulders and hands shaking.

"They ordered it," he repeated. "Haven't you heard the cries? They've captured our wounded, as we have captured theirs. They've not offered to ransom them back, nor to trade prisoner for prisoner. Don't you see their fires? Haven't you heard the screams?"

Dehaev looked from face to face at the circle of warriors who surrounded her, the prisoners, and the men who were killing them.

Tired, bloody, worn-out faces; eyes that had looked into death.

"I didn't order this," Dehaev said.

"My brother fell today," the swordsman said. "But he was still alive. This evening I heard his cries. I felt it in here when he died! I know that he was in pain."

The swordsmen pointed to his chest; his eyes were wild. The tension among the men and women who stood watching was like a palpable thing; Dehaev felt it breathing on the back of her neck.

"Then you'll have to kill me first," Dehaev said. Wincing, she drew her sword. She was so fatigued she could barely hold it up, but she managed to point it at the swordsman who had done the talking.

"My brother and I followed you!" the swordsman said. "We've killed for you. Today, he died for you. And tomorrow, I'll probably die for you."

Dehaev nodded. When she spoke, she spoke in a flat, even tone, but projected her voice so that all of the men and women encircling them could hear.

"If you're going to kill them," Dehaev said. "Then you're going to have to kill me first."

For a long moment, everything was still. Dehaev could feel her heart beating against her broken ribs like a panicked bird fluttering against the bars of its cage.

And finally the swordman who had done the talking threw down his weapon, turned, and stepped through the crowd. The other swordsman sheathed his weapon, and the hammerman untangled his fingers from the hair of the prisoner.

Dehaev lowered her sword.

"Give these prisoners water," she said to a camp orderly. "If there's food to spare, give each a half ration of bread."

The kneeling prisoner, who had just been released by the hammerman, stared into Dehaev's eyes.

You had hope, and tonight your hope was founded, Dehaev thought, but she didn't say this out loud. Instead, she gave the prisoner one last glance and said, "You were lucky."

As night fell, the lieutenants of Princess Dehaev forced her to her tent to rest.

She lay back on her bedroll, taking care to spare her ribs as much as she could. A few hours. That would be all she needed. If she could but have a few hours not as a Princess, not as a general, not as a contender for the kingdom of Therault, but a few hours as an ordinary woman. A few hours of peace.

A few hours of rest . . .

As she lay there quietly, she noticed a tiny speck moving in the lamp-cast shadows above her head. The speck dropped downward, suspended by a thread, slowly, slowly toward her.

A spider.

She managed a grim smile. One of the best-loved tales of Sprakgist the Storyteller had involved a King who lay wounded after battle, and who was inspired to win back his rightful kingdom after watching the travails of a spider overhead.

"Are you here to inspire me, eight-legs?" she whispered.

The spider held fast for a moment, then dropped swiftly to a place on Dehaev's pillow beside her face.

"No," the spider said.

Dehaev's eyebrows arched.

"Not at all," the spider said in a voice like a soft wind through a tin flute. "I'm here to make you an offer."

Dehaev lay back on the pillow. Her ribs still ached; the lamps still cast shadows about the interior of the tent. She could still hear the creak of leather and the clanking of steel from people moving around the encampment outside. She could still smell the smoke of low fires. She was sure she wasn't dreaming.

"What sort of offer?" she asked. "Just what can an eight-legs do?"

"Little eight-legs is the part you see. I'm an avatar of someone else."

"What is your offer?" Dehaev asked again.

"And so now your stepsister has designs on the throne. What do you think the Kingdom of Therault will look like if she takes power?"

Dehaev scowled. "I know exactly what it will look like. She'll make the land and the Kingdom over into an image of herself. What she can't tax to death, she'll prohibit. She'll set herself up as a goddess. Those who won't worship, she'll burn alive as heretics. If she doesn't destroy the kingdom—and don't think that she necessarily will, because the people there are human, and so feel fear just like anyone else, they may go along with her—she'll turn it into a war machine. I know her too well. She's mad."

The spider crawled away from Dehaev and walked onto the mapboard. It took its place in the exact center, between the two arrayed ranks of warrior pieces.

"So from *that* direction," it said, pointing northwest with one of its legs, "came Jhalyn and the Kavonian barbarians and mercenaries she seduced into following her with promises of plunder and displays of ruthlessness. And from *that* direction," (pointing southeast) "came you and the army you put together from allies and followers of Therault."

Dehaev nodded.

"And she is stopped here or will not be stopped at all, correct? If she gets past you, the Kingdom of Therault will be hers?"

"She won't get past me," Dehaev said, forgetting herself and leaning forward, then immediately slumping back and grimacing. "At least not as long as I live."

"So there's the rub," the spider said softly and with a hint of slyness in its voice. It walked around and around the board, walking over the warrior pieces in a manner which struck Dehaev as being somehow obscene.

"Who or what are you an avatar for, eight-legs?" Dehaev asked.

"Someone knowledgeable," the spider said. "Someone who can help."

"How can anyone help? If you know something that can save Therault, you must tell me."

"Now today the forces met, you and yours standing over there, and Jhalyn and hers advancing from over there. And you battled all day, and two of every five of your people were cut down today, but you fought so skillfully and well that she lost an equivalent number. And the battle tomorrow will be less crowded, but no less bloody, and there will be a similar result. And the day after. And the day after. I think that by the time of the next full moon your forces and hers will each kill the other off. I foresee two warriors meeting in the middle of a great pile of carrion, one killing the other, then dying of her own wounds."

"Eight-legs, you're telling me nothing my lieutenants haven't already told me."

"But there is a way to avoid that bloody scene, Princess Dehaev. There is a way if you could but see it, and have the courage to agree to use it."

"And what is the way, eight-legs? Surrender?"

"Neither you nor Jhalyn would ever do that, Princess."

"Trickery?"

"She is as guileful as you are clever, Princess. No such tricks would work."

"A new tactic?"

"You are equally matched in knowledge and ferocity. No tactic exists which can avoid the spilling of blood."

"What is the answer, then? Tell me quickly, eight-legs, for I may die before you finish."

"I offer you a deal from my master. There is magic to be had. A certain magic which can turn the tide of battle."

"And what would be my part of the deal? What would your master want in return?" Dehaev asked.

"Jhalyn and her soldiers would be dead. You—provided that you survive the battle, of course, and that wouldn't be guaranteed—would be required to allow my master the freedom to live unchallenged in the kingdom after the battle is done. Realizing that you might not survive, you would make each of your lieutenants swear that the Kingdom of Therault would be required to leave my master unmolested."

Dehaev nodded. "I don't like the fact that your master will not show his true aspect."

The spider shrugged.

"Now if I should agree—and I am not agreeing—just how would your master turn the tide of battle?"

"Reinforcements," the spider said.

Dehaev frowned. "Every man or woman of warring age and condition is in the battle already."

"Not true," the spider answered. "There are a few thousand nearby ready to rejoin the battle. And these soldiers would not exhibit the failing that so many of your soldiers have shown already."

"And what failing is that, eight-legs?"

"The failing of getting themselves killed."

The spider walked over to the stack of warrior pieces which sat to one side of the mapboard. They were the pieces which Caerghal had pushed off the board in order to represent the soldiers who had died that first day. The spider climbed to the top of the stack.

"So these warriors won't be killed?" Dehaev asked.

"These thousands won't be killed—again."

Dehaev stared at the spider for a long moment. The lamps still cast deep shadows about the interior of the tent. She could still hear the groaning of leather and the knelling of steel as people moved around the encampment outside; she still smelled the smoke of low fires. This was no nightmare; it was really happening.

"Begone, pestilent!" she hissed through clenched teeth.

"Then say good-bye to the Kingdom of Therault!" the spider piped. "Is there something that you love beyond the kingdom? Why do you refuse my help?"

"Tempting vermin," Dehaev said, reaching around

for something with which to swat the offending creature, but it scurried away, or perhaps disappeared.

Again Dehaev fell back on her bedroll. She lay still for a moment. There was much she had to think about, and many things she needed to do.

And yet . . .

There was so much pain. . . .

And yet . . .

It felt good to lie still and to close her eyes. . . .

Dehaev stood up. Her ribs no longer hurt. She no longer tasted blood in her mouth. She looked down to see if she still bore the bruises and cuts which she had been given on the battlefield. The external marks were there, but she felt no pain associated with them.

The interior of the tent fell away.

Dehaev stood on a vast plain. The sky was overcast.

In the distance, a figure stood, hand outstretched, seemingly waiting for her.

Dehaev took a step toward the figure, which was somehow familiar.

The figure waved.

And Dehaev recognized him. King Therault the Just stood beneath a gray sky.

Dehaev ran to him, her feet kicking up fine crimson and purple dust which fell soundlessly to the ground behind her.

He still wore his burial shroud, keeping it wrapped about him like a cloak. The structure of his face had not changed, with the strong brow, the jutting nose, the prominent cheekbones, and the fringe of white beard.

Yet, there were differences, that much Dehaev could see right away. Therault no longer shook with the palsy which had cursed his later years. His back was not even slightly bowed with the wounds and age which had conspired to be carried by him into the dusk of his life.

"Yes, come to me, my Dehaev. Come and listen to me," he called in a steady and strong voice which the barren landscape could not echo.

Within seconds Dehaev caught up to Therault.

"Oh, Father," she said, holding her arms out to invite a hug from the tall King.

He backed away and showed Dehaev the palm of his right hand, stopping her in her tracks.

"You are not to join me, Dehaev. I can only tarry here for a moment."

"Where are you headed, Father?" Dehaev asked.

Therault pointed to the range of mountains in the distance. "I'm to travel there, walking one day and one night for every year that I lived. What I am supposed to find or see or do there, I do not know."

"Am I to follow you, Father?"

"No. You are not dead. I have been allowed to wait in order to tell you that you have done the right thing in refusing the spider's offer."

"Then we will win against Jhalyn?"

The King shook his head sadly. "I did not say that. I have only said that you have done the right thing."

Dehaev's heart fell. When the King turned away from her, she could see the mountains in the distance through his body. She held her hands before her face; she could see the ground at her feet through her hands when she held them a certain way.

"I see so much now," King Therault said. "I know so much, but it's hard for me to feel anything. The entirety of my life was so small, so fleeting. . . ."

He looked Dehaev in the eye. His own eyes were

clear and calm. As Dehaev looked into them, she was struck by how blue and peaceful they seemed.

"But this painless world is not for you yet, my child. Some borders may not be crossed. One may glimpse the world across the border, or one may walk for the briefest period on the other side, *but some borders may not be crossed.* I have but one more thing I'm allowed to give you. I will give you a command which you will forget, but later there may come a time when you must do something you desperately do not want to do, something which is against your very nature. . . ."

The King raised his left hand and pressed his palm against Dehaev's forehead.

Dehaev reeled under his touch. The barren land became a jumble of gray, and the face of the King became more and more distant.

"How strange that I have loved you so much, you a child that I found starving in the forest in a foreign land, while Jhalyn, my own child, has always been a stranger to me," the King said, his voice reaching Dehaev like a distant echo.

Chaikev the page tugged at Dehaev's tunic, while bending over her chest and sobbing.

"Here, page," Dehaev croaked hoarsely. "Is this a new way to show respect?"

"Princess," Chaikev choked. "I couldn't waken you! I did not see you breathing!"

Dehaev sat up gingerly. Her ribs ached; blood was crusted all about her gums and lips.

"Wipe away those snot bubbles, child. Fetch my weapons and armor. This is a day of battle."

* * *

The vale was darkened. The moon had set. The eastern horizon began to blush with crimson light which crept upward like a spreading bloodstain. Mist lay across the low areas like sleeping gray snakes.

Dehaev breathed as evenly as possible, feeling her ribs burn with every inhalation, and watched her breath form little puffs in the early morning air. All around her was the creak of leather and the muffled clanking of steel and iron. Any warriors who spoke did so in low tones, giving Dehaev the impression that her army was a great, multivoiced beast, mumbling or perhaps praying to itself.

Dehaev's soldiers stood in ranks, ready to be deployed when orders would be called or blown on horns.

Dehaev's lieutenants stood around her.

"Can you see anything of their deployment, Caerghal?" she asked the short warrior standing to her right.

He peered into the darkness.

"As far as I can see, they've not formed up. They're ready and armed and facing the field, but they seem to be waiting for something."

Dehaev felt cold fingers of fear plucking at the edges of her mind.

The sun rose through the mist, and as it did so, the troops arrayed on the opposite side of the field slowly emerged from the darkness and mist to become visible to Dehaev and her forces.

"What in the world are they doing?" Corrandin said. "They've got some sort of barrier line erected—do you see it?"

"Are they mad?" Maastracht whispered. "They've set up low bundles of some kind, or spikes."

Caerghal shook his head. "Those aren't spikes. They look like spears and swords. The bloody fools have set up a wall of scarecrows, and given them swords and spears to hold."

Dehaev gasped; her heart felt as if it were shrinking within her chest. "The spider," she said.

"Those aren't scarecrows," Corrandin said. "The barbarians! The superstitious, sick-minded fools. Can't you see what they've done?"

"I see it," Maastracht said. "Sickening."

Dehaev whispered to no one in particular, "Jhalyn took its offer. Jhalyn felt no boundaries of decency. All she saw was a chance to win the battle. Jhalyn took its offer."

None of her lieutenants said anything, or even indicated that they heard her, as the four of them stood there staring at enemy soldiers who stood behind ranks of slumped over, slack-jawed, stiff, dead warriors.

But only as the sun came fully out from behind the clouds and its rays hit the dead warriors, only then did Dehaev's lieutenants and troops realize what she already suspected.

As the sun hit each dead face, the heads raised, the arms twitched to raise swords and spears were level and pointing toward their opponents, backs were straightened, and splayed legs were drawn up and forced to carry the dead weight of armored, unfeeling bodies.

A murmur ran through Dehaev's ranks of soldiers.

"Hold your positions," Caerghal called.

In the distance, a horn sounded behind Jhalyn's

soldiers. The dead troops advanced with jerky, clattering motions.

On Dehaev's left flank, a few troops broke ranks and ran.

"Hold your positions," Corrandin shouted.

As the dead troops advanced across the vale, the live troops fell in and formed a rank behind them, following them toward Dehaev's position.

Somewhere to the left of and behind Dehaev, there was another commotion among her troops.

Maastracht lifted his longbow above his head, and called for attention from the archers. "On my signal," he called.

Slowly and deliberately, Jhalyn's troops closed the distance. Dehaev took the time to turn around to find the source of commotion on her left flank. Something was happening far behind the front line.

As Jhalyn's troops closed to within two hundred and fifty yards, Maastracht threw his hand forward and shouted, "Shoot!"

A hundred bowstrings sang and their arrows flew with a sound like the gasping of a multivoiced giant. A few seconds later the shafts fell among the ranks of Jhalyn's soldiers. Several in the second rank dropped as the ashwood arrows found their marks. Many more in the first rank were hit, but these soldiers didn't break stride as the arrows decorated already dead flesh like pins in pincushions.

Dehaev saw it and realized that the battle was lost.

"Defensive deployment," Dehaev said to her lieutenants.

"Castled block," Maastracht called to the squad leaders. "Castled block, linked phalanx!"

The soldiers seemed to welcome the familiar orders.

Well-trained and drilled by rote, they shifted position in order to form the interlinked disposition that Maastracht had called for. Within a minute they were in position, except for the left flank.

Dehaev walked back to wave her sword above her head and shout at the troops there. "Position! Position!" she screamed.

And then she saw the source of the disturbance. The dead bodies of fallen comrades had been hit by the sunlight, and were twitching and stirring. Soldiers stood around them with swords drawn and spears held at shoulder level. No one knew whether to hang back, or to take action.

They didn't have to wait long to find out. The swordsman whom Dehaev had confronted the day before knelt beside a dead man—whom Dehaev recognized by his similar hair and features as his fallen brother—who lay wrapped in his cloak as in a burial shroud, with his hands folded across his chest, a necklace with the signet of his clan and his region intertwined in his fingers.

The living swordsman set down his blade and pulled his dead brother up by his shoulders, to embrace him. As he did so the dead man blinked his eyes against the sun, reminding Dehaev for all the world of a man awakening from deep slumber, while he felt around on the ground with his left hand.

"Careful!" Dehaev shouted.

The dead man let drop the signet necklace as his hand found the handle of his brother's sword. He neither said anything nor changed expression as he took up the sword and plunged it into his brother's side.

This was all the signal Dehaev's soldiers needed as they set upon the newly-stirring dead men with blades and spears and hammers, realizing that no matter which side of the battle they were on when they left the world, they came back as allies of the evil Jhalyn.

And yet what good can they do? Dehaev asked herself. *See that soldier being pierced through the heart for the second time in two days? He no longer needs his heart to move and fight. See that hammerstruck corpse which has pulled a sword from his own back? See him turn the stolen sword on the hammerman, then on the now-defenseless swordsman. And now an arm is taken from this other soldier, yet he neither bleeds nor calls out in pain. He fights on, while the arm flops along the ground to grasp at the ankles of its body's opponents.*

Horns sounded in the distance, and the advancing army of Jhalyn broke into a run, the live soldiers shouting, the dead simply clanking and stomping along the distance of the vale, closing on Dehaev's army in their defensive formation.

We've lost, Dehaev realized.

Her troops, disciplined and loyal fought on, but the outcome was not in doubt. That they were so well trained, in fact, stood against them. The tactics of individual combat which were so deeply ingrained in Dehaev's soldiers were useless against enemy soldiers who could not be killed. Likewise, on the squad and phalanx level, numerous maneuvers relied for success on the fact that they allowed the skirmish line to be clogged with useless enemy corpses, but these dead fought on after being killed. What good was a storm of arrows if it had no more effect than a summer rain? What good was a ten-foot spear if an enemy soldier was able to take its tip through the chest and slowly make his way up the shaft to the spear holder?

The battle unfolded as a whirl of unforgettable images for Dehaev. Enemy troops pouring through the broken left flank . . . a knot of headless corpses wrestling the hammerman and swordsmen who had decapitated them the night before to the ground . . . Maastracht and Caerghal going down before a ring of gray-faced warriors, two and three deep, using their swords without art or precision, but with deadly effect . . . Chaikev (the dear child! Dehaev could recall taking the orphaned girl from the war-destroyed farm of her dead parents) being run through by a dispassionate corpse spearman who saw neither combatant nor child, but only saw a living thing, and therefore an enemy.

Through it all Dehaev fought. It would have been easier to lay down her sword and give herself up to the blades of the overwhelming numbers of dead warriors. The pain of dying would be over in an instant, and then she might have peace. She could join Therault on his sojourn to the distant mountains he had shown her last night.

But surrender was not an option. How could she give up when so many thousands had fought to their deaths in her name? And then, too, there was a selfish reason. On this cursed day, what release did death offer? Could she not come back immediately as a slave of her step-sister Jhalyn?

Suddenly the wave of fighters parted. Through the dust and clamor and blood fog over the battlefield, Dehaev could see the standard of her mad stepsister now, approaching her. Jhalyn had changed the crest of the family Therault. Where the family had once displayed the seahorse, symbol of wisdom, there now was a representation of a spider. Likewise, the eye of justice was now replaced by the fang of strength.

The dead warriors backed away from Dehaev, without a signal to be seen, nor a command to be heard. Theirs was some deep link, some hidden channel which tied them to the Princess who had brought them to this, Jhalyn.

"Dear sister," Jhalyn called, stressing the word like a sweet obscenity.

"You've taken on some miserable helpers," Dehaev replied, gesturing toward the retreating warriors. "I've been trying to get them to kill me, but they're no more skilled after death than they were in life. What do I have to do? Throw down my sword? Wouldn't that be particularly artless?"

Jhalyn laughed, holding her hand out to one side. A page, dead, with a mutilated face, placed a gleaming steel sword in it.

"You'll not goad me into letting them hack you apart, dear sister. I've saved you for myself." With that, Jhalyn raised her sword.

Dehaev, her ribs still throbbing, held her own sword forward. "I can't ask for anything more," she said. "I know I can still beat you in a fair fight."

Jhalyn's eyes blazed, but she said nothing.

There was movement to Dehaev's right. She made an effort to avoid the blow, but wasn't fast enough. One of the dead warriors used the flat of his sword blade to strike her wrist. Dehaev couldn't be sure if it was broken. The bones didn't come through the flesh, nor was the wrist crooked. Still, she couldn't move her right hand.

Jhalyn bared straight teeth and hissed through her lips, "Fair fight? You dare talk to me about fair? Ser-

pent taken into my father's home. Adder warmed by
my father's fire. Wicked outsider. You poisoned his
mind against me. You and he were both weak. I hate
you both with a passion that's brighter than the sun."

Dehaev bent down to try to pick up her sword. Her
right hand wouldn't grasp, so she put her left hand on
it.

One of Jhalyn's dead spearmen reached out with the
tip of his spear and pushed Dehaev's sword out of her
reach.

"I don't even think I feel like a fair fight, anyway,
dearest sister," Jhalyn said. "I know that I want to kill
you, and I want to kill you slowly and painfully, maybe
even carving you up like I did this servant." (Here
Jhalyn indicated the page with the mutilated face.)

Dehaev felt that she had two slender chances left.

"Then please kill me quickly, Jhalyn, so I don't have
to live and be tortured by seeing you inherit the Kingdom of Therault, which may be yours by blood, but
which I've longed for as you can't imagine."

Jhalyn sighed. "Of course I can imagine, and of
course a part of me would like to let you live and suffer in ways that these meat men—they're very loyal,
know that?—that these meat men can't suffer, but then
you'd be alive and you'd have a chance to hurt me,
and I can't allow that. And another part of me is interested in what it's going to be like having you as fleshy
skeleton, maybe even serving me as a kind of page, or
even some sort of orderly, watching me. Now that will
be interesting. And even though you'd be dead, I'll be
able to imagine that deep inside there's a tiny part of
you, the *real* you, which watches me rule the kingdom
and suffers because of it."

Jhalyn smiled sweetly. "That thought cheers me. What of it, my warriors? Can the dead suffer?"

As she shouted this last, the warriors gathered around muttered and stirred in a way which would have frightened Dehaev, had she not been tired and desperate beyond the point of feeling any additional fear.

Dehaev braced herself, but tried to not let Jhalyn see that she was tensing. There was no way to survive, but if Jhalyn was to personally kill her, she'd have to get close enough. If Dehaev could get her sword . . .

"Sweet sister," Jhalyn said, smiling again. "We were always so evenly matched. Remember all the strategy games we played, almost always ending in a draw?"

"What are you saying, Jhalyn?"

"I'm saying don't bother trying to take my sword and use it on me. Hold her down!" she called to the warriors.

A few stirred and stepped forward, but they didn't get close enough to touch her. There was a sound like an old man leaning forward and whispering.

Jhalyn cried out.

An arrow was sticking out of her left breast.

Dehaev turned. In the distance she could see a man holding a bow. He wore the garb and hair of a Kavonian warrior.

"I'm dying," Jhalyn croaked, tugging at the shaft of the arrow. "Do you hear me? I'm dying."

She slumped to her knees.

The bowman and another warrior advanced on the little group around Dehaev. These warriors immediately surrounding Dehaev stood still, and the din of battle settled and diminished like the last echoing of an old man's call off of distant mountains.

Jhalyn sank to her knees, and put one hand out to feel for the ground and steady herself.

"Kill her," she said. "Kill my stepsister, warriors. Cut her to ribbons. Send us to the land of death together. I'm dying, do you hear me, I'm dying."

The dead men and women and children standing around the fallen Jhalyn made no move toward Dehaev, but a few made tentative, stiff steps toward their fallen leader.

Dehaev was hauled to her feet by rough hands.

On one side was the Kovonian warrior, still holding the bow. Dehaev recognized him as the man she had saved the night before.

On the other side was her stepcousin, Corrandin.

"Can you walk, Princess?" Corrandin asked.

"I can."

"Well, I think we'd better run."

Jhalyn slumped over further. With what seemed like agonizing effort, she forced her head back to look up. Blood ran down her arm to stain the dust around her hand. With the other arm she reached out to Corrandin and Dehaev.

"Don't leave me," she said.

The dead warriors shuffled closer, their glazed-over eyes fixed on Jhalyn's face, as if they were looking there and seeing the only light in their universe.

"Run!" Corrandin shouted to the stumbling Dehaev.

"But we have soldiers still alive here," Dehaev said. "The battle must not be quit."

"Run," Corrandin repeated, and it was as if the word released something in Dehaev's mind. She got to her feet and staggered along with Corrandin and the Kavonian. As she ran, she passed some of her own soldiers who were desperately fighting, and others who lay wounded, but these were rare.

Most of those she passed were the dead warriors of Jhalyn, and these all seemed to be turning their frozen faces toward the spot Dehaev had left.

"Run!" Corrandin shrieked again.

And now the warriors were quitting their individual fights and turning toward the place where Jhalyn lay dying.

The three ran unmolested, as the warriors raised their swords and spears and hammers and madly rushed toward their queen.

Corrandin and the Kavonian dragged Dehaev up the nearest hill, as if she were a sack of stones. At one point they dropped her on the slope and she rolled over to look back upon the vale.

A din and clamor rose from that land like a thunderstorm trapped on earth. The warriors one and all were madly hacking and carving on themselves and on the tiny figure which lay in their center.

They swarmed around this figure like moths around a flame.

"She's their queen," Dehaev said, gasping. "She's their gate. She's their way back to the land of the dead, where they know they belong."

Some borders can't be crossed.

And then Corrandin and the Kavonian pulled her farther up the slope, and she passed out.

The sky was dark when she awoke, and her two companions lay gasping and wheezing on the ground beside her. She rolled over, and pushed her head up to look at the battlefield.

It was gone.

What had been trees were now twisted structures of fragile ash which fell apart in the slightest breeze; what had been waves of grass were now crumblings mats of dessicated blades; what had been rolling meadows were now jagged outcrops of rock.

In the center sat a creature which made Dehaev queasy to even look at. At one time it had probably been a human, but that time was long past, as the thing had evidently fallen prey to practices which had caused it to transform.

It had a great humped body, about as large as an ox. On the front of the body was a great slab of a face, like a man's face hastily drawn by a crude and angry child. It had eight limbs, four on each side, weirdly articulated and jointed things which looked both like human arms and human legs and also much like things which were neither.

So this then was the thing of which the spider—the tempting, treacherous spider—had been an avatar.

"Someday," Corrandin said, her chest heaving, sweat rolling from her face as she touched Dehaev on the wrist. "Someday we're going to have to take care of *that*," she said, tilting her head toward the spider beast which, even as the two exhausted warriors watched, slid beneath a pile of bones and abandoned armor.

Dehaev sat up and looked with obvious disgust at the place where the creature disappeared.

"I agree. It can't be allowed to live. And it probably won't be content with the territory it has now. When it tricked Jhalyn, it got what it wanted—a foothold in the Kingdom."

Corrandin lay back down and gasped. "But not today."

Dehaev grimaced in a bitter smile. "No. We'll travel back to the city, and heal, and do some research. In the meantime, you'll have to send some guards, if we can find any."

The man who had accompanied the two from the battlefield got to his knees, then, shakily, to his feet. He looked back over his shoulder at the vale of the spider creature, then looked toward Dehaev.

"Your problem," he said. "Lucky."

Then he turned and started off.

Dehaev and Corrandin watched him go, heading southeast, in the general direction of his homeland, Mag-Kavone.

"What do you think he meant by that?" Dehaev asked.

Corrandin shrugged. "Maybe he meant, 'Good-bye, Dehaev, Rightful Queen of Therault.' "

MORE THAN ONE WAY
by Heather Rose Jones

It seems to me that half the women I know are named Heather; my second son married one, and my daughter takes voice lessons from another. Then, of course, there's the talented young woman who works in our office and has provided us with this fine tale of shape-shifting magic. It's set in the same universe as "Skins," which appeared in *Sword and Sorceress XII*.

Heather works part-time for my magazine while attending UC Berkeley, where she is a graduate student in the Linguistics Department specializing in Medieval Welsh. She is active in the Society for Creative Anachronism and publishes a journal of Welsh research for reenactors. Prior to that, she had, as she puts it, "a lucrative career in biomedical research," which leads me to wonder what strange and interesting stories we may see from her in the future.

Heather is also a musician and a songwriter. She has written some very fine songs indeed, including one of my favorites, which concludes: "The years slip away like cats in the dawn; it's not 'till you miss them you know they are gone." She should know, since, like most writers, she has cats. She has recorded two tapes, and performs at science fiction conventions and SCA events.

In addition to her story sales, Heather has published a number of articles on Welsh names and some poetry. "Like everyone else," she says, "I'm working on a novel or two. After all, it would be nice to have other options if I find the market is slow for Medieval Welsh linguists!"

I waited in the hut most of the night, hoping that I was wrong and that dawn would find me sleepy but undisturbed. But there had been murder in Ashóli's eyes when they met mine over her grandmother's grave. I had no intention of stealing the inheritance that she thought hers by right, but I could not tell her so—not yet. So I waited, fashioning a song of binding that I hoped would hold her long enough to make her listen. Night had always been my element, and though I could no longer use an owl's eyes and ears, there was little danger that she would catch me unaware. No, this night held little danger for me—but for her? Would she cross that threshold and put herself beyond my help?

We had crossed the river around midday two days before—Dyoan and Ale'en and I—and rested a while on a grassy bank overlooking the wide water. Dyoan would have put on his wolf-skin and run ahead exploring, but there were trails and human footprints along the shore, and I persuaded him to caution.

It wasn't until after we had crossed that I felt a weight drop away that I hadn't known I carried. Ganasset was well and truly behind us now; a land too uncomfortable with what they considered magic to have made us comfortable there. I watched Ale'en dancing in the sunlight with his cloak of eagle feathers floating out behind him. He was delighted at having borne us across the water, as only a child can be at having done a grown-up task. And though I was the one who had sung his eagle-skin around the three of us, it had been his wings that carried us, and his generosity that brought us across dry and safe. It was hard not to presume upon that generosity, after the years when neither of them could wear their own skins except by my word. But after our narrow escape the year before, I had set all my skills to crafting skin-songs for the two of them. And now that they could sing their own shapes into fur and feathers and back again, I kept my tongue behind my teeth and did not order that part of their lives. But, oh, it was hard, now that I was the slowest one, walking only on two legs.

From this side of the river an open woodland rose slowly toward distant mountains. I squinted into the distance looking for signs of habitation. The rumors behind us said that our people were known here, and I hoped to find a family that would take the boys in. But in a land frequented by Kaltaoven, strangers could as easily be kin or enemies. We are not always comfortable neighbors.

A thread of smoke lifted from behind a hill in the distance and farther up the riverbank a narrow path led in the same direction. And though we steered our steps toward the smoke, it was they who found us first: a woman flanked by two snarling hounds who stepped onto the path before us. Dyoan stiffened beside me and fingered his wolf-skin cloak, but I laid a restraining hand on his arm. "Gently," I hissed. "We are the strangers here." He relaxed with effort and I could see the strange woman smiling in amusement.

"Are you come far, then?" she asked in our own tongue, her choice of words including us as distant kin. Disconcertingly, it was to Dyoan that she addressed her question.

He stared slack-jawed in amazement to hear that language from any lips but ours. I answered in his stead. "A long ways indeed since the beginning. From Dyelenol, but most recently from Ganasset."

She frowned, but it did not seem only in confusion. "Dyelenol?"

"Near Karscar in the north. Too far from the lands of our people, as it turned out. We are searching for a friendlier home."

She seemed to consider this and then make a decision. "We will offer you guesting, of course. It may be that the council will offer you more." She left that thought hanging vaguely and snapped her fingers at the hounds. They shed their skins and stood—a young man and woman who might have been twins, grinning at us as if to apologize for their earlier growls. She introduced the two of them and then sent them running back to the village to announce us.

So it was that they all turned out to welcome us—or almost all, as we learned. There were nearly fifty in the village, a circle of thatched huts set in a broad meadow. I could see Ale'en and Dyoan comparing it to their parents' fine stone house, but that house lay in ruins now.

It took me a few minutes to put my finger on the oddness in these folk: the two hounds were the youn-

gest who wore skins. There were no children at all
with a furred or feathered cloak, and even a few adults
went without. *They have no singer,* I thought. *No one
to fashion new spell-songs. And so they are left only to
pass down the old ones.* I'd heard of such clans before,
of course, but it was a perilous way to survive. If
someone died while cloaked, if no one learned the old
song, there was one less skin for the tribe. And an old
song never had the power of one made for the wearer.
Then I counted up the people I saw who wanted skins,
and thought how long the making would be if they
bound me to the task. It frightened me more than a
little.

They led us into the long central hall, apologizing
for the lack of merrymaking. "Grandmother is dying,"
one of the hounds explained, gesturing toward the
hearth as they seated us and brought in food.

I looked where they pointed and saw a young
brown-haired woman, and then looked again and saw
that she held in her lap a bone-thin wildcat that she
stroked slowly and gently. The woman who had come
to greet us—Boesen, she was called—went over to her
and said something sharply. The young woman looked
up with tears in her eyes and answered, "It eases her
pain. Why should you begrudge it?"

"Because we cannot afford to lose her skin," Boesen
said, less sharply. "She knows that; don't encourage
her."

The young woman gathered the cat in her arms as
gently as possible and laid her on a pallet by the fire.
"Gran, Gran," I heard her say, then something too soft
to be understood. The skin fell away and a withered
old woman lay on it, her gasping breath a pain to hear.

Boesen laid a hand on the younger woman's shoulder. "Ashóli, come to dinner. There is nothing you can do here."

"There *is* something I can do," she answered, taking the old woman's hand and settling herself by the bedside.

The other woman shrugged and turned away.

I felt as if I had been intruding, though no one else seemed to mark the exchange. Dyoan and Ale'en had been ensconced in the place for honored guests—much to their astonished delight—while I was seated down along one end with the younger folk. Knowing what I had seen, I guessed the reason. They fed us on roasted pork and porridge and passed bowls of fresh milk around the table. And then when the meal was done, and the bowls were being filled with beer instead, the children and those who wore no skins drew back against the walls and Boesen began the chant that opened council.

They asked Dyoan our names—since it would have been rude to inquire before feeding us—and he gave them the full and formal names with clan and parentage attached. But when he would have given me the honorific of a singer I interrupted him with something inconsequential about my homeland, and made sure to catch his eye and shake my head in warning.

Boesen frowned in my direction. "You are a stranger and so we forgive your ignorance, but children may only speak in council when asked."

It was hard not to laugh—seeing Ale'en sitting there stiff with eight-year-old dignity in their midst—but she meant the other sense of "children," those who did not yet wear skins. In a clan where those were limited, it would be an important mark of adulthood. I looked over at the woman called Ashóli and wondered why she wore none when several younger than she sat in council.

The talk went much as I could have predicted: where did we come from; where were we going; did we know of kinfolk in the area? It seemed they were isolated here and were as eager as we to learn of others of our race. Dyoan was handling the questions as well as I would have, so I set myself to studying the people instead, until my attention was jerked back by my own name.

"You are not Laaki's kin, you say, but surely you could serve as such for her. Is she married or betrothed?"

Dyoan looked wildly in my direction for help, but I only shrugged, so he answered simply, "No."

"Ah," Boesen said, nodding. "Then perhaps we can make a three-fold bargain with you. Your friend lacks a skin. We may soon have a skin available." She made a sign to ward off evil, but it was clear it was an empty gesture. "And my son, Goalnen, would like to take a bride. As the first bargain, perhaps Laaki would take a skin as a bride-price?"

Dyoan had no chance to respond, for Ashóli had risen from the old woman's bedside and shrieked, "No!"

"Ashóli, be still!" Boesen snapped.

"No! You can't . . . she said it should come to me."

" 'Should' is not 'will.' We have to think of what's best for the family."

"And Goalnen is family, but I am not!" I could see Ashóli was shaking with rage, but she said no further word and dashed out the door. Boesen made a calming gesture. "We needn't decide now. Tomorrow will be soon enough to begin the bargaining." Then she closed the council and we were shown places to sleep: the boys in the young men's lodgings and I alone in the guest house.

Dyoan slipped out to see me before going to sleep. I was expecting him. He looked around outside to make sure no one was in earshot, then asked me quietly but heatedly, "Why did you let them treat you like that? You're a *byal-dónen,* a song-maker. They have no right to call you a child!"

"Peace!" I said. "We're guests here and you know only your own family's ways. I've seen this before: counting only skin-wearers as fully adult."

"But you had a skin, and you'll have one again." I could see a flicker of guilt cross his features, even in the dim light of the hut, as he recalled his own foolish part in the loss of my owl-skin.

"And if they know I am a skin-singer ..." I wondered how much to tell him of the geas laid on my kind. "When your father left you and Ale'en in my care, it was not only kindness that made me care for you—though kindness would have been enough, I swear to you. Those that know the way of it can bind a song-maker to her task. He knew it, and bound me to make songs for you and I could not have left you until the task was done. Oh, I don't blame him for it," I said hastily, seeing the expression on Dyoan's face. "He was being hunted and needed to know you would be cared for. And if he had lived, he would have paid me for the work. But there it is. I could be many years making songs for these folk if they know. And I'm not so sure yet that I would be happy settling here."

"I didn't know ..." Dyoan began.

"But now you do, and you will hold your tongue."
He nodded and slipped back to his own quarters.

On the next day they were to talk further of the
three-fold bargain. It was a ritual of our people, to bind
clans together with a triple exchange. A marriage offer
would be a tricky thing to refuse, but if we insisted on
an exchange they would not countenance, we could
force *them* to withdraw the negotiations.

But that morning Goalnen began courting me and I
began to think of other things than escape. He was
only a little older than me, and not at all bad to look
upon. And though I put little stock in his flowery
words, I could see he was intelligent and generous and
knew how to laugh. So I told Dyoan to stall them with
details while I considered what answer I wanted to
give.

And then, in the midst of that bright day, the old
woman died and all else was put aside to mourn her.
There was little to prepare; they had been ready for
her death most of the spring. They took turns singing
her soul on its journey, and Ashóli stubbornly insisted
on watching through the night along with her uncles
and aunt, although she had no true right to be there.
The next day, they buried her with her belongings—
except, of course, for the cat-skin. Boesen had taken it
from her body before it was cold, lest it bind her soul
to the world, and—perhaps—to lay claim to its dis-
posal.

The boys and I did honor at her graveside, though
we had not known her. But when I looked up across
the fresh earth and met Ashóli's stare I knew there
would be trouble. It was hard not to sympathize with

her, for I had gathered her story from whispered gossip. She had been her grandmother's favorite and yet, because her mother had been a second wife and clanless, no one else would take her part. She had been passed over for skins several times. This was likely her last chance. Even now there was no guarantee it would go to her if I refused Goalnen. If I accepted him, the skin would be mine, and there was nothing to say I had to keep it for myself. But she could not know that I had no need of another's skin.

And so I lay awake that night, alone in the guest house, and made a small song of power. She came, finally, as the sky was just beginning to brighten, the time when most people sleep the deepest. I heard a rustling by the door too loud and deliberate for a mouse. I tried to breathe slowly and evenly as I heard her cross the floor. There would be no excuse for what I did unless she acted first.

She stood for a long time, accustoming her eyes to the dimness. Then she bent over me and raised one hand. That was when I chanted the binding song all in a rush. I heard her gasp in surprise and fear, but she did not move, and when I lit myself a flame from the coals in the hearth, I could see her frozen where she crouched by my bedding, a knife raised in her hand. She trembled as she fought against the spell. I settled myself comfortably before her, then released her with a word. She collapsed to the ground, the knife still clenched in her hand, and breathed *"Byal-dónen!"*

I nodded, wrapping myself in what I hoped was intimidating dignity.

"Then why . . ." she began. I saw hope chase the questions from her eyes and they grew wild with want-

ing. "Take me away with you. Make a skin for me—
I'll pay whatever you ask. I'll be your servant, I'll do
anything . . . only don't leave me here to see another
wear my skin."

"Your skin?" I was surprised by her possessiveness.
"Did the old woman name it yours, then?"

She dropped her eyes but dared not lie to me. "No.
Boesen forbade it, and Gran didn't have the strength to
oppose her. But I could not bear to see it go to another
after—" Her voice trailed off and she seemed frightened at what she had begun to say.

I made a guess and finished for her. "—after you
have worn it yourself."

She nodded miserably.

"And what good would killing me have done?" I
asked.

She looked at the knife in her hand as if she had
never seen it before. Slowly she let it fall to the floor.

"Did you think no one would figure it out," I continued, "with a guest slain under their own roof?"

She stared at me in dawning horror. *Guest-slayer:*
the very word was unthinkable. The depth of her
desperation showed in her failure to admit, even to herself, what she had planned.

"How did you learn the skin-song," I asked curiously. "Did she teach you or did you overhear."

"I didn't . . . I didn't mean to. It wasn't like that,"
she stammered. "It was one night when Gran was
asleep. I only put the skin-cloak around me—to see
how it would feel. I didn't mean any harm. I think I
just *wanted* too much. And then . . . then I changed."

I think some of my astonishment must have shown
on my face because she flinched back, thinking my reaction was to her transgression.

"But don't you see—I can't stay, not if they give Gran's cat-skin to someone else."

My mind was racing. Clearly she had no idea what it meant—that she had worn another's skin, without a changing-song, by will alone. They had the answer to their problems at hand and no one here had the wit or knowledge to see it.

A plan formed in my mind. I picked the knife up and put it back in her fingers, heedless of her confusion. Then I dragged her by the wrist out into the growing dawn. A few early risers stared at us curiously. I took a deep breath and began chanting the call for the three-fold bargain.

> *"Geol-dón, geol-dón anaol,*
> *Geol-dón, geol-dón byenol,*
> *Geol-dón alyen ambol."*

As I began it a second time, people were boiling out of the buildings like angry ants. Boesen broke through the clustering throng, took in the frightened Ashóli, still holding her knife, and demanded, "What does this mean?" She tried to ignore me and searched out Dyoan in the crowd. "What is this disturbance?"

He stepped up beside me. "Laaki has a tongue of her own. Ask her—she called for the bargaining."

"Does she speak in your name, then?" Boesen asked.

"If you like," he said with a shrug. He went back to stand by Ale'en and waited with eager curiosity.

When Boesen turned her attention to me, I sat on the ground before her—as one does for bargain-making—and pulled Ashóli down to sit beside me.

"I have a set of bargains to propose," I began, following the traditional words. "For each, you will tell me whether you think it a fair bargain or not."

I could tell she was angry, but now she was caught in the ceremony and would have to see it through. She sat before us and the rest of the village gathered round.

"This one," I said, pointing to Ashóli, "has broken your hospitality."

Ashóli shot me a terrified, pleading look as the crowd began to mutter.

"You owe me a price for the attack made against me while I was under your protection."

"She will die," Boesen said flatly.

I held up my hand in ritual denial. "I do not accept the bargain. It is your tribe that must pay the price."

Boesen pressed her lips together grimly. "She is a miserable creature, but she is one of our tribe."

"Is she?" I asked sharply. "And if she is of your tribe, why was she denied the skin that should have been hers? Was that not a rejection of her as much as if you had closed your doors to her? I say she has no tribe and cannot pay your price for you."

It was a subtle argument, and I would have been hard pressed to convince a law-singer with it. But there was guilt here over how they had treated Ashóli, and I blew that from embers into a flame.

"Will you suggest a bargain, then?" Boesen asked warily.

I pretended to consider for a minute. "As the price of the crime against me, I will take your vengeance." There was confused talk all around me, but Boesen only waited patiently for the explanation. She saw the game, though not how the pieces moved. "Give me your right to revenge against Ashóli as the price of your failure to protect me. Though she did not break her own hospitality, she broke yours, and owes you a price for that. Give me her debt in exchange for your own."

Boesen gave Ashóli a look that suggested she was not entirely unhappy to let it go. "I accept this bargain," she said.

Then I turned to Ashóli herself. "Now your debt is to me. I will bargain for it. For the price you owe, I will take three years of your life."

I could see the relief sweep over her, though she did not yet understand the whole of it. "It is a fair bargain," she answered.

Boesen cut in hurriedly. "For the third bargain, will you consider the one we spoke of before? The skin as your bride-price?"

I looked up at Goalnen and smiled faintly to try to soften my answer as I made the sign of refusal again. "I do not accept the bargain. I find I have no wish to be a bought wife. But bring the skin and I will offer for it. You will tell me if the bargain is fair."

Boesen frowned, but she signaled to her son. Goalnen went and got it and laid it on the ground between the three of us. As he passed, I could see that my choice had disappointed him. I reached out and touched the soft, spotted fur of the cloak. It took all Ashóli's will not to do the same.

"Here is my bargain," I said. "Give me the cat-skin and in three years I will trade you a song-maker for it."

There was a stunned silence from the crowd. Boesen finally found her tongue to speak. "It is a handsome bargain, as you well know. There would be no fame for me in refusing. You are a *byal-dónen?*"

I shrugged. "Perhaps I am, perhaps I'm not. It will

84

be Ashóli I trade to you for it. She has the talent, and in three years she will have the skill as well."

Boesen looked the girl over with a newly measuring eye. Ashóli in turn was gaping at me in surprise. But understanding crept over her, and she turned to face her aunt with a quiet confidence born of her new status.

I knew then that my meddling would bear sweet fruit, not bitter. There was no hatred between them, only an uneasy reassessment of their positions.

Boesen nodded, answering the unspoken question. "The bargain is well-made. *Gyel-dón a-don.* And I think we have all received more than we have given."

"The best sort of bargain," I agreed. *"Gyel-dón a-don."*

I took up the skin-cloak and draped it over Ashóli's shoulders as she rose. I could see Goalnen watching approvingly from the edge of the crowd. *And perhaps,* I thought, *when three years are done I will return them two skin-singers after all.*

DAELITH'S BARGAIN
by Cynthia McQuillin

When I printed Cynthia McQuillin's first story, I inquired rhetorically, "Is there anything this talented young woman can't do?" Now, many years later, I am convinced that there probably isn't. In addition to being a fiction writer, she also writes and performs songs, makes beautiful hand-crafted jewelry, and runs her own recording company, Unlikely Publications. She and her partner, "Dr. Jane" Robinson, have appeared on many tapes, including: *Mid-life Crisis, This Heavy Heart,* and *Bedlam Cats.*

Cynthia and Jane live here in Berkeley with three creatures who purport to be cats, but which I personally suspect are really poltergeists; in their presence small objects fly from the shelves, untouched by human hands. Cindy also enjoys reading, sf conventions, and cooking, and is one of the few people I have ever met who cooks as well, if not better, than I do.

She recently completed her first novel, *Singer in the Shadow.* This is the first book of three, she tells us. Having committed a few trilogies myself, I can understand the impulse, and certainly sympathize with anyone breaking into the field these days. But selling a first novel has always been difficult; I recall that Madeleine L'Engle's award-winning novel, *A Wrinkle in Time,* was rejected thirteen times before it found a home. I believe that Cynthia's novel is of the same quality, and would certainly take a chance on it myself, if I were a book publisher. As it is, I wish her every success.

*S*urely, this must be the spot where Mad Maedie *lairs,* Daelith thought, throwing herself down beside the turgid water. Old and winding, the River Tael had many cutoffs and oxbows turned halfway to swamp or mire. She'd already tried every overgrown backwater from Temaene to Delaerue, but none had been nearly so loathsome as this.

"Oh, why have the gods cursed me with such useless beauty?" she wailed and began to weep, hoping she sounded properly insipid and self-pitying. Her tears were real enough, though born of anger and grief rather than despair. Taeran, her promised husband and dearest friend in the world, lay two weeks in his grave, the seventh victim of Mad Maedie's spite in as many years. Even with the help of her aunt, the wisewoman Genae, Daelith's hunt for the witch had been frustrated at every turn.

As if in answer to her cry, the hot summer air grew suddenly very still. Nothing could be heard save for the low, ominous drone of insects; a sense of pressure and stifling heat seemed to envelop the place. The droning grew louder as the water began to swirl into a small eddy. In moments, the disturbance grew into a whirlpool of amazing proportions. Mouth falling open in astonishment, Daelith sat up to stare at the apparition which arose from the center of the whirlpool.

"Who dares to wake me!" the hag croaked as she stepped to the shore, glaring balefully about her.

Mad Maedie was the ugliest woman Daelith had ever seen. Her visage might have been shaped by the cruelty and spite that permeated her being—snaggle-toothed and pasty, she had a carbuncle the size of a prune on her nose. Her unsavory appearance was made even less appealing by the river-weed tangled locks that hung over her baggy breasts and stomach, not quite covering the splotchy flesh beneath.

"I . . . I," Daelith stammered, revolted by the woman's appearance. Not a little afraid, now that she actually faced the witch, she scrambled to her feet. Though Daelith had steeled herself for this meeting, she was unprepared for the reality of such malice.

"Well, speak up before I turn you into a leech, or something even nastier!" the witch demanded in a voice like a rusty hinge. She leaned toward Daelith, fixing her with red-rimmed eyes that might have been watery blue or gray.

"I beg your pardon, ma'am. I didn't know there was anyone here," Daelith lied, wiping at her tear-stained cheeks to cover their sudden, guilty flush.

"Tears?" the witch laughed. "What does a creature like you have to weep about? *You* could have the love of any man you chose, while *I* am so cursed that none but the most desperate would even seek me out for the knowledge and power I command. I should hang you this very minute for your impudence!"

But Mad Maedie's lack of sympathy and blatant self-pity only served to rekindle Daelith's anger and harden her resolve.

"Do your worst!" she cried, sinking to her knees in a rather contrived display of maidenly distress. "I have no use for love, take my beauty! It has brought me nothing but shame and despair." With this she began weeping again.

"What's this, girl?" The witch stared at her in disbelief. "What do you say?"

"It's true," Daelith sniffled. "Had I been high-born, perhaps it would have been different. But what does a miller's daughter need with such beauty? No honest man will have me for fear I will be vain and lazy. Those who *will* have me will not wed me, so I must become a rich man's whore!"

The witch considered her for a long moment, then said, "If *I* had such a body, I would make better use of it."

Daelith almost smiled at that, but instead she paused in her weeping and looked up to face the witch.

"Then," Daelith said, defiant gaze meeting Mad Maedie's own, "since you value physical beauty so highly, let us trade. *I* would far rather possess the knowledge and power *you* wield than be the most beautiful woman in the world."

Her words rang true enough, for with Taeran gone there was no one now she wished to please, and what else was beauty good for? Daelith was gratified to see the witch's eyes narrow with a calculating gleam.

"Done and done!" Mad Maedie cried, at last, capering about. "Oh, what fun I shall have with such a pretty, pretty face and young ripe body. Ah, ha! But, how will you enjoy inhabiting this toad-flesh of mine, I wonder?"

"I shall like it well enough so long as it serves me,"

Daelith replied. "But you must swear that all your knowledge and power shall be mine."

"Yes, yes," the witch assured her, waving Daelith's demand away as if it were of little consequence. "All of it. You shall have it all, I swear it by the dark of the moon and the river's flow."

Daelith could scarce believe it had been so easy to trick her. But she knew from all that Genae had told her that the most dangerous part was yet to come.

The next evening, Daelith returned just before moonrise, as the witch had instructed. There she found Mad Maedie pawing through a filthy burlap sack and humming tunelessly to herself as she squatted on the river bank in the gathering dusk. Upon seeing Daelith approach, she leaped to her feet and motioned her eagerly forward.

"Ah, ha, my pretty maiden, you came after all. I thought perhaps a night's consideration might change your mind."

"Never fear, my resolve has not wavered. But what is all this?" Daelith nudged the bag Mad Maedie had dumped on the ground.

"Just a few odds and ends I need for the magic," the witch said, thumbing through the ragged grimoire. She paused, having found the spell she required. But rather than reading the spidery scrawl that covered the page, she simply listed the required implements and herbs under her breath.

"And the book?" Daelith pressed, reminded of the way her friend Elmaenie would check the ingredients in the cookbook, then begin mixing things without bothering to read the recipe. She hoped that Mad Maedie would achieve better results.

"The book is called the *Tome of Jaedith*," the witch muttered, closing her eyes to mouth something over and over as if she had trouble remembering it. When she was satisfied, she set the book aside, then took up a wicked-looking dagger from the sack.

With this she cut a large circle into the damp sod around the spot where they stood. She set the dagger aside and began walking clockwise around the circle. Three times around the inside she went, muttering a short invocation to the four guardians as she lit a candle at each of the cardinal points of the compass. Daelith paid careful attention to each thing Mad Maedie did, for fear she would miss some clue that might alert her to treachery on the witch's part.

"What purpose does the circle serve?" Daelith asked as Mad Maedie paused before stooping to light the small brazier she'd set in the center.

"It protects us from evil spirits and such like," she replied, sprinkling three generous pinches of a fragrant herb mixture into the flame as she hastily murmured another invocation.

"The spell I've chosen is simple enough, if you have the power for the doing of it, that is," the witch laughed, stepping back from the brazier and fixing Daelith with a meaningful look. "First, we must make a blood sacrifice beneath the light of the full moon."

Daelith's stomach knotted, and Mad Maedie grinned, revealing long misshapen teeth.

"Not to worry, dearie. A drop or three of blood from each of us will do." She wiped her dagger on the long grass, then held the blade up to catch the firelight.

"Why must it be blood?" Daelith's voice sounded faint even in her own ears, and she could see the impatient look in the witch's eyes. But Genae had said her

91

best chance was to keep Mad Maedie distracted if she could, so Daelith kept on. "I mean couldn't it be something else? They use wine to symbolize blood at the Harvest Festival."

"Harvest Festival, indeed! Pointless, empty ritual. The books says blood, so we use blood. I suppose you'll be one of those meddlesome, goodie-good witches, making the magic all nice and harmless like that soft-heart Genae." Mad Maedie paused to scowl at her, then her eyes narrowed suspiciously. Had she noticed Daelith's start when she mentioned the wise-woman's name?

"What a tiresome little creature you are. Why do you ask so many questions?"

"Because I want to understand how the magic works," Daelith replied, seeming as guileless as she could. "Knowledge is power, after all."

"What fool has filled your head with such nonsense? Power is power. Without the power, this book and all the knowledge it contains is useless, and the power comes from me. I was born with it, just as I was born with this useless, ugly bag of bones for a body. When you have my body, you will have the power. *That* is all you need to know. Now, hold out your right hand."

Trying not to flinch, Daelith held it out, and Mad Maedie pricked her forefinger with the surprisingly sharp point of her dagger. She held it for a moment, to make sure the blood would flow free, then demanded, "Speak your full, true name!" as she allowed three drops of blood to fall into the brazier where it sizzled in the flame.

"Daelith kinMartin."

Pricking her own finger, the witch murmured, "Maedie kinShero," and dripped her blood into the fire. Then she pressed her hand to Daelith's, palm to palm, muttering, "Blood to blood, body to body, soul to soul.

"Now our souls are bound," she said, possessively fingering a lock of Daelith's soft golden hair, before turning once more to look at the grimoire.

"But where did the book come from?"

"I stole it from an old fool who didn't have the power to use it. Now be quiet!" Squinting, she stared uncertainly at the page.

It must be hard to read in the dim light of the brazier, Daelith thought, wondering why she didn't just memorize the spells. But then, if Maedie couldn't be bothered to read them, she could hardly memorize them.

When the witch found what she was looking for, Daelith leaned forward to listen as she read the final words of the incantation. A sickly green mist rose up from the edge of the circle, shrouding them in an unearthly chill; it seemed to Daelith that she swooned for a moment. When she came to herself once more, she stood staring at the lovely, full-fleshed body she had inhabited only moments before. Maedie kinShero blinked back at her with Daelith's own periwinkle blue eyes from beneath a familiar cloud of blonde curls.

"It is done!" the former witch cried in glee, wresting the grimoire from Daelith's hand to kiss its moldy cover.

"The book. Give me back the book!" Daelith croaked as Maedie began to spin and leap about with joy at the strength and grace of her body.

"Take it, fool!" Maedie laughed, pressing the volume into Daelith's gnarled fingers. "It is of no use to me now." Then she turned and, as Daelith watched open-mouthed, simply danced away.

Genae had instructed her to kill the witch as soon as she was transformed, and Daelith *had* meant to kill her—by the gods, she had even longed to. But seeing her own face so rapt with joy, and the softly rounded limbs, breast, and belly that had given her such pleasure at Taeran's touch, she simply could not bring herself to pick up the dagger and strike. Now it was too late.

"That was ill done, niece of mine."

Startled, Daelith turned to find Genae standing at the edge of the clearing. The old woman came forward shaking her head, dark eyes sad as she carefully unmade the circle. Though not as hunched as Mad Maedie, Genae was small and narrowly built.

"But how?" Daelith blurted blushing furiously.

"Surely you didn't think I'd let my only living blood face that demented creature alone?"

"But you said I had to face Mad Maedie by myself because she would never allow you near enough to harm her."

"That is true, my dear. You were our best chance to bring her down. If she had known I was here, she would never have come." Daelith looked guiltily at the dagger which lay where Maedie had discarded it on the ground.

Following her niece's gaze, the wisewoman quietly said, "Never mind, girl. What's done is done and we've work to do." She stroked Daelith's cheek with a slender finger before turning away.

"But Mad Maedie?"

"Will do whatever evil it is within her power to do, but she will not find the world to her liking. Never fear, she will return for what she has foolishly traded away, and next time you will be better prepared to deal with her."

Daelith glanced at the grimoire with a sigh, then began helping Genae gather up the rest of Mad Maedie's things.

Much too early one morning, some five years later, Daelith was startled from a deep, pleasant sleep by the most piteous wailing. She had kept the witch's residence and identity, brightening and expanding the hole in the riverbank and cleaning up the surrounding area. She had also, with Genae's help, established a healer's shrine above. Accustomed to callers at odd hours, she was hardly surprised that someone had come to summon her, although most people used the bell in the shrine. The local folk marveled at the change that had overtaken Mad Maedie, but never questioned their good fortune.

"What is it? What do you need?" she demanded, peering groggily at the bedraggled woman who lay before her on the thick, damp grass. Daelith was both astonished and dismayed to see that it was Maedie who peered up at her—beaten, bruised, and looking quite desperate. Daelith leaned down to help her to her feet.

"Have pity!" Maedie cried, clutching at the sturdy homespun of Daelith's robe. "You must give me back my power that I might punish those who've wronged me!"

"Enough time for that later. First we must see to those cuts," Daelith insisted, helping her into the shrine. Dampening a cloth in the water of the healing pool, she tried to bathe one of the cuts on Maedie's cheek.

"Leave off," Maedie snapped, pushing her away.

"Very well, but what has befallen to you?" Daelith backed away, seating herself on one of the benches that lined the interior of the small stone building.

"Much has happened to me," Maedie spat, pushing the hair from her eyes, "and all of it evil."

"But I don't understand. You were so certain that beauty would bring you all you desired." Daelith watched with troubled eyes as Maedie paced angrily back and forth.

"I have found that beauty holds little power. Men become bored with it too quickly."

"Wealth is also power," Daelith said, her tone quiet and neutral. "Surely you attracted men of substance and did not scruple at using them as they would use you? When first we met, you vowed you could have any man if only my body were yours."

"Indeed, I did!" Maedie declared. "I amassed a goodly fortune before I chose to wed Delaen kin-Kellan. He seemed perfect, a wealthy merchant-trader—the last of his line—come to Kaelie's Bend to settle down. Even better, he was an old man with no sons and soon to die, or so I thought! Worse luck, he expected me to give him an heir!"

"But neither of us may bear children," Daelith said, comprehending the root of the problem. "That was part of the price we paid for the magic you wrought."

"So I discovered," Maedie hissed. "When his fancy, city-educated healer-man declared me to be barren, my dear husband turned from my bed and took another wife, as the law allows. When I complained of this, the brute beat me and told me that I was free to go whenever I chose. But of course, all the assets of our marriage were by law *his* property, even those *I* had brought into it."

"That may not be fair, but it is the law," Daelith replied. "What did you do?"

"Never fear, a solution soon presented itself. You see, I also learned that if I were widowed, I should have half of everything he owned. It seemed quite simple, really, a bit of something in his food or wine, and there would be two grieving widows left to share and share alike. But then, I doubt that my sister-wife would have lived very long." Her mouth twisted into an ugly grin.

"Unfortunately," Maedie continued, "I was not clever enough with the herbs I mixed—I had always relied on the book to guide me in such things before. Though he grew deathly ill, the kinKellan men have the constitution of oxen and Delaen lived despite my best efforts. My intentions were discovered before I could make a second attempt, so I fled."

"Now you've come begging for help, and expect me to give up the power simply because you ask it?" Daelith's voice held a note of incredulity.

Genae was right. I should have destroyed her when I had the chance. Look at the evil she's wrought for all my kindness. Daelith reproached herself, eyes hardening as she gazed upon the failed murderess. But Maedie was so caught up in the fury of her own desire for retribution that she failed to notice.

"If you will not return to me that which is rightly mine," she exhorted Daelith, "then at least give me the means to regain the fortune I've lost. Money, which I now see is the true road to power in this world, will comfort me well enough."

"You could go elsewhere and start again," Daelith

said, considering what she should do with the woman. It was clear she could not allow her back into the world to create more sorrow.

"My fortune was years in the making. I do not have those years to give again to the task. Already the bloom of this body is fading. Do you think that such bait ripens with age?" Maedie sneered. "It does not!"

"Well, I cannot help you regain your wealth," Daelith said, making up her mind. "But if you desire it, I can prepare a draught that will solve the problem of your aging."

"Ah, no," Maedie said with a bitter laugh. "I know that trick too well. Your draught would be poison, and truly I would never age another hour after I'd taken it."

Daelith sighed inwardly, shaking her head as if in reproach for Maedie's accusation. *So it must be the most dangerous way. Why is nothing ever easy?* Assuming the simpering, maidenly affectation she'd used to trick Maedie before, she said, "Your tale has touched me. I was only testing you, after all, to discover if your desire to trade back was a true one. For surely, were I you, I would do anything to keep what beauty I could."

"My desire is true indeed, kind, good friend," Maedie said in a most ingratiating tone, hope coloring her expression.

"I can see that now," Daelith said, then she sighed for effect. "In truth, as you suspected I would, I have grown weary of this joyless form, and would take up my old life again.

"But," Daelith said when she saw the crafty, eager gleam in Maedie's eye, "you must swear that when our exchange is complete, you will help me get safe away to some distant place, where the trouble you've stirred up in Kaelie's Bend will not pursue me. And you must allow me to prepare the potion I offered you, for I have no more desire to lose the charms of youth than you have."

With little choice in the matter, Maedie agreed.

They met again two days later, just before moonrise. Once again the circle was drawn upon the ground; the two women stood within its confines, wreathed in incense and candlelight. The blood flowed, and Daelith spoke the words of changing. But unlike Maedie, she spoke the incantation from memory. This left her hands free to grasp the cup of dark liquid she'd prepared before their meeting.

As the mist rose from the circle's edge, she raised the cup to her lips and drank down the bitter fluid. The poison burned her throat like acid, but she smiled a cold triumphant smile. Seeing this, Maedie screamed in rage, knocking the cup from Daelith's hand, but it was too late.

"Foolish woman," Daelith murmured sadly, looking down at the deformed corpse which lay at her feet. "If only you had bothered to read a little further in that book you thought so worthless, you would have discovered that to keep the power for yourself, you had only to destroy your own body when your spirit entered mine."

With a gesture like setting a bird free to fly, Daelith whispered the words of unbinding, then cast a simple fire spell to burn the remains of the body she had inhabited for five long years. It had been a good body after all, and deserved the dignity of the fire for all else it had suffered. Perhaps Maedie would even find some peace for her tortured soul now that the flesh she'd so despised was finally destroyed. Daelith hoped so, but somehow she doubted it.

Carefully washing away the ashes with water from the pool in the shrine, she replaced the Tome of Jaedith and all the rest of the tools in her carry sack. She paused for a moment to look out over the moon-silvered flow of the river. Watching the light play across its dark surface, she thought, as she often did, of Taeran and of all that had befallen her since his death. But this time no tears came to fill her eyes; instead, Daelith felt inexplicably free.

With a sigh, she hefted the sack to her shoulder and stepped into the whirlpool she'd created with the wave of her hand and a mumbled word, then disappeared beneath the swirling water.

THE SPIRIT ARROW
by Deborah Wheeler

I think Deborah has been featured in most of these anthologies, except the year she and her family were all in France. I've read Deborah's first book, *Jaydium,* and it was excellent. That's not just words, either. I've made it clear I'll do anything for anybody except say their book—or short story—is good when it isn't. I've lost friends by this attitude, but the ones who know me also know how objective I can be. They know my good reviews are not because the person is a friend or a brother or a sister.

And now Deborah has another novel out, also from DAW, entitled *Northlight.* Both of her books were science fiction, and I've enjoyed them thoroughly. And based on *my* opinion of science fiction (and my limited attention span toward anything with rivets and robots), then you *know* they were good.

The rising sun, sullen and gray, cast eerie shadows across the Azkhantian badlands. To the north, jagged hills slashed through the haze. An old woman sat on a solitary crag of black granite, gazing down at the valley where the Geloni Imperials had set up their

101

encampment. She wore a cloak of black wool over her tight-fitting jacket and horseman's trousers, so that from a distance, she seemed to be part of the rock itself. Her skin was creased and her almond-shaped eyes faded from looking at the sun. Across her lap lay a short, curved bow, the wood worn into a soft gloss.

She remembered sitting like this with her mother, many years ago, learning to shoot an arrow straight up in the air and catch it in her bare hands as it came down. She remembered teaching her own daughters to do the same. It was not a test of courage, but an act of surrender, of perfect balance and stillness.

At moments, the old woman imagined she caught the noises of the soldiers below. She had heard them in her dreams for so many nights now—the strangely accented speech, the shouted commands, the clanging of bronze swords and buckles. And the smells—the fetor of unwashed men's bodies crowded together, of leather harness and boiled wheat-meal.

She ran her fingertips over the bow, stroking it like an old friend. It resonated to her touch, as if eager for her to use it again. Beside the bow rested her arrow case. The leather sides were flat, as if empty. It was not empty. She drew out a single arrow, an arrow without a flaw, straight and smooth, each vane of its feathering perfect.

She had carried it since the day her youngest daughter had gone to war.

Outside the circle of Azkhantian tents, watchfires of dried camel dung hissed and flickered. The wind, laden with the smells of horse dung, wild herbs, and charred camel meat, burned cold. A dog barked at a passing shadow. Hardy roach-maned ponies stamped their feet along the tether lines and nickered, as if scenting what lay ahead.

Earlier that day, bonfires of precious ironwood had been lighted, a young camel sacrificed and its entrails examined by the *enaree*, who pronounced the omens auspicious. Then the animal was roasted whole in a pit dug in the earth and everyone who was to ride against the Geloni invaders ate the meat to share in the good fortune. The strong young men and women drank *k'th*, fermented camel's milk, and danced to the music of drums and reed pipes.

Aimellina Daughter of Oomara Daughter of Shannivar stood on the side and watched, her hands curled into fists. The rhythm of the drums pounded through her body like a fever. Her right breast, bound tightly across her chest to keep it from her bowstring, throbbed. Shadows cast by the dancers flickered across her face. Dancers leaped and spun in front of her, their ebony braids flying. They were her friends, her age mates, even the bully she had challenged so many years ago. Now they were all to ride to glory.

All except her.

"The *enaree* made a prophecy the night you were born," Aimellina's mother, Oomara, had said when she forbade her to ride with the others. "The midwives had feared we both might die because a star fell from the sky. The *enaree* said you would live, but die young and far from your own tent."

Aimellina went to find the *enaree* in his tent. She brought a length of fine camel-wool cloth of her own weaving in token of her respect for his powers. Her heart beat unaccountably fast as she waited for his permission to enter.

Ruddy light filled the tent. A brazier of beautifully

wrought bronze held a bed of glowing coals upon which cones of sandalwood incense smoldered. Carpets woven in dark, intricate designs symbolizing the Tree of Life covered the floor.

"I knew that some day you would come to me, Aimellina Daughter of Oomara Daughter of Shannivar." The *enaree* gestured her to sit. "You are grown into a fine strong archer, just as I foresaw."

"Ar-Dethien-Gelon marches on Azkhantia with his army and my mother has forbidden me to ride in our defense!" Aimellina burst out. "All because she fears your prophecy."

"And *you* fear that your friends will get all the glory while you sit at home milking your camels and making curd-cheese, with no chance to kill a man and earn a husband."

Aimellina flushed. "I care nothing for a husband!"

"Then why have you come to me? Not to invite me to dance?" The *enaree* cackled, his voice as hoarse as the cawing of a carrion crow.

Aimellina's shoulders tensed, but she kept her hands open on her lap. "Surely in all your knowledge, with all your powers, you can give me something that will set my mother's heart at ease."

For a long moment, the *enaree* sat silent. The orange light shadowed every seam and line of the old man's face, turning his eyes into those of a strange animal, one of demonic aspect. Aimellina tried to imagine what he was thinking, whether he saw how much Oomara loved her, whether he cared, what secret purpose her own life or death might serve. Finally he said, "And that is all you wish? Your mother's blessing, not the protection of your own life?"

Aimellina's heart shivered. Then, like all brash

young things, she shook it off with a proud toss of her head. "I want to ride, to fight, to serve my people. To win glory. The rest is in the hand of the gods."

Later that night, Aimellina came to her mother's tent. The bonfires had died down. Only a few of the young warriors still danced. The rest had gone off to sleep away the *k'th* and dream of battles to come.

Oomara noted how her daughter held her head, the lightness of her step and the laughter just below the surface of her voice. She'd heard it before, when the girl had made up her mind to take on the tribal bully, even though he was half again as big as she. Or when her father, Oomara's third husband, told her that if she could ride the big dun gelding, she could have it.

"I have come once more to ask your blessing," Aimellina said. "You need have no fear, for the *enaree* has given me a charm that will guard my life through any peril." She held out an arrow, perfect in balance and the smoothness of its shaft.

Oomara picked it up in both hands and tried its strength. To her surprise, the shaft did not bend in her grasp.

"It cannot be broken or burnt," Aimellina said. "It must take a life to—to end mine. So you must keep it for me, for as long as it is safe in your care, so am I. The *enaree* has sworn it so."

"Why would the *enaree* do this for you? What price did you pay?"

Aimellina laughed. "For love of you and pity of me, I suppose. Or perhaps he fears what will become of him if the Geloni triumph. They are not overly fond of his sort, or so it is said."

Oomara closed her eyes, but she could not shut out

the vision of her daughter's face, so filled with the brassy certainty of youth. She had no choice but to give her consent now. If she refused, the *enaree* would hear and take it as a personal insult.

Yet Oomara mistrusted the *enaree,* for she knew his ways were devious and his motives were his own. His loyalty was to his hidden gods and the welfare of the entire tribe, not one headstrong woman archer.

She remembered the last part of his prophecy, the part she had never breathed aloud, that Aimellina would die at the hands of one who loved her.

The Azkhantian clans sent their families and camel herds north, to the summer pastures. Hares, wild boar, and swift-footed gazelle roamed freely over the empty plains. Cloud leopards, emboldened at the retreat of the tribes, came down from the high reaches to hunt. Black-winged hawks soared overhead to dive upon the unwary. The land was broad and wide under the endless sky.

Aimellina rode out with the Azkhantian host, mounted on the same dun pony she had won from her father. She wore a pointed felt cap and jacket of camel-wool, stitched with the stylized lioness of her family totem. The Azkhantian riders sang as they rode, and Aimellina's voice rose higher and wilder than the rest.

They rested their ponies on a ridge overlooking the flat river valley. Aimellina, near the front, rocked forward on her saddle pad and shaded her eyes with one hand. In the distance, the Geloni army inched forward, barely moving except for the clouds of dust thrown up at its passage.

"By all the gods of fire and thunder," one of the men

beside her murmured, "there must be thousands of them."

"Five thousand at least," someone else said.

"No, ten!"

"Aiee! They are locusts, filling the land beyond counting."

Aimellina's heart leaped like a startled gazelle in her chest. The Azkhantian defenders numbered no more than two thousand. Then she calmed, remembering her life was safe in her mother's strong hands.

She tossed her head, sending her braids swirling. "What have we to fear from locusts? Ten or ten thousand or a hundred thousand? We are the fire in the sky, the hawk which hunts where it wills!" She raised her bow and the dun pony pranced underneath her. "Who rides with me to glory?"

The men beside her lifted their bows and shouted. The one who had likened the Geloni host to locusts hesitated for a moment, then joined them.

They waited all day and then the next as the Geloni Imperials crept closer and closer. Aimellina wanted to charge them, but Itheryas Warleader, son of the Azkhantian chief, held the young hotheads back.

"There will be glory enough in its own time. If we cannot be a raging lion, we will be a dancing wolf."

For days, Aimellina thought she would go mad with waiting. She went to camp and offered herself to Itheryas as a scout. That night, she took her dun pony and rode for the Geloni encampment.

She got closer than she expected before she spotted their sentries. She slipped from her mount and hushed it with a hand over its nose. The Geloni had no horses, only supply carts pulled by onagers. The camp looked well-ordered, with latrine pits dug well away from the living areas. The smell of boiled grain arose from the cookfires. She studied the sentries, their weapons and armor, overlapping plates of metal on leather. As silently as she came, she slipped away to give her report.

Itheryas called his swiftest riders, Aimellina among them. "Before we fight the Geloni invaders, we must know their strengths. You will lead a troop to just beyond the reach of a long arrow's shot of the foremost. Go no closer. As soon as they answer, head east as fast as your ponies can run."

"We are not to stay and battle them?" Aimellina protested. She had not yet killed anything more fearsome than a brace of plains-hares.

"There will be glory enough to go around," he repeated. "For now, let us see how easily we can outrun them."

Aimellina led her troops as the warleader commanded. The Geloni Imperials lunged after them, spears and shields upraised. They shouted slogans she could not understand. But laden with armor as they were, their first burst of speed quickly faded. The Azkhantians paused just beyond the reach of the Geloni arrows. Their ponies jigged and pranced with excitement, their necks arched. Again the Geloni charged and again the plains riders retreated.

"Stand and fight! Cowards!" shouted the Geloni.

Aimellina laughed as she rode away. She presented herself to the warleader with shining eyes and glowing cheeks.

"Pah! They are nothing to fear! They are slow and stupid!"

Itheryas, sitting on his chair of stretched camel-hide, stroked the coils of his beard. "Yet even a slow and stupid beast can turn deadly if it gets you within its claws. We must not underestimate the power of this one. Let us lead him ever onward, farther and farther from his own land. Let us see if the Geloni can eat grass and conjure water from the stones."

That night, the Azkhantians danced and mocked the stupid, cowardly Geloni. *K'th* flowed freely. Aimellina danced as wildly as any man, and that night she lay with Itheryas Warleader in his tent.

Far in the northern hills, along with the families and camel herds, Oomara awoke with a start. Her breath caught in her throat, her heart pounded, and there was a sweet melting ache in her loins. She had not taken joy in a man's arms since her last husband died of a poisoned wound while hunting wild boar. Yet this was no memory of a tender lover which had come to her in the night. This was something more, tainted with magic. . . .

Moving by touch in the velvet darkness of her tent, she found her arrow case and drew out a single, perfect shaft. The wood, once polished so smooth, was damp, as if with sweat.

Farther and farther, Itheryas led the Geloni army, always taunting them, always beyond their reach. The Geloni charges grew shorter, as they learned they could not catch the swift plains riders. One day, Aimellina's scouting party saw that the Geloni had split their forces into three parts. One continued on its present course, thrusting deep into abandoned Azkhantian territory. The others went north and south, one toward the fever-ridden swamplands of the south, the other toward where the Azkhantians had sent their herds and families.

Itheryas called his captains to discuss strategy. Although he had granted Aimellina no special favors since they had become lovers, he listened to her now, stroking his beard thoughtfully, as she urged that a small party—no more than three hands of riders—remain behind as a ruse to hold the main body of Geloni, while the rest raced north. At a fraction of their full strength, the northern Geloni contingent alone could not overpower the Azkhantian host.

The young men and women cheered Aimellina's proposal, hoping they would be chosen to stay behind, a few against so many. Itheryas gave Aimellina the command. That night, he kissed her as tenderly as a daughter and sent her to her own tent alone.

The old woman shifted on her position on the chunk of black rock. Below her, smoke curled skyward from the cooking fires of the encampment. The sun was slowly burning off the morning's haze, and the outlines of the hills grew sharper. Morning's chill hung about her still, clinging to her like a familiar garment. Under her fingertips, the arrow felt warm. It quivered under her touch.

The Geloni Imperials made camp by the Doharra Springs in the shape of a huge circle. They stayed there for many days. Aimellina rode closer and closer, jeering at them, calling them cowards, shooting arrows into the sky and then catching them with her bare hands. She led her troops on a hare-hunt just beyond arrow range to show how little regard she gave the Geloni. Nothing would budge the Imperials.

Then, the next morning, they were gone, fled in the darkness. The dust of their retreat could be seen in the far distance. Nothing remained of the encampment except latrine furrows and discarded packs. In places, the wiry plains-grass had been torn and beaten. Much of the campsite looked as if an army of moles had been at work, throwing up burrows and heaps of loose soil, only to have them smoothed over by the passage of men's feet. Dust swirls arose like ghosts from the dry dirt.

Aimellina and her riders sat on the little rise beyond the campsite and cheered. "Come on!" she cried, slinging her bow across her back. "Let's see what gifts they've left for us!"

She urged the dun gelding down toward the trampled earth. The pony bucked, fighting her. She dug her heels into its sides and forced it onward. Giving her ululating battle cry, she galloped toward the stretch of smoothed, bare earth. Her riders pounded close behind her, headed for the abandoned cart which was piled high with baggage.

Without warning, Aimellina's pony plunged to the ground. She looked down as the earth gave way beneath it. A ditch gaped beneath her. Instinct sent her scrambling off the pony's back just before it crashed down upon the spearpoints braced in the ditch.

Aimellina's boots slipped on the shield which had covered the ditch, masked by a thin layer of dirt. The pony shrieked as it landed full force on the spears. Blood spurted from its neck and sides. It thrashed wildly. One hoof caught Aimellina on the side of the head. Her vision whirled and her stomach lurched. Pain lanced through her skull.

Around her, she heard more ponies neighing, someone screaming, then the guttural battle chant of the Geloni.

Aimellina clawed at the edge of the ditch. The dirt crumbled in her hand. Her feet tore and slipped on the slope. Then, as if some invisible hand caught her, sustained her, the earth grew steady beneath her toes. She scrambled up.

The next instant, she'd drawn her knife from its sheath on her thigh. A Geloni soldier lunged at her with a heavy bronze sword. Under his helmet, with its feathered crest, his shaven face was flushed and grim.

Aimellina twisted, parrying the Geloni's thrust as best she could. Her knees felt slippery; her heart pounded.

All around her, the earth boiled over with Geloni in full battle armor. A hundred spear points clashed in the sun. As she turned to face her attacker, she caught a glimpse of one of her riders—only one—an instant before he was buried under a dozen Imperials.

More Geloni—five or six—formed a circle around her. In one hand, each held a sword, angled so she could not pass their reach. Each protected his own body with a shield. She tried lunging this way and then that, but could not reach them.

"Cowards!" She sliced through the air with her long knife. "Are you afraid to fight one woman?"

The first Geloni—at least, she thought it was he, the way her vision blurred now and her ears sang high and sweet—straightened his shoulders.

"Surrender!"

"Never!" Aimellina cried. "Come at me, one to one, and I will spit your eyeballs on my blade and eat your liver raw!"

"Surrender or death," rumbled the Imperial.

"Death, then! Death for both of us!" Her knife extended to its fullest range, Aimellina hurled herself at him.

Something thudded against the side of her head and everything went black.

In her tent in the northern hills, Oomara woke screaming. Pain, endless pain ... Her chest and belly were a mass of oozing burns, her left nipple torn out by pincers, her joints twisted until the bones splintered. A hundred moments of searing agony, a hundred moments of looming blackness from which something always held her back ...

And still she did not die.

And always came the questions, thundered at her in a voice she could barely understand.

Where is the Azkhantian host? Where have they gone? North or south? Where? Where?

Oomara pulled off her loose robe of camel-wool, clawed at the soft shift beneath it. She lifted her arms, surprised at the easy motion of her shoulders. Trembling fingers smoothed over her unbroken skin, traced the outlines of her unscarred left breast.

She lit a lamp of camel tallow and dressed, shivering in the cold. Her arrow case lay as always beside her sleeping pillow. She reached inside. Her stomach curled as her fingers closed around the single, perfect shaft. As before, it was wet. She held it up to the light.

Droplets of blood oozed silently from the wooden shaft.

She took only a single mount, a tough old mare like herself, a bag of grain and dried mutton, her bow and arrow case. As she left, the *enaree* watched from the edge of the camp. She wondered what curse might come if she strangled him with her bare hands. But something in the lonely figure, the way he hobbled from his tent, caught at her heart. It was said the *enarees* saw many things, and for this they paid a terrible price. The *enaree*'s death would not buy back Aimellina's, or change what Oomara must do.

The Geloni would not know which way they had gone, not yet. Aimellina had bought them that much time. The Azkhantian force would arrive that day or the next and move them all farther into the northern badlands, where any pursuit could be countered by ambush.

The arrow drew her south, as unerring as a lodestone. The mare trotted on, untiring. Hours melted into days of gray sky, gray dust, gray fear in her heart.

Day by day, the arrow wept blood.

Night by night, she awoke screaming.

Where have they gone? North or south? Say the word and we will end your pain.

By death, she knew they meant. But she could not die.

A woman sat on a crag of black rock, looking down on the broad flatness where the Geloni had set up their encampment. The sun was well up now. The night, with its tortured sleep, was over.

Another day. Another day of pain.

She drew out a single arrow, an arrow without flaw, straight and smooth, each vane of its feathering perfect. Like a lover, her bow welcomed her touch, the wood worn silken by years of use.

Her left breast ached, as if filled with milk. She remembered the tug of a petal-soft mouth, the sweet moments of guiding the pony for her daughter's first ride.

The hot fierce pride as she watched Aimellina's dancing swordplay, the way she sat her big dun pony, the eagle steadiness of her gaze, the sureness of her aim.

Oomara stood and searched for a place to stand among the crannies and loose rock chips. Her feet came to rest, well apart, balanced, as if this place in the rock had always been waiting for her.

She looked into the sky. The blue was so clear, it hurt her eyes. She imagined a hawk flying free, just beyond the limit of her aging eyes.

She strung the bow and notched the arrow to the bowstring. Slowly, she drew the bow. She felt its power matched by the strength in her arms. A great stillness came over her. The haze overhead parted. The wind hushed.

She looked unblinking at the sun and aimed. Loosed, the arrow shot free. The bow quivered in her hands. She soared with the arrow, straight to the heart of the sun's brilliance. The earth fell away below her, the tiny figure of a black-cloaked woman on a rock as craggy and weather-seamed as she.

Slower and slower she rose, until at last she curved back toward the earth. Each instant, she gathered strength and sureness.

The returning arrow fell so straight, it was a mere dot against the bright splendor of the sky. She did not need to see it. She felt it singing in her blood, in her bones, in the pit of her belly, the center of joy.

Air whistled by as the green and golden plains rushed to meet her. Then, at the last moment, she opened her arms, as if to welcome a lost child, and arched her chest to embrace the falling arrow.

Silver pain shocked through her. She gasped and fell to her knees. Her body tumbled down the slope like a broken doll. She landed in a heap on a clump of jagged rocks. Below, in the Geloni encampment, another body shuddered, another mouth curved in a smile of relief, another chest grew suddenly still. Her vision blurred and her eyes stung with unexpected tears. She had been prepared for the pain, for the fading of the day, but not for the sense of inexpressible tenderness which swept all through her, carrying her to the last.

THE CHOOSING
by John P. Buentello

John says that, like the character in his story, he's
currently at a number of crossroads in his life. He's
just coming out of a spell of teaching, which I, as an
editor, apologize for interrupting. There's probably
only one thing this country needs as much as good
literate writers, and that's more good admirable
people in the teaching profession. Having been a
dropout from three teacher's colleges—SUNY in Al-
bany, New York, Hardin-Simmons in Abilene, Texas;
and University of California in Berkeley—this is a
subject on which I feel qualified to speak. Actually, it
was the unfortunate and certainly atypical classes I
took to become a teacher that made me decide not
to go into that most honorable profession. The first
session of one such class we spent all the period
discussing—I swear I'm not making this up—the rel-
ative worth of tacks or Scotch tape for making bulletin boards, a second period discussing on which
occasion we should make bulletin boards, the third
period we began a discussion of whether we should
use a psychological or a psychoanalytic model for
giving our students self-esteem. I walked out, went
up to the office and changed my major. I was also
told by this unusually misguided department that I

could not teach without a remedial speech course, because I had a "Flat A"—whatever *that* is. I eventually graduated with a triple major; Education, Psychology, and Spanish, and have never taught regularly since. I probably should be grateful for the bad experience because my true calling is *not* teaching, but writing and editing. For the record, I believe children matter more than any amount of tacks or tape or bulletin boards, and nothing on Earth or elsewhere would induce me to treat them as if they didn't.

Laira saw the edge of the sword descending in time to deflect the blow. The force of the attack drove her to her knees, and she winced as the hard rocks of the practice square bit into her flesh. She pushed the vision of the spell she had been conjuring from her mind and fought to regain her balance. Athan's sword continued to beat down on her, until she held up a hand of supplication and lowered her own weapon.

"Gods, Laira! What were you dreaming about? I could have cut your head from your shoulders!" The swordmaster sheathed his weapon and helped Laira to her feet. There was anger in his gray eyes, but there was also a touch of concern. He looked down at her sword hand and saw it was shaking.

"Are you ill, Laira?"

Laira shook her head. She raised her eyes to meet the swordmaster's gaze and sighed. "I'm fine. I was thinking about that spell of summoning I practiced in the wizard's hall today."

Athan's hands balled up into fists. "What have I told you about magic and swordwork, girl?"

She nodded, feeling her cheeks burn. "Mix not one with the other."

"Lest your head fly away from your body," Athan said sourly. His tone softened a bit. "The time of choosing is close, isn't it, my pupil?"

Laira nodded. "The Council told me yesterday that I would have a week to choose. Oh, Master, what will I do?"

Athan put a rough hand on Laira's shoulder. He smiled and brushed a strand of brown hair from her eyes. "You will make the right choice. Both Master Kirn and I know you will walk the right path."

Laira's eyes grew wider at the mention of her spellmaster's name. "Oh no! I forgot that I promised Master Kirn I'd help him with the sorting of the herbs this morning."

"Then you'd best tend to your duties, student." Athan nodded and turned toward the dorm. "I'll see you this afternoon on the dueling grounds."

Master Kirn was already dividing the bundles of dried herbs when Laira finally arrived at his study. The white-haired master smiled at her as she took a seat at the bench next to him, and watched as she plucked the dried, bitter herbs from the fresh.

"You're late, student."

Laira nodded and dropped her eyes. "I was busy with Master Athan. I'm afraid I did badly in practice today."

Kirn laughed and resumed his sorting. "Athan was never one to let a student get through a practice unscathed. Even one as skilled as you, Laira." His eyes became suddenly serious. "Did Master Athan talk to you about your choosing?"

Laira nodded. She wished everyone would stop asking her about it. She knew she was already past the time of choosing. Every novice who came to the Masters' dorm was trained in a variety of skills. As the young apprentices gained in experience and skill, their individual talents began to come to the surface. Most chose a path to walk much earlier than Laira. She had early on shown her skill with a sword and dagger. As a fighter she was virtually unbeatable. But her talents for magic had kept pace with her fighting skills, until now a time of choosing was upon her.

Kirn looked at a bundle of herbs as it dried on the table before him. The magically-treated plants withered into a black pile of useless ash. The spellmaster looked at Laira and shook his head. He reached over and tapped the short silver dagger sheathed at her side.

"You know the rules, Laira. Please remove your weapon from the room."

Laira stared at the drying herbs before her. She let out a gasp and hurried from the room. Unsheathing the dagger, she placed it on a shelf in the hallway and stood holding herself, trying to keep from shaking. How could she have been so stupid? Everyone knew that to use magic required the user be free of any other kind of power. Metal weapons were the worst. A dagger would warp the intent of any magical spell. First she had almost lost her head because she couldn't stop thinking of magic while she practiced, and now she had forgotten to shed her weapon before sitting with Master Kirn. The mage probably thought her a fool. If she weren't careful, there would be no choosing for her to have to make. She'd be thrown out of the dorms for incompetence.

"Laira?" Master Kirn's voice sought her in the hall. He stepped from the study and shook his head. "Don't be so hard on yourself, girl. There are plenty in the world who will fill that role for you."

"I'm sorry, Master," Laira whispered. "I didn't mean to spoil the herbs."

"The rest will surely spoil if we don't sort and store them," Kirn replied. He reached out and took Laira's hand. "Child, there is no shame in being confused. When I was your age I had as much trouble knowing which foot to place in front of the other. Your choice is a much harder one."

Laira looked up into the old master's eyes. "But what if I make the wrong choice?"

"As long as you make the choice with your heart, it cannot be wrong," Kirn told her.

Finally the day arrived. Masters Kirn and Athan announced that Laira would have to choose the path she would follow in her life. The next steps in training would require total dedication. Laira learned that she was to ride with one of them to the Master's Temple, to pray for guidance in her choosing. As she dressed that morning in her room, she felt her body shake from more than the coolness of the air.

When she came down, Master Athan was waiting for her in the courtyard. He held the reins of a pair of horses and smiled when he saw Laira dressed in her ceremonial robes. His smile grew broader as he noticed the dagger tied to her waist.

"Remember to shed that thing if you decide to pray for the power of a mage," he told her as he handed her

121

one set of reins. "The gods might not take such an omission as kindly as we do."

Laira nodded and climbed onto the animal's back. "Is Master Kirn going to at least see us off?"

Athan pointed to the stairs leading to Kirn's chambers. The older man was already making his way slowly down to the courtyard. "Kirn is not here to see you off," Athan told her. "He is the one who will take you to the temple."

"Will you not come?" Laira asked.

Athan shook his head. "There is too much work at the dorms to allow two Masters to be absent. Don't worry, Laira. You will make the right choice." His face grew slightly sad. "And if it must be the path of a mage, then I pray you, make me proud, girl!"

"I will," Laira replied. "I swear it."

Kirn nodded at Athan as the other turned to help the older man to his horse. The swordmaster waited until the two were both settled in the saddles, then turned and disappeared back into the dorms. Kirn turned his horse toward the road leading to the woods and spurred it. Laira, with a final look back at the dorms, followed after.

They had ridden for more than two hours before Kirn reined his horse and slowly slid from his saddle. He sat on the ground and stared up at Laira. "Let's rest a while," he said, his breath coming in short pants. "At my age, riding is more of an exertion than it seems."

Laira nodded and dismounted. She had been preoccupied with her own thoughts during the journey. Kirn had asked her nothing about her decision. Indeed, he had said almost nothing once they'd left the surrounding walls of the dorm. Laira guessed he was trying to be fair to her. Anything he said at this point might influence her choosing.

As she sat and watched the horses graze, Laira realized she had not even come close to choosing a path. It wasn't so much that she hated the thought of giving up one way of life for another. The masters had taught her that the choice would be the most important moment in her life. Being so divided between two callings was tearing her apart inside. If she chose wrong, she might never feel whole again.

Master Kirn stood up and stretched his arms. He smiled down at Laira and said, "While we're resting, why don't you practice some of your spells of power? The practice will do you good."

Laira nodded and closed her eyes. She slowed her breathing, mentally seeking out that place within her where only quiet peace dwelled. She felt her muscles relax and began to recite the spells to herself. She hadn't finished the first when she felt a tap on her shoulder.

She opened her eyes to see Kirn frowning at her. "Remember what I said about weapons?"

Laira's hand went to the dagger at her belt. She quickly pulled it off and laid it on the ground. Master Kirn nodded and went back to see to the horses. Laira sighed, closed her eyes, and tried to calm the hurried beating of her heart. She scolded herself silently, telling herself she would be neither a mage nor a warrior if she kept this up. And now she knew why Master Kirn wanted her to practice. The power spells were the most complex form of magic for a novice to control. That she had forgotten her weapon again was not a good sign. She had to concentrate, prove to both the mage and herself that she could handle the raw power.

Perhaps if she successfully completed this exercise, her choice would be clear.

Laira had finished the first of the seven levels of spells and was beginning to let her mind sink into that murky darkness that signaled her arrival at the source of her powers when she heard a sound. It was faint, just at the edge of her perception, and she fought to push it away. The sound would not leave. It grew louder, filling her mind until it registered that it was a cry she was hearing; a cry of pain.

There was the sound of bramble snapping close to her, and Laira opened her eyes to see two things at once. Where the horses stood, Master Kirn had fallen to his knees. His left hand clutched at his right shoulder, where an arrow had buried itself deep into his flesh. A red stain was flowing across his tunic. Not more than two paces in front of her was a very large man. He wore stained leather and fur, and in his hands he held an upraised sword. This he was bringing down toward Laira's head.

She moved without thinking. Her hands went up, even as the power spell she was shaping fled from her mind. She caught the man's wrists as he dropped the sword, and let his weight carry him over her to the ground. Before he could rise, she was on him, twisting him up and back. His eyes held a wild, angry look, and he pawed at her with a free hand. Laira ignored it. She kept turning him, until his torso went over the end of the blade in his other hand. Laira jumped up and slammed her body down on the man, driving the blade deep into him.

She was rolling free from his corpse even as two other men broke through the brush. One was holding a bow, already nocked with an arrow aimed straight for

Master Kirn. Laira finished her roll and came to a sitting position as her hand caught the hilt of the dagger she had placed on the ground. She threw with the aim of countless hours of practice, following the arc of the dagger until it came to rest squarely in the bowman's large chest. The man gave a muffled grunt and fell to the ground.

The third man was on her then, pushing her back to the hard ground, trying to pin her arms. Laira relaxed for a moment, letting his weight settle on her, then shoved him backward with her feet. She reached out toward where the first man lay and gripped the exposed hilt of the buried sword. Pulling it free, she regained her feet even as the other man charged with his own sword. Laira parried the clumsy thrust, closed the distance between her and her attacker, and slashed the edge of her weapon across his neck. The man looked down at the red life seeping away from him and fell dead.

Laira dropped the sword and ran for Master Kirn. The mage sat on the ground holding his shoulder. He had pulled the arrow free and was trying to staunch the wound. Laira bound his arm tightly enough to stop the bleeding and helped him to his feet.

"Come, Master Kirn, we must get you to a healer."

The mage nodded and let her help him to his horse. Laira grabbed the free reins and remounted her own animal. She turned them back toward the dorms and slowly led them back down the road. Master Kirn seemed to be in some pain, but after a moment he closed his eyes and seemed to relax. He opened his eyes again and smiled at Laira.

"Don't worry, child. We'll make it. The wound will

not flow until we reach a healer. At least I have enough strength for that."

Laira shook her head in disbelief "That's a lesson you never bothered to teach me, Master."

Kirn nodded. He reached to take the reins in his good hand. "And I'm afraid it is one you may never know."

Laira didn't believe what she had just heard. "What are you saying? Am I to be expelled?"

Kirn laughed. "No, Laira. But you have chosen your path. You will be a warrior, not a mage."

"But we haven't reached the temple," Laira began.

"There is no need. You fought against three bandits and defeated them, as a warrior born to the talent would. When you saw those men attacking, why didn't you use your powers?"

Laira opened her mouth to speak, but she suddenly understood what the mage was telling her. "I reached for my weapons."

Kirn nodded. "Out of pure instinct. Out of pure heart. Master Athan will be pleased to hear he has his student back. And a most promising one at that."

Laira felt a mixture of joy and sadness fill her. She knew Master Kirn was right. She looked to him and said, "Will I never be able to work magic again?"

Kirn frowned. "You know the rules. Weapons and magic never mix." Then his face slowly softened into a smile. "So if you ever come to my study to practice, leave your dagger in your room!"

TORTOISE WEEPS
by Marella Sands

Marella Sands has just sold two novels to Tor in the same universe as this fine, subtle story. She graduated from Kent State University with a master's degree in Anthropology (am I the only writer in the whole world who doesn't have a master's degree?), and has a pet rat and an iguana. There's one for the collection—the first iguana, I think; writers have cats, dogs, wolves, mongoose (is the plural of mongoose mongeese?), and even a turkey who so far escaped Thanksgiving, but no iguanas.

Marella says that this story and her two novels are set in Tikal during the fifth century. This story began based on the story of a historic woman. "Frog Spring is my fantasy version of a woman known to archaeologists as Woman of Tikal. She actually had architecture dedicated to her. She is shown standing on the right (the honored side) of her husband, and her tomb is the only known one of its kind dedicated to a woman in the Classic period of Tikal. Although no one knows her name or what she did with her life, she must have been a remarkable woman."

Frog Spring leaned against the wall of the palace and stared at the cloudless sky. The sun shone so brilliantly the sky was almost white, as if all color had been scorched out of it. The heat damaged everything. Even the red and orange paint on the palace wall chipped a bit more every day. Some of the paint flakes fluttered down onto Frog Spring's dress. The orange flakes stood out in stark contrast with the purple cotton.

Her son beat the dry ground of the courtyard near her feet with his tiny hands. He had just discovered how to walk and run and loved to practice both. But right now he was more interested in the thumping noises the ground made when he struck it. Dust rose from the ground where he played and drifted lazily around him in the still morning air.

It was the month of Yax—normally the height of the rainy season—but day after day, no friendly black clouds came to drop water on the farmers' *milpas*. The priests had prayed for rain, had burned rubber and copal to make black smoke to attract the *chacs,* the givers of water. They had pierced their own bodies and dedicated the blood to the gods. Sacrifices, both animal and human, had been offered at all the temples of the city. At night, the croaking of the *uo*-frog boys could be heard all over the city. But none of it had done any good.

Even Frog Spring's husband, Claw Bark, the king, had personally offered his blood to the gods. Not that his blood should do any good—Claw Bark did not honor the gods as the previous kings had. Why should they accept *his* blood? If Frog Spring were one of the gods, she would be insulted by his offering.

Four maids knelt in the center of the courtyard, their

black hair piled on their heads with wooden hairpins. Frog Spring suppressed a surge of anger. When her father had been king, even the maids had been decked with beautiful jewelry. Frog Spring had begged Claw Bark to let the maids wear finery in order to honor the household and the gods. He had refused. Frog Spring had even spread her own meager store of finery amongst the servants, but that had made Claw Bark angry. He'd beaten her for it. She hadn't been able to walk for a week.

That her husband had the right to beat her she accepted. That he would beat her for trying to honor the gods and the kingship she would never forgive.

All the maids were soaked with sweat, which made the flour they ground on their stone *metates* stick to their arms like a coating of mud. But their hands were still quick and the pile of maize they had ground to a fine powder was already large.

The eldest among the maids, a woman whose corn flour dusted hair was also streaked with the gray of age, rocked back on her heels and pointed. "Mistress! Look!"

"Yes?" asked Frog Spring. She glanced toward the corner of the courtyard the maid indicated, but she saw nothing. Her son ran to her and grabbed her around the knees. She reached down and stroked his hair.

"A tortoise, Mistress—there, see?" The maid's eyes were wide in awe.

Frog Spring looked again. Yes, a tortoise was there. Excitement rose in her breast. Frog Spring extricated herself from her son's arms and walked toward the corner. A large tortoise sat there, head up, apparently studying the scene. Dark streaks marked its face where its tears had flowed.

Frog Spring fell on her knees before the tortoise. The shell beads of her earrings clinked together as she bowed to the tortoise. The tortoise was always good luck, for he was a friend of mankind. He pitied men and wept for their afflictions. His tears could call up miracles.

Frog Spring bowed her head again to the reptile. "Father Tortoise," she said. "Thank you for visiting this courtyard. Thank you for your tears."

She looked up. The tortoise sat just as it had. Frog Spring stood carefully and backed away several steps. She turned and walked back to the maids, careful to maintain proper decorum. She felt like running, like laughing—good luck was sure to come to the palace now. But it wouldn't do for the wife of the king to act like a child.

"Girl, go fetch fruit for the tortoise," she ordered one of the maids. The girl stood and ran to the storeroom quickly and was back with several selections of fruit. Frog Spring frowned. The fruit was old and bruised, but she took it from the maid and said nothing. She knew there was little fruit left in the storeroom. Considering what the servants had been bringing to supper lately, this was probably the best of what was left.

Frog Spring took the fruit and walked back to the tortoise. She laid the fruit on the ground before it. The tortoise blinked its eyes slowly and watched her. Frog Spring hoped the tortoise was not insulted by the condition of the sacrifice she offered it.

"Please, accept this offering," said Frog Spring, swallowing her embarrassment over the condition of the food. To make up for the bruised fruit, she removed her wooden bracelets and her earrings and laid them beside the fruit.

The tortoise blinked again. Frog Spring left it there with the fruit and the jewelry. Her son glimpsed the tortoise and ran forward. Frog Spring grabbed him and swung him into her arms.

"No," she said. "Never bother Father Tortoise, or he might get angry. Leave him in peace."

Frog Spring went into the dark, but in no way cooler, palace, hopeful for the first time since the rains had failed.

Frog Spring left her son with his nurse and returned to the quarters she shared with her husband. Claw Bark sat in the center of the room next to the small fire, a piece of bark paper in his lap, a stingray spine in his hands. His eyes were closed.

Frog Spring stood still, unwilling to interrupt her husband while he prepared to sacrifice his blood. She waited while Claw Bark raised the stingray spine to his face and plunged it into his ear several times. Claw Bark's face drew up in pain, but he didn't cry out or open his eyes. He lifted the paper to his ear and let the blood drip onto it.

After a few moments, Claw Bark opened his eyes and threw the paper into the fire. It flashed up briefly, and the fire consumed it eagerly.

Claw Bark stood and walked over to a pile of cotton towels. He picked up one and held it to his face. Blood dripped from beneath the cloth.

"Bah," he said. "I give blood and the priests give blood, and still the rains do not come."

"Husband, your wound is still bleeding," said Frog

Spring. "Let me call one of the maids to tend it for you."

Claw Bark's handsome face snarled. "Let it bleed."

Frog Spring marveled anew that anyone as beautiful in form as her husband could be so repulsive in manner. She wished her brother had lived to become king, so she could have been free to marry some lesser noble of Tikal and not this ambitious foreigner who had so impressed her father with his eloquence and knowledge of arcane things.

Claw Bark dropped the towel into the fire and wrapped himself in a brilliant red skirt with the pattern of yellow and white birds woven into the cloth. Large jade beads dangled in several strands around his neck and a small bone ring hung from his nose. Purple abalone shell beads had been woven into his elaborately braided hair. Even his ankles were heavy with strands of shell and jade beads.

"Then let me give blood, too," said Frog Spring softly. She knew it wasn't proper, but she wanted to do something—anything—to help her city.

"The gods do not want a woman's blood. You will just make them more angry."

"Sometimes the gods want a woman's heart. Why not a woman's blood?" Frog Spring knew all the arguments, but she was tired of them. Giving fruit and jewelry to Father Tortoise was a small gesture; she wanted to do more.

"Silence! If you had not been Kan Boar's daughter, I never would have married you." Claw Bark dismissed Frog Spring with a wave.

Anger overwhelmed Frog Spring. She had turned enough heads as a maiden to know she was not ugly. Nor was she lazy. Claw Bark implied she would have been unmarriageable if she had not been a king's daughter, and she knew it wasn't true. She spat into the fire in defiance of his derision. "No, you would have married any woman whose status would make you a king!"

Claw Bark snarled, strode quickly across the room and slapped her. Frog Spring reeled with the force of his blow and her ears rang, but she didn't fall. She would not go on her knees before this upstart foreigner. She was a king's daughter, not a peasant woman.

"You are willful, woman," spat Claw Bark. "Your mother raised you without manners. In my city, the son of a willful woman will also grow up to be willful." His eyes narrowed. "Perhaps your son is the reason for the drought."

Cold fear clutched Frog Spring's heart and her knees wobbled. One of the foreign ways Claw Bark had brought with him to Tikal was the sacrifice of children. He couldn't—he wouldn't—dare threaten their son, would he? Despite her fear, Frog Spring would not bow before Claw Bark. She straightened her shoulders. "Our son is too young to anger the gods," she said.

"My blood does no good," he said. "It's because of your son."

"Our son," said Frog Spring, wondering why Claw Bark suddenly refused to acknowledge his son. If her husband truly thought her unfaithful, she would die an adulteress' death in the courtyard before sunset. There was but one punishment for adultery, yet Frog Spring did not deserve it—as much as she detested her husband, she had been faithful to him.

"Your son," said Claw Bark.

Frog Spring walked up to face her husband. He was

133

a head taller than she, and she had to crane her neck to see his eyes.

"If you think I'm an adulteress, then accuse me!" she said. "And if you accuse me, then I spit on your accusation. I am Frog Spring, daughter of Kan Boar, of the line of the great Jaguar Paw! I know my duty, and I know the law. I am blameless in this."

Claw Bark raised his hand, but Frog Spring did not flinch. Claw Bark lowered his hand slowly and turned away. "Our son," he said. "Well, then, my wife, it is time to do something more about the bad luck. We must offer a sacrifice."

"Sacrifices have already been made. Blood, hearts, copal . . ." said Frog Spring, afraid of what her husband would say next.

"It is our son who shall be sacrificed," said Claw Bark. "Only the son of a king can intercede for us now. He must go to the bottom of the sacred *cenote* and talk to the *chac*. He must beg the *chac* for rain in his small child's voice."

"No," whispered Frog Spring, her heart cold in her chest. Not her son! To be sacrificed was an honor, but still, she could not bear to see her son cast into the water. "No—I will go instead."

"You?" Claw Bark sneered. He sat down on a bench and wiped more blood away from his face.

Frog Spring waited in silence.

"All right," said Claw Bark. He smirked. Frog Spring bit her tongue in anger—that had been his thought all along. He hadn't wanted to sacrifice the boy; he wanted to be rid of her. An adulteress or a sacrifice—he didn't care, so long as she was gone.

Too late now. She had offered and the king had accepted. Frog Spring nodded and kept her anger to herself.

"Then go prepare yourself, woman," said Claw Bark. "The sacrifice goes into the *cenote* at midday."

Frog Spring bit back the words she wanted to say. She turned and left the room. Claw Bark's laughter followed her down the corridor.

The midday sun sent out blistering heat. Frog Spring stood on the edge of the *cenote* as the priest bound her ankles. Another held her wrists. When her ankles were securely tied, the second priest bound her wrists. Frog Spring tried not to look at the deep blue water sixty feet below.

Frog Spring stood still, eyes staring straight ahead, desperate to turn around and steal one last glimpse of her son, but determined not to give in. She would be a proper sacrifice—brave and unmoved by the heat or the cries of her son behind her.

"Accept this sacrifice!" shouted the High Priest, a man who had come to Tikal with Claw Bark. He was dressed in a bright blue skirt with a jaguar skin draped across his shoulders. A shell-and-jade-bead mask obscured his face.

Someone picked up Frog Spring from behind. She closed her eyes as the man's strong arms lifted her up and threw her forward.

Pain lanced through her as she hit the water. She opened her mouth to scream and water rushed down her throat. Desperate for air, she pulled at her bonds, but they were tight, so tight. Her ears rang and a strange pulling sensation tickled her heart. Panic robbed her of her reason and she twisted furiously, but blackness swept over her and the ringing drowned out the sound of her heartbeat.

Frog Spring thrashed again, and then her spirit pulled free. Suddenly, Frog Spring felt as light as air, as free as a cloud. She had no sensation of weight, or of her body. She had escaped it.

Through spirit-eyes, the water was a bright, dazzling blue. Frog Spring floated through the water, amazed by the shimmering colors. Finally, she remembered her task and looked around for the home of the *chac*. It should be at the very bottom of the *cenote*. Frog Spring swam through the water as sunlight turned bubbles into floating jewels. She laughed. The water slid against her spirit in a way that was warm and friendly and much more pleasant than any dress she'd ever worn.

The *chac*'s house was small, but looked very much like a miniature palace. Frog Spring's spirit feet sank to the bottom of the *cenote* and she stood before the *chac*'s house. She strode forward bravely, determined to discover the reason for Tikal's bad luck.

The *chac* sat on a bench in his house, tending his fire. The fire glowed blue rather than orange but its tongues of flame danced the way a true fire would.

The *chac* stood. He was tall and blue-skinned. His skull was elongated to an ideal degree, and his eyes crossed slightly. His black eyes burned with anger. Frog Spring stopped, awed by him. She had thought her husband a beautiful man, but the *chac*'s beauty put Claw Bark to shame.

"So the king sends his wife to speak to me. Should I be honored or insulted that he doesn't come himself?" The voice of the *chac* shimmered with the small clear voices of the streams and the loud rumble of the waterfall.

Frog Spring knelt before the *chac*. "Noble *chac*, I have come to ask you to intercede on my people's behalf. There has been no rain this year, and the crops refuse to grow. The *milpas* are cracked and bake under the face of the sun."

The *chac* adjusted his blue and green striped skirt and sat back down. "Of course it hasn't rained," he said. "I asked my father Kumku Chac to withhold the rains this year because I have been gravely insulted. He and the rest of the great *chacs* wait beyond the borders of the *holhum taz muyal* in the land of *chun caan,* where they shall remain until I call for them."

"How have you been insulted?" asked Frog Spring. "Who has done this?"

"Your husband, of course," said the *chac*. "He has been king for four years now, but he has yet to truly honor me with a ceremony worthy of my greatness. No jade has been thrown into my *cenote* for me to wear. No fine cotton or beautiful feathers have made their way to me. And the sacrifices he has offered have not been adequate."

"But the people have offered animals, tobacco, and copal—even their blood and their hearts! My husband has offered his own blood as well," protested Frog Spring, cringing at the thought that her husband's miserly ways had brought Tikal to the brink of ruin.

The *chac* strode around the room, pacing as he spoke. "Bah. What about the children he has been sending me? Disgraceful! A sacrifice should be a brave young man or a virtuous woman—someone with whom I should be honored to converse. Someone who has earned the right to petition me. A child patters into my home without knowing why it was sent or how to ask my favor."

"How can I redeem my people?" asked Frog Spring. "Shall we all starve on behalf of Claw Bark?"

The *chac* grunted. "I considered it. But today, another has interceded for you. Father Tortoise tells me you have been kind to him and have shared what little bounty you have left in your stores."

"I am always willing to share anything of mine with Father Tortoise," said Frog Spring.

The *chac* laughed. "Most people do not mean it when they say that, but I see you do. So. I offer you a way to escape my anger."

"Yes?"

"If Claw Bark ceases to be king before dawn tomorrow, I shall ask my father Kumku Chac to fly forth from the *holhum taz muyal* and bring the rains. If Claw Bark remains king, I shall not ask."

"How can Claw Bark be overthrown?" asked Frog Spring. "The High Priest is his creature. Do you mean you want his life as a sacrifice?"

"No, most certainly not. He has not earned such an honor. As to how, you must do this, not me. You are a Jaguar Paw woman, daughter of Kan Boar. You are worthy. Rid yourself of this foreigner and rule for your son until he is grown."

"Rule? But I am a woman. No woman has ever ruled Tikal!"

"No woman has been king," said the *chac*. "Which is not to say no woman has ever ruled. It is an unusual fate, but it could be yours. Father Tortoise believes you are worthy. And now that I have spoken with you, I tend to agree with him."

Frog Spring was silent for a moment. She bowed her head to the floor. "I shall do as you ask, mighty *chac*," she said.

The *chac* nodded. "Then go, woman. Time passes and you have only until dawn."

Frog Spring stood and backed out of the house. Once in the open water, she floated back to her body just as a rope was lowered into the water. Frog Spring melted back into her body. The feeling was like returning home.

Her bonds had fallen away and she reached out to grasp the rope. She pulled her head out of the water.

"She's alive!" someone on the rim of the *cenote* shouted. Others crowded around to see. Frog Spring held on to the rope and stared blearily at the people. She blinked. It was so dark—could it be night already?

A man climbed down the rope and dropped into the water beside her. "Mistress," he said. "The gods have been kind. They have sent you back to us!"

Frog Spring took a breath to answer him and choked. She coughed up water. The man wrapped the rope around her chest and signaled to someone on the rim. Frog Spring felt herself being lifted out of the water. The feeling of having weight again seemed oppressive. She felt clumsy and longed briefly to feel as light and graceful as a spirit again.

Hands grabbed her and pulled her over the rim. Frog Spring lay on the ground, coughing. Someone removed the rope.

When she could speak, Frog Spring raised her head. "Where is the king?" she asked.

"In the palace, Mistress," said someone near her. "The priests are with him."

Frog Spring pushed herself up slowly. She tried to stand, but something had lodged in her shoe. She reached into her sandal and extracted a small, tear-shaped stone. It was a deep green, as green as a tortoise's shell. Or a tortoise's tear. Frog Spring clutched the stone and tried to keep her own tears at bay. She still had much to do tonight. She had to save her tears for later.

She struggled again to stand. Her limbs felt weak and her knees trembled, but she managed to pull herself to her feet. All around her, the people fell on their faces in the dust to honor her. Frog Spring felt warmed by their faith. She only hoped she would prove worthy.

She walked toward the palace. Her wet dress clung to her body and her hair lay plastered against her neck and shoulders. But the air was so hungry for moisture that she could feel the water evaporating off her skin. By the time she neared the palace, her dress was no more than damp, and the ends of her hair floated about her head once again.

Frog Spring felt as weak as a newborn, barely able to hold herself upright, but she would not collapse now—not in front of the people, who followed her silently in awe. Their reverence was almost as hard a burden to bear as the pronouncement of the *chac*.

The proud warriors who guarded the palace, armed with their spears and slings, stared—unabashedly stared—at her. Normally, they kept their eyes on their feet when she passed, but she knew they had never seen a sacrifice returned before. She ignored their stares and walked into the palace alone.

Frog Spring felt a moment of uncertainty as she entered the palace. She had never been to the throne room of the king before—women could not go there. But if Claw Bark were there, she had to go. Frog Spring gathered her courage and walked to the throne room. The warrior standing guard held up a hand to stop her, but she ignored him and he let her go. No doubt he did not know what to do with a sacrifice returned, either.

Frog Spring found Claw Bark on his dais, throwing divination bones with one of the priests. As she entered, he turned to stare at her, sweat dripping down his face. His jaw dropped open in surprise and he tried to speak, but only a squeak escaped him.

The courtiers in the room edged away from her and bowed to her as she passed. Claw Bark stood on the dais, making himself tower over her. A snarl of rage marred his handsome face.

"Get out of here, woman," he shouted, though his voice was high and nervous. "No woman may come here."

"I am the sacrifice, come back with the words of the *chac* to relay to you," she said evenly. "There is nowhere in this city I may not go tonight."

"Even so," said the High Priest, though that cost him a dirty look from Claw Bark. "Speak, sacrifice. What is the word of the *chac?*"

Frog Spring pointed at her husband. "The rains do not come because the sacrifices you send the *chac* are unworthy. He does not delight in the company of the children you send him. Nor does he have new beads and baubles to wear. You are stingy with your wealth. The *chac* is stingy with the rain in return."

Claw Bark laughed. "That is ridiculous," he said. "Now get out of here."

"No," said Frog Spring. "It ends tonight."

"What ends?"

"Your reign," she said evenly. "The *chac* has made it clear to me that as long as you remain king, there will be no rain. My son must be declared king before morning."

"Blasphemy," shrieked the High Priest. "No one but the gods may depose a king." Frog Spring comforted herself with the thought that the High Priest was more worried about his position as a priest of the highest status rather than any blasphemy she might utter.

"The gods have spoken," said Frog Spring. "He will be deposed."

The High Priest stood in front of the king. "I say he will not be. You are lying, woman. Get out of my sight. The gods talk to me, not you."

Frog Spring thought of the tortoise and its tears on her behalf. "No," she said. "You are wrong. Go out to the people and declare my son king or there will be no rain."

The High Priest spread his hands and closed his eyes. "The powers of darkness will overtake you in the night. The *Bolon ti ku* shall take charge of your rebellious soul in the twilight of Xibalba."

"No one is sending me to Xibalba," said Frog Spring.

The High Priest reached into the leather pouch at his waist and pulled out his sacrificial knife.

"The Hand of God shall condemn you to the afterlife," said the High Priest. He raised the black glass blade above his head. It glowed blue, first faintly, then grew stronger.

Frog Spring held onto the green stone and fought back her fear. She had never dared oppose a priest before. But the *chac* had said to do it. She had faith that the *chac* knew what was right for her to do. The *chac* and Father Tortoise.

A strange lassitude crept into her limbs and curled around her heart. Frog Spring felt her heart beat slower

. . . slower . . . The High Priest smiled and pointed the knife toward her.

Frog Spring squeezed the stone and her heart jumped. The room looked clearer, sounds were louder. She took a deep breath and threw her shoulders back.

The High Priest frowned and began chanting something in a language Frog Spring did not recognize. The lassitude crept up her limbs again and grasped her heart. Her chest constricted as if a strong rope had been wrapped around her many times and tied tightly. She couldn't breathe.

Anger boiled inside Frog Spring. She was the sacrifice returned—this priest had no right to oppose her. With her last bit of strength, she reached her arm back and threw the green stone at the High Priest.

The stone struck him in the face. He screamed and dropped the knife. The knife shattered into a thousand pieces as it hit the stone floor and the shards flew in every direction.

Frog Spring gasped for air, released from the spell. All around her, junior priests and royal attendants whimpered in fear and pulled sharp slices of glass out of their skin. Frog Spring looked down at herself. None of the glass had touched her.

Confidently, she walked forward to the High Priest where he lay sprawled on the floor. His eyes stared widely and his mouth was open, but there was no breath in him.

Claw Bark scuttled forward. "What did you do?" he screamed. "You shall die for this!" He picked up the green stone but immediately dropped it, shrieking. In the confines of the room, the sound was deafening.

Frog Spring reached down and grabbed the stone, reclaiming it.

Her husband held out his hand. His skin was black and smoked where he had touched the stone.

"You are no longer king here," said Frog Spring. "You will leave Tikal tonight, and you will take nothing with you but some food and water. You will have nothing to wear but a loincloth and your shoes. You will leave all your jewelry and your fine clothes here and I shall give them to the *chac* of the *cenote* at midday to make up for all that you have kept from him these years."

Claw Bark held his burned hand to his chest. "You can't. I am king. These men are my attendants. They do as I say!"

Frog Spring turned to the whimpering courtiers slowly. None of them would meet her eyes. "Anyone who wishes to accompany my husband into exile may go. Anyone who agrees to acknowledge my son as King of Tikal and myself as his regent may stay—after you have touched the stone and declared your loyalty to the new king and the gods. But be warned—the stone will not tolerate treachery."

Claw Bark reached for Frog Spring, but she stepped away. "Get out," he whispered. "Get her out of here."

Frog Spring watched the courtiers, but none moved to obey Claw Bark. She walked to the first one and held out the stone. The man cringed but reached out a trembling hand and touched it.

"I will be loyal to your son. And the gods," he said through chattering teeth. He jerked his hand back after touching the stone, but was unscathed.

Frog Spring nodded. "Then you may stay." One by one, she repeated the procedure with each man in the room. Every one of the men pledged his loyalty and touched the stone without harm. Several showed fear, but some displayed relief. So she had not been the only one angered by Claw Bark's foreign ways.

Frog Spring turned back to Claw Bark after the last man had touched the stone. "It is you who must get out, Claw Bark. Now."

Her husband licked his lips; his gaze darted from side to side, but no one came to help him. He stood and stepped down from the dais.

"No," said Frog Spring. "The clothes. The jewelry. Leave them."

He glared at her, hate in his face, but he said nothing. He stripped off his crown of feathers and his fine cotton skirt. He removed all his necklaces and his ear spools. Finally, he stood before her clad in nothing but his rope sandals and white loincloth.

"Now, get out of this city," said Frog Spring. "And never come back. If you do, I shall have you killed."

Claw Bark walked slowly past her, and out of the room. The courtiers kept their eyes to the floor and did not watch him go. Frog Spring followed him at a distance. The warriors at the entrance of the palace jerked in surprised to see him almost naked and without his symbols of office.

"He is no longer king here," said Frog Spring. "My son is. This man is leaving Tikal, never to return."

"She lies!" shrieked Claw Bark. "Kill her! Kill her!"

The warrior on Frog Spring's left hesitated, but the one on her right raised his spear. Frog Spring stepped close to him, too close for him to use the spear, and held out the stone.

"My son is king now," she said. "This stone is my proof. If you touch it and are unburned, you may stay. Otherwise, you will be exiled with my husband."

The warrior stepped back from her, confused, but

raised his spear again. Frog Spring's anger rose up and overwhelmed her. She ran to the warrior and pressed the stone against his tattooed chest.

The man screamed. Where the stone had touched him, only a raw red burn remained. The man raised the spear again, but the other warrior jumped in front of Frog Spring and held his knife on the burned man.

"No," he said. "Don't harm her." The second warrior turned to her. "Mistress. I'll touch the stone."

Frog Spring held it out and the man reached back with his left hand and touched the stone briefly. He drew his hand away unharmed.

"You can't believe her," said Claw Bark.

"She has died for her people and been returned by the gods," said the warrior. "She has the proof. Now you and this other man will leave Tikal, for you show by your burns that the gods reject you."

Claw Bark spat, but backed away. The burned warrior followed him, fear in his face.

Frog Spring heard a rustling behind her. She turned. The courtiers stood grouped together at the entrance to the palace.

"Mistress?" asked one. "Will it rain now?"

"Yes," she said. "Provided Claw Bark leaves immediately."

"Then you had better leave," said the courtier to Claw Bark. "I will call out the rest of the household guard to make sure you do." The man turned and disappeared into the palace.

Claw Bark turned and walked away, back straight and fists clenched. The burned warrior followed him at a distance.

The first rays of dawn touched the eastern horizon.

Frog Spring raised her head to the sky, afraid the *chac* might not keep his promise.

But she need not have worried. On the horizon, she saw a gathering of clouds. They poured forth into the sky as the great *chacs*, released from the *holhum taz muyal,* flew forth behind their father Kumku Chac to gather the clouds, the winds, and the waters.

Frog Spring clutched the green stone and laughed. All around her, drops of rain fell from the sky and splashed against the dry tiles of the patio. The courtiers sang a song of joy and the remaining warrior knelt at Frog Spring's feet in homage.

Frog Spring wanted to run through the city, feeling the rain run through her hair and along her skin, but she was the mother of a king and not a child.

But what was the harm? Father Tortoise had interceded, and the *chac* had kept his promise. Rain had come again to Tikal; the corn would grow and the people prosper. Frog Spring ran through the downpour into the Great Plaza and joined the people of the city in their shouts of thanksgiving and joy.

WHAT THE GODS WILL
by Kathleen Dalton-Woodbury

Kathleen Dalton-Woodbury is the director of the Science Fiction and Fantasy Workshop, a national network for new and aspiring science fiction, fantasy, and horror writers, for which she writes a marketing column in their monthly magazine. She also publishes a small fiction magazine, *Promises, Pro-mss,* which consists of science fiction, fantasy, and horror stories and three critiques of each story by professional writers.

Kathleen is the wife of a chemical engineer and has three daughters. She has a B.A. in Mathematics and a M.E. degree in Mechanical Engineering.

Kathleen's main character is something of a shapeshifter, but with an unusual twist. Like most shapeshifters, this story is not what it seems. . . .

Late afternoon and First Daughter Moratiri sat in her tent, feeding Dancer, her mongoose, holding bits of meat high enough above her lap that its long, sleek body stretched full-length, the small, clawed paws resting on her shoulders for balance. The curtain to the outer chamber twitched, and a maidservant whispered, "Zeraphane, servant of the House of Elmirais, my lady." Moratiri froze as a tall woman stepped past the curtain and dropped to obeisance before her.

Dancer snatched the half-raised piece of meat, and Moratiri lifted the mongoose from her lap, placing it and the bowl of food on the carpeted floor beside her seat. Elmirais had been given Moratiri's hand in betrothal in honor of the many lands he had conquered for her father. Even now he was feasting with the other lords and warriors in the great tent at the center of the encampment, and at dawn the First Father would give her to him in marriage. So why would his servant come to her now? All was ready. What more needed to be said?

She leaned forward from her high cushioned seat and tapped the servant on her bared shoulder. "You may speak."

Zeraphane sent a pleading glance at Moratiri and then looked down again. "Gracious First Daughter of the Almighty First Father of our land, hear me!"

"I hear."

"Gracious First Daughter, I was born in far Zenoby, and before it was conquered by the First Father, I was taught the ways of my mother and her mother before her and so down through time from the beginning. By those ways I have discovered that Elmirais, the son of my Blessed mistress, Illiandra, may she rest with the gods, is conspired against."

Moratiri frowned. "Conspired against? In what way? Forget the forms and recitations." A conspiracy against her betrothed was a conspiracy against the First Father, and as such was not to be borne.

Zeraphane nodded. "There is a deathserpent in the

processional wagon. When the procession begins, it will kill the son of my Blessed Illiandra."

Moratiri wanted to ask how this woman knew such a thing, but she realized that was a waste of time—no Zenobite woman shared the ways of her mothers with someone not of her family or people. There were more important things to determine anyway. "Do you know who put it there, and why?"

The handwoman shrugged. "There are many who would want to kill the favored of the First Father. All I know is that you can help me save him."

Could she? And did she really want to? What if Elmirais had changed? What if his pledge to win glory and honor so he could win her had changed when he earned the glory and honor? What if he no longer cared for her, but only for the sound of battle, and the joy of winning? She had had no chance to speak with him since his triumphal return, only the look in his eyes when the First Father had betrothed them. And that glow could have had many sources.

But what other choice did she have? If war had changed him, then he was changed. If it had become his new love, he would go off again to seek it. And she would stay behind, the wife of a hero honored of the First Father. Unless he died on the morrow.

"Have you spoken to anyone else of this, to Elmirais?"

Zeraphane shook her head. "He is not yet returned from the ritual baths and feasting." She brought her hands up in the prayer sign. "I was sleeping—I am no longer young—and the vision of the serpent came to me in a dream. At first, I didn't know what to do, then I worked my arts and the gods sent me to you. I came straight away."

And to whom should Moratiri speak of this? The First Father would be involved in the ritual feasting, but he should know of the plan. It was, ultimately, directed at him. She would have to seek him when he retired to his tent.

"Thank you for your wisdom, Handwoman. You may go now. See if your arts can determine the mind behind this evil. I will prepare to visit the First Father and tell him of your warning. You are to be honored."

After Zeraphane left, Moratiri sent a serving girl with the order that she notify her when the First Father left the feasting. Then she began to prepare herself for an uninvited visit to a man who could kill her for disturbing him. She would have to plan carefully.

The way to the tent of the First Father seemed longer than usual. As wise and powerful as he was, he bore many years and could no longer feast late into the night. The fact that he had retired this early, barely giving Moratiri enough time to prepare for his presence, made her especially concerned. He would very likely not want to be kept awake past the time necessary to ready him for his bed. Was the life of Elmirais worth the risk of angering the First Father?

Moratiri had to tell herself it was. If after taking her as his wife, Elmirais died, Moratiri would no longer be First Daughter. Instead she would be the widow of a hero, forsaken of the gods and no prize for any who might follow his path. She had to do this for herself as well as for her betrothed.

The guards at the tent entrance stood without moving as she passed between them. The servant who met her in the front area of the tent only bowed and gestured her toward the curtain to the receiving area. A guard pulled the curtain back for her and she stepped in to find the First Father seated on his throne, staring at her as if he expected her. In her surprise she faltered, but he raised his hand to beckon her closer.

She stepped up, knelt before him with her robe pulled off of her shoulder, and felt with relief the touch on her skin. "What brings me the pleasure of the First Daughter's presence on this joyous night?"

Moratiri glanced up at him and suddenly remembered a similar glance from Zeraphane. She hid her smile. She had been merciful with the handwoman, perhaps the First Father would be merciful with her. "Oh, Great and Hallowed Father of this Mighty Land. Oh, Conqueror of the World. Oh, Song of the Heart of Your People. Oh—"

"Yes, yes. That's enough." He put his finger under her chin and lifted so that she met his gaze. "You are a fitting bride for Elmirais, my child. What do you ask of me?"

Moratiri blinked. She had not looked into her father's eyes since she was a little girl. Her heart warmed to the love and kindness still there for her. "Oh, Father, I have learned that there is a plot against my betrothed: A deathserpent waits on the processional wagon. If nothing is done, Elmirais will be dead by this time tomorrow."

The finger slipped away from her chin. Before Moratiri could lower her gaze, she saw sadness replace the love in her father's eyes. "So."

She waited, but he said no more. She had dared so much already. Did she dare interrupt his thoughts? She peeked at him through her eyelashes. He sat frowning and didn't notice her childish look. She would wait for him to speak.

Finally she heard him shift on his throne. "What do you want me to do, my child?"

She blinked again. "Oh, Father, can you not stop this plot?"

"How?"

Yes, how? He was supposed to think of something, not her. "Have your men find and kill the death-serpent?"

"How could anyone place a deathserpent on the pro-cessional wagon? The priests blessed and purified it this morning and the ritual guards have been set around it that no man may come near. To disturb the wagon would not only delay the procession, but insult the priests and the gods."

"But, Father—"

"Even I can do nothing against what the gods will."

"But if he dies in your wagon, riding in the proces-sion in your robes, bearing your rod of office and wearing your crown, then he dies as you. And your enemies will bring Onaziah from his prison to reign in your stead."

"Onaziah. Your brother would like that, wouldn't he?"

Moratiri suppressed a shudder at the thought of Onaziah. His mother had terrorized all of the other wives and concubines of the First Father and raised her son to do the same among their children. Why did he, of all her father's sons, have to be First Son? And then she thought of the accidents. Maybe they had been no more accident than the deathserpent finding its way onto the wagon of the First Father. "The will of the gods, Father, or the will of the First Son?"

The First Father sighed. "I am an old man, First Daughter, and the gods have called me home. I am not strong enough to stand up against Onaziah. I had hoped that with you, Elmirais would be strong enough. After the wedding, after I give him the sigils of my power, I am leaving for the halls of my ancestors. I will be dead either way." He stood and Moratiri dropped into obeisance again. This time he did not touch her on her bared shoulder. "If the gods will it, you will find a way to stop the death of the First Father, my child. I leave it on your head."

Moratiri listened to his footsteps, slow and measured, as he walked into the inner areas of his tent.

As Moratiri left the tent of the First Father, Zeraphane dropped to obeisance before her. The first daughter touched the handwoman's bared shoulder as she passed. "Rise and walk with me."

When Zeraphane insisted on staying the required three steps behind, Moratiri suppressed a sigh. There was no time for this, but Zeraphane was right. It would not do for the First Daughter to be seen treating a servant as an equal.

Once they had entered Moratiri's tent, gone to her bedchamber, and Moratiri had sent her servants away with the promise that Zeraphane would attend her, the women could relax their pretence. "You know what the First Father said to me, don't you?"

Zeraphane nodded but did not speak. Still cautious? Whom did she fear? Moratiri shrugged. "If your arts can tell you what he said, can they tell you how we might deal with this threat? You may speak."

Zeraphane stared into Moratiri's eyes for a moment, searching for something. Moratiri, in her turn, stared back and saw something that reminded her of Elmirais, what little she had seen of him since his return from conquering. A way of frowning? A piercing under-standing of who she really was in her heart? Suddenly Moratiri wanted to look away, but she was First Daughter and she would not be the first to drop her gaze.

"There is one thing we may do, but it has risks."

Moratiri smiled. "Does not everything? Tell me."

Zeraphane seemed to shrink toward obeisance again, but then she stiffened. "Forgive me, my lady. I have not been treated this way since the Blessed Illiandra went to the gods." She gave a great sigh. "I must trust you as you are willing to trust me."

Moratiri nodded.

"What we must do is send a fighter to find the ser-pent. A fighter the priests and the guards will not no-tice. A fighter whose presence in the wagon tent will not be detected. And who else can fight a deathserpent but your wily friend?" Zeraphane turned to where Moratiri's pet mongoose lay curled on her sleeping couch.

The First Daughter smiled at the creature. "Dancer loves to fight serpents, but can your arts tell her where to find this one?"

Zeraphane gave another great sigh. "My arts could do that if Dancer were bound to me as she is to you. But I have no mongoose as my companion. We must walk another path. And that is where you need to trust me. You will have to allow your Self to leave your body and enter hers, while her Self waits in your body for your return. *You* must be the one who fights the deathserpent."

Moratiri sat down on the couch next to the animal. Leave her body for another, smaller one? How could she fit? And how would Dancer like waking in

Moratiri's body? Could Zeraphane's arts truly do this thing? What if she could not restore them each to their own bodies? Would Elmirais want to marry a mongoose in a woman's body? She smiled as she imagined the look of horror on his face. But it wasn't really funny. "What would happen if we could not go back to our own bodies?"

"The only thing to prevent that would be the death of one of the bodies." Zeraphane knelt beside the couch and stared up into Moratiri's eyes. "If the serpent were to kill you, the Self of the mongoose would have to remain in your body, and it would appear that you had gone mad. I have heard stories . . . the body dies after a while with the wrong Self in it."

So, she was risking her life to save that of Elmirais. But if she did not kill the serpent, her life as a widow, with Onaziah as First Father, would not be worth living. "Then I will have to trust that the gods will protect me, that they will help me keep the serpent from killing me. I have seen Dancer fight enough serpents. I will just have to move as quickly as she does." She tried not to think of all the times she had watched that dance of death and feared that the mongoose would not survive.

"And the body will know what to do, if you allow it."

Moratiri frowned at the handwoman. "You have done this yourself."

Zeraphane smiled. "We have little time. You must be ready for Elmirais before dawn. Let us prepare you for sleep, my lady."

Moratiri lay holding Dancer, though the wakened animal struggled to get away and about her nightly business. Zeraphane patted the mongoose and the animal stilled. "Only a few more moments and you may be off, little one. Close your eyes, my lady."

The First Daughter closed her eyes and waited, trying to tell by sound what Zeraphane was doing. As she'd undressed for bed, the handwoman had busied herself at Moratiri's dressing table, mixing ingredients she produced from a pouch hidden in her robes. Now that Moratiri's eyes were closed, all she could hear was a soft humming. Then came the touch of a finger on each eyelid, on her ears, her nose, and her lips. Zeraphane had daubed something there because Moratiri could smell a strange, sweet odor. "Lick your lips, my lady." The taste was tart and made her mouth water. She could hear the mongoose flicking her tongue in and out as well. "Now sleep. Sleep until the hour before dawn."

Moratiri felt heavy, dropping as if into a deep chasm, spinning as she dropped. She wanted to reach out, grasp for a handhold, but she couldn't move. And then she landed, on all fours. She opened her eyes and looked around. She was kneeling—no—standing on the rug in her bedchamber, but everything was so much larger. And the smells! Her nose told her that Zeraphane and Moratiri—herself?—were in the bedchamber, and that no one else was in the tent. Her ears pricked at the sound of a voice. "Go, little one. Find the serpent." *Yes! The serpent. There wasn't much time.* She started for the doorway of the bedchamber. She was hungry and needed to relieve herself, and then she would find the serpent.

No. No time to eat. Moratiri flinched as the guard outside the tent shifted when she ran past him. *No food. Find the serpent.* She had to wait while this body

157

ran into a bush and rid itself of what was no longer needed. *Now, find the serpent! Where was the wagon tent from here?* She forced herself to ignore the interesting scents that beckoned to her empty stomach. *Over this way, the tent is there.* Maybe if she told herself to look in the wagon tent for food. Dancer's body quickened its steps till it reached the place along the tent wall where the serpent had entered and she slipped under a flap to follow. *Yes! Smell the serpent! Where is it?* The tent was cold, unheated by the braziers that had warmed her own tent after the setting of the sun. The sharp, dusty tang of serpent hung on the motionless air.

Moratiri allowed the body to follow the smell toward the wagon. The ears caught the gentle scrape as scales moved across the wagon floor. Then the ears heard a hiss, and the smell overwhelmed all other scents. The deathserpent had reared up to look over the wall of the wagon. Eyes that glinted with an inner fire stared down at her. And it was *huge!* Open jaws wider than the mongoose head that held her Self, length of neck showing above the wall of the wagon longer than the body she wore. That body froze, and Moratiri forced herself to stillness within it.

For a moment neither animal moved. Moratiri had never seen a deathserpent this close. How could the gods will her to fight such a monster? Did all serpents look with such cold intelligence and scorn at what they saw? Part of her wanted to turn quickly and flee, but the body resisted, and the part of her that remembered why she had come helped in that resistance. The gods *must* intend for her to do this thing, else why would they have sent Zeraphane to her?

Then the serpent's head was gone, back down to the floor of the wagon. Did it hope to force the mongoose to follow it? Moratiri turned her will to holding the mongoose on the ground. What chance did she have in such a small area? But how could she get the snake to come out where she would have more room?

Rearing up to stand on just the back feet, Moratiri used Dancer's sense of smell to assure herself that the serpent was coiled against the near wall of the wagon. As she worked her way around to the other side, she reared up every so often to check that the serpent wasn't following. No, it stayed against the same wall. That seemed strange to Moratiri, but then she remembered being told that serpents sleep when it's cold. Perhaps the cold would make the serpent tired, slower.

On the other side of the wagon, Moratiri jumped to the part of the wagon floor sticking out before the wagon wall. She held her position there and sniffed, waiting for any sign that the serpent had moved closer to this side. But no. It stayed where it was, so Moratiri dared to rear up and look over the wall. The serpent raised its head and lashed out its tongue, but otherwise did not move.

Moratiri scrambled to the top of the wall and jumped to the royal seat before she could fall. The serpent raised its head higher, to look over the seat at her, and hissed. Moratiri jumped to the high back of the seat. The serpent hissed again and darted up at her. The mongoose flinched, but didn't leave the high seat back. The serpent fell short, and Moratiri swiped at its head before it had fallen away.

Her claws stung with the feel of serpent skin, so she licked them. She had blooded it! She looked down into the eyes that seemed too close—the serpent had moved behind the seat. It lunged at her again, and she jumped down onto the cushion, placing the back of the seat between them. The serpent thudded against the barrier and then fell to the wagon floor.

It would come around to the front now, but on which side? Moratiri jumped back up to the top of the seat. The serpent had risen and was swaying back and forth. This time it spit at her, and she dodged the venom, wrinkling her nose at the smell as it passed. She hissed back.

And the serpent lunged again. Dancer's mouth closed on the serpent's head and Moratiri jerked in surprise. *Don't kill it! It must not die here and offend the gods.*

Muscles bunched and jerked as the serpent tried to get loose. Moratiri added her will to that of Dancer's body and hung on even though the spasms threw them off the high back and onto the seat. Claws dug into cushions to resist the thrashing coils of serpent. If she could hold on long enough, the serpent would tire, and be easy to remove from the tent.

The cushion was not secured to the seat, but when the serpent's exertions knocked Moratiri off, the softness padded the jolt of landing on the floor of the wagon. Moratiri had an instant to wonder what the priests would think when they found the cushion out of place. More thrashings and whipping about as the serpent tried to raise its head and lift the mongoose with it. Moratiri scrabbled at the wagon wall, trying to find somewhere else to hold on, when with one last shudder the serpent relaxed.

Moratiri crouched beside it, its head still in Dancer's mouth. Was this a trick? How could she have caught the serpent so easily? She waited a moment longer before trying to move. The serpent did not so much as twitch, though she could feel the gentle rumble as it breathed. Well, if it had given up, even for only a little while, she had to take advantage. She looked around the wagon, trying to decide how to get herself and the serpent out. Finally she jumped up to the seat. It would be easier to get over the wagon wall from there than from the wagon floor. And so it was, barely. She leaped to the wagon wall and then to the ground, almost hanging by her teeth for a moment as the weight of the serpent still in the wagon resisted her own meager weight. But the scales were slippery and that helped. Slowly, the coils edged over the top and down, almost catching her as they fell. Moratiri was grateful for the quickness of this body, even cumbered with a serpent's head in its mouth.

She rested a moment beside a wagon wheel, wondering what to do next. And then she knew. She would show the priests what to think. She would take the serpent out of the door of the tent and show them a miracle: a mongoose dragging a living deathserpent out of the tent of the royal wagon. It would insult the gods to bring death to a place sanctified by the priests, so she would take the serpent out, and let the guards deal with it. And then she could return to her tent and rest.

Even though she was ready for it, the loud cry as she walked through the doorway startled her into freezing outside the tent. Moratiri twisted to see its source. Someone large and noisy loomed over her, a sword flashing as it fell. She dropped the serpent's head and dashed for the shadows of a nearby bush. Once there, she turned to look out. Both guards were beating at the serpent's body with their swords as threshers beat the grain with their flails. Pieces of serpent flew into the air with each stroke. Moratiri gave a sigh of relief, and allowed herself to feel how tired she really was. Dancer's body wanted to curl up under the bush, but Moratiri thought of her own cushioned bed, and hurried away, keeping tents between herself and the frenzied guards.

"I place upon your shoulders the robe of the First Father. I place in your hands the rod of office. I seat you in the royal seat, and name you First Father in my place." The First Father turned and gestured toward the crowds. "Behold Elmirais, the Son of the Great God, the protector of the People, the honored of the First Father!" The crowds roared their approval.

Moratiri's hand still tingled with the touch of Elmirais' hand as they were joined husband and wife. Now she watched the First Father honor her husband. Soon the procession would start and Elmirais would ride as First Father before all the people. And later, he would return to find no one waiting to receive back the robe and rod, no one to reclaim the seat. She wished her father well in his journey to the gods, his fathers. No one would notice his departure in all the glory and excitement of the procession, and no one would dare say anything about there being a new First Father in his place. No one, except Onaziah.

The trumpets sounded and cymbals clashed. Reed flute and tambourines, songs of triumph, and the procession began. Moratiri watched as the oxen pulled the wagon away from her. Elmirais waved the rod in blessing over the crowds and the servants seated on the wagon floor threw sweetmeats and coins out in token of those blessings.

Moratiri felt something brush her skirts and looked down to see Zeraphane's huddled form. She tapped the woman's bared shoulder and then followed her to the back of the platform, behind those who watched the procession. "What is it?"

The handwoman refused to meet Moratiri's gaze. "My lady, I have just received word that the First Son is ill. It seems that he writhes and hisses in his bed, and has to be restrained." And finally the eyes glanced up at the wife of the new First Father. "They say he seems as one possessed of a serpent."

Moratiri felt her eyes widen, and then she saw Zeraphane's smile. It would not do to return it. She lowered her gaze and nodded. "I see. Thank you for bringing me such news. I will rest easier knowing that the gods have willed no opposition for Elmirais." Then she reached out her hand and took the hand of the servant. "You have served me well. May the gods bless you, Zeraphane, chief of the servants of my household."

Zeraphane bowed her head, still smiling.

DOUBLE BLIND

by Syne Mitchell

Syne Mitchell says she is currently living in a 1920s farmhouse in the middle of an orange grove in central Florida. She says that in March she finished her first novel, which is hard science fiction. "I put my M.S. in physics to good use writing it."

Now, for all you people who ask, "Where do you get your ideas?" she says that she got the idea for this story from one that was rejected for *Sword & Sorceress X*. "I struggled for a month to write a story for this anthology. I read all the old volumes and wrote the first half of about five different stories that led nowhere. Then I was soaking in the tub and it hit me; start this story where the first one ended . . . and I wrote 'Double Blind' in a manic burst of energy—a two-hour fit of inspiration."

Have you ever noticed how often inspiration arrives when you've been doing some good hard wrestling with work? Stated otherwise; put brain in gear before engaging typewriter.

Last year, Syne sold us a short short called "Amber" that had quite a twist in its tail; this year, she sold us "Double Blind," which has some twists of its own.

The demon's laughter resonated in the forest. A hot wind stirred the leaves and battered them against Lillain. Twigs stabbed her skin. She fell to her knees. When the wind died, she opened her eyes . . . to darkness.

"Who's there?" a man's voice called. "Lady, is that you?"

Lillain cried out in relief. It was Haverick, one of the few knights who remained loyal to her. "I cannot see," she called. "Help me."

She heard splashing and the dull thuds of hooves. She imagined how he must look, leading his horse over the wet earth.

"Lady, where are you?" His voice was within arms' reach.

"Here. I am here. Can you not see me?"

The horse shrieked. Lillain crouched back into the underbrush. It reared and thudded into the earth.

Haverick swore as he tried to control his mount. "Lady, thank the gods. Show yourself."

"I am here, can't you see me?" The branches rustled about her and scratched her naked skin.

Mud sucked wetly on his boots as he walked over the damp earth. She felt the heat of his body. A hand brushed her forehead.

Lillain grabbed it.

Haverick cried out and struck her hand away. He fell back, cried out. Lillain heard his body sprawl on the dirt.

"Gods and goddesses defend me. This some trick of Jurlic's."

"No, Haverick. It's me. I'm here. I need your help."

"Begone, unseen spirit." There were tears in the soldier's voice. "Remind me no more that my Lady is missing." With a jingle of stirrups he mounted. The horse thundered past her.

"Wait—" She reached out. A hoof caught her in the ribs. Something inside cracked. Lillain dropped to the ground, the wind knocked from her. The next breath was agony. Pain flared along her side and sent white lancets across her empty vision. She gasped. Lillain pressed her forehead against the ground until she could breathe again.

She had come to the woods desperate, to command more power from the demon she controlled. Her brother, Jurlic, was too ambitious. She saw how the captains of her army looked to him. It was only a matter of time before he moved against her. She had wanted to be able to walk unseen among her men, to sort the treacherous from the true. The demon's words returned to her. She heard its chuckle, like an old man's death rattle. "Light-doess-not-touch-you-nor-doess-it-touch-your-eyess. It-iss-what-you-asked. In-viss-ssi-bil-ity."

Blind, Lillain stumbled over the lines of the pentagram. The precise cuts in the earth blurred. With a sputtering hiss, the demon broke free and was gone.

Now she had nothing, no magic, no retainer, even the clothes she had worn were lost.

She felt along the ground. Her long fingers filtered rotting leaves and a beetle's wing, bits of twigs until she found a crescent-shaped depression in the moist earth. She crawled on her knees, hands out, until she found a second. Haverick's trail should lead her back to the army's encampment. She might be walking to her death, but she had no other place to go.

Hours passed and the air warmed. Lillain heard songbirds call to each other,. It must be dawn. She smelled wood smoke and horses and guessed that she was near her army's camp.

"Goddesses breath!" The voice was a woman's, in middle age.

Lillain paused, crouched. "Is someone there?"

"What sort of creature are you?" the voice said. "Half earth and half maiden?"

"Tell me, what do you see?" Lillain stretched closer, not wanting to miss a word.

"Cor, you're a sight. Look like half a painting of a woman, barely sketched in with smears of dirt and mud. You've an arm and your belly and legs are with us. There's a swatch in the air, might be part of a head, I don't know. What kind of ill-fetched wight are you?"

So the demon had not lied, she was invisible. Lillain stood up and, remembering Haverick's reaction, she asked, "Aren't you afraid?"

The voice laughed nervously. "Cor, no. I've wenched at the Boar's Tit. Seen sights a lot stranger than you."

Lillain scraped mud off her thigh and rubbed it on the back of her hands.

"Creating more of yourself? Eh? You run afoul of that wretched witch-lord and his twice-cursed sister?"

Lillain paused. "What's happened?"

The woman's skirts rustled. Lillain heard the slap of liquid in a jar. "The witch-lady hied off and no one's seen her. Some say her own demons ate her. Some say the Lordling done her in. Whatever is the truth, it's certain that the Lord's worse now than his sister ever was. That's why I'm leaving, and you should have done a while ago by the look of ye."

"I need your help."

The woman barked a short bout of laughter. "That's

a surety, but what do you offer in trade, Earth-woman?"

"Coffers of jewels. Six piles of gold coins as tall as yourself. Silk dresses of midnight blue—and more. If you help me."

Again, the woman laughed. "What would an honest woman such as myself do with this finery? Where would I keep it, or how long? I'd be a robber's dream."

Lillain reined in her frustration. In other circumstances, she would have had the woman beheaded for insolence. "What do you want?"

The woman thought a moment and said, "A man's true love. Can you fetch me that, Demon?"

Lillain shook her head, then realized the futility of the gesture. "No."

The woman sighed. "Ah, at least you're an honest demon. What kind of help do you need? Perhaps that will help me set a price."

What she wanted was clear: revenge on the demon that had tricked her, and her brother Jurlic's treacherous black heart. "I need to be led into the witch-lord's chamber."

"Cor, why not just ask for the moon itself? That one's a danger, evil as marsh-gas. No, Earth-maiden, I cannot help you."

The water in the woman's pack sloshed again as the woman picked up her walking stick.

Lillain grabbed her.

"Goddess' teats!"

The woman's body was soft and smelled of sweat. A pack was slung over her shoulder. The bar-maid battered Lillain's head and shoulders with her walking stick. Lillain pushed her hands up the woman's back and grabbed the pack. She wrestled the jar free. With a swift motion she upended it above her head.

The mud sluiced off her body. The woman gasped. Lillain stood before the older woman, invisible.

"Yes. You can."

"Cor. You're mad. It'll never work."

They were inside Fiona's tiny house. It smelled of baking bread and bitter ale.

"I must reach the source of his power. That is the only way to stop him."

"His whole army camps about him, he continues the siege that his sister began. What if the she-bitch returns? There'll be two witch-spawn to fight."

"I assure you. His sister will not hinder us."

Lillain sat near the fire, trying to shake the fen's chill. "All you need do is carry a letter I will write. I will follow close behind you in the camp. When I am in his tent, you may leave."

"It's not as simple as all that. Many a woman of the town's gone into that tent and not come back. You yourself have suffered his spells. As much as it would please me to see the witch-lord and his armies destroyed, I would rather see me in my old age."

"I will protect you."

Fiona snorted. "I've seen such protection as you can afford yourself. No thanks."

"You must. The whole country depends on you."

"Ha! If that's so, they're late with their tributes. It's not my face I see on the coins. Let the lords fight their own battles. Fiona can find other taverns to wench."

"I'll build you your own tavern."

"A woman barkeep—I like that. Still . . ." The woman paused. "My own place? No more pinching and slapping and carrying heavy trays? I'm listening, Earth-demon."

Fiona was stopped at the perimeter of the army's encampment. Lillain did not recognize the voice of the soldier on watch.

"This isn't going to work," Fiona whispered to the emptiness behind her.

"You say this came from the Lady's own hand?" the soldier asked.

"Yes, Mesir." Fiona curtsied joint-crackingly low.

The paper rustled as the soldier inspected it.

Lillain had written the pass along a straight stick. Was it legible? Fiona said that the scrip was clear enough, if a bit sloppy. Would the soldier accept it? Lillain held her breath.

"It's poorly scribed, but it could be her hand. Where did you get this?"

"That I can only tell to the Lord, Mesir."

"He is a busy man, not to be bothered with the likes of you."

"What I have to tell—he wants to hear."

"It will be safer for you if you tell me." His scabbard clinked against his brigadine as he stepped forward.

Fiona retreated. "Mesir, what I have to say is for the Lord's ears alone."

"You will tell me, wench—"

Fiona gasped in pain.

"Let go, dog." Lillain commanded from behind Fiona's head, "Lest I strike you down where you stand."

The man scuttled back. Lillain smelled his fear. "My Lady—I had no idea—we thought you were—"

"—To my tent."

The guard led Fiona into the encampment. Lillain held onto the woman's elbow and followed.

The first change Lillain noticed was the silence. The men whispered around the fires in the darkness and drank from wine skins, but they no longer sang or talked of victories past. Gone was the rowdy laughter.

Her tent had changed as well. It stank of blood. Her arms hairs tingled when Fiona led her across the threshold. Jurlic practiced blood-magic in this room. Lillain wanted to spit into his face. Fool, he had defiled her tent. She heard the popping of a fire from the center of the tent and its heat prickled her skin.

"I do not like this place," Fiona said when they were alone.

"Tell me what you see."

"There is a cauldron in the center of the room, and chains. The floor is stained—"

"Are there lines carved into the dirt?"

"Yes."

"Avoid them. Where is the war-throne?"

"Across the room."

"Take me to it."

Fiona walked a wide circle to the other side. Tent canvas rustled. The woman stiffened.

"The mistress of disguise returns." Jurlic's smooth voice wept sarcasm. "I must say, sister, I've never seen you look better."

Lillain shifted to Fiona's side, closer to Jurlic's voice. She slid her feet slowly to avoid disturbing the dust.

"A dowdy peasant matron, I would have never known. Fortunately my demonic allies told me that you would come tonight."

Lillain heard a hissing pop. Heat and the screaming of a thousand souls flared from the center of the tent

"Gods and goddesses forfend," Fiona swore. The woman stepped back. "What is that?"

"Do you not recognize your former servant?" Jurlic asked. "You would have done well to feed your demons better, as I have done."

Lillain lunged for Jurlic. Her hands missed his throat and hit his shoulder.

He gasped and spun in place. A dagger sliced her shoulder. She hissed in pain.

"What foul trick—" Jurlic gasped.

Lillain flailed for his hands, grabbed his wrist, and grappled for the knife.

The demon in the fire pit chuckled. "I'll-feed-tonight-on-royal-blood." Its voice was the rustle of leaves on a gravestone.

Pain burned in her arms as Jurlic forced the dagger down to her invisible throat. The blade dragged along her cheek. Lillain tasted blood.

Her brother laughed. "A clever trick, Sister. Pity you were never strong enough to hold onto the power you wield." The point of the blade pricked the hollow of her throat.

A loud clang resounded. Lillain felt it vibrate through Jurlic's shoulder. He slumped forward in her arms.

Lillain hefted her brother onto her bleeding shoulder. "By the bargains made in my own blood, release the spell, old one." She threw her brother into the center of the tent.

A hot wind blasted the tent. Dust bit into Lillain's skin. When the air cleared, Lillain saw Fiona. The peasant woman stood open-mouthed, staring at the burnt out fire pit, a cast iron skillet in her hand.

Four soldiers burst through the tent flap. The sight of Lillain, stopped them. They fell to their knees. "Milady," said the captain, "we heard you were dead." If he noticed her nakedness, he gave no sign.

"No longer. Tell the company that it is Jurlic who is dead." Lillain eyed the empty fire pit. "Order the men to pack the horses. The siege is ended. We ride home in the morning. Go. Now."

The leader whirled to obey, his soldiers following.

Lillain sat with a whump on the war-throne.

"Like that and you're leaving?" Fiona asked.

"I've no more taste for war, and I find that my ambition, like my taste for dealing with demons, has faded." Lillain wiped blood from her cheek with the back of her hand. "Where would you like your tavern built?"

Fiona shook her head, "Not much call for a woman barkeep around here. I thought that I might try the north, some kingdom where a grateful queen might keep the thieves from stealing my tavern from under me nose." Fiona picked up a silk robe. "You'd best get dressed. I don't pay taxes to naked queens."

Lillain snorted. "Still, there is one thing I don't understand. When Jurlic and I wrestled over the dagger, you couldn't see me. How did you know where to aim your blow?"

Fiona lowered her head and blushed. "Tell the truth, Lady. Once I learned it was you, I just swung. I figured I was doing the kingdom a good stroke, wherever the blow landed."

PATCHWORK MAGIC
by P. Andrew Miller

Since receiving his MFA (Master of Fine Arts) in creative writing, P. Andrew Miller has been teaching and writing. He writes both fiction and poetry—who doesn't? Don't we all have an epic verse tucked away somewhere? He also writes fantasy and mainstream, humorous and serious. He has appeared in such varied places as *Dragon Magazine, The Magic Within, Nuthouse, Plot,* and *The Journal of Kentucky Studies.* He has also been an attending author in the International Conference on the Fantastic in the Arts.

He says that he hopes this sale will mark the beginning of a profitable career of writing so he doesn't have to "go back to the mall and stalk shoppers with his clipboard asking them to do surveys."

And I thought myself badly off scrubbing floors!

This is my first memory of Aunt Cordelia's quilt: I had just turned five when the Lord Margon's raiders came to our village. For my birthday, Aunt Cordelia, in truth my mother's aunt, gave me a quilt she had sewn over the years. I sat on my bed in the corner feeling the soft yellow piece of cloth in the upper right corner when the first screams reached me.

Mother turned from the kettle over the fire as another scream tore the afternoon's haze. She ran to the door, but it fell upon her as one of Margon's brutes kicked it in. I screamed as the man advanced over my mother, his sword drawn.

I ducked under the quilt, not wishing to see what came for me. Under the quilt, I noticed that the gold stitching on a square of soft leather started to glow. The thread seemed to radiate both light and a slight warmth.

In front of me, I heard the swordsman gasp and then came the noise I would later learn was steel glancing off steel. I heard the man grunt and curse but heard no other sound from the room. Suddenly, the man cried out and I heard his heavy boots clomping through the house and out the door. The glow faded and I looked closer. The embroidery had vanished. I stayed under the quilt for several minutes. I was afraid the man with sword would come back. But I also knew my mother needed me.

Finally, I peeked over the top of the quilt and saw no one in the room. Jumping from the bed, I ran to her. I called to her, shook her, but she didn't answer. Tears flooded my eyes and overran my lids. I heard another scream from outside and I crawled under the bed, taking the quilt with me and pulling it up over my head once again.

I must have eventually cried myself to sleep because I next remember a pale woman shaking me awake. She handed me a cup of water and an apple. Taking both, I stared at her, then realized I stared through her. The kettle, the wooden cabinet my father had built for my mother, I could see these between the woman's shoulders, right through her chest!

Then I glanced down and noticed that another one of the squares glowed, a soft purple this time. The square itself was pink with small flowers woven in it.

I looked back at the woman in front of me. The faint see-through dress she wore looked to be of the same print, if not the exact material.

The quilt continued to glow and the woman stayed and cared for me until Lady Croma's people came to our village. At the sound of the horses' hooves, my transparent nurse faded away and the quilt square became blank, all the embroidery gone.

Lady Croma's retainers found me a few minutes after that. I was the sole survivor of the village. My father and the rest of the men had been killed in the fields. The rest of the women, including my Aunt Cordelia, had been cut down in their homes. They asked how I survived since the raiders sole purpose was to terrorize by killing everyone in the villages they attacked. I told them I hid under the quilt. They believed me and I carried it with me when Captain Hawkins took me to his home.

The Captain and his wife raised me as their own child as they had none of their own. I kept the quilt always on my bed, but the embroidered runes, for so I believed them to be, remained quiet, plain things of thread.

Until my thirteenth year when the blight struck our crops. The corn turned black on the stalks; the wheat withered in the field.

None of us knew what to do. Then as I lay in bed unable to sleep because I could hear my father and mother whispering in the main room, the quilt began to glow again.

The glow came from a gray square of coarse homespun cloth. I waited to see if an apparition would appear before me but nothing appeared.

Then the glow vanished and the square was blank. I felt disappointment. Had the magic failed? I fell asleep beneath its comforting weight believing that.

In the morning, I awoke feeling strange. Something buzzed around inside my head, like a wasp trapped in the house. Mother asked me if I felt all right. I told her yes and went outside.

Something drew me toward the woods and though I had wandered there many a time, this felt different. I went with a purpose, passing by the wild flowers that I normally gathered for the table. I walked past the tree that I always climbed. Back beneath the shadow of the plush canopy, I found several small plants growing in the shade. I had never seen them before nor knew their name but I picked them just the same.

Bringing them back to the house, I put a kettle on to boil.

"What do you do, Marya?" mother asked.

In truth, I didn't know the answer, so I just told her that I had a feeling that I needed to do this.

She looked at me askance and watched as I crushed the plants from the woods with a mortar and then tossed the pulp into the kettle.

The odor that arose made me draw back and mother came over to remove the kettle from the house.

I stopped her. "Please, let me finish," I said.

She looked down at me, frowned slightly, then wrinkled her nose and nodded.

The odor increased and we both had to leave the

kitchen. After an hour, I pinched my nose between my fingers and went and took it from the fire.

I let it cool, then went to the fields of our village. I walked about the field sprinkling the mixture on the new-forming ears. The grayish-green mixture soaked into the plants and when it touched a blighted ear, it bubbled.

I sprinkled all of the corn I could and then went and gathered more of the plant, brewed more of the concoction. The end of the day found me weary and I slipped beneath the quilt with joy.

The next day, word spread that the blight had vanished. New ears were unaffected and the old ones had fallen off and withered.

Mother glanced at me, a question forming in her eyes. I shrugged and went to look at the quilt. I rubbed my hand over a few of the embroidered squares. Its magic could not only conjure spirits, but it also imparted knowledge. And not for the first time I wondered how Aunt Cordelia had made it.

The quilt again showed its magic when I caught fever. My skin cracked and my eyes blurred so that I couldn't make out Mother's face.

"Please," I asked, "put me under the quilt."

Mother shook her head. "We need to keep you cool," she said.

I grabbed at her hand, squeezed it. "Please, mama. Remember the corn."

She drew back and I let go of her hand. She disappeared, then returned with the quilt.

No sooner had she placed it over me than the silver embroidery on a blue square near the center began to shimmer. Then it gave forth light like the moon when full.

Mother stared at it, put her hand out but drew back before she touched it.

My fever broke the next day, but the glow remained. I wondered why until father and then mother came down with the fever as well. I placed both under the quilt and both got better.

I always slept beneath the quilt after that. Sometimes in the morning, I would notice that a square was blank. In the next few days I realized I knew how to do something else, usually how to make a sleeping potion or fever remedy. Sometimes I would awake knowing a particular story like the history of the Lady Croma's family or of the ancient heroes.

By the time I was a young woman, many in the village came to me for potions or stories. Mostly the other young women came, but sometimes the men came as well. Such as Doran.

He used to come and sit at the far edge of the circle when I would tell my quilt tales. I pretended not to notice him and he pretended not to really listen though I think neither one of us was fooled.

Then one night, I awoke sometime after midnight to a red glow from the quilt. A plain white square contained a red rune and it faded quickly while I watched. I went back to sleep and in the morning I had the knowledge to brew a love potion that would last for eternity.

I rubbed the edge of the quilt. "No thank you, Aunt Cordelia. This I do on my own."

And I did. Doran and I wed when I turned nineteen. We moved from the village to Ringold City, Lady Croma's seat. Doran joined the guard and with my father's encouragement and backing, as well his own skill, he soon made it to Captain himself. And I became pregnant.

The quilt had remained quiet during this time. In fact, only three squares with runes remained. A solid gray, a blue-and-white striped, and a black. The black square made me uneasy whenever I touched it and I wondered what essence Aunt Cordelia had trapped in it.

Then came the news that Lady Croma had died in the night. It saddened us all, but it came as no surprise as she was past her seventieth year.

Her grandnephew, Lord Nelvon, became the Keep Holder in her place, and his wife, the Lady Shira, took up her residence as well. One day soon after, I worked in my house, brewing some of the quilt potions when I heard a knock. Brushing my hands against my apron, I pulled open the door and stood face-to-face with the Lady Shira.

She had green eyes set too far apart over her wide nose. She tried to hide that with too much blue powder. Likewise, her thin yellow hair was clasped by sapphire and gold combs. Because of her homeliness, some in town gossiped that she had used witch power to trap her husband.

Whatever I thought of her appearance, however, I still curtsied and gave her proper welcome. Then I asked, "What brings my lady to my humble house?"

Lady Shira motioned her escort to stay outside and walked over to my work table. She put out a finger, then quickly withdrew it before she touched anything. I saw her lip curl before she turned to answer.

"I was told that you have knowledge of certain potions and drinks, such as love draughts. I came to see if it was true."

I nodded to her. "I have limited knowledge of such things, my lady. Do you have need of such things?"

I could tell she blushed even beneath that coating of red she had plastered across her face.

"No, no, I have no need of that. My lord and I are very happy. However, sometimes I do have trouble sleeping. Perhaps you have something for me?"

I nodded. "I believe I have some. If you will pardon me?"

She gave a curt nod and I left the room and went to my bedroom where I kept such potions safely hidden. I was about to go to the safe spot in the wall when I heard her say behind me, "What a lovely quilt!"

I spun about to see that Lady Shira had followed me and now fondled Aunt Cordelia's quilt. She picked it up from its place on the bed and pulled it closer, rubbing her face against it. I thought of her face paint rubbing off, and I am sure I blanched.

"How much will you take for it?" she asked, turning her attention to the rune stitched squares.

Then I know my face turned white. I reached out and steadied myself by the bedpost.

"The quilt is not for sale."

"Nonsense. I will pay you well for it." She started to trace one of the runes.

"I'm sorry, my lady. My aunt gave that quilt to me before she was killed. I couldn't possibly part with it."

Then I turned to the portrait on the wall, swung it out, and grabbed a vial of sleeping potion from the hidden shelf. I gave it to her and said, "Here, my lady, take this with my compliments."

I forced it into her hands and pulled the quilt from her grasp. Luckily, none of her paint seemed to have rubbed off on it.

"Now, my lady, if you will excuse me, I am very tired," I said, rubbing the bulge of my stomach. I began walking to the door, herding her with my bulk.

"Oh, yes, thank you," she said. "Are you sure I can't change your mind about the quilt?"

"No, I'm afraid not," I said as I nudged her out the door. I thought I saw her eyes narrow and her lips part as if she would speak as I said good-bye and closed the door.

I tried to forget her visit by concentrating once more on my brewing and had succeeded by the time Doran came home. As he walked through the door, I turned to greet him with a smile. It died before it reached my lips.

"Doran, what is it?"

"Marya, did the Lady Shira visit you today?" he asked, his eyes shadowed, his mouth puckered at the corners.

I put down my ladle and answered. "Yes, she stopped by for a potion and I gave it to her."

"Why didn't you sell her the quilt?" he asked and I could tell he was serious.

I know the color fled from my face and my legs buckled. I fell upon a chair with a thump.

Doran rushed to my side and grasped my hand in his.

"Marya, are you all right?"

I yanked my hand from his.

"How," I said, "how can you ask me that?"

He shook his head and a small crease appeared between his eyes. "You look faint. I want to know if you're well."

I waved my hand at him.

"Not that. How can you ask me about the quilt? How could you ever think I would sell it?"

Doran stood up, his face flushed.

"It's just a quilt, Marya. And she is the Lady Shira; her husband rules us all and is my employer. Would you like us to be without a job when our baby arrives?"

I didn't want to hear anymore.

"Just a quilt? Just a quilt?" I screamed. "There is nothing 'just' about it. It's special. Very special to me. Apparently, more than you are," I said and immediately wished I hadn't.

The concern that had been on Doran's face before transformed into a quiet anger. He didn't speak; he never did when riled. Instead, he turned and walked out the door. I watched him go, then ran to the bedroom. I collapsed on the bed and pulled the quilt close to me. I looked at the three remaining squares, hoping one would come to life and solve this problem for me as it had so many times in the past. But the quilt remained dull.

I huddled under the quilt until I fell asleep. In the middle of the night, I heard Doran come in and stumble into the kitchen table. Glass shattered against the floor and I wondered which potion now lay spilled on the floor.

The door to the bedroom creaked open and I knew he was staring at me. My eyes remained closed and I pulled the quilt tighter. After several minutes, Doran closed the door and scuttled back to the kitchen table. I heard him scrape a chair across the floor then it creak as he sat in it. I listened for a while longer only to hear snores erupt from the other side of the door. Finally, I went back to sleep myself.

In the morning, Doran was gone before I awoke. I found the kitchen empty and the broken glass swept up. For that much I was grateful, but I had hoped to see Doran and apologize.

Instead, after I had my breakfast, I took up my herb basket and set out for the stretch of woodlands that flanked the keeptown. I planned to gather as many as I could before my time came upon me.

The walk took me twice as long as it usually did, but I had packed a lunch and had planned to spend the day. The weather was warm under the midsummer sun, and I enjoyed being out of doors. I gathered up my herbs at leisure, often needing to rest in between, so that the sun had nearly disappeared when I made it back home.

I knew as soon as I opened the door that Doran wasn't there. Once again I regretted my words the night before.

I placed the basket on the table and went into the bedroom to check and see if he had come home at all. I saw no coat or signs he had been there. Then I noticed the bed. Nothing lay upon it. The quilt was gone.

I tore through the room, searching under the bed, in the closet. Nowhere. Then I knew. Doran had been home. And no doubt my quilt now rested on the Lady Shira's bed.

I fell back on the bed surprised to find my eyes dry. I think shock had stolen my tears. I lay there remembering what the quilt brought me and wondering what gifts those last three squares held. What treasures would I miss?

A noise from the outer room roused me from my thoughts. The door had creaked which meant someone stood in the kitchen. I sat up, and Doran poked his head around the door.

"Marya?" he asked.

He started to come in when my shoe skimmed past his nose. He yanked his head back before the second could strike.

"Marya! What are you doing?"

"How could you," I screamed, "how could you give it away?"

His voice came from around the door. "I had to Marya. Lord Nelvon made it plain that either his wife had the quilt or I would have to find a new place to work and live."

Finally, the tears starting pouring from my eyes.

"So why didn't you tell him you'd move? We could have gone elsewhere."

"What are you saying? Are you serious? Is your quilt more important than everything I've worked for? I'm worth less than your precious quilt?"

I rocked on the bed and I almost shouted back, yes, it means everything to me. Instead, I stayed quiet which may have been worse.

"Fine, Marya. I think I'll go see what lodgings I can make in the barracks. Perhaps I'll even find a bed with a wench."

I know he spoke to sting and it almost worked. But before I could answer or he could leave, the pain hit, like a sword plunged through my gut, and I screamed.

"Marya?" Doran ran into the bedroom and fell down on his knees next to me as I sat on the bed. He grabbed my hand and held it.

"Marya, what is it? I was only joking."

I sat panting and finally managed to tell him that I thought it was the baby.

"But you have another month to go."

"Tell that to the baby," I said.

"Here, lie down," he said and grabbed me about the shoulders and pulled me back on to the bed.

"Doran?" I asked.

"Yes, Marya?" he answered as he smoothed my hair back.

"Go get Midwife Larisha. Tell her I need her."

He started to shake his head.

"Go, Doran. I'll be okay until you get back. Please, I need her help."

He made a few more swipes at my hair, then stood up. He held my hand for a moment and then left.

He hadn't been gone for more than ten minutes when another pain struck me. I held back my scream so he wouldn't hear me and come running back.

Oh, how I wished for my quilt then. I felt sure that its weight alone would make things all right. For I felt sure that something was wrong, but part of me didn't really want to know what.

It was another fifteen minutes before the next pain struck. I waited for Doran to come back any minute as the Midwife didn't live that far away. But still he didn't come.

An hour went by and the pains kept coming and still no Doran. Where had he gone?

Finally, I heard the door open and I lifted my head to greet the midwife. But Doran was alone when he entered the bedroom. He came over and immediately fell down on his knees next to the bed. Tears slipped from the corners of his eyes.

"I tried," he said. "I went looking for her, but she has another patient in delivery this evening and it looked like a difficult birth. She said she would come as soon as she could."

I dropped my head back on the pillow.

"Oh, Marya, darling Marya, is there anything else I can do?"

I shook my head even though I wanted to yell at him, go get my quilt back, it will make everything all right. But he wouldn't have believed me and I knew that the quilt was already a painful subject between us.

I spent the night in frequent spasms of pain, like someone twisting my stomach in circles. Doran stayed with me, holding my hand, wiping my head with a damp cloth. We both flitted in and out of sleep between the contractions.

Occasionally, the wind would rattle the door and we would both jump, hoping it was the midwife. But even though Doran would fly to the door, he found no one there.

The sun came through the window in time with another pain. I gripped Doran's hand and could see him grimace through his fatigue as I squeezed.

Then we both heard a knock on the door. At last Doran jumped up, but I kept my grip as the pain stayed with me. Finally the feeling of tearing stopped, and I let go. The knocking came again, harder. Doran ran to the door.

It was not the midwife he brought into the bedroom, but the Lady Shira. She wore a dark cloak as if she had come in secret and when she threw back the hood, I could see why. Thick red blotches decorated her face and her wrists looked swollen. Then I realized she held my quilt in her arms. Hope shot through me like the pains before.

"Do something," she shrieked. "Make it take them away."

Doran stood still, holding the doorknob to the bedroom, blinking. I knew he thought she had gone mad.

Lady Shira turned away from him and spotted me lying on the bed. She came toward me. Doran moved to block her path. I'm sure he thought I was in bad enough shape without her giving me whatever it was she had.

However, she pushed him aside. She threw the quilt on my bed and again screamed "Do something!"

A contraction grabbed me then and without Doran to squeeze, I screamed.

Lady Shira backed away, her eyes snapping wide open. I think she thought I was mad. Doran rushed to me and brushed her aside. He grabbed my hand, and I squeezed back. Finally, when the pain stopped, I told him to cover me with the quilt.

"Why, what will that do?"

"Please, just do it," I said.

He looked at me sideways, then pulled the quilt up and over me, tucking the upper edge under my chin. I put my arms over it and caressed the old fabric, feeling worn places in some of the cotton squares.

Then I noticed that the black square near the bottom, the one I never liked, was blank. I looked over at Lady Shira, now ignored and cringing against the wall and I knew where that square had gone.

A glow I caught in the corner of my eye brought my attention back to the quilt. The silver embroidery on the gray square was coming to life.

I held out my hands to it, watching the silver light play on my fingertips. I looked up at Doran and smiled. He stared at the square, then turned to me.

"No wonder you valued it. I'm sorry."

I reached for his hand and took it. "I'm sorry, too," I said.

"No! Let it fix me, let it fix me!"

The Lady Shira ran to the bed and tried to yank the quilt off of me. I held on to it and wouldn't let go. She started to scratch at my face when Doran seized her and dragged her back.

"No, my Lady. You must calm down," he said.

She struggled in his grip and raked her nails against his arm. I saw scarlet lines spring up and I wondered if the infection she carried now entered Doran.

I didn't have long to think on it though before another pain squeezed me. I screamed and clutched the quilt in handfuls. Doran looked at me and I could see turmoil slither across his face. He wanted to come to me again but dared not release the lady.

The pain continued burning through my middle and as it did, the silver glow grew brighter until it choked the sunlight out of the room. We were all lit by the argent light. Even Lady Shira relaxed in its grip.

The light coalesced at the side of the bed. It shrank in upon itself, forming into a human shape, a female shape. In a few minutes a silver-haired woman dressed in gray stood next to me. The silver glow hung about closer than a shadow.

"Shh, relax, dear one," she said.

At her touch, the pain lessened. Then she turned to Doran. "We will need water and some linens."

Doran nodded to the swollen lady. "What about her?" he asked.

"You need hold her no longer."

Doran released her. Lady Shira cringed once more against the wall and didn't come near.

I felt another pain coming and reached out for the woman. My hand fell on solid flesh and she turned back to me.

"It will be all right."

189

The pain once more flowed through me and dissipated. I smiled at the woman and she smiled back.

"Now it's time for the baby to come," she said.

My smile left and my eyes grew wide. I was too early.

She seemed to read my thoughts. "Nonsense," she said, pulling the quilt up toward my head. Then she reached out and traced patterns over my swollen stomach. They reminded me of the quilt square embroidery and glowed silver on my stomach.

I could still feel the contractions as they racked my body, but the pain vanished.

"Now push," she said, so I did. I could feel my body helping me, and I went with it. The woman had now assumed the role of midwife and I was glad.

Doran came bustling in with a kettle of water and some blankets, but when he saw what was happening, he dropped them. The silver woman glanced at him and chuckled.

"I think you need to get more," she said.

He stood there a moment and than vanished back into the kitchen only to reappear and snatch the kettle from the floor before ducking out again.

"We're almost there," she said and I pushed as hard as I could. I saw her lean over and then I felt as if something broke free. I looked, and she held a baby girl still covered in blood. The midwife rapped her across the buttocks and she screamed, taking in lungfuls of air.

Doran ran back into the room with his kettle and a small blanket. He stood before the quilt woman as she took the blanket and cleaned the baby. Then she handed my child to me.

"Thank you," I said.

"You're welcome, great-great-granddaughter," she said.

"What . . ." I started to ask but the apparition quieted me.

"Who do you think your Aunt Cordelia learned from?" she said.

Then Lady Shira came to life again.

"What about me? Do something for me," she screamed.

Great-great-grandma looked over at her and said "Hush, woman," and she did. Then she walked over to her and traced a pattern on her forehead. It also glowed silver, and I saw a black web, like embroidery, lift from her forehead.

"Now go home and rest and you will recover."

Lady Shira's eyes still held a silver glow as she turned without a word and left.

"She scratched Doran," I said. "Will he get ill?"

Great-great-grandma shook her head. "That square was there to keep the quilt from anyone but you. He will be fine," she said.

Doran sat down next to me to look at the baby.

"Isn't she beautiful?" I said.

He nodded his agreement and stroked her cheek.

I looked back to great-great-grandma only to find her half there. She faded as I watched.

"Wait, don't go yet," I yelled, but she only raised her hand and then vanished. Doran also watched her go.

"Well, I guess that's it," he said, but I knew there was one more thing I had to do.

I pulled the quilt up around me until I found the last blue and white striped square with gold embroidery and pulled it up over the baby. The runes leaped to life with a golden flare that made us both blink. When we opened our eyes, the embroidery was gone.

Doran shook his head and smiled.

"What should we name her?" he asked.

"Cordelia," I answered.

TWILIGHT
by Diana L. Paxson

There are not too many in my generation or younger
who take on an unfamiliar mythology; a good deal of
current fantasy seems to take place in the Celtic Twilight. This one is set in the twilight of a society, but it
is certainly not Celtic. It is Norse—somewhat more
unusual.

But then, Diana's stories are always a little different than expected. That means among other things
that they're never hackneyed, and she has now become a very solid writer on her own. She has two
sons, now both working, and she has become the
first in my generation of the family to become a
grandmother. Her grandson, Evan Raphael Kelson
Grey is a very charming infant—but then, that's typi-
cal of a baby; they have nothing else to do but be
charming. I often fancy that that's how the race sur-
vives.

At midsummer the sun circled round the sky, barely
dipping beneath the horizon. The folk of the
Tronds who had answered Jarl Sigurd's summons to
the Allthing spent the long twilight talking and drink-

ing in the tents of skins and bothies of woven branches that had flowered in the meadow below the grave mounds of the ancient kings. Bera Steinbjornsdottir, searching the woods above the encampment for pot herbs, envied them. But the Vœlva must have something that grew in this place in her dinner so that the landspirits would help her to see truly when they performed *seidh* tomorrow, and Bera was under orders to gather what she could find.

She peered through the shadows and jumped as she realized that what she had taken for a fallen log was a man. He lay sprawled on his belly, the skin over his back and arms the blue-black of a bruise. Bera held her breath, afraid she had awakened him, but he did not stir. After a few moments, it occurred to her that if someone had come up here in search of a quiet spot to rest, he would have worn a tunic, or at least folded a cloak to lie on. This sleeper would never waken again.

She bent over the body. There was no blood, but there was something wrong about the shape of his skull. Shuddering, Bera drew back. From the field below she heard the shrill squeal of a stallion and the shouts of the men who were watching the horse-fights, but the wood was silent. The body had that indefinable air of abandonment that comes when a man has been dead for some time.

Bera bit her lip, stifling the impulse to run. Men who killed for honorable reasons proclaimed their deed and paid the weregild. This was secret murder, the worst of crimes. A man who left his victim's body out of sight might well return to hide it more effectively, and would hardly hesitate to kill her, too!

Behind her a twig snapped. Without looking to see the cause, she picked up her skirts and ran.

In moments she was among the tents. She caught her breath, heart pounding, and forced herself to move slowly from fire to fire. She was small, with a mass of dark curly hair. Wrapped in an old shawl, anyone who saw her would have taken her for someone's serving maid.

She heard snatches of conversation and song, and gradually they began to make sense to her. Five years it had been since Groa had taken her from her father's hall to teach her the craft of the seeress, moving from steading to steading as need called. But she had never before been to one of the great assemblies where men settled claims at law and raised armies for kings. If she listened to their talk, perhaps she could forget what she had seen.

Over in England King Aethelstan, who had made Eric Blood-Ax lord in Jorvik, was dead. Folk said that the new king Edmund hated him and would drive him from the land. And if Eric was landless, he might well turn his mind back to Norway, where his younger brother King Hacon ruled. The harvests had been good since Hacon came, and no one wanted Eric and Gunhild back again.

It was clear, thought Bera, what kind of questions they would be asking the Vœlva when it came time for *seidh*. The king might be a Christian, but his chieftains were not. They would want the seeress to tell them whether Eric would attack, and if he did, to which brother the gods would give victory.

She passed the tents of Jarl Sigurd, on a rise nearest to the field of assembly. Inside the largest someone was arguing. The tent swayed as a burly man in a skin vest burst through the door flap. She scrambled out of the way as he lurched past. The tent flap twitched again, and for a moment she glimpsed a pale, pinched face above a dark robe. The sound of men's rough joking grew louder as they returned from the field. Suddenly this did not seem a good place to be.

She paused for a moment, extending her awareness to the earth and drawing up stillness as Groa had taught her, wrapping it around her like a cloak of shadow. *I am not here . . .* she thought as the warriors neared, tall men, half-drunk already. *You see nothing but twilight.*

"What took you so long?" Groa was stirring gruel when Bera returned. She looked up, the firelight turning her strong-boned face to a mask of light and shadow.

"I walked through the camp," answered Bera. "I have never seen so many folk together in one place before." She dared not speak even to the Vœlva of what else she had seen.

"And what did you hear?" asked the older woman, taking the basket of herbs and beginning to strip off the leaves and cast them into the pot.

"The folk are divided." She settled down by the fire, feeling her tension ease. "They like the king, but they fear his brother. Some say the gods will turn against Hacon because he leaves it to other men to make the offerings."

"Eric and Gunhild let themselves be baptized," observed the Vœlva.

"True, but no one believes they mean it. Eric Blood-Ax puts his faith to his own right arm, and everyone knows that Gunhild is a sorceress. But you

196

know all that, don't you? Did not Jarl Sigurd himself summon you?"

On Groa's bed lay a new cloak lined with sable. Was it the jarl who had sent it? It was rumored in the camp that she had wintered with him many years ago and they had been lovers.

"It is the future that men fear, not the past. I have not spoken with Sigurd since I came here. What else do the people say."

"Perhaps I should not tell you." Bera frowned. "If you know too much, how can you tell if your visions are true or your own imaginings?"

It was a question that had begun to weigh on her. She had not doubted Groa's powers when she began her training, and indeed, she had seen the Vœlva do remarkable things. But as she became more accustomed to such journeys, she had begun to wonder. How did the visions of seidh differ from dreams or her own imaginings? She knew that she would never intentionally deceive, but how could she *know?*

The Vœlva straightened, and suddenly Bera could not look away.

"When I perform seidh at a farmstead, what do I do?"

"You wander about and look at the fields . . . and you eat their food . . . so that you can feel the spirits of the place."

Groa nodded. "Most of the questions will be about the crops and the herds, and so I must know them. But here the questions will have to do with the needs of men. Yet I cannot go among them—even my protections would falter before the passions of so many. But you can be my ears. You are right to fear distortion—I cannot say myself how I tell the difference between true sight and my own desires. But you know that most often the knowledge comes only as pictures, no good to anyone until we can say what they mean."

"It is not up to us to decide what that is!" Bera exclaimed.

"Truth has many faces. Is it better to speak in riddles which may be misinterpreted, or to seek the meaning of the vision and, if I can see it, to counsel the best course. In times like these, where armies may march and men die because of my words, it is vital to know which truth to tell."

Bera scowled. She had always believed that truth lit up the inner landscape like the noonday sun. These words were like the twilight, neither night nor day. As she got out the wooden bowls and spoons of horn so that they could eat, she thought about the nameless corpse that lay beneath the trees, but she did not tell the Vœlva what she had found.

If the murderer had meant to hide the body, he delayed too long. At the hour of greatest darkness, two men, wandering off to relieve themselves after an evening's drinking, stumbled over the corpse and awakened half the camp with their cries. Soon an even more interesting rumor swept the encampment. The body was that of Brynjulv Hjaltison, one of Jarl Sigurd's men. But this was no drunken quarrel. Had the man been struck down because of what he might do, or because of what he knew?

"Surely they'll find the killer soon. Jarl Sigurd will not suffer such a thing to be done to his own." said Bera, weak with relief. Her sleep had been haunted by visions of the murdered man. If he had not been found, she would have had to report it. But now she could rest, for what, after all, did she know?

Groa nodded distantly. By the time of the seidh ceremony, she would be completely detached from the concerns of the world. But Bera had plenty to occupy her. It was up to her and Haki to see to the construction of a high seat from which the Vœlva could prophesy. By the time the sky faded to the long northern twilight, physical labor had driven most other thoughts from her mind.

She straightened the folds of her old blue cloak and twitched at the amber necklaces that lay across her breast as the bonders—the noble farmer-chieftains of the northern lands—came in. The more prosperous had brought benches to sit on; the others stood behind them, talking softly. Folk were always a little on edge as they waited for the seeing to begin, but Bera had never felt so much tension.

It is because of the king and his brother . . . she thought, watching them. And then, *It is the murder. If Jarl Sigurd does not find the guilty one, the others will not support the king.* The men of the Trond were like wolves. If their leader weakened, they would sense it instantly and bring him down.

Men began to murmur and turn; she looked up and saw Jarl Sigurd, his blunt, pleasant features set in a scowl, coming in with his houseguard. They all looked grim, she thought, recognizing the young men who had been at the horse-fights—Sigurd's nephew Orm Einarsson and black-browed Rogn, who was said to be a berserker, in the lead. With the warriors came the rest of the jarl's household. Bera recognized the man who had run from the tent, a smith called Skagi who men said was the murdered man's brother, but she did not see the other figure she had glimpsed inside.

"The Vœlva is ready?" asked the Jarl. Bera nodded, swallowing. Sigurd turned to survey the gathered crowd and the mutterings stilled. "Are you here because of curiosity or because you have questions? It does not matter. It is I who have paid for this seidhkona to come here. Perhaps she will be able to see an answer to our mystery. When I am finished, if the woman has still the strength for it, you others may question her." He took his place, and Bera cleared her throat.

"When the Vœlva has been seated, I will call the spirits." Her voice sounded thin in her own ears; she hoped she would be able to sing.

She nodded to Haki, and he led the Vœlva out from beneath the shadows of the trees. A veil concealed her face, a cloak her form. The servingman made a stirrup of his hands and lifted the wisewoman onto the raised seat they had lashed together from saplings. The long rays of the sun, slanting through the trees behind it, left the seidhkona a shape of shadow, as if she herself were part of that darkness in which the visions appeared.

Bera began to sing as once she had sung her cattle home, the high notes chill and sharp, cutting a path between the worlds. The people grew still, avoiding each other's gaze, as the song stirred feelings that warriors were not allowed to recognize. Above her, the Vœlva sighed and shifted on her cushion of goose feathers, letting awareness of self slip away. Bera felt the spirits of field and forest pause, and drift toward the circle, more and more of them gathering until the hairs prickled on her arms. The Vœlva yawned; wood creaked as she slumped against the frame. And still Bera sang, holding onto the high seat for balance as the earth seemed to shift beneath her, feeling the pressure of still greater powers as that part of Midgard which was the seidh circle aligned itself with the greater Midgard which lies within.

The last notes thinned and whispered to silence. The Vœlva was as motionless as the dead. Bera felt a momentary thrill of fear, but she could still sense the other woman's spirit.

"Margerd—" she whispered, "do you hear me? Ancient One, awaken from your dreaming. There are those who need your wisdom here."

A wind rustled the branches above them, then there was silence. Bera drew breath to call again.

"It is dark here, and quiet . . ." Groa's voice seemed to come from very far away. "Here there is peace. Who calls me? Who would disturb my sleep?"

Cloth rustled. Bera turned and saw Jarl Sigurd rising to his feet, frowning.

"It is I who call you, Sigurd of Lade, Jarl of the Tronds. By the bond we once shared I bid you tell me, who has murdered the man called Brynjulf Hjaltison and why?"

"How . . . did he die?"

"Struck down like a dog in the forest," rumbled the Jarl. "I fear that you must seek him in Hella's realm."

The Vœlva sighed. "That is a far and fearful journey, but I do not go alone. Blackmane, Blackmane," she whispered to the horse spirit that was her helper. "Spirit steed, I summon—" she whistled, and almost immediately Bera heard the sound of hoofbeats and a low whickering. Some of the others heard it too; she saw them tense, staring around them.

"Three great roots anchor the Worldtree. Blackmane

bears me beneath them," said the seeress. "We pass through mists and veils of shadow. The roots of the moist mountains of Jotunheim we pass, splashing through icy streams, through the charred forest of Myrkwood, past the Well of Wyrd. Around and down we descend, and around. . . ." Her voice rose and fell, noting the landmarks that marked the way. Bera blinked; each time they did this, it grew harder to keep from being drawn into trance herself. But she could not allow it. She must stay on the threshold between the worlds.

"I come to Hella's gate; the great doors swing open to my touch. The dead are drifting toward me, men made of mist; ghosts are gathering now. I will call Brynjulf—" The Vœlva twitched and muttered. Bera felt the air grow cold. "I see him . . . he tries to speak—"

"No! Unholy!" another voice cut across hers. Bera swayed, dizzied by the shock of the interruption. A man in a dark tunic leaped forward. Haki, startled from his own daze, scrambled after. "To raise the dead is abomination—" The assailant clutched at the Vœlva's robe.

Groa shrieked as he touched her. Bera, recovering her senses, leaped at him, bearing him back. Haki snatched up the Vœlva's staff and brought it down across his forearms with a crack. The man cried out and as he let go, Groa moaned and slumped into Bera's arms.

"Treachery!" cried some, but others were arguing.

"He did well. It can only bring bad luck to disturb the dead."

"But he might have told us the name of his murderer!" Voices clashed and rumbled around them.

"This witch has lain in Jarl Sigurd's bed. How can we trust what she will say?"

"That's so—this is an evil thing—" came the murmur. "The king's justice is not served by seidh."

"It is you who betray justice!" roared the jarl. "Did you fear what she would reveal?" Bera looked up as he bent over her. "Is she hurt?"

"I don't know—" stammered the girl. "She is alive, but she has fainted, or worse. I don't know if her spirit can find the way home." She bent over her teacher once more.

"Margerd!" she whispered. "Can you hear me? Come back!" Above her, the Jarl was ordering the others away.

"She will find the way!" he said harshly when they had gone. "She has been journeying so since before you were born, and her spirits have great power."

Bera nodded. "Guard me—" she murmured, then bent over the motionless body of her teacher. "Margerd, come out, and let Hella's gates close behind you! Blackmane, bear her swiftly to safety!"

Groa sighed and shuddered, then relaxed again. Bera's pulse leaped, but she kept talking, calling the Vœlva's allies to aid her. As she spoke of the otherworld, she found herself being drawn into it once more. She felt the warmth of the bear who was her own guardian behind her. Now she saw Hella's gates before her. With Bear's strength she thrust them open and called.

For a time, it seemed, there was nothing. Then she heard a horse's neigh. "Blackmane, bring her!" she cried. Now she could see the horse, a dark shape slumped on its back. She grabbed for the mane, and

hanging on, drew the animal through the gates. Together they began to climb the rocky path to the world
of humankind.

When Bera opened her eyes once more, only Haki
and Jarl Sigurd remained. Groa was breathing deeply,
evenly.

"Groa—it is time to awaken now. Your body and
spirit are united. Come back to us! Please—I need
you ..." Her breath caught on a sob.

The jarl gripped her other hand. "Groa, in the name
of all we once shared, I call you—" he rumbled.
"Come, my dear, you are safe now."

The Vœlva sighed, her head turned restlessly against
his arm. "I hear you. What happened to me?"

"You were in trance," said Bera. "You were interrupted."

"You were seeking Brynjulf," said Sigurd. "Did you
find him? Who was his murderer?"

"I ... found him," came the answer. "But ... the
blow that killed him came from behind. He did not
know ..." She shivered. "Oh gods, my head hurts."
She struggled to sit up, turned suddenly, and retched
onto the ground.

"What can I do?" asked the jarl. "Some mead?"

"No," whispered the Vœlva. "There is tea. Bera
knows."

"Can you carry her?" asked the girl. The Vœlva was
strongly built and tall. "We must put her to bed. She
needs to rest now."

He nodded. "I will leave men to guard you." Grunt-
ing, he got his arms under the Vœlva and lifted her.

"The only protection we need is for you to let it be
known that she failed," said Bera. "Those who don't
believe in our magic would not be convinced even if

she had given you a name. This way we'll escape accusations of deception."

"And those who do believe?" he smiled grimly.

"If the guilty one is among them, he might be willing to kill again to keep her from giving evidence." She tucked the wool blankets around the Vœlva.

"If she had given me a name, I would know who to accuse, who to challenge. Then the gods would decide."

"But she didn't," said Bera. "And she will need time to recover. A long time. Tell everyone—whoever did this deed has nothing to fear from her now." There was a silence. Bera felt the jarl watching her.

"And what about you?" he said then.

"I am only her apprentice," Bera said quickly.

"There is power in you. You remind me of Groa when she was young."

"Should I be flattered? If you say that to others, I will be doomed as well. What skill I have will be used to heal *her.* I can do nothing to help you, lord. Leave us alone."

"Do you think I ask for myself? It is for the king, who gave the bonders back their rights when he took the crown. If suspicion divides us, Eric Blood-Ax will find us easy meat when he comes. And Gunhild will allow no magic but her own. . . ."

Bera shook her head, her gaze still fixed on Groa, who had passed into an uneasy slumber. "I am sorry. There is nothing I can do."

The next day Groa stayed in bed, waking from time to time to drink willowbark tea and then falling back into uneasy slumber. Still, by twilight the older woman was well enough for Bera to go down to wash clothes at the stream. She found the physical labor of beating the soiled linen curiously satisfying, as if she could take out all the fears and frustrations of the past few days on the unoffending cloth.

But eventually she could do no more. She wrung out the wet clothing and rolled it into a bundle to take back to camp. Though there was still light, the camp had grown quieter. Most folk were eating now, gathered around their fires. Bera let her thoughts drift while her feet found the way up the familiar path.

The part of her mind that was thinking heard nothing, but some other sense, honed, perhaps, by her training, alerted her just before the shadow behind the trees darted forward, steel flickering in its hand.

A knife. With a jolt Bera's consciousness focused completely on the here and now. She dropped the laundry and turned to run, but an arm like iron clamped around her and against her throat she felt the cold edge of the blade. *If he had wanted to kill me, I would be dead.* She swallowed and stood still, waiting.

"Will the Vœlva recover before the end of the Thing?" came a hoarse whisper from behind her. She was abruptly certain her captor, whoever he might be, was the murderer.

"What is it to you?"

"It would be better if her weakness continued . . . if she remains too ill to practice her craft until it is over. No talk with the dead."

Bera bit her lip, realizing it would do no good to tell her captor that Groa had learned nothing. Sometimes people could hear only what agreed with their hopes or fears.

"If she does more magic here, her next sickness will be death. Tell her!"

She felt his muscles tense, then he thrust her away and she went sprawling. There was a rustle of branches, twigs snapped beneath running feet. When she caught her breath sufficiently to look up, he was gone, and the light had faded to a featureless dusk in which she could hardly see her way.

Bera lay wakeful while the sun crept round behind the hills, reliving the attack again and again. She had made the wrong decisions, she realized, from the moment she discovered the murdered man. Some things must be confronted, and you only made them worse if you tried to hide. She had not told Groa about the threat; the Vœlva knew better than to take the spirit paths until she was fully recovered, so why worry her?

But neither could they afford to simply sit and let things take their course. Besides, the attack had angered her. Groa would do no more in this—even had she been up to it, the accusations of partiality had stung her. But Bera herself had learned to walk between the worlds. It was forbidden to seek Hella's home alone, but she did not need to. The Vœlva had proved there was nothing to be learned there.

With a sigh she sat up. Groa lay still on her pallet on the other side of the tent, sleeping peacefully. Moving quietly, Bera took her cloak, made her way out of the tent, and took the path that led to the mounds.

Though the Assembly was held in their shadow, few men cared to spend time near the grassy humps that were said to house the bones of ancient kings. The tallest had a hollow on the far side. Once she reached it, Bera had no fear that she would be disturbed. She set her hands upon the turf and asked permission and protection from the spirit that dwelt within. When she felt

207

the odd shift, like a change in the air around her, that told her she had been heard, she lay down upon her cloak and wrapped it carefully around her.

The wool was thick and tightly woven, smelling of horse and grass. When she drew it up over her face, Bera found herself in the dark for the first time in weeks. She twisted and turned, willing taut muscles to relax, let her breathing deepen, counted her breaths until awareness of the wool that cocooned her and the hard ground beneath her fell away.

"Honey Paws, Wintersleeper, Brúnbjorn, wisest of helpers, come to me . . ." All her being bent to summon the Bear who was her *hamingja,* her ally in the other worlds. Her heartbeat was a silent drum. *"Your daughter calls you, old one. Come and I will give you lingonberries as an offering!"* Again she waited, until she heard the familiar sighing grunt of the bear. She sighed, more relieved than she would have cared to admit, and with that last release of tension found herself sinking completely into trance.

Gradually the darkness behind her eyelids became the featureless illumination of the Midgard that lies within. A plain stretched before her, in its midst a great tree. Three great roots plunged through the soil. Its upper boughs brushed the heavens. Radiance glimmered through those distant branches when they stirred in the breeze. At the foot of the Worldtree, sitting with his back against the trunk and licking honey from his paws, was a great brown bear.

Brúnbjorn looked up with a deep whuffling sigh. Bera ran to him and her own breath went out of her as he clasped her. Within, she heard words— *"At least you waited until I finished the honey. What trouble are you in now?"* Bera caught back a sob of laughter as he released her, and began to tell her tale.

"And so I came to you," she ended. "Until the murderer is caught, Groa will not be safe. It must be someone still in camp—any sudden departures would invite suspicion. But the jarl would not condemn a man even on Groa's word alone. Unless I have proof, to speak would only increase my danger!"

Brúnbjorn grunted. *"You already know . . ."*

"What do you mean?" She sat back, staring at him.

"You humans—you walk past good mushrooms. You look at the surface of water and do not see the fish in the stream. Foolish child, the proof is there—you have to understand what you see." His paw shot out suddenly, scooped from the soil the stalk and bulb of spear-leek that had been growing among the grasses, and carried it to his jaws.

"Think, fearful one—what did you learn from the body of the murdered man?"

Brúnbjorn's solid strength warmed her; for the first time, Bera found herself able to deal with the memories without flinching, and things she had seen without noticing appeared with unearthly clarity.

"Brynjulf's back was all mottled and blue. He must have been killed elsewhere and lain on his back for some time before he was moved. In a tent . . . in Jarl Sigurd's tent—there was a pattern on the woven mats I saw when the flap was opened that matched the mottlings. They said that the jarl had been at the Thing and then at the stallion-fights since early morning. It was not he who killed the man. I think Brynjulf heard what he should not and was struck down, then kept in the tent until everyone went out to watch the horses." She sighed and let memory range farther.

"The man who ran from the jarl's tent when I passed smelled of the forge, and so did the man who threatened me. It was the smith, Skagi, Brynjulf's brother. The man who laid hands on Groa was the one in the tent, but then—" she could see clearly in memory, "—he was wearing a cross. I think one of them killed Brynjulf, but which, and why?"

"You don't understand what you see, or what you hear. You heard them speaking. Allow yourself to remember what they said."

For a moment Bera wanted to protest. She had been too far away! But Brúnbjorn was watching her with implacable patience. She made herself remember the murmur of voices, and this time she understood the words.

Time runs differently in the Midgard that lies within. From vision, Bera passed into a deep sleep. When she woke, she could not at first imagine where she was or why. She thrust aside the folds of the cloak and sat up, drawing in deep breaths of the warm summer air.

The sun had moved all the way around the sky and was shining brightly. From somewhere nearby she could hear the rumble and clash of men's voices raised in argument. Still dazed with sleep, she stumbled to the top of the mound. The men below her fell silent, their stillness communicating itself from one group to the next until they were all staring. Later, she realized how she must have appeared to them, with the folds of her blue cloak twisted around her as if she had arisen from the soil of the mound.

"The Vœlva . . ." came the whisper, "she rises from the grave!"

Bera rubbed her eyes and sneezed, and someone laughed. "No—it's only the girl—"

"But she's seidh-trained," came the answer, "and she's been sitting out on the mound!"

"Maiden!" Jarl Sigurd pushed his way through the others and halted at the foot of the mound. "Do not be afraid. Speak, child. What visions have been granted you?"

Bera stared at him. Slowly, for her mind was waking more slowly than her body, she made her way to the gray stone that had poked through the earth of the mound and sat down. Several of the men murmured uneasily. She found that she wanted to laugh. She had accused Groa of imposing her own interpretations on the strange images of her visions. The information she herself had found on her journey was quite factual, but she knew that for the bonders to accept it she would have to dress it up with some mystery.

But she did not have to pretend for her first words to come out a moan. She coughed and tried again.

"The Worldtree bends to a wind of change . . . Ratatosk bears strange rede from root to crown. War is coming, and woe to men!" Gods, she sounded like Groa on a bad day. She took a deep breath. "A blade of blood brings sorrow to many. Beware the day when brother fights brother. . . ."

Even the most dedicated warriors had some skald-craft. A hiss of commentary ran through the assembly as they began to understand her.

"I see your meaning—" said the jarl. "When Eric fights Hacon all will suffer."

"Do you?" she asked. "The kings war already in your hearts. . . ."

He blinked, and a little of the high color receded

from his brow. "That is so, to our sorrow. Have you seen aught that will help us deal with the troubles we have here?"

"Do not listen to her," came another voice. Bera turned and saw it was the smith, Skagi, his hard-muscled arms bare. "Here men meet beneath the rule of Law. This is no place for women's sorcery!"

"She has sat out the night upon the holy mound," said Jarl Sigurd. "And that gives her a right to be here that is older than this assembly." He looked at her expectantly.

But Bera's gaze was on the smith. "Volundr's sons are strong and subtle. The hammer's blow blocks one betrayal, but cannot kill all who could threaten. The White Christ's counsels trouble conscience."

Skagi's pale glance shifted nervously, and Bera followed his gaze to where a shadow was easing away from among the watching men.

"Strange words, Lady," said Sigurd. "Can you tell us what they mean?"

"Bring Skagi's sib to stand with his brother," she said coldly. She had their attention now.

"His brother is dead!" said someone.

"His brother flees—" she pointed. There was a commotion at the edge of the crowd, and a cry, and then she saw men dragging a struggling figure toward the mound.

"Who is it?" came the murmur. "Isn't that Hjalti's youngest son Kol? I thought he was dead long ago in Frankland. What's he doing here?"

For a moment the man in the dark tunic stared at her. In the struggle the cross he had worn beneath his tunic had pulled free; it winked in the sun. Then he made the sign against Evil and turned to face the other men. "I will face your judgment," he quavered, "but do not heed this demon's deceptions!"

"Why are you afraid," said Bera. "If you follow the faith of your fathers, I am a holy woman and you ought to honor me. If you belong to the White Christ, then you must obey his law above all others and it is you who will be the sinner if you do not speak now."

"What do you mean?" Sigurd's gaze went to the brothers. Kol stood with bent head, shivering, but the muscles in Skagi's arms knotted as his fists clenched, and perspiration glistened on his brow. No man might bear weapons to the Thing, but the men of the jarl's houseguard drew closer, like mastiffs surrounding a wolf.

Bera looked from one brother to the other. Had the time come to bring the truth into the light of day?

"Skagi has taken King Eric's gold to speak for him among the bonders. Brynjulf learned of it and they quarreled, and as he turned to go, Skagi in his anger struck him down. Kol had returned in secret, hoping to win men for his god, but to save the living brother he kept silence about the deed and hid the body of the dead one away. Is that not so—*Gregorius?*" she asked.

There was a stark silence. Skagi stepped away from his brother, his big hands opening and closing, and the jarl's men stiffened.

"Kol Hjaltison—in the name of whatever god you serve now, I call you to say if this is so!"

"Miserere nobis!" The man who was now Gregorius sank to his knees, shaking. "By my own faith Satan snares me! The witch speaks true!"

Skagi roared and leaped for him, but the jarl's men bore him down. Now everyone was shouting. Bera sat back with a sigh.

Groa had told her once how Heide prophesied the twilight of the gods. *"Brothers will battle to bloody end, and sisters' sons their sib betray. . . ."* Was this the end of the Age, or only of the world they had known?

Men were pointing at her, gabbling of seidh-craft. But the only magic she had used here was that which had enabled her to see what she herself already knew.

"You have done well." Jarl Sigurd held out his hand to her. "Perhaps now the bonders will believe that Eric is dangerous."

"No longer," whispered Bera. The jarl stiffened. She gripped his fingers and pulled herself upright, remembering what Brúnbjorn had told her, the one thing she had not known. "Eric Blood-Ax is dead in England. He will not return to trouble you."

Bera let the jarl lead her away from the mound. The sun beat down upon her head, but she knew now that its clarity was an illusion. Truth was a twilight creature, and from now on nothing would be simple anymore.

PERSONAL NEED
by Lynn Michals

People have different levels of comfort food, but most of my close friends prefer chocolate. Lynn's is rice pudding, apparently, since her fiancé Bob (whom she'd like to dedicate this story to) went out in the night and got her some when the story before this one was rejected. She says, "We're getting married at the end of June on a mountaintop in Virginia. We're both college teachers and the closest jobs we've been able to find so far are in Washington and North Carolina."

I've published two of her other stories in Darkover anthologies, and one in *Sword and Sorceress XI*. During the past two years of commuting between North Carolina and DC, she says she had two bright blue and green parakeets named Patience and Comfort who kept her company during the semester, shrieking like peacocks and kicking seeds at her computer whenever she tried to grade papers or write. Well, better her than me. Misty Lackey, whose first stories I bought when she was just starting out, rehabs birds of prey by the dozens. I imagine if you're fond of that sort of thing, you might as well do it, but give me a cat or dog any day of the week and I'm happy.

215

Cora landed on the barren island, set fire to her boat, and waited. She waited in tranquillity and perfect faith, fasting for three days. Then a skiff scraped onto the flint of the beach and a tall young man splashed ashore; he handed Cora a water bottle and a loaf of her favorite rye.

"You could've just sent a messenger pigeon, you know," he said. "You didn't have to put your life in danger to make me drop everything and come running."

Guzzling water, Cora snorted in disbelief.

"Liar. You wouldn't have budged for anything less, not with twelve mayors and twenty ambassadors howling for audiences, and a blight in that ridiculous little cornfield you call your western province."

Cora's ruthlessness was one reason why she was well on her way to becoming a full mage, while Prince Arn of Oland had left Para House with only the powers of a very minor sorcerer.

"Well, now that you've lured me here without scruple, what crazy scheme are you going to drag me into?"

"I'd almost forgotten how much fun it is to lead a respectable young prince astray," Cora said thoughtfully. "You're going to steal the great key from Weland and return it to the High Queen of Iria, to whom it rightly belongs."

"That's impossible! And anyway, we've been at bloodfeud with Iria for generations, the Queen's greatuncle murdered my grandfather, my cousin killed her paternal aunt—"

"All the more reason for a progressive young aristocrat like you to end the feud now with a grand gesture. Anyway, Iria's lost too many of its things of power;

their border-magic and crop-magic are weakening. And Weland's hoarding up too many talismans for anyone's good."

"You're supposed to be becoming a mage," Arn said, troubled. Minor sorcerer or not, he knew the law. "Why are you meddling in human affairs?"

"Me? I'm just the Archmage's messenger pigeon. It's your quest, not mine—absolutely no magic allowed beyond your own illusions and charms. I'm just along for the ride."

"I'll give you a ride back to shore, my dear, but that's all. If I hadn't shown up, would you really have let yourself starve to death on this rock?"

Cora sniffed.

"Of course. One mustn't break the Pattern for personal needs. One mustn't even *feel* personal needs."

"I used to think kings were hard men—and then I met the mages. Thank all the dying gods I'm only a minor sorcerer," Arn said, and kissed Cora's hand. "You know I can't possibly go questing with you, darling Cora. I have to get back to the twelve mayors and the twenty ambassadors."

Cora laughed. She recognized the irresponsible eagerness lurking behind Arn's responsible words; it had been the prelude to every splendidly disastrous bit of rule-breaking she had hauled him into as a student.

So, a fortnight later, Arn ended up with his back against the wall of the King of Weland's treasure-house and a dozen of the King's guards closing in on him with drawn swords. Despite his fear, Arn's spell of illusion held steady: he would die as an insignificant barbarian thief, not as a Prince of Oland whose blood would require countless generations of Welander blood in vengeance.

But Cora threw off the shape of the barbarian thief's climbing-monkey and blazed forth as herself, a half-made mage in a blind rage.

"Touch a hair on his head and I'll drown the pack of you in molten rock!"

That threat was unnecessary: the little treasure-house seethed and crackled with danger, with half-unleashed hurricanes and electrical storms and earthquakes.

The guards fled.

Cora put her head in her hands, overcome by a flood of insight, a mage's first privilege and first duty.

"That was some bluff," Arn said, his voice uncertain. He looked down at the glittering crystal key in his hands as if he had forgotten what it was. "Even I half-believed you'd do it."

Cora faced him, putting aside the urge to rock and moan and howl with grief.

"I wasn't bluffing. We always thought I was your weakness, my dear, always leading you into trouble. But the truth is you were my weakness—and you still are. That's what the Archmage sent me here to learn. You're my last personal need."

Cora paused for a moment, watching the Pattern unfold before her. "Take the key to the High Queen of Iria, she'll marry you on the strength of it, and end the old feud, and you'll rule wisely and well with her. And I'll spend the next year in the sevenfold labyrinth at Para, unlearning the idea that each breath you take is worth more than the entire Pattern itself, present, past, and future."

Arn began to protest, then choked down his words. He took Cora's hand and kissed it, not with the old gallantry of a friend and a lover, but with the humility of a minor sorcerer recognizing a mage.

CATRIONA'S DAUGHTERS
by Andrea J. Horlick

Andrea Horlick says, "I have a nine-year-old son, Danny, two cats, and a warped imagination. I live just north of Boston, and to pay the bills, I work as a pediatric EEG technologist."

I collect peculiar jobs at which people work to pay the bills before they manage to make it writing, but that's a new one on me. She explains that she tries to persuade babies to sleep with electrodes on their heads. Heck, neither of my older sons would sleep, even without electrodes on their little heads. Only when my daughter was born did I ever find out how much time babies can spend sleeping—especially when you want to take their picture or something.

Andrea adds, "The first piece of writing I wrote in school, the teacher commented, 'Fine, now I'll be depressed all day after reading this,' and my output ever since has been similarly cheerful and uplifting." Andrea is a new writer to me, and unusual in that most of my new writers sell me short and funny pieces. This piece is neither short nor funny (unless you have a *very* strange sense of humor).

I never thought to end up a prisoner in Castle Remor. The first time I set eyes on the ancient, yet still impressive, pile of gray granite rising so suddenly from the Plain, I had thought more in terms of being welcomed as an esteemed guest. Or perhaps—if Old Perry, master of Remor, was susceptible to feminine charm—even as its prospective Lady. More realistically, I looked at Remor as a place to bide a while, to find some work and raise some coin. It had been a long, wet walk from Halthern.

I was, and had been since the age of fifteen, an herbalist. I couldn't claim the title of wisewoman, not at my tender age, and I refused to be called a witch. There was nothing of the magic in what I did. I healed the sick and helped women to conceive or not conceive, as was their wish, but love philters, curses on enemies, luck charms, all that was beyond my skill. Not that Luke, magistrate in Halthern, would have any of it. When I refused to sell him either a vial of poison or my virtue, he had threatened me with a charge of witchcraft. There'd been nothing for a lone, defenseless girl to do but leave the city and hope for the best.

"Ah, guess again, Jerika," my brother Rafe would have said, had he been still alive. A witch trial, even one as plainly rigged as Luke's would have been, would have been far preferable to ending my life chained to the slime-covered stone walls of Remor's dungeon. Execution would have been a quicker, cleaner way out than slowly rotting in this cell. But that drizzly morning in the spring of my nineteenth year, as I stood outside Remor's walls calling for admittance, I had no clue. I kept on calling till the guards came and threw open the gates.

Clearly, the guards didn't know what to make of me.

My feet were shod in fine leather boots, and dirty and mud-caked as they were, my garments were not those of a peasant. Likewise, my vocabulary and diction belonged to no ignorant, unschooled maid. But no woman of position traveled unescorted. And I was bedraggled and unwashed. The two guards deliberated amongst themselves in loud stage whispers before finally allowing me through, and even as they conducted me to their master, one kept carefully behind me, his hand on his sword.

I sucked in my breath as they ushered me into Old Perry's presence. The few stories I had heard of him in Halthern—not to mention his moniker—had led me to expect a withered geezer, but the man before me, shaking dice out onto a handsomely tiled table, was of no more than middle years and plainly in excellent health. My fantasies of marriage seemed at once more plausible and more appealing.

He looked up at me, his thick black curls falling back from his face, and grinned, his teeth white against his beard. "What have we here?"

The guard in front of me mumbled what explanation he could, not raising his eyes from the floor as he did so. Very servile for a fighting man, I thought, but Perry was speaking to me and I pushed the observation aside.

"Wandering the Plain all alone, my pretty one? How odd of you. But I'm sure you'll enlighten me presently. Right now, let us get you some refreshment." As I murmured my thanks and sank into the chair he proffered, he was already clapping his hands for a serving woman.

I attacked the mulled cider and thick stew she brought, very nearly forgetting my manners. The food I had left Halthern with had lasted only three days.

And though I well knew which wild plants were edible, this early in the year there hadn't been much to find. As I shoveled the food into my mouth, Perry watched me with an expression of amused tolerance. "You wish more, my lady?" he asked, as I scraped the last of the gravy from the bowl. There may have been just a bit of mockery in his voice, but if so, I was too grateful for my full belly to register it.

"Thank you, no, milord," I answered, sated enough just then to wipe daintily at my mouth with the cloth provided.

"Then perhaps you are ready to tell me who you are and where you might be going."

"My name is Jerika of Halthern, milord, and I am the best herbalist in that city." I had enough experience with these lordly types to know that a little honest swagger was not misplaced. Show too much humility and they were glad to treat you like a menial.

"Ah. And how do you come to be so far from that fair town? And all alone?" His eyes were heavy-lidded, sensual.

I'd certainly had time in my week-long walk to consider how to answer that. "I had some difficulty, lord, and was forced to leave my home. My people are all dead. I've no one to shelter me. I hope to reach Kelm eventually, start anew."

"You run from the law, then?" he said, as if it mattered not to him, but my gut still twisted.

"Oh, no, milord." It wasn't a lie, not really. Luke had only threatened; as far as I knew, no warrant had been issued. "I'm just an honest woman in need of temporary shelter. And I can repay you for your charity. I am, as I said, an herbalist of some note. You perhaps require some medicines for Remor's people?"

"You will repay me in some fashion, I am sure, Jerika." He smiled, another flash of white teeth. So it was like that, eh? So sorry, milord, but as Luke found out, my virginity wouldn't be sold so cheaply. But put a marriage ring on me and that was another story. A woman could live quite comfortably in a keep as rich as Remor.

"Would it be possible for me to bathe and rest a bit?" I asked, changing the subject.

"Of course, my lady." Once more, just a touch of irony. He clapped sharply again for a servant. "Take the lady Jerika to a room and make her at home. You, my dear, I will see at dinner."

The maid lugged bucket after bucket of warm water to fill my tub, and found me soap, finer even than I knew how to make, and a hairbrush, sponge, and linen towels. The hearth was laid with some aromatic wood that perfumed the very air. As I slid into the bath, the privations of the last few days and the uncertainties of the future seemed very far away. How could the rich ever be unhappy?

After my bath, I found an even greater pleasure. A soft, thick robe of green velvet had been thrown across the bed. Sweet heavens, if Perry had sent that, he did think me a lady. And desirable. I allowed myself to daydream about being Remor's mistress as I dressed. *Ah, Rafe, things're looking up.*

But if Perry had romance on his mind, I couldn't prove it by dinner. We ate in the small, private dining room instead of the hall, true, but we were certainly not alone. No, three others persons were already at table when the maid brought me in. The first was a fighting man, like Perry of middle years, and not in Remor's colors. The second was a skinny, sour cleric, crowlike in his black robes. And the last was, astoundingly, a dwarf girl, no taller than my waist. They were duly introduced to me as Gillen, Father Todd, and Marielda.

Father Todd frowned at me, then at Perry. "Milord! Surely you've noticed the—"

Perry cut him off. "Watch your tongue." There was no deference in his voice. Interesting. Even great lords usually showed a pittance of respect to the priests. "Gillen, you observed archery practice this noon? What think you of the new bows my weaponer has fashioned?"

"Aye, Perry, I saw the drill. As for the bows, I think what you gain in range, you may lose in accuracy."

"Accuracy will come with experience and hard training."

"Perhaps. But, still—"

Dinner went on like that, Perry and Gillen talking of military matters, Father Todd glowering at me in silence and finding himself largely ignored or interrupted whenever he did speak. As for the dwarf girl, she was so quiet, I questioned her wits. A few times I tried to strike up conversation, but she would merely nod at me and duck her head. So I contented myself with enjoying the plentiful meat, the expensive wine, and the occasional heavy-lidded glance from Perry. After my third cup of that fine wine, he was becoming more and more attractive, and not just for his money.

Gillen appeared to enjoy the wine as well. He quaffed two cups for each of mine and by the time the servants cleared the plates, his eyes were glassy and unfocused and his answers to Perry's questions less pertinent. "Do you wish to seek your bed, old friend?" Perry asked. "We can finish this conversation at the morning's hunt." The same maid who had prepared my room had come in with another flagon of wine and Perry ordered her sharply. "Take Master Gillen to his room, Gemma. Make sure to see to his . . . comforts." There were implications in that order that I ignored, not without some difficulty.

"May I retire now, too, Papa?"

I choked on my wine, almost as surprised by the full sentence from the girl I'd presumed dumb as by the content of that sentence. None of the stories I'd heard of Perry had suggested he'd ever been married. Though marriage, of course, was no precondition of siring a child. And if Marielda was his daughter, I could see why I'd heard no mention of her. Perry didn't seem the type of man to advertise a malformed child. Not that she was uncomely, actually. With her thick, reddish hair and big brown eyes, she bore some passing resemblance to myself.

"Of course, child. You've earned your rest this night. But on the morrow, perhaps you might show the lady Jerika around the keep while Gillen and I hunt."

The girl ducked her head again and went out. Somehow I got the feeling that the prospect didn't fill her with joy.

"Isn't your bed waiting for you, too, priest?" Perry asked, raising his eyebrow wickedly. My heart leaped to my throat. He did want to be alone with me. I'd have to be very careful. Careful not to allow him anything improper, while still holding out hopes that my mind could be changed. I shouldn't have had *quite* so much wine. His fleshy mouth looked absurdly tempting. And surely a few kisses wouldn't be improper. . . .

"It's early, milord. And I have the Lord's work to do," Father Todd said bluntly.

226

"Save your own soul, priest." But Perry didn't force the issue. "Do you like music, Jerika?"

I woke the next morning to the maid, Gemma, staring shyly at me from outside the bed curtains. My head was still vaguely muzzy from the wine, and I had confused memories of whirling around the dining room in Perry's arms as his piper played, Perry's fingers splayed intimately across my lower back, and the priest glowering at us all the while. "Excuse me, lady," Gemma said. "Lady Marielda awaits you in the hall. At your convenience."

Well, it seemed rude to keep the poor dwarf girl waiting. I forced myself from the bed and found my own clothes laid across the chair, all miraculously cleaned and mended. *Ah, Rafe,* I thought, *life in a keep like Remor grows more and more inviting.* Rafe was gone from me for over two years, but I couldn't yet lose the habit of conversing with him in my mind, and most probably never would. The bond between orphaned twins was stronger than most.

When I entered the hall, Marielda tossed down her sewing and rose immediately to greet me. She was still skittish, still plainly afraid to speak to me, but she was making the effort. Apparently fear of disobeying her papa ran deeper than any apprehension of me. "Do you want tea or breakfast before I give you the tour, Lady Jerika?"

"No, truly, I'm not hungry," I said. It would be cruel to prolong this.

"Very well. I thought we might start with my workroom." She glanced cautiously at me. "If that pleases you."

Workroom? I followed her down some steep stone stairs, frankly surprised at the quickness of her stunted legs. When she pushed open the heavy oak door, I saw why Perry had seemed amused by my offer of medicines. Marielda had an herbary far more extensive than any I'd seen. Dried plants hung in profusion from the walls. The two long tables were covered in jars, bottles, and vials, all neatly labeled in a spidery handwriting.

"You must have a great knowledge of the healing arts, madam," I said.

She merely smiled, the first smile I'd seen on her face, and spread her hands out. "What would you like to see first, lady?"

By the time I'd finished questioning her and inspecting her inventory, it was dinner hour. My head ached, no longer from the after-effects of the wine, but from attempting to cram all the information she'd offered into my brain. As we'd spoken, all her timidness had melted away until we were just two professionals exchanging shoptalk, or, more properly, student and master, for there was little I could tell her that she didn't already know.

"Where did you learn all this, Lady Marielda?" I was a little jealous. She was a good three or four years younger than I.

"My . . . nurse." She smiled again and for just an instant, I imagined I saw some slyness in her face. "And then later, Papa brought me books from his travels. He's been everywhere."

Well, I comforted myself, there it was. Knowledge could be bought, like any other commodity. The rich could always get what they wanted.

"You should go up to dinner, Lady Jerika," she said then, some of the awkwardness edging back into her voice.

"Aren't you coming?"

"No. Papa asked me to do something for him."

I was tempted to argue with her, to say that surely Perry meant her to eat before she got to whatever task he'd set. But then, I remembered my own agenda. The fewer people at dinner, the more intimacy. Perhaps I'd be the girl's stepmother someday. I'd make Perry treat her better. With that sop to my conscience, I left her at her worktable.

But there proved precious little time for Perry and me to be alone the next few weeks. Gillen and the captain of his guards, Quincy, were forever hunting with him, drinking with him, dicing with him. And even when they were not, Father Todd was lurking about, peevish and disapproving. Perry insulted him, mocked him, and ignored him, but never, I couldn't help but notice, sent him away. Meanwhile, I grew comfortable and contented, almost drugged. I whiled away whole days reading from the books Marielda loaned me or just staring out the window of my room and dreaming. And every evening, attired in another beautiful garment left across my bed, I drank and ate and danced. And when Perry's hand slipped from my back to rest on my buttocks, I didn't pull away immediately. When he brushed his lips across my throat, I let him.

Perhaps things could have gone along that way indefinitely. Perhaps the seasons could have slipped away, and I could have slipped with them, slipped ever so slowly into becoming Perry's mistress, slipped into this life of ease and privilege, ever hoping for a marriage proposal and losing more of myself each day. But the day came when I saw the marks on Gemma and things changed all at once.

She was filling my bathtub, pouring out what was

probably her twentieth bucket of water. I'd been watching her in silence, vaguely admiring the muscle in her arms. All that carrying was bound to make a person strong. But as she bent to empty that pail, her blouse slid down off one shoulder, exposing a couple of nasty red welts crisscrossed on her pale skin. I gasped. "Sweet heavens, Gemma, how'd you get those? Do you want me to—"

She whirled around, yanking her shirt hastily back up. "I'm fine, my lady. It's— It's nothing." There was a touch of panic in her voice.

"Gemma," I said slowly, "did Gillen do that to you?" Much as I'd tried to push the knowledge back into some hidden corner of my mind, I couldn't pretend not to know that Perry had been ordering her to Gillen's room every night.

"Oh, no, madam," she said. "No. Please. It's nothing." She still clutched her clothing tightly to herself, as if she was afraid to let me get another look.

A wave of queasiness washed over me, but I didn't let it show. I forced my voice into a gentle, encouraging, professional tone, the one I used when ministering to small children and dying patients. "Even if you've been disobedient, Gemma," I said quietly, "even if you made the master punish you, you ought to let me have a look at that. You wouldn't want to scar."

She looked at me, wide-eyed and mute.

"And if, like I think, you're a good girl, and you didn't deserve that," I continued, "well, you don't need to stand for it. You're a hard worker. There're other places you could go."

She stared at me a moment longer, then shook her head, just once. "No," she almost whispered. "No. They wouldn't let me leave. He'd make her stop me."

She clamped her mouth shut, like she could swallow the words back, then snatched up her bucket and bolted for the door.

The bathwater was a touch too hot, but I was so numb, I'd not have noticed had it scalded me. *Oh, Rafe, how could I have been so blind?* How could I have ignored the rot, the putridness underlying the richness here? Yes, women were brutalized everywhere. And, yes, peasants were routinely used by their betters. But there was more here. Maybe Gemma thought she couldn't leave, but I'd be off soon enough now.

Perry eyed me brightly when I went into dinner. "Sweet Jerika, you look so fine. But a trifle pale, pretty one. Are you not feeling well?"

I composed my face and forced my voice steady. Father Todd was glowering at me as usual and Marielda was playing with her spoon. "Perhaps, milord, I just need some sun. Some fresh air. Perhaps I'll go riding tomorrow."

"Perhaps." Was it my imagination or was his smile more a baring of the teeth? I was sure he knew something, sensed something. "But come, conversation has been lagging at table. What say you, Jerika? Tell us a story. Tell us of your family."

Father Todd inexplicably sputtered on his cup of ale. "There's nothing to tell, milord," I said. "My mother died when I was just a babe. My father died of a fever when I was twelve. My only brother died at the Battle of Creadon." If I'd still meant to marry Perry, maybe I'd have told him more of the truth. Maybe I'd have told him that my mama had run off and left us when Rafe and I were barely weaned and that we'd never heard another word about her. Maybe I'd have told him

231

that my grandfather was minor gentry until he lost his fortune gambling and had to sell his title. But now it was none of his affair.

"I have a story to tell," the priest said suddenly. "Some may find it instructive. It's about evil men who steal other men's wives and do murder in the name of their pride."

"Enough," Perry said in a low, threatening voice, but for once Father Todd wouldn't be stopped.

"An interesting story, to be sure," he said. "About spawn of the devil who instruct their own children in the black arts and mock God's Holy Church."

"Enough!" Perry growled, slamming his tankard onto the tabletop. "I should have rid myself of you long ago, priest." My mouth dropped in horror as I saw Perry's hand on his sword hilt, but I was distracted by the sound of Marielda's head hitting the floor as she slid bonelessly out of her chair, eyes rolled up white.

"Please," I said, my glance darting from one man to the other. "Please. Lady Marielda is unwell." I picked her up from the rushes myself, cradling her light body in my arms like a child. "We must help her."

"She's prone to fits and fainting," Perry said coldly. "Put her in her bed. She'll come out of it soon enough."

I slept not at all that night, just sat on the edge of the bed, my pack containing my few possessions on my lap, waiting for dawn. As soon as first light came, I crept down the back stairs and out to the stables. One of the young grooms was already awake, but he seemed to find nothing odd in my request for a mount. Neither did the guard who opened the gate for me. I smiled charmingly at him and explained that I had a headache and had slept poorly and wanted some air.

"Don't go too far, madam," was all he said. "There're dangers on the Plain."

So now I was a criminal, well and true. Stealing a horse could get a person executed as sure as witchcraft. Perhaps when I was far enough from Remor to feel safe, I would dismount and send her back. Ridding myself of every vestige of Remor was attractive in its own right.

I rode across the Plain all morning, away from Remor, away from Halthern. At midday I stopped at a small stream to water the horse and have a rest. My fear was fast being replaced by exhilaration. No one had followed me. Perry was probably unaware of my absence as yet; I often stayed abed this late. As the mare grazed on the stream bank, I stretched out on my cloak, my head pillowed on my pack.

I woke with the little hairs prickling on the back of my neck and the sickening realization that I was not alone. I cautiously opened my eyes to find Perry sitting on a rock to my left, cleaning his fingernails with his knife. "Well, well, Jerika," he said. "Leaving so abruptly and without even a good-bye."

I sat up, trying to control my trembling. "I was going to send back the horse, my lord. I'd keep nothing of yours."

"Be that true or be that false, pretty one, we still aren't squared. You said you'd repay my charity, but I've seen no payment yet." He came off the rock and sat beside me, his hand resting in the heavy mass of my hair.

"You know I'm a maiden, my lord."

He chuckled then, a sound so far from humor it chilled the blood. "Are you truly that stupid, girl? If that's what I wanted of you, I'd have had it long ago.

But maidenheads are ten for a copper penny. You've a far greater value than that."

"I don't know what you mean."

"You've been very naughty, Jerika. Running off, taking my property. Oh, and lying to me last night." I opened my mouth to protest, but he shook his head. "Your mama didn't die when you were a babe. No, you must have been five or six when I beat the life from her."

I gaped at him, but instead of his face, it was Marielda's I saw before me, her eyes, her coloring so like mine. "I'm not much given to regrets, but I do regret that. It was a fit of temper. When it became clear the child wasn't growing properly, that she was abnormal, I blamed Catriona. Of course, it was the child I should have killed, not her." He gave me another chilling smile. "When a man has found his soulmate, he shouldn't be so quick to discard her. A black heart in such a lovely body is difficult to come by."

I tried to scoot away from him on the ground, but he pulled me back by the hair cruelly. "What do you want of me?" I asked, no longer able to keep the shaking from my voice.

"Marielda grows proficient in her craft," he said. "When I saw you in the market at Halthern, looking so like your mama, I set her to casting a drawing spell. How well it worked. No more than a fortnight later you were banging on my gates."

His eyes glittered. Evil or madness or perhaps both. *Oh, Rafe,* I thought, *if he speaks true, how can I fight it? I know no magic. I've no defense against the black arts.*

"The other task I've set her is harder, of course," Perry continued. "She searches the texts, all the knowledge of the East, to find just the right incantation. It's no easy thing. No easy thing to call a soul back from Hell. No easy thing to put it in another's body. Ah, but when she is successful, pretty one, I'll have my dear Catriona back."

I've lost track now how many months I've been chained in this dungeon. I know it's been a long time; summer's heat has come and gone and the wind that seeps through the chinks in the stones is frosty. And when Marielda comes to see me, she sometimes bears evidence that her father grows impatient—a bruised face, a welt or two showing under a sleeve. I've given up on trying to convince her to turn her powers on Perry. She's been cowed too long for that. But she does have powers. Who else has kept Father Todd in heel all these years? Who else has hidden the evil in Remor from all the outside world?

I don't know if what Perry seeks is possible, if it will ever be possible. But I hope Father Todd prays for my soul. I hope if my sweet Rafe is in heaven, he intercedes with the blessed saints for me. I hope I die soon.

Before I find out.

THE WHISHT HOUND'S BONE
by Laura J. Underwood

Laura Underwood is one of "my" writers: writers I seem to have discovered (and of whose work I am inordinately fond). She is a librarian and a book reviewer for the Knoxville *News Sentinel,* and she owns a harp that, incidentally, was designed and built by her father and modeled upon Glynnanis, the harp in several of her stories that have appeared in my magazine.

Laura is a former state fencing champion, and she hikes the mountains of her native East Tennessee. One of my housemates, Stephanie Shaver, says that she met Laura at Dragon*Con '95, and met the harp as well. It was a lap-harp, and from the description, it sounds as if the unicorn on the harp had a seashell for a horn, and some sort of pale blond wood for its frame.

This story seems to be based in a Scottish society, which I am admittedly fond of.

The woman who sat on the broken wall of the old rath had black tresses and eyes of amber. Though Brighid Nic Cooley did not recognize the woman, the young lass gathered her courage like a warm cloak and marched across the heather. No Keltoran in her right mind—though some folks in the other kingdoms of Ard-Taebh would sneer and call that a rare contradiction of nature—would be caught crossing the moors on such a night. A full moon rose over the dark stones and coarse ground, shedding baleful light. A bogie night to be certain, but Brighid was not to be swayed. She thought of her cousin Liam going on about her being as dumb as stone, but she was determined to go into the rath and seek the Whisht Hound's Bone.

"Madness!" Liam had sneered. "No man has ever taken the Bone. The Whisht Hound will have you for supper."

"I don't care," Brighid retorted. "I'm tired of sitting around and watching the men of this village cower beneath their plaidies before that filthy bloodmage. The Bone is our chance to defeat Ultan Mac Narr."

"Haud, lass!" Liam said. "You dinna even know how to make the wretched bone work. You're not one of the mageborn, you know."

That truth stung even now. Brighid's father was descended from one of the mage families scattered throughout Ard-Taebh. His kin birthed at least one mageborn in every generation. Brighid had always hoped she would be the one in whom the power manifested. At fifteen, she was beginning to doubt her own fortune would turn out so well. Most mageborn found their powers stirring as soon as they came into adolescence, and kept to their own. In Keltora, women were respected, but they did not have holdings or choose their own husbands as was allowed in some other kingdoms of Ard-Taebh. Mageborn, at least, chose their own mates, if they chose them at all. Brighid feared her father would marry her off to cousin Liam. He was only a year her senior, and like most young Keltoran males who had earned their plaids, he tended to be quite a bore.

Brighid was already looking beyond such prospect. Hidden under split skirts, an overtunic and the tartan shawl wrapped about her shoulders, her figure was blossoming more than she liked. Her stormy gray eyes and fiery hair, which Liam swore matched her temperament, were already garnering attention from the village lads. She didn't want to be stuck in Banbriar for the rest of her life, birthing babies and tending an ungrateful man like her cousin. She wanted with all her heart to be a mage.

As Brighid climbed to the edge of the old hillfort, the eldritch creature on the rath wall did not stir, but the yellow-gold eyes, catching moonlight to become twin embers in the dark of night, followed Brighid until she crested the embankment and stopped. The young lass clutched a staff of rowan in her hand, good, according to her granny, for thrashing bogie folk believed to inhabit the Keltoran moors. Brighid used it as a brace, pausing to catch her breath.

"Well, well," the woman said, her teeth were extraordinarily white as she flashed a brief smile. "What a bold lass you are to come to the rath at night."

"Some would say *fool* lass," Brighid said. "Are ye one of the mageborn?"

The woman threw back her head and laughed, a sound that echoed like an eerie howl. "Mageborn generally know mageborn, don't they?" she said.

"I'm not mageborn," Brighid said.

"Not?" the woman said, brows rising as if she did

not believe. "Then I am mistaken. What brings a foolish *mortal* lass out on such a night as this."

"I seek the Whisht Hound's Bone," Brighid said plainly, and the woman's brows shifted into a single line over her nose.

"A foolish quest," the woman said. "Why would you risk your life to claim the Whisht Hound's Bone?"

"To stop a bloodmage," Brighid said.

"A bloodmage?" the woman repeated. "Which bloodmage?"

"Ultan Mac Narr," Brighid said. "He has declared himself Laird of Banbriar and uses his magic to steal our lives. The men of Banbriar cower before him like whipped dogs. And we are too far from the great duns of the nobility to hope for *their* help. With the Bone, I can stop his senseless destruction."

The woman's lips drew back in a snarl. "Ultan Mac Narr," she growled in her throat. "So the wretch still lives, does he?"

"You know him?" Brighid said.

"All too well," the woman said. She shook her head. "He and I have had our differences on various matters over the decades. Were it not for him . . ." Then she stopped and looked elsewhere as though angry over what she had been about to reveal.

"Decades?" Brighid said. She hardly thought the woman so old as she glared at the dark of night. The long ebon hair seemed to blend into the black wool tunic and trews she wore, so Brighid almost could not tell where one ended and the other began. The gleam of those strange feral eyes reminded Brighid of the first time she ever saw the Whisht Hound on the moors.

She'd been ten at the time. Liam dared her to go

down to the long moor road with him in the dark to hunt fox. She boldly took up the challenge, but once they were out on the lonely stretch that passed below the rath, a mournful howl had sent them scattering for cover. Brighid did not see where her cousin went. She hid herself in the heather, covering her head as Granny said one was supposed to do when one heard the unseelie beast howling. Still, the curiosity of a child prevailed, and Brighid lifted her head in time to see the giant black dog tearing down the road at a gallop. Its flaming eyes had looked right at her, and with a whimper to the gods to spare her, she hid her face again. The hot breath of an animal assailed her then, its cold nose moving up and down her back with inquisitive sniffs, and she waited, expecting the Hound to seize her by the neck and drag her to her death.

Instead, it leaped away, and after a time, she convinced her trembling legs to carry her home where Father and Mother had words of anger and concern to share with both her and her cousin. Liam had beaten her back to the farmstead by an hour, leaving her to her assumed doom, but his noisy return had awakened both parents, so he did not escape their rage any more than Brighid.

"Do you know how the Bone works?" the woman asked, leaning forward.

Brighid looked at the woman's ember-bright eyes and shook her head. "No," Brighid said. "Do you?"

Again the woman laughed. "Oh, yes, my bonny lass," she said. "I even know where the Bone is buried."

"Then tell me," Brighid said.

"I would gladly see Ultan Mac Narr's throat torn to

shreds by the Hound, but knowledge has a price, my child," the woman said, shifting her head sideways.

"What price?" Brighid said. She tightened her grasp around the rowan.

"Burn that stick of *ferlie* wood for a start," the woman said, "for the sight of it galls me."

"Then you *are* one of the bogie folk, and not mageborn after all," Brighid said.

"You could say that," the woman agreed.

"You're an *unseelie!*" Brighid said. "I'd be a fool to burn my rowan, for you would take my soul to feed Arawn!"

"I could do that anyway if I *really* felt like it," the woman said harshly, "but the wood that protects you from *most* fae whims also prevents me from revealing what you wish to know."

"How do I know you'll tell me the truth?" Brighid said.

"As I said, I have many differences with Ultan Mac Narr." The woman shifted on the wall, sitting straight. "I would gladly assist any who sought his destruction."

"Then name the price," Brighid said.

"The burning of your ferlie wood," the woman said. "And a bit of your blood."

"My blood . . ."

"Not much," the woman was quick to say. "Have you a dagger?"

Brighid nodded, uncertain.

"And tinder and flint?"

Brighid nodded again.

"Good," the woman said and slipped off the wall. "Then break your ferlie wood against the stone of this wall. When it's small enough to burn, light it with your tinder and flint. Wait until the fire is hot, then thrust your dagger into the flames. Call to whatever gods please you, but when the blade turns red, slash it across the palm of your heart hand and let the blood run into the fire. Then call the hound."

"By what name?"

"Dubh Whisht will serve, or Black Shuck, if you please. The Hound will never give you its True Name, but if you bargain well, it might give you the Bone."

With that, the woman started into the rath.

"Where are you going?" Brighid called. "I thought you were going to show me where the Bone was buried."

"Only the Hound can do that," the woman said as she disappeared into the shadows of the rath. Brighid listened, but with the whine of the wind on the moor, she could not tell if the woman moved at all. For many heartbeats, Brighid held to her place. Her glance fell across the moor to the dark silhouette of the lone square tower that rose over Banbriar in the distance. Like the rath, it had been built long before Keltora found its name, some said by the Old Ones from whom mageborn claimed to have descended. It now served as a grim reminder of the man who had come to their remote village and stolen their lives with his greed.

This was her chance to end his reign, to stop his slaughter of her folk to feed his spells. What the woman had told Brighid she must do had the sound of witchery. *But mageborn do such things to enhance their spells,* she reminded herself. Granny, whose brother was mageborn, had told Brighid so. *But I am not mageborn.* How could she use such magics to free her village from Ultan Mac Narr's tyranny?

"It can't hurt to try," she told the wind. With a sigh, Brighid approached the wall. She slammed the rowan against the rocks until it snapped several times, and then she took a loose stone from the wall and battered those smaller portions into kindling. Gathering them on the path close to the wall, she put her back to the wind and tindered a flame. It flared more easily than she imagined, and in that brief moment, she felt a strange kinship with the fire. How odd. Weren't mageborn supposed to feel such things?

She took the dagger from her belt and squatted in the heather to thrust it into the flames until it was hot. Gritting her teeth, she slashed it across her left palm. Heat seared her and she bit back a scream, forcing her hand over the fire to let droplets of her blood spatter the flames as hot tears grazed her cheeks. The angry hiss did not stop her from hearing a howl that sent shivers up her spine. *Cernunnos and Arianrhod, protect me,* she thought, hoping a plea both to the Protector and the Lady of the Silver Wheel would be doubly strong. Rising to her feet, she shouted into the wind. "Dubh Whisht! Black Shuck! Come, Hound of the Dark Road and show me your Bone!"

The howl came again from much closer. Brighid turned and put her back to the fire, pressing her bloody hand to her split skirt. Her other hand clutched the dagger tightly as a black form glided out of the mist toward her. The Whisht Hound's eyes glowed like embers. Its great black tongue lolled from its mouth as it stopped to face her. It stood taller than her favorite pony. The Hound snarled at her, and fangs whiter than pearls glistened in the flickering lights. She took a startled step back, stumbling at the edge of her fire. The Hound sat down and glared at her with those frightful eyes.

"Why have you summoned me?" the Hound asked.

243

"I . . ." Brighid hesitated, clearing her throat, for she did not wish to sound as frightened as she felt. She drew herself tall and glared at the beast. "I have come for your Bone," she said.

"There is a price, young lass," the Hound said.

"Another?"

"What do you wish to do with my Bone?" it asked.

"To end a bloodmage's terrible reign," Brighid said.

"The price is a life."

"Whose?"

"I will choose," the Hound said. *"Will you agree?"*

"Whose life will you choose?"

"Does it matter?"

"Of course, it matters," she insisted, running her injured hand through her hair and wincing when the knife wound stung. "I can't just let you kill innocent folk."

"That matters not," the Hound said. *"I will choose the life. Will you agree?"*

Her eyes teared as she nodded, desperately wondering who among her kin and the village she had condemned by her act. She could not turn back now. Ultan Mac Narr had to be stopped. Banbriar had to be free. Slowly, she nodded, blinking tears. "All right," she said. "I agree."

"Follow me," the Hound said, and turning, it trotted into the shadows of the rath. Brighid wiped her tears on the back of her hand. With a deep sense of regret, she followed the Black Beast into the old hillfort's depths. The buildings had long ago crumbled to ruins, the result of the Cataclysm that was believed to have nearly destroyed the Old Ones and forced them to mingle their blood with humans to continue their leins of power. Briefly, she looked around, wondering if the

woman were near, but of that strange unseelie, there was no sign.

The Whisht Hound stopped before a cairn of stones. There, it began to dig a hole, sending great clumps of dirt and stone flying in the process. Brighid stepped aside, raising one arm to protect her face from the flurry.

Within moments, the Hound stopped. It had dug a hole nearly as deep as a grave. The thought made Brighid shiver, but she watched. The Hound's neck seemed to grow long like a snake as its head dove into the hole. She heard the clatter of teeth on bone, and the Hound's head withdrew, hauling a whitish object nearly as thick as her forearm. The Bone was oddly clean for something that had been buried in the ground. The Hound laid it at Brighid's feet, like a playful puppy offering its favorite toy to its owner in hopes of a game of fetch.

"Take it straight to the tower now," the Hound said. *"Give it to Ultan Mac Narr with my blessing."* And with that, the beast turned and leaped away into the dark, disappearing from sight.

Brighid stared at the bone, afraid to touch it, fearful of the burden it cost. A life. Whose life? Father? Mother? Granny or Liam? Or someone she knew in the village. They would be found bloody and torn, their throats missing, if the stories Granny told of Whisht Hounds were true. *And I shall be to blame.* Was Ultan Mac Narr's destruction worth such a terrible price?

Cautiously, she picked up the bone, wrapping it in her tartan shawl and drawing it into her arms like a child. Her throat was still thick, and her heart felt heavy as the Bone she carried away from the rath. She descended to the long road. Now and again, she looked about, still curious as to what had happened to the woman, when a figure broke into the road ahead of her, tall and slender and dressed in black. *And grinning like a pup,* Brighid thought sourly.

"I see you have it," the woman from the rath said. "Well done, lass."

"It came with yet another price!" Brighid snapped and continued her march along the road. She would take the low path below the village and come around to the tower rather than boldly walk the streets of Banbriar explaining what she was about to do.

"You expected none?" the woman said, blithely following like a friendly shadow. "I *told* you to bargain well."

"It offered no chance to bargain," Brighid said stiffly. "It demanded a life, but it would not say whose."

"What does it matter?"

"It matters to me!" Brighid insisted. "Someone in Banbriar is going to die, and I am to blame."

"Would you rather the many died at Ultan Mac Narr's whim than for one to die and save all?" the woman asked.

"Do you have a name?" Brighid said.

"Duvessa will do," the woman said. "And yours?"

"Brighid."

"Brightness and darkness, aren't we a pair," Duvessa said and chuckled. "And you have not answered my question."

Brighid frowned. "No unwarranted death is right," she said.

"But the Old Ways have their price, and the most powerful magics, such as that you carry in your arms, require a powerful price," Duvessa said. "Bloodmages have known this as far back as given time. Even the Old Ones knew that great magic has its price—or should I say they found out the hard way?"

"I still don't know how to use it," Brighid said.

"Do what the Hound told you. Give it to Ultan Mac Narr."

"And then what?" Brighid said fiercely. "I don't know what words will cause the Bone to destroy him."

"The Hound does not give its Bone to just anyone who wants it, child," Duvessa said. "Give the Bone to Mac Narr with the Hound's blessing. The rest will happen as it should."

"But . . ."

Brighid's protest died on her lips, for even as she turned to ask *what* would happen, Duvessa stepped back into the darkness and was gone. None too soon, it seemed, for walking angry meant Brighid had walked fast. She was at the gate of the wall surrounding the tower base before she knew it. The rectangular structure rose like a box on end. She took a deep breath and moved around to the opening in the wall, and there, a man with a halberd suddenly stiffened and raised his weapon in a threatening manner. Seeing his attacker was nothing more than a young lass with a bundle in her arms, he stopped and leered.

"Well, what have we here?" he said.

"Please, sir, I must see the Laird Ultan Mac Narr," Brighid said, trying not to wrinkle her nose. The guard had not bathed in some time. The plaid he wore kilted over his tunic and trews was as ill-kept as his thick beard and hair.

"On what business, my wee bonny lass?" the guard said.

"I've something for him," she said hesitantly. Then

pulling the bundled bone to her breast, she looked up with innocent eyes. "I hear the Laird Mac Narr will pay silver for a newborn child."

"A child?" the guard said with a snort. "I know who you are, lass. You're Manus Mac Cooley's daughter. And I haven't heard of you birthing any babies."

"I found it up in the rath," Brighid said. *Idiot!* she scolded herself, for she realized she had seen this man around the village often enough.

"Here, let's have a look . . ." He reached for the edge of her shawl, and she was about to draw back lest he discover the ruse, when a savage snarl broke the black of night. Brighid gave a startled gasp as the Whisht Hound materialized out of the dark. Its growl was more than enough distraction, and its presence caused the guard to swear and swing around. Before he could act in his own defense, huge paws thumped his chest. Brighid took advantage of the moment to slip inside the wall and march toward the tower. She threw a quick glance over her shoulder in time to see the guard fall, crashing his head into the stone wall. Of the Hound, there was again no sign.

"I'm beginning to believe the beast is naught but mist and imagination," she murmured as she stopped at the tower's double doors. She knocked on the wood, only to have one side drift open under her hand. *As if I'm expected?* she wondered. She hoped not. Brighid waited until her eyes had adjusted to the dark, and found they adjusted better than normal.

The air around her came alive with a strange glamor that made the small hairs stiffen on her neck. Did magic feel that way? She smelled livestock in this lower chamber, and heard them shuffling in their stalls.

Carefully, she picked her way across the straw, then clambered a stone staircase leading upward.

The hall on the next floor was heavily lined in shadows cast by the glow of firelight at the far end. There, she perceived a chair, and saw the end of a man's plaid drifting onto the floor.

"Well, don't just stand there, child," a somber voice said. "Come here to the fire that I might see you better."

Brighid took a deep breath to still the flutters in her stomach. She paced the length of the room like a timid mouse, keeping distance between herself and the chair as she looked at its occupant.

Laird Ultan Mac Narr looked as if he weren't much older than her cousin Liam, but she had heard mageborn looked young a long time. Ultan had shoulder-length gold hair and deep blue eyes. They flashed up at her, and a wicked grin spread. "Well," he said. "You are a lovely lass. It shall be a shame to give you to Arawn, but the moon is full and I need a sacrifice."

He rose from the chair, the seven ells of his black plaid with its thin red and white stripes sweeping the floor as he reached for her.

"I'm not here to be sacrificed to your dark god!" Brighid said forcefully as she stepped out of his grasp. "Too many have already died to feed your power!"

"Then what *are* you here for, child," he said, still grinning. "For though I sense the mage blood in you, I know your powers have not yet blossomed. Do you, untrained as you are, believe you can challenge me?"

Brighid blinked. Mageborn? Untrained? Could it be true? *Mageborn generally know mageborn, don't they?* Wasn't that what Duvessa had said. If so . . . Brighid's courage welled within her. "Maybe I have come to challenge you," she said in a forceful voice. "Here. This is for you."

She thrust the shawl at him. He frowned, taking the heavy bundle from her hands and throwing back the edges to reveal the end of the Bone. His face flared with a mixture of terror and mad rage.

"I give this Bone to you with the Whisht Hound's blessing!" she said and stepped away.

"Bloody bitch!" he snarled. "How dare you send this to me!"

His angry words drove Brighid to turn. The last of her courage evaporated like morning dew in the face of his fury. She'd seen before what Ultan Mac Narr could do in a rage. He would rain fire on her, or use magic to tear her limb from limb, if he did not steal her life to feed his own. Running for the stairs, she realized there was little hope of escape.

A darkness suddenly came rushing up the stairs, flying past Brighid. The wind of it knocked her back and sent her tumbling against the wall. The darkness swelled and shifted until it became a woman with tresses like midnight whose eyes glowed with the fiery light of the Whisht Hound.

"I hope you haven't forgotten me, Ultan Mac Narr!" Duvessa snarled.

Ultan threw the bone to the floor and raised his hand, preparing to call a spell. Before he could utter more than a word of the arcane tongue, Duvessa lunged. Her form shifted in midair to become the huge Whisht Hound as she swiftly bore down on Ultan. She seized his throat and shook him like a rat. He screamed, and Brighid covered her eyes, unable to watch the bloodmage's terrible demise.

Only when silence fell did Brighid dare lower her hands from her face. Ultan lay on the floor, and even though he was limp, the Hound continued to shake him before she finally released his corpse and turned. Hellfire eyes settled on Brighid, and her throat constricted. The monster would take her now! The Hound would claim *her* life as the price it demanded. She froze against the stone and waited for what would come. *Better me than those I love,* she thought.

But the Hound did not attack. She shook her head, flinging blood everywhere, then picked up the Bone and stepped over to face Brighid. There she laid the Bone at Brighid's feet, and sat, tongue lolling. The Hound dissolved, leaving Duvessa who brushed her black hair from a face both young and old with its eldritch beauty.

"You need not cringe there, child," Duvessa said. "It's not what you think. As I told you, I have known Ultan many years, and I have sworn I would repay him an old debt, if I could just get to him. I just needed for him to touch the Bone so I could pass the magical barriers he set about this tower to keep me at bay."

"The Bone . . ." Brighid said.

"All I have left of an old suitor Ultan sacrificed for bloodmagic," Duvessa said.

"But you're *unseelie,*" Brighid insisted.

"Aye, child, but that does not mean I cannot love. Now, go home to your farm and your family. In a few years, I dare say, your mageborn powers *will* finally blossom. Not all who are mageborn come into their power at the same time."

"But the price . . ."

"The blood price is paid. I chose *Ultan's* life. Now, I will take my Bone and leave."

With that, Duvessa shifted like smoke back into the Hound. She seized up her Bone and trotted for the stairs, tail wagging just slightly as she descended from view.

Brighid just sat there, staring first at Ultan, then at her own hands. Mageborn after all. She couldn't wait to tell haughty Liam. But first, she needed to tell the villagers of Banbriar that their dreaded Laird was dead.

All because of a bone Duvessa had to pick with him.

THE WEREWOLF'S FINAL LESSON

by Joette M. Rozanski

As I stated before, one of the themes of this year's submissions was the shapechanger. This story involves that theme. (But I imagine, gentle reader, that you could tell that from the title.)

Joette Rozanski says of herself that she was thrilled when she received the contract. Have fun—I doubt if I'll ever grow old and hardened not to be thrilled by a sale. One's first sale is one of the few pleasures that's neither illegal, immoral, nor fattening. She is a legal assistant with a taste for fantasy which she's had since the day she could read Grimm's fairy tales, (for me, it was Anderson) and she blames Tolkien for the urge to write her own stories. Many of us have started with JRR Tolkien; he's inspired whole generations of us, hasn't he? Think what his karma will be—would he really want to take responsibility for all of us young people starting to write?

She is a member of Mensa, and also has a Maine coon cat named Zenda. I've met one before and thought of it as the largest feline I ever saw outside a cage at the zoo, though I understand they have very sweet tempers. Emerson—or was it someone else?—once said that God had created cats to give man the pleasures of petting the tiger.

The squirrel's russet body lay curled up at the base of a walnut tree. Fahren bent down and cradled the small creature in her hands; she marveled at the perfection of the unseeing black bead eyes, the softness of the dense fur. She never tired of Father Forest's gifts to her.

"Oh, little one," she whispered, "I am sorry your days are done, but part of you may serve me yet."

She carefully inspected the body, but there were no signs of violence. Violence, whether of man or beast, could not provide the conduits for her magic. Misfortune, in this life, was unavoidable.

Straightening up, Fahren turned around and strode back to her soul cave, her knotted-grass skirt making whispering sounds as it brushed against the tall weeds on either side of the path. Enchantment cloaked the cave's entrance, transforming the cleft into an ivy-covered, sandstone wall. Her eyes alone could pierce the deception that kept her holy place safe. She squeezed past the narrow entrance and walked into the cavern.

Fahren had chosen this particular cave because, unlike so many others, its air was pure and dry. Her white birch-bark sandals scuffed through fine golden sand. She ascribed this arid condition to the cave's position on the edge of the vast Waste, where no green thing grew.

Several shafts of early summer sunlight cascaded through fissures in the stone ceiling, revealing Fahren's skins on their wooden forms. These figures were cleverly carved representations—complete with talon or fang or inquisitively-cocked ear—of the creatures who once owned the pelts now draped over them. Most were small beings such as voles and mice and birds, but the occasional badger or forest cat reclined in the corners. Willful death had no part in their demises, for Fahren eschewed evil enchantment.

Fahren squatted before the knives on their altar, said her prayers, and set to work. A short time later she took the skin to an empty form, then carried the remains into the Forest and, with many whispered thanks, buried them.

She still had her rounds to complete and so returned to the cave. After tracing certain signs in the sand, she selected a cat's spotted skin, lay down, and spread it upon her torso. She closed her eyes.

Fahren breathed deeply. Soul-stuff pulled away with each exhalation and slowly filled the cat's skin with consciousness. In just a few moments, Fahren looked down at her human body, now stiff and cold. She stepped away, then padded out of the cave.

She paused a few feet away. Fahren always needed a little time to become used to her new world, a world crowded with smell and sound and furtive motion. A thin, shining soul-cord unraveled behind her; it could stretch around the world if need be, but once severed she would die. Fahren didn't worry about it, for the only ones who had that power were other spirit-beings—arrows and spears passed through her like stones through water. That was the glory of her magic: she could act upon the world, but the world could not affect her.

She moved forward, then stopped. Her spirit-sense

burned, a small flame tickling behind her eyes. At first she thought that a spy from one of the many surrounding hostile clans lurked nearby, but she soon decided that no physical being caused her distress. An intruder had entered her spiritual landscape.

Then, like a cloud passing before the sun, the alien presence disappeared. With many misgivings, Fahren proceeded upon her way.

At dawn, her mind filled with information, Fahren walked down the path that led to her village, Jofam. Her senses felt dull, but this torpor would soon pass away. She hummed as the scent of wild roses floated upon the wind and the chill prickle of dewy grass slapped against her ankles.

Fahren turned a sharp corner and nearly ran into her younger sister, Nonny. This young woman, who felt cold even in summer, was wrapped in a long red shawl from neck to foot. She yelped and jumped aside, her arms flung wide like an immense scarlet bat.

"Fahren! You scared me half to death!"

Fahren smiled at Nonny's flushed round cheeks.

"What brings you out at such an hour? Story-weavers have no reason to rise with the rooster."

Nonny, whose prodigious memory qualified her as the village's oral historian and gossip-monger, snorted at this comment.

"I've got tremendous news, Fahren! Dar's returned to Jofam. He's meeting with the elders in the market-place this very moment. I knew you'd want to see him."

Again, the flame burned behind Fahren's eyes. Dar had once been apprenticed to her; he had clever hands and made most of her skin-forms. But he'd been headstrong and willful, prone to violence, and so she'd sent him away. He left Jofam vowing to best his teacher.

Nonny guessed her thoughts. "Yes, he's become a skin-walker like you, and the elders are most interested in the services he has to offer."

"He means them no good," Fahren said and she hurried toward Jofam, afraid for her people.

Dar stood in the center of an excited crowd of elders, and Fahren couldn't help feeling a rush of fondness at the sight of him. He stood tall, brown and leanly muscled. His shaggy black hair fell over wide brown eyes, eyes that always made him look surprised. He wore tunic and trousers of knotted grass, but his feet were bare. A beautiful white wolf's skin hung from his shoulders like a cape.

He turned toward her and cried, "Fahren!"

She stopped several feet from him and trembled at his voice; she heard echoes of wildness, a howling in the waste.

"Hello, Dar," she said. "What brings you to Jofam? Five years ago, you were none too happy with us."

Dar grinned, baring his sharp white teeth. "I had a teacher who refused to teach, so I had to find someone who would. And, as you can see, I've become a skin-walker. Like you."

Fahren glanced at the wolf's hide and said, "That stinks of blood. You killed it. You're no skin-walker." She turned to the elders. "He's a werewolf."

Dar threw back his head and laughed—a feral sound. "Call me what you will, but I'm the answer to Jofam's prayers. I'm here to protect them."

"Protect them? From what?"

Kehann, elder spokesman, stepped forward.

257

"Fahren," he said, sweat rolling down his round face, "you yourself have seen thieves assault caravans, have warned us of attacks against our families as they tilled their fields."

"Creeping rat!" Kehann's scrawny wife Lan hissed her derision. "Spying is all you're good for. We need real protection! Dar will give us that."

"He'll give you nothing!" Fahren shouted, enraged at the sly smile that creased Dar's full lips. "He'll take! I warn you. He's tasted blood to become what he is. Sooner or later, he'll taste yours."

"I've tasted power," Dar said. "You're afraid of that, aren't you, Fahren? Play mouse as the lion roars."

"Just let him be," Kehann told her sternly. "You've sworn to obey elder directives, and we're binding you now to our wishes. Let Dar do his work."

Fahren kicked dust at them, signifying her rejection, then turned and walked away.

As Dar began his campaign against rival clans and thieves, Fahren kept out of his way. She did not agree with the elders, but she bowed to their will.

Rumors of terror and carnage mounted through summer and fall, rolling through the skeletal gates of winter. Nonny usually kept her current with the news but, soon after the solstice, Fahren saw for herself.

On raven's wings that bitter morning, she flew toward the Great Meeting Oak. It was the tallest tree on the western plains, often used for truces and trading pacts. On this day, two of the most prestigious clans—one being Fahren's own—were to meet and pledge friendship in the new year. Fahren wanted to see if Dar would enjoy the fruits of his labors.

And see she did. The sun shone its pale light on

scores of bodies in the snow—bodies dressed in black and brown woolens, the colors of Jofam's future allies. Bloody halos surrounded their torsos; entrails were looped playfully about their necks.

Fahren perched upon a branch, but saw no sign of her own people. Except for Dar.

No longer white, but wholly crimson, the great wolf paced around the oak. He glanced up and grinned at Fahren.

What have you done? Fahren asked in spirit, anger radiating through every thought. *This meeting would have brought peace.*

I have brought peace, Dar responded. He glanced at the bodies behind him. *Can they be any more peaceful?*

They meant us no harm.

And I have ensured that they never shall.

When will you be satisfied, Dar?

He squinted his dark eyes at her. *Stay away from me, little Fahren. Or I'll deal with you in the same manner.*

She spread her wings. *I will never allow you to do such things again.*

Dar laughed. *How? As a mouse? A sparrow? You don't have the courage for anything stouter. Besides, the elders wanted this. You've sworn to obey them.*

They're terrified of you, Dar. But I'm not. And you've yet to learn that size does not determine power.

Her wings beat the air and brushed snow from the branches as she rose into a shower of gems bright enough to veil the werewolf's red gaze.

* * *

The spring thaw brought flood, and mud, and whispered tales of horror. Surrounding clans had moved away; caravans followed brigands into safe country, leaving Jofam poorer than ever and Dar hungrier for more carnage.

At last, when Nonny came barging into Fahren's hut at the Forest's edge, Fahren knew she could no longer ignore the werewolf's savagery.

"The children!" Nonny wept, wringing her plump hands. "He's demanding children. And they're giving them to him!"

Fahren felt a cold anger. "Where and when," she said.

"I don't see why we can't have a hunter bring back a she-bear for you," Nonny said as she trotted along the sandy rim of the Waste. "What you're doing is madness."

Fahren chittered from the depths of her sister's skirt pocket. She knew that her mouse-form seemed less than impressive, but it was all she needed. Apparently many people had to learn the werewolf's lesson.

After a short while, Nonny stopped. "I daren't go nearer," she whispered. She dug deep into her pocket, scooped Fahren into the palm of her right hand, and lifted her out.

Fahren shuddered when she realized how near the werewolf's den was to her own home. It was a terrifying place. The sunset's lurid red light spread thickly over the bones and rotting flesh strewn before the entrance to a high, narrow cave. But she sensed that the werewolf was not there.

A child's piercing wail trembled from behind a pile

of tumbled rocks. Fahren leaped from Nonny's hand and scurried toward the sound.

A small boy, no older than six summers, was tethered to a short wooden post. Dar, his white fur resplendent in the day's fading glow, lunged at him, then retreated. Fahren heard his spectral laugh at the boy's screams.

Dar turned and looked down. *I knew you'd come.* He drew his lips back from his teeth. *Is this the best you could do? Will you nibble at my ankles?*

I want you go away, Dar, she told him. *You've turned against your own people, fools that they be. You are a monster whom I should have destroyed in the very beginning. But I loved you.*

Dar growled and backed away. *To think that I once considered you a mother. You sent me away, Fahren, but you won't do it again.*

He turned his head and snuffled at the crying boy. Seizing the moment, Fahren scuttled to Dar's soul-cord and took the shining strand into her small jaws.

The werewolf's head snapped around and he began to leap at her, but he was too late. Fahren bit down.

At the cord's severance, the wolf's skin collapsed and Dar's soul soared up into the air like dandelion silk. She heard him scream for a long time before the wind tumbled him away.

Nonny ran to the child, released him, and gathered him up into her arms. Fahren watched them, and realized how foolish her love for Dar had been. Even theives and enemies hadn't deserved to die helpless before his power; individuals should be punished for their crimes, not vengeance visited upon entire peoples. Because of her devotion to him and her own clan, innocent lives were lost.

The former Dar had died long ago and now so did Fahren.

The villagers discovered Dar's body in the cave and burned it, along with the wolf skin, at a place far out in the Waste. In their righteous anger, they cursed him for deceiving them and impoverishing Jofam. Then they marched back to their homes, congratulating themselves on a job well done.

Nobody noticed the red-breasted thrush that perched upon a thorn-bush and filled the air with its plaintive song. It watched the embers cool, then flew away.

THE CURSE OF TANIT

by Dorothy J. Heydt

Dorothy Heydt lives in Berkeley with her husband and two children. I became a writer because I wanted to stay home with my kids; I didn't want them raised by a woman with less commercial value than mine.

Dorothy has a pair of kids that, judging by the results, turned out very well. They're all—both hers and mine—almost frighteningly intelligent and articulate. In fact, in one of the issues of *Marion Zimmer Bradley's FANTASY Magazine* we published a first story by her daughter in the "Writers Talk Back" section, and her son sold a story to one of my anthologies. My kids are now all grown. My "baby" is now nearly thirty, and a musician—the only profession harder to get established in than writing.

This story features Dorothy's heroine "Cynthia," a favorite of our readers and a favorite of mine.

D ay was breaking, a calm perfect sunrise without a cloud in the sky, in shades of rose and gold. Cynthia and Komi sat with their arms around each other, watching the growing light reveal the planking of their boat, the path along the shore, the blocky shapes of the city of Panormos rising to the west.

As the light grew they could see how many merchant ships lay in its harbor, putting off or taking on rich cargoes for the ceaseless Punic trade that bustled all over and around the Mediterranean Sea. One could also see how many of them were no merchants, but ships of war: a fair number. Ten, twenty, thirty of them. No one doubted that the Carthaginians and the Romans meant to go to war sooner or later: maybe it would be sooner.

There was now light for them to see each other by. Cynthia saw a small dark man with a broad brow and a narrow chin, light-footed, deft-fingered, a sailor of small boats since he could walk. Komi saw—well, the gods knew what he saw, under the surface of a tall hawk-faced widow of twenty-two, but he had found it fair.

Without a word they embraced and parted; each knew what was to be done. Komi must find a better docking place for the boat than he could have found in the dark, while Cynthia made her way into the city.

Komi had given her careful instructions, a chart in words for navigating those treacherous shoals, the streets of Panormos. *Just inside the gate the streets branch five times. Take the second to the left, passing between the inns called the Fortunate Ferret and the Winepress. . . .*

She had lived in Punic cities before, during her father's long wanderings, and had never taken harm; but it might be different now. She had fought the priest of Tanit in the streets of Syracuse, cat to rat, and killed him. Though she had told no one, the word had somehow leaked out into Punic lands. She paused at a crossroads. There was the fountain with the blue tiles; she turned left here.

The sun was warm already, promising furnace heat by afternoon. Between two buildings Cynthia caught a glimpse of the center of the city, rich houses and temples, and a shining dome that housed a furnace of another kind. The Tophet they called it, the fane of the god they called the King: in Punic, Moloch. Cynthia made to spit, and then held back; someone might see. *Dirty Punic gods.*

Word had made its way back to her, eventually, that the priests of Tanit knew how she had slain their emissary in defense of Syracuse. But how had they known? Had there been witnesses, hidden in the dark from even a cat's eyes?

Unless Tanit herself had been the witness—assuming she wasn't dead, like most of the gods these days. Zeus and Hera, Hermes and Apollo: their names were still sung, their rituals carefully performed; but the gods men really adored were Peace and Harmony and other goddesses whose names were abstract virtues.

She glanced down at the ring of black iron on her finger, the gift of Arethousa, patroness of Syracuse. Cynthia had never seen the nymph again after the day she had received the ring, but its power to shield from magic still held. From any ill-wishing of Tanit the ring should protect her; and against the actions of mortals she would simply have to use her wits.

But if she ever got back to Syracuse, then by Prudence and Virtue, she was going to get out those books of magic and study them. She knew only a handful of spells, none of them helpful at the moment. Three chants for taking away the toothache, and one for bringing it on. She knew many tricks for easing child-birth and gripes in the gut, little bits of village witch-ery. And the shape-changing spell, which she would never try again without Komi at hand to take it off from her. And the enlarging spell that had turned tiny bubbles of mist into the semblance of a fogbank. And the one that turned a curse back on its sender—but the curse had to accomplish itself first before it could be returned, so that was no good for protection.

When she reached the house she knew it, from the pattern of the windows on the walls to the crack in the paving stone at the service door. But caution and their plan made her say to the woman sweeping the pave-ment, "Is this the house of Hanno, son of Barca, the oil merchant?"

"It is. What's your business with the master?"

"Not with him; with a woman named Enzaro. Does she still live here?"

"And if she does?"

"I'm a midwife," Cynthia said. "I met her brother Komi in a foreign port, and learning that I was coming to Panormos around his sister's time, he asked me to look in on her; and I have come."

The woman squinted, peering at Cynthia against the morning brightness. "You're a Greek, aren't you? Never mind, you may be sent by the gods for all of that. Enzaro has lain in childbed these three days, and still lies there; her womb will not open. Will you come and see her?"

"Of course." Now came the tricky part. "What of Komi, then? Is he at home, or is there any news of him?"

"No. He and the young master, Myrcan, they went to Carthage in the spring and haven't returned. The gods grant they are well." The woman didn't seem at all confident of it.

As Cynthia stepped toward the doorway, she stumbled on the hem of her long gown and fell against the wall. She slapped it once, twice, and got her balance back.

The woman's face had gone ashen. "A bad omen."

"No, a good one. I stumbled outside the doorstep, not on it. So may all ill-luck fall short and remain outside this house."

"May it be so. Come with me." As she entered, Cynthia cast a glance at the wall: the smudges from her charcoal-smeared hand were not very dark, but visible enough for one who was looking for them. The slaves in a household know everything that happens in it: if this woman knew nothing of what Komi had been up to in the past month, she could be sure Hanno knew even less.

The woman led her, not to some little dark room, but up a flight of tiled stairs into the better part of the house. Seeing Cynthia's lifted brow, the woman said, "It's Myrcan's child Enzaro's bearing, you see, and the master thought to acknowledge it in Myrcan's name by letting it see the light of day in Myrcan's own room."

"That's quite an honor. Does he mean to bring up the child as if it were legitimate?"

"Oh, no." The woman looked shocked. "The child is Myrcan's first-born, and Enzaro's, too, for that matter. He'll give it to the Lord, as is proper. Not that it'll do him any good."

"Why not? Is your master not a pious man? Does he not fear the gods?"

"Pious? He's all of that, now, when it's too late. Sacrifices and mortifications and prayers at all hours; he's up in the Lady's shrine now, begging her for mercy. Fear the gods? He'd better.

"It was Myrcan, you see, who should have gone to the Lord. He was Hanno's first-born, and his poor lady's, too, and she died in childbed, and the baby was all he had left of her." The voice dropped to a whisper. "So he withheld him, and did not give him to the fire. And the gods will punish him."

"Hmmm," Cynthia said. "He seems to have prospered so far."

"Of course," the woman said scornfully. "Don't you know *anything?* Well, you're a Greek. The gods have raised him high, the better to cast him down. They are jealous, and quick to anger."

"And best of all," said Cynthia dryly, "he's never been able to enjoy any of his success."

"Of course not. Come, it's this way," and she led Cynthia into a pleasant room with a window that looked out over the sea. There was a bed in it, and a painted chest, and a birthing-stool. An old woman lay curled up asleep on the floor: the local midwife, worn out after three days and nights of watching.

The girl in the bed could have been no more than fifteen, and she had Komi's triangular face and dark lashes. As Cynthia watched a shadow passed over her face, and she said, "Uh!" and awoke.

"It's all right," Cynthia said, slipping her hand under the bedclothes to feel the rigid abdomen. "Just another pain; you've had no little few of them so far."

The girl nodded, breathing shallowly till the contraction passed off. "It's morning, isn't it? What's the weather like?"

Stepping over the sleeping woman, Cynthia peered out the window. "Well, well. At dawn this morning there wasn't a cloud in the sky; now there's a big mass of them in the west.

> *"The one thing we know of the weather,*
> *if fine, or if stormy, it will change,"*

the girl quoted. She had Komi's sparkling eyes, too, and much of his cheerful disposition. "Maybe it's an omen. Burst open, you clouds, and give forth your rain. I wish I could."

Cynthia turned back the covers and cast a practiced look between Enzaro's legs. Nothing doing there yet. The old woman still slept; Cynthia sighed and put a hand on her shoulder. "Grannie, wake up."

The old woman woke, confused and frightened. "Don't worry," Cynthia said. "I've come to help. Nothing's happened yet. Has her water broken? Was there a bloody show?"

The crone shook her head "no." "As you said, girl, nothing has happened. The doors of her womb are shut. I begin to think it's witchcraft."

"Who would pay a witch to hold back a slave's baby? Even when—"

"Even when it's a firstborn, destined for the fire? Maybe nobody gives a curse about Enzaro. Maybe someone wants to torment Hanno—him up in the shrine, bowing and bellowing and pleading for the gods' favor."

"Maybe. Well, grannie, you're worn out, and I'm young and fresh. Go home and rest. Maybe tomorrow will bring better news." The old woman crept away.

The day wore on. From time to time someone would come by to see how things were getting on, usually bearing in hand some excuse for being on this floor at all. The old woman who kept the door, carrying a broom. A young man with a basket, peering round the doorframe ("Get out of here, you scamp! This is women's business!") The door stood open, of course; to close it might close up the womb that now should open.

An older man came by, carrying a chamberpot, his eyes well averted as he asked, "No luck yet?"

"Good morning, Chamboro," Enzaro called out. "No, no luck yet. Pray to Tanit for me. (He's very pious," Enzaro murmured as the old man shuffled away. "Notice how he's too modest to look inside the door.")

"It's getting hot, I'm afraid." Cynthia removed most of the bedding, covering Enzaro with a single layer of linen, gave her a sip of water. "Whatever happened to that storm?" But it was still hanging off in the west. And the day wore on. Cynthia had time to think.

Never mind the *why* someone would pay to block Enzaro's labor; *how* was the question. The old herbwife who had taught her never mentioned such a thing. But then Cynthia had never consented to learn any of Xanthe's favorite abortifacients; maybe she had assumed she wouldn't be interested in this, either. Nor was she, except in how to undo it; and there was nothing about it in old Palamedes' books of magic, not as far as she had read in them. When she got back to Syracuse she must go on with those books.

—*If* she got back to Syracuse. She had never decided how to explain that her man was a runaway Sikel slave; maybe there was no graceful way. Maybe they would do better to set up as metics in some Greek or even Roman town where they weren't known. But she must get this child born somehow, get out of here before someone in the house found out about Komi.

There was a song creeping forward now on hesitant feet from the dark back rooms of her memory. A song about a young wife who'd had this trouble, and the way her man solved it. Oh, she remembered only bits and snatches, but he had gone out into the street, bidding all his neighbors congratulate him on his new son. And the witch had cried, had cried,

"What rascal has combed out the witch-knots I tied in her hair for safekeeping?
"Or who has unknotted her sandal, to let her go light of a baby?"

—and the husband had gone and done those things, and the child was born before he could turn round. It was worth a try. She found a pair of worn sandals at the foot of the bed, spread the laces wide. She found a comb in the ornamented chest and combed the girl's hair smooth and plaited it. But still the contractions came and went without effect.

Ah, but the gods must be on somebody's side after all: there was Komi, peering through the doorway. Enzaro cried out in delight, and Komi stepped round the birthing-stool to kiss his sister's cheek.

"Komi, I'm so glad to see you. I didn't expect you back till autumn, if then. Where's Myrcan? Oh, gods, and here I am lying-in in his bedroom." She started to get up, but another contraction set in and she lay down again, panting.

"I wish I could do this and get it over with," she said when she could breathe freely. "I don't know why it won't *come*. Do you suppose it knows something?" The sparkle had gone out of her eyes. She reached down to cradle, as best she could, her swollen abdomen. "Poor little scrap, I carry you safe for nine months, and go to all this trouble to bring you into the world, and then in the same hour of your birth you've got to have your little throat cut and go into the fire. Is that why you're afraid to come out? But it's a hard world, child, and death is everywhere in the midst of life. You may be getting the better deal." The girl looked up, and the corner of her mouth twitched. "Oh, look: I've made the midwife weep. I'm sorry. Komi, you never said: where is Myrcan?"

"Ah, he's not here. I've been telling them downstairs about the beautiful Carthaginian lady he's smitten with, and how he's forgotten all about boats and the sea, and how his father mustn't know of it—"

"That's not answering my question!" Enzaro snapped. "Komi, you're in trouble, aren't you? *Where is Myrcan?*"

"I told you her wits were quick," Komi said. "To the best of my knowledge he's still in Carthage. There really is a lady, and the gods really should forbid his father ever hears about her. And I'm not in trouble yet, though I shall be soon."

"What have you done?"

"Why, I've stolen a boat," he counted off on his fingers, "left Myrcan—come to Syracuse and abducted Cynthia here—crept by stealth into Panormos harbor and brought her here—all to steal your baby the moment it's born, and Hanno can buy off his dirty old gods some other way. That's all." He spread out his hand as if the whole thing were childishly simple.

"Oh!" Enzaro's face flushed, and her body went limp. Cynthia knelt beside her, all alert: if pity for the child's fate had been holding her back, this news might be all she needed to set her going. But a contraction came on and went off without effect.

"Cynthia," the girl said. "Are you the one they call the Witch of Syracuse?"

"Miscalled, yes, once or twice."

"Then you must walk carefully here. You've been spoken of in Panormos, and not well spoken of. They say you slew a priest of Tanit who went to set a plague in Syracuse."

"Did I? Who told you so?"

"Oh, I've heard it. You know, the fine folk talk of this and that; they don't think slaves can hear, and so we hear everything. And Chamboro has spoken of it; he's an older man than Hanno, and fears the gods." Another contraction came on and went off without effect, and Enzaro spoke a bad Punic word under her breath. She sat up a little higher, and patted her abdomen like a naughty puppy. "Come on, child, you've got an unusual bit of good fortune here; you mustn't miss your tide."

"It may be there's something unnatural in this," Cynthia said: "you're young and healthy and you ought to have given birth two and a half days ago. The old woman said she suspected witchcraft, and there's an old song—" She told them the fragments she remembered, and how the story came out. "Hanno's got plans for your child; maybe someone's out to foil them. Someone other than us, that is. Sandals, hair, doors and windows, I can't think of anything else. Komi, you're going to have to do what the young husband did in the song. Go downstairs and tell everyone it's done: mother and child alive and well. Tell them it's a boy. And if someone starts shouting, 'Oh, who's undone this, that, and the other?' for the gods' sake listen. If that doesn't fetch anything, you may have to go out in the street, though that's risky."

"Do you think I care?" Komi said, and was gone. Presently they heard his voice ringing downstairs, echoing through the house: and the sound of cheering, and a wail of indignation, and running footsteps. "Quick," Cynthia said. "Your back to the door. Here, take this." She rolled up one of the discarded blankets into a bundle of suitable size and put it into the girl's arms. And the footsteps were loud on the tiles outside, and in through the door burst the old man Chamboro.

"Who?" he shrieked. "Who loosened her sandal straps, to let the child go free? Who took the knotted serpent from her bed—? He stopped, seeing Cynthia. "Oh. It was *you*." And Komi ran in and twisted his arms behind him.

"No, but it's about to be." Cynthia looked under the low bedframe; seeing nothing, she rolled Enzaro to one side and slid her hand under the mattress. Her fingers touched a small round box; she grasped it and pulled it out. The box, of copper with an openwork lid, had inside it a little snake, dead and dried, and tied in a knot. She opened the box, broke the knot apart, and threw box, fragments and all out the window. And Enzaro said "Oh!" with a sound of great surprise.

The old man laughed. "Go ahead, 'Zaro, you'll have no more trouble. You and I have served our purpose: the Witch of Syracuse has come here to her death."

"Have I? And what is a Punic sorcerer doing, carrying chamberpots in the house of Hanno the oil-merchant?"

"Why, I'm not the sorcerer, witch. The priest of Tanit himself made these charms, and I laid them out at his bidding. The Lady herself told him how you slew her servant in Syracuse, and how she sought your death. But you have some foul magic about you that turned all her sendings. But it won't turn spears, and you shall die for the offense you've done the Lady—"

"Cynthia!" Enzaro interrupted. "I think we are getting somewhere."

"Turn your backs, you two." Komi turned the old man forcibly to the wall, while Cynthia helped Enzaro onto the birthing-stool. And not before it was time: one contraction and the head appeared, round and dark, and then the child fell into Cynthia's hands with a gush of blood and water.

The infant drew in a breath and let it out in a thin gurgling cry. In the silence that followed they could hear the commotion downstairs, with cries of "It's a boy!"

"In fact, it's a girl," Cynthia said, clearing the baby's mouth and face of blood and slime. "Everything else in order, though." She cut and tied the navel cord and wrapped the child in the long strips of linen that lay at hand.

"I don't mind," Enzaro said. "Good luck to her."

"Are you all right, 'Zaro?" the old man said. "Good." And shouted at the top of his cracked old voice, "Help! Help! Witch!" Komi clouted the side of his head, and he fell in a heap to the floor.

"Have you killed him?"

"Have I? No. But he'll sleep for a while. They'll have heard him below, though. Take the child and run—" He listened. "No, they're coming up the stairs. The front stairs, too. Hide somewhere till this blows over."

Voices floated up the back stairs and the front. Here was another stair, leading upward. Any port in a storm:

she picked up her hems with her free hand and scurried up the stairs.

It was dark here, with only a faint glimmer of light from above. She drew a fold of her stole over the small bundle in the crook of her arm, and began to climb.

In the upstairs room a dozen oil lamps had been set in a half circle. Now they were guttering out, some of them dark already. By what was left of their light Cynthia could see a man lying on the floor.

His clothing was dark, his face hidden in his arms; he lay flat on his belly in a pose of utter exhaustion. Gold glinted on his fingers. Cynthia was certain this was Hanno, the master of the house, worn out with prayers and entreaties and fallen asleep in the shrine of Tanit.

As for Tanit herself, there was nothing to be seen of her but a wooden image, rather larger than life size, arms outstretched, the head covered with a veil of fine linen.

Ah, curse it, here came someone up the stairs. Cynthia edged her way up shallow steps, avoiding the line of flickering lamps. Just what she needed, to send one of them crashing to the step below. The image of Tanit had full skirts of heavy silk; she settled down behind them and pulled her stole over her face.

"My lord? My lord Hanno! We have some trouble." The man's voice was smooth, even in his present distress, and he spoke with an upper-class accent. The steward of the house, maybe; a lifelong servant at any rate, grown up with Hanno as Komi had with Myrcan, and the likeliest of all the slaves to survive bringing the master bad news.

"What is it?" Hanno had woken quickly, without confusion. (Well, the man was a successful merchant, he could not be an absolute dolt—except where it touched his gods.) "Is the child born? There's trouble on your face. Don't fear to tell me: is the child dead?"

"Don't think so, my lord, but stolen. The midwife snatched it up while the mother was still on the birthing-stool, and ran off with it."

"The midwife? Old Pitti? She couldn't run to save her life."

"Another midwife, my lord. A Greek, a younger woman. The mother says her brother sent her to aid in the birthing. And there's no doubt the child was born under her hand, whereas Pitti could accomplish nothing in three days."

"But a Greek, and the enemy of the gods. And the mother's brother sent her? Is this Komi we're speaking of? Komi's in Carthage, with Myrcan."

"There seems to be some difference of opinion about that, my lord. Some of the household say, yes, he's in Carthage. Others say, no, they've seen him here today. And the old fool says the gods blew him here on the wings of the mistral: she says that's what he told her. Things are a bit confused downstairs."

Hanno made a little sound like a sniff. "That boy always would say anything. Find him. Find the midwife. And tell the household to collect themselves and keep their minds on what they are doing. I'll stay here and pray till you find them: I'm not fit any more for running up and down stairs and chasing mysterious Greeks."

"Yes, my lord." She heard the steward go, his feet whispering down the stairs.

"Not that I'm fit to pray, either," Hanno went on, as if continuing a conversation. "I have sinned, against the Lord and against you; I withheld the sacrifice. But he was all I had, all I have. Have mercy on him, Lady. Intercede for us with the Lord King. Let us find the child. In the same hour it is found, I will give Myrcan's firstborn to the fire. Then spare us, in your great mercy. Let me live to see my son's children growing up in my house. Have mercy, forgive me, for I have sinned against you—"

This is indecent. No Greek cared much about nakedness in public or in private: Cynthia had nothing to compare the crawling feeling of wrongness Hanno's prayers gave her. It was as if the man had taken off not merely his clothes but his skin, and laid his soul bare. She uncovered one eye and peered cautiously round the edge of Tanit's draperies. Oh, this was not good at all: Hanno was no longer lying prostrate, but kneeling, upright, sitting back on his heels, his eyes fixed on Tanit's image. His little nap must have done him good: his eyes were wide open and he looked fit for another three days at least.

As she drew her head back, a corner of the image's veil brushed her face. The idea struck her, full-formed, like a wave of the sea. The enlarging spell.

The only problem was that Hanno was watching the image already; she was not sure just how the transition would look to him. There was some dust on the floor behind the image, dust in the folds of its skirts; she would do the best she could with that. She recited the enlarging spell, counting on her fingers, and with the last count pulled the linen veil from the image and draped it over her own head.

Hanno at first saw nothing: the billowing clouds roiled in the shadows, untouched by the feeble lamplight. Then a light began to shine through them, pale at first and then brighter, the white shape of the Lady's veil, gleaming in lamplight suddenly a dozen times brighter than it had been. The veiled figure also was taller than it had been. It was moving, coming closer, descending one shallow step to tower over him. It was a wonder his heart did not stop on the instant. He bent down and covered his eyes and waited to die.

"Hanno, get up." The voice was near as a whisper, vast as wind over the plains. Hanno obeyed.

"Look at me, Hanno. Do not be afraid: you will not see anything to harm you."

Trembling, he raised his eyes. The veil shone white above the dark shape like snow atop a tall mountain seen far-off in his youth. Beneath it he could see only a shadowed hint of dark eyes.

"Hanno, your sins are forgiven." The words washed over him; he could not understand. "Because of your long faithfulness, I have forgiven you," the voice said again. "I have interceded with the Lord, the King: the life of Myrcan will not be held against you. I chose that he should live to beget this child for me." Under the veil something dark was drawn aside, revealing a white shape in the Lady's arms, a bundle wrapped in linen. "This child will never go to the fire, it is mine. Hanno, do my bidding." Not daring to speak, he nodded shakily.

"Go downstairs. Tell your servants only to stop their foolish searches and go back to their duties. As for you, eat bread and drink wine and give thanks for the bounty of the earth; then go to your bed and sleep. When you wake again, you may tell them all you have seen. Tell them your grandchild is in the arms of Tanit. Go now."

Somehow he got to his feet, somehow made his way

down the stairs despite the mists in his eyes. And he was gone.

Cynthia let out a long breath and made the gesture that broke the spell. She took the dusty veil and draped it again over the image (the wooden thing had no face at all). She would wait here a while till the household went back to normal, then sneak away. She covered the child with her stole again, smiling at the little wrinkled face. A good baby; she had slept through the whole thing—

"Oh, very clever," a voice said, gentle as breath, and Cynthia felt the hairs stand up on her neck.

Without changing, the shape of Tanit had changed. The idol had grown no larger; it did not move; but it seemed to reach backward into the darkness, back and back into a lightless gulf that was before the world began. Not surprising that Hanno, seeing Cynthia in her magical seeming, had thought he was seeing the goddess, but if he had seen this, then Cynthia could never have beguiled him.

"Hide behind *my* skirts, will you? Now I lay my curse upon you, and its fulfillment shall be swift."

"If I understood correctly from your toady downstairs, you've been cursing me this year past and I still live. Arethousa wrought well."

"Arethousa's dead, her magic fading. You have no power against me."

"Am I Hanno, to believe whatever I'm told? If you had the power to burn me to ashes where I stand, you'd have done it without so much talk. It is you who have no power over me."

"Insolent mortal, you shall see what power I have on things around you. Get out of my shrine."

Cynthia opened her mouth and closed it again. The

goddess could have the last word if she liked; words were only words. It was very quiet below. She crept downstairs and heard nothing but a faint murmuring drifting up the back stairs. *She was trying to scare me to death, like any gutter-priest. She's good at it, too; if I believed in her it might have worked.*

After the quiet outside the house, the noise outside came as a shock. Men were running about in the street, shouting "Here!" and "Hurry up!" and a lot of rough Punic swearing. Cynthia shrank back against the wall, but no one paid her any heed. Either all this turmoil had nothing to do with her, or Arethousa's ring still protected her.

She found the place easily enough—an old weathered pine blown nearly flat against the hillside. She crept in under the branches and lay down on a thick mat of fallen needles. She would wait out this day, maybe two.

She should have brought water with her—but she was not thirsty yet, and the baby slept peacefully, not needing anything yet but to be kept safe. If Komi didn't come, she would set off by herself, begging her bread as she went. The countryfolk would be generous to one in need, so long as she didn't stay for long. Finding milk would be a harder task—but it was midsummer and the last few years had been prosperous: there should be a good crop of babies among the farmfolk, their mothers full of milk and willing to share. She began to calculate how many days lay between her and Syracuse, and how she would avoid the Mamertine fortress and General Hiero's army that lay besieging it.

Time passed, perhaps as much as an hour. Then the old pine's branches rustled. Before Cynthia could die of fright, Komi's face appeared, surrounded by greenery like a satyr's, saying cheerfully, "There you are! You have the baby? Good! Come on out. Things have gotten a bit more complicated, but I think we'll cope."

Cynthia crept out and got to her feet, brushing pine needles from her clothing. She saw at once what the complication was: beside Komi stood Enzaro. She held out her arms, and Cynthia surrendered the baby without a word.

"I thought you were staying."

"I did, too, at first," Enzaro said. "But after all the noise started up and Komi made himself scarce, I had some time to think. And I thought, 'No one is going to believe I wasn't in on this, I shall be beaten at the very least.' And I thought, 'Why should I stay? There's nothing in this house to hold me.' So I put on my clothes, bundled up those bits of linen, and went to find Komi."

"She knows all my old hiding places."

"As long as you feel fit enough to travel," Cynthia said. She had seen women who languished in bed for days after a birth, and others who got up an hour afterward and finished doing the laundry. Enzaro's color was good, her eyes clear, and she carried her baby in the crook of her arm, with an air of confidence; if this was the first child she had borne, it was not the first she'd cared for.

Komi led the way down a ravine into the bed of a glittering stream. "We'll do well to get clear; I think the fleet is headed out for Messana at last." He ducked under a tangle of bushes to a place where a tree fallen into the stream had given him something to moor to. "Look, that storm is finally moving in."

Komi and Enzaro walked confidently down the

trunk and hopped into the boat; Cynthia followed more cautiously. Komi pushed off with the boat-hook and paddled out till he could raise the sail. A good west wind was blowing ahead of the storm, and it filled the sail and carried them along briskly.

A shadow fell over them, and they looked up. The westering sun had gone behind the storm clouds as they billowed up, a dozen shades of blue and gray and purple, robust as cabbages. And below them a score, a hundred white and colored shapes. Sails: a fleet of ships: a Punic war fleet. "There they are. So we don't want to go through the Straits of Messana till it's over. Maybe we'll go to the Aeolians. I told you I had friends on the north coast of Phaneraia. For the present, any place that isn't Panormos is good enough for me."

He made the sheets fast and sat down beside Enzaro, who sat in silence holding her baby. Cynthia sat on her other side. The young mother seemed hale enough, neither gasping from exhaustion nor pale from excessive bleeding. Slaves seldom got the chance to lie about idle and grow soft. By all the signs Cynthia could read, Enzaro would be all right.

There would be time enough later to explain everything. Thinking that Enzaro would see Komi only briefly and Cynthia never again, they had thought it best not to mention that Cynthia was more to Komi than a midwife hired for the occasion. That he was more to her than all the world put together. They would find time to tell her later, when they had found shelter.

The wind at their backs strengthened and grew colder, and a few drops of rain fell, big juicy ones.

Then the whole storm hit them, a drenching from Poseidon's largest bucket. Komi jumped up and took the sheets, keeping the sail in trim. The women pulled their stoles over their heads.

"Better go below," Komi shouted through the howling wind, but Enzaro shook her head. "You know I get sick if I can't see the sky."

Now the storm slacked off a little, dropping only moderate rain instead of rain by the tubful, and they could see through the rain's veil the Punic war fleet, still well behind them.

"We're going to have to make for shore," Komi said, "while we still know where the shore is. That village up on the cliffs is Kertyra—I don't know if you can see it—and there's a little tiny harbor down below. Well-shielded with rocks, but I know where they are. Hunker down, you two, if you won't go below, and keep out of the way."

He gathered the sheets in one hand and took the cords of the steering-oars in the other. As a stable-groom, sent to bring two high-spirited horses to the chariot, takes the bridles each in one hand, turning and bending as the sleek-bodied beasts rear and lunge, but always drawing them onward on the way he wants them to go: so Komi guided the boat by its sheets and steering-oars between the glistening rocks into Kertyra harbor. Cynthia watched him with pleasure, as one might watch a skilled and well-loved dancer, seeing in the dance the image of the dance they danced in the dark—

And the storm hit them again, the full force of the winds and a lash of rain, pushing the boat sharply sideways. It bowed and shied like a frightened horse. In the sudden darkness Cynthia heard Komi shout, "Oh, gods—" and a great thundering crackling sound drowned out his voice as they struck a rock. The boat cracked like an eggshell and the sea poured in.

The waters closed over Cynthia's head. Kicking hard, she rose to the surface; spluttering and cursing, she flailed about in the dark. Her hand struck something, painfully hard, and she grabbed it and pulled herself in close. A timber from the boat, a side-rail perhaps, riding high and buoyant. She got her arm over it and groped around in the water with her other hand. On her third pass she touched sodden wool, and Enzaro bobbed up like a cork. Cynthia got her to the rail (or the rail to her; in this wet floating darkness it was hard to say which), and both women shouted like a well-trained chorus, "The baby! Is the baby all right?"

A wail from the folds of Enzaro's stole answered them. The sudden soaking in cold water had woken the child, and she didn't care for it at all. They would have to get to shore quickly, before she took a chill.

Now the raging storm was moving on again; it was merely cloudy, merely raining. Kicking steadily, pushing the timber and all its passengers through the water, Cynthia brought them to a sandy beach in the lee of the harbor. Such backward glances as she could spare gave her no sign of Komi, but she knew the man could swim like a fish; she would not begin to worry yet.

They took off their clothes, wrung most of the sea water out of them, and put them back on, wrapping the woolen stoles to cover as much of them as possible. Wool is warm when wet, and it cut the chill of the wind. Enzaro draped the swaddling bands over a bush, to rinse out in the rain and dry in the sun when there was any, and tucked her daughter naked into the warmth of her stole. The child went back to sleep.

Cynthia paced along the shoreline, watching the water. Well out to sea, safe from shallow shoals and lurking rocks, the Punic war-fleet sailed by. There was a scattering of broken timbers floating on the surface, a half-empty amphora, a purple cushion that floated for half an hour or so before it finally went under. But nothing moving: nothing human. For a long while Cynthia tried to reassure herself: Komi had been carried farther downwind, or out to sea, clinging to the mast; presently he would come swimming in to shore, blithe as a dolphin, or come strolling down the beach, jaunty as a conquering hero coming home. But her heart knew the truth already.

She twisted the ring of Arethousa this way and that on her finger, pulled it down as far as the first joint and then pushed it back again. The curse of Tanit had glanced away from her, reflected like sunlight off a mirror; and from Enzaro also when Cynthia touched her with the hand that wore the ring. But nothing had shielded Komi, and the curse had struck him down. Now here she stood like a reed, whole and hale to the eye, but empty inside. How the faceless goddess must be pleased.

Empty and dark inside, empty as a gourd, dark as a well shaft. There were caverns by the sea with pipes and crevices that pierced the rock to the upper air: when the tide came in the air rose in these pipes and whistled like whole phalanxes of Furies. Something was rising in Cynthia now, grief perhaps, or rage, or something without a name, hidden in darkness, but she knew it could break worlds if properly applied. And the spell came to her mind, the spell for turning a curse back the way it had come. Such a little spell: only five words. They were rising from her throat; they were trembling on her lips. She strove to hold them back as one strives not to vomit.

In the darkness within a sound echoed, rebounding and reechoing with no way to get out: Komi's last despairing "Oh, gods—" in his resonant voice. She heard it and heard it again; she could not bear to hear it. To drown it out, she spoke the five words.

And the sky burst open, the storm falling again like a landslide, the winds howling with deafening noise. All the rage of Tanit's curse, funneled through Cynthia's spell, resounded like an actor's voice through his wide-mouthed mask, a dozen, a hundred times its real force. It blinded and deafened her, but scarcely ruffled her clothing; it could not touch her; it was bound away from her.

Once she had seen a Punic trireme wreck upon shoals, its back broken, its crew milling about like ants, and sink into the sea. She could see nothing now, but her memory told her the tale again a hundred times. Again the masts snapped, again the oars fell idle, again desperate men scrambled and fought to reach the upper deck or drowned in the dark below, as the ship's heavy ram pulled her prow underwater and the sea closed her fierce eyes in death.

The clouds were melting away into the sky, as pale as frost in the morning sun. Cynthia felt tired, and sick, and ashamed. Some of those sailors had women who loved them, as she loved Komi: not yet, but tomorrow or the day after, they would learn the terrible news and weep. You could call it poetic justice.

The water was warm on her ankles, after the chill of the wind. Below, there would be no wind at all, no conflict of Greek and Punic and Roman, where all the dead were dead alike. And Komi was down there somewhere. His voice still echoed within her: "Oh, gods—" Could she not stop that? Not to drown out the voice, all that was left to her, but to give the patient actor Memory a different line to read?

"I say it who know:" he had said it the first day they met. *"It is better to be alive and a poor slave than dead and wrapped in silk and gold."* Yes, he had said that, and prayed for long days between himself and the end, but they had not been granted. But the deathless actor Memory stood mask in hand, to speak her lines, his words, to an audience of all the immortal gods so long as breath should last.

Well: she would simply have to make breath last as long as possible. She stepped back out of the water and turned away.

Night was falling, a calm perfect sunset without a cloud in the sky, in shades of apricot and lemon. Enzaro sat with her daughter at her breast, one finger propping her tiny chin, teaching her to suck. They would beg shelter in Kertyra for the night, and begin their journey in the morning. Cynthia plucked the drying swaddling bands from the bush and folded them against further use. And the sun went down, and nothing was left but memory and the wind.

DUAL

by Quinn Weller

Quinn Weller writes that the, "whoops of joy you undoubtedly heard yesterday were coming from me."
Well, they could equally likely be coming from me; dis-
covering a really fine story in the slush is not an every-
day experience, and I tend to react to them
uninhibitedly. Just ask my house mates . . . four of us
are writers: I, Elisabeth Waters, Stephanie Shaver, and
Cynthia McQuillin. Raul Reyes writes, too, and very
well, but he's usually busy chasing the dog around the
yard and garden, doing everything from lawn mowing
to keeping the magazine's books. But all of them who
live here are aware of the effect on me when I find
something in the slush that I want to keep.

Zhi studied the knee-deep indentations in the snow,
clearly visible even through the new accumulation.
She smiled with satisfaction. The toddler was falling
every few steps now; his mother would soon be forced
to carry him. Her quarry's five-hour lead would dimin-
ish to nothing in no time. Zhi brushed ice pellets out of
her eyelashes and continued her hunt, keeping her eyes
riveted to the tracks in front of her.

"Stupid sorceress," she muttered, staring at the two pairs of boot prints. "Doesn't know enough to steal winter gear before she bolts. She'd freeze to death with her bastard child even if I weren't going to kill them." She pushed her skis forward with powerful thrusts, skimming easily over the icy crust. A few more strokes brought Zhi to an outcropping of pines where the trail led to a dished-out place in the snow between two tree trunks. Much of the snow around the area was melted or compacted.

"Uh-huh," grimaced Zhi. "Had to rest a bit here, didn't you? And you even risked a tiny fire." Zhi guessed they were only two or three hours ahead of her now. She skied briskly onward, poling with her pair of spears and watching the two sets of prints, the big set and the little set, counting how many times the little set disappeared in the outline of a tiny body part. Usually the child seemed to land on his seat, but several times Zhi detected the print of two little arms and a face. At each fall-spot, Zhi could see the mother's footprints, dug in firmly behind the child outline where the woman must have stood to drag the baby to his feet once more.

After another hour of even skiing, Zhi came upon more evidence of the pair she followed. She skidded to a stop and squinted at the snow, chuckling grimly. This time, Marran herself must have fallen, taking her son down with her. "Sat here in the blizzard for a while, did you, Marran? Holding him close, trying to persuade him to walk a little farther?" Zhi stifled a pang of sympathy as she took advantage of a brief lull in the storm to look down the trail. The tracks leading away from Marran's fall had only the mother's set of prints.

"You won't make any progress now," hissed Zhi.

"Not with a thirty-pound load on your back—especially when the load is probably kicking and screaming."

She spotted them a half hour later. Marran crouched on the lee side of a hillock. She had wrapped her son in her own meager cloak and was cradling him beside a small fire. Zhi squatted, unbuckled her skis, and kicked them off in one fluid motion. She pulled her bow off her shoulder, notched an arrow, and took aim.

Marran looked up and saw Zhi. Quickly, she set the sleeping child on the ground and flung herself in front of him. "Don't even try it, Zhi," she called. "You know I can spell your arrows away long before they come near us."

Zhi took a step closer. "I also know," she called back, not lowering her bow an inch, "that you're still a good two miles from the border of your homeland. You don't dare use your magic while you're still in range of the castle. Not with the King's Magician attuned to your tiniest spell." She pulled back the bow.

Marran considered for a heartbeat, then jumped behind her son and held him up before her like a shield. "Go ahead and shoot Canual, then," she shouted over the shrieking wind. "But if you kill my son, I will use every spell I hold to destroy you, and I won't care any more if they trace me."

Zhi hesitated. The point of her arrow dipped slightly. The wind abruptly died down; the snow slowed to a flurry. Zhi slung her bow back over her shoulder and plodded toward Marran, wielding her spears. She advanced until she was less than a quarter of her average throwing distance.

"I can get you both with one throw," said Zhi. "I won't miss from this distance."

Marran balanced Canual on her shoulder, quietly watching Zhi aim. As Zhi reached her right arm back to power her throw, Marran remarked casually, "I was hoping I could get you to come close enough to talk."

Zhi checked her throw awkwardly. "Don't try any of your tricks on me, sorceress."

"You know I won't use magic—except in desperation. The King's Magician could spell me back to the castle in an eye blink if he senses me. Besides, I won't need magic to keep you from killing me."

Zhi's face burned. "You always try to humiliate me," she snapped. "It won't work this time. I'm sworn to the King's service, and today my service requires me to kill the bastard and his mother."

"Canual wasn't a bastard until the King's pitiful excuse for a Queen finally managed to carry a child to term."

"Be that as it may, I will carry out my duty."

"You won't kill us."

Zhi felt as if she could obliterate the winter with her rage. "Don't be so cocky, sorceress." She hefted both spears again. "You can't intimidate me. Not this time."

"Zhi, Zhi, look at me: I'm exhausted, half-frozen, helpless without my spells. If you really wanted to kill us," said Marran gently, "you would have done it by now."

"That—that's not true . . ." began Zhi, but she knew that Marran had heard and noted the hesitation in her voice. Zhi cried out and fell to her knees, pressing the point of the spear to her abdomen. "I have failed you, my King," she moaned. "My life is worthless. I must condemn myself."

"Zhi, wait!" commanded Marran. The sorceress laid her slumbering son near the fire and ran to Zhi's side.

"Stay back! Don't try to talk me out of this!"

"Please put down your spears. I don't want to have to resort to a spell to save you."

Zhi started, her hands behind the spear point relaxing slightly. "You'd risk being caught to spell me safe?" Marran said nothing. Zhi began to laugh bitterly. "If only I'd known! I could have tricked you into betraying yourself."

"You still could."

Zhi threw the spears away with all her strength. "Please tell me you bewitched me somehow. Please tell me I didn't fail because of my own weakness." She cast a pleading look at Marran. "Did you spell me before you ran away, hoping the King would send me after you? If so, you were very lucky. I'm not his favorite warrior, you know."

"But you are his best." Marran smiled sadly. "I did cast a spell before I left, but not on you. I just made sure the King would be certain to select you to follow me."

Zhi was beyond surprise. "I see. You did know my weakness."

"Not your weakness. Your strength." Marran took Zhi's face in her hands and forced her to meet Marran's eyes. "You're the only warrior in his service," she whispered, her voice burning, "who's strong enough to know when it's time to break an oath. The only one with the courage to do something about the way he treats the women in his castle."

"I have no complaints about my treatment," protested Zhi weakly.

"The King does not think of you as a woman. Except occasionally, when the candles are out and all his concubines have bored him."

Zhi squeezed her eyes closed. It had been so long since she had shed tears that she remembered it no more than she remembered nursing at her mother's breast. She would not cry now, either. When she trusted her voice again, she murmured shakily. "How do you know about that?"

"Would you like to hear what else I know? Haven't you wondered, along with everyone else in the kingdom, how Canual came to be born? You must know all the other concubines have been spelled into barrenness by the King's Magician."

Zhi stumbled to her feet, kicking pinecones into the fire as she paced. "I suppose you blame me for that, too. I didn't ask you to come and visit me; in fact, I warned you away. I told you the King was likely to enslave you." She kicked another pinecone furiously. "He takes all foreign female visitors for his harem, except those who are too ugly to—"

"Stop it, Zhi."

Zhi grabbed Marran's shoulders roughly. "You said I'm strong. Well, I'm strong enough to face the truth about myself. I failed as a sorceress, I failed as a concubine, and now I'm about to be a failed warrior, too." She pushed Marran into a snowbank and ran to the sleeping child. "Not this time! I'm going to finish something, for once." Zhi jerked the boy from where he lay in Marran's cloak and dangled him over the fire. Canual awoke and wailed. "You see? I do remember, Marran. You chose the water elemental for your spellway and therefore have no power over fire. You won't be able to save him from this."

Zhi turned slightly so she would not have to watch Marran's face. But she could still hear Marran's gasp. "The King asked me to set a counter spell against the

Magician's," Marran said rapidly. "He was finally beginning to fear that the arrogant imbecile he married could never give him an heir. He promised me, if I bore him a son, that he would recognize the child."

Zhi tried to drop Canual, but her hands would not unclench. "You're using a spell," she warned. "The Magician will take you, and I'll kill the boy anyway."

"I considered running then," Marran continued as if she hadn't heard, "but by then I had made friends with some of the other concubines. I didn't want to leave them in that awful place. I started thinking about what my son might be able to accomplish if he were to become King. I decided to acquiesce to the King's request."

Zhi attempted to shake Canual from her arms. To her astonishment, the little boy stopped crying and began to giggle. "Marran, unspell me, now! You can't save him!"

"At first after Canual was born, I thought I'd chosen correctly. The King left me alone, and I had the raising of the boy. It looked as though I'd have a free hand to teach him as I saw fit until the King recognized him as the heir—which he promised to do when Canual reached his fifteenth year. But I overlooked the Magician's jealousy. He plotted against me, somehow managing to spell a successful pregnancy on the Queen."

Zhi closed her eyes and prepared to throw Canual into the flames. "You'd better cut off your spell on me, now, or your enemy will have you." She heard Marran stomping through the snow toward her.

Marran walked slowly around Zhi and stood across the fire from her. "Zhi, I haven't used any spells on you," she said calmly, making no attempt to take her son.

Zhi crumpled to the ground, sobbing, clutching the baby to her chest. "I can't kill him," she wept. "I can't kill my sister's baby."

Canual burst into tears again and cried out for his mother. Marran knelt beside her sister and her son. "Zhi, you are not a failed warrior." She was weeping now as well. "I made sure you'd follow me, not only because I missed my sister, but also because you're the most capable warrior to help me with the mission I am facing."

Zhi raised her tear-streaked face, unable to utter her questions. But Marran answered them anyway. "The Queen's son will not live to adulthood," Marran said. "That insipid woman was never meant to bear children. The Magician was forced to use spells with a serious price: her son was born with barely enough mind to keep his body breathing. He'll be lucky to survive his first birthday."

"Does the King know?" said Zhi hoarsely.

"Not yet. I expect the Magician will be able to keep up the pretense until the boy's death."

"And then what?"

Marran leaned forward and stroked her son's hair until he quieted. "Then, I come back," she said. "With the rightful heir to the throne."

Zhi reached up a hand and tentatively touched her nephew's head. "Do you really think the King will accept you both back?"

"Yes," declared Marran. "If I come back after having studied enough sorcery to overthrow the Magician. And if I've raised an army led by the most courageous warrior I know."

Zhi was silent a long time. Finally, she met her sister's eyes. "I swear my service to you, sister sorceress," she vowed. "And this time I will keep my oath."

Marran embraced her sister for the first time in many years. "I put all my trust in you," she whispered.

SPIRIT QUEST

by *Kathryne Kennedy*

Kathryne Kennedy says that her first story was about witches, printed in a school paper when she was in first grade. She says, "Contrary to common belief, *salable* writing is hard work, and there's a lot to learn! Having a mother who was a published writer helped. The biggest problem was I was always running out of things to read. Finally I decided that the only way I'd get enough to read was to write it myself." I think many of us can relate to that—I know I can. Somebody once came to sell me a speed-reading course and I said, "Get out of here! I read too fast already—I'm always running out of things to read!"

Kathryne lives with her husband Chris in Arizona and her two sons named Jordan and Langdon Lee. She has appeared in several small press publications and received honorable mentions in contests, but I gather this is her first professional sale. Congratulations. Enjoy it. That's the greatest thrill you'll ever have—till the day you go on a best-seller list.

The beast growled and shook its head, sending spittle flying to land with a hiss in the snow. Blue fur rippled in the wind and it spun, seeking a way out of the trap it had been lured into. But behind stood the smooth wall of the glacier, and in front the pointed spears of the villagers. It extended talons from the pads of its hands and growled again. The sound escalated into a scream that echoed off walls of ice for miles.

Kallaka's grip tightened on her weapon, yet even fear couldn't keep the small smile of satisfaction from spreading across her face. She lowered mismatched eyes; one green, one brown, the mark of a true Shaman, and glanced at her beloved. Alloc stood frozen like the sea they stood on, his amber eyes wide in astonishment, his perfectly-shaped mouth hanging open. His wife, To'nua, moved slightly in front of him, trying to protect him with her small form. She smiled up at her husband, revealing black, crooked teeth. He glanced at Kallaka and returned her smile instead.

The Traveler finally broke the spell, screaming aloud his own challenge. His hooded parka fell backward, exposing his odd, golden hair to the glow of the clouded sun. Kallaka's winged eyebrows rose in surprise. This stranger from a distant tribe seemed to have no fear of the beast. Slightly ashamed, the villagers quickly formed a circle surrounding the monster, stabbing with their spears and taunting it with their own cries.

"Foolish girl," grunted the Shaman, his arms trembling with the weight of a spear. He glanced at Kallaka, one black eye sparkling with anger, the other brown one reflecting something else. Pity mingled with understanding.

Kallaka bristled at the look, then moved closer to the old man, helping him with his place in the circle.

"They wanted dinner," she panted. "Now they've got it."

"Don't try to bluff me, apprentice. I sensed a fat bear you could've Called for them." Binuu wheezed and spat, his wrinkled face twisted in pain. "And it would've taken a lot less effort."

The monster lunged and Kallaka quickened her efforts, warning the prey back. *Binuu's right,* she thought. *A renegade beast's nothing to trifle with.* But now the villagers couldn't doubt the strength of her Gift, for it took a strong Shaman to tame that savage mind to answer a Calling. Kallaka flicked ebony hair over her shoulder. Why couldn't Alloc have waited for her to come of age? Perhaps *now* he would set aside his wife and marry her! After all, To'nua's only a Chieftain's daughter, and today Kallaka proved herself to be one of great power.

The beast shook with fatigue and sensed that the villagers wanted to tire it. It stomped in renewed anger, cracking the frozen layer of ice. The fissures spread so quickly that the villagers barely had time to react. A snaking hiss sounded in Kallaka's ears and she felt herself grabbed roughly from behind. The ice she'd stood on had disappeared, instead there gaped an opening with the turgid waters of the sea at the bottom of it.

Kallaka looked up into the green eyes of the Traveler, words of thanks dying on her lips. The stranger had saved her from certain death, yet he frowned at her with anger, as if he'd like to toss her into the water himself.

"You Called it," he gritted from between clenched teeth. "Now you get rid of it!"

He spun the girl around, showing her the chaos that the beast had created. Most of the villagers had fallen to their knees, and now looked up with dazed expressions. The Shaman lay on the ground, his chest heaving from the exertion of avoiding the sudden rift, unable to gather the strength to rise. The Chieftain and a few others still fought the beast with drawn swords, but the snow gleamed scarlet beneath their boots.

The Traveler sprinted around the gaps of broken ice, and drew from his scabbard the oddest sword Kallaka had ever seen. The blade rippled with eerie lights and seemed to radiate power, yet she'd no time to study it further. Her hand had emerged from her pocket empty, and she hastily searched the rest of her clothing. Surely she'd brought the little flute with her!

Kallaka cleared the panic from her mind with the discipline the Shaman had taught her, then remembered her boot. She'd stuck it in the top of her boot! She dug her hand beneath the fur trim and heard the soul-rending scream of a dying man. Please let it not be Alloc, she begged the Spirits. "Alloc," breathed the girl. "Alloc!"

Her fingers closed around the carved whistle and she straightened, slapping the hair from her eyes. She searched the snow, squinting against the sudden glare of the sun. Alloc ran slightly behind To'nua, away from the battle that still raged. The beast saw the opening, lunged for freedom, and headed straight for Alloc. Kallaka gasped, unable to move. If the monster harmed him, it'd be her fault!

Alloc grabbed his wife's arm and pushed her into the path of the beast, dropped his weapon and ran faster. Kallaka sighed with relief. To'nua raised her spear and plunged the point into the monster's leg. It screamed and pulled at the shaft, then the Traveler sliced it from behind, and the beast whirled to fight this new menace. The rest of the villagers joined the battle.

Kallaka screamed at Alloc too late. He ran blindly, and fell over the edge of a crack into the water with a splash. To'nua ran to him, lay flat on her belly, and reached for her husband, desperately trying to pull him out. Her arms strained against the dead weight, and Kallaka could see her body slide forward with agonizing slowness.

Kallaka glanced at the flute in her hand, a miniature carving of the beast with a hole pierced through the length of it, smaller holes ranged along the belly for sound variation. *It won't work anyway,* she thought. It took hours of preparation for a Calling; certain herbs had to be drunk, certain mind techniques enforced. To just stand and whistle seemed pure folly. Her decision made, she took off at a run, away from the villagers who fought for their lives. Toward the only person who really mattered.

Suddenly everything but Kallaka seemed to slow down. One minute she ran, screaming Alloc's name, the next she knelt at To'nua's side, and pulled on her beloved's parka. The parka she'd helped him get, Calling the snowcat from his mountain lair, knowing the danger but not caring because Alloc wanted the fur. She screamed his name again and summoned physical strength she hadn't known she possessed. She'd do anything for Alloc, anything!

He lay facedown on the ice, only his legs dangling over the edge, when Kallaka heard another scream and a roar of satisfaction from the beast. Her back prickled, but still she knelt over her beloved, checking the extent of his injury. A purple knot on the side of his temple, a small trickle of blood.

"You can't do anything else for him now," cried To'nua. "Help the others!"

Another scream and Kallaka finally turned, watched with rising guilt as another villager fell. How many had died while she saved Alloc? Only two men remained standing, she recognized the red fur of the Chieftain and with surprise the blond hair of the Traveler.

Kallaka raised the whistle to her lips. It might not work, but she had to try. She closed her eyes and went through the mental disciplines, not with the slow thought that normally paved the way but with reckless speed. She had no herbs but pictured herself preparing them, the way the tea warmed her belly and brought light beneath her lids. Then she blew on the flute. The power spread through her chest, fired her blood until her skin tingled, and she could picture it running out of her mouth, into the whistle and across the frigid air to reach the beast.

This Calling was different, less controlled, and Kallaka fought with all her strength to keep it tamed. To keep it a part of her, not to be let loose across the land, a wild thing with no purpose. The melody from the flute rose and fell, a haunting tune that no human could compose. The song of the beast.

Kallaka opened her eyes, saw the beast quiver, try to fight the Calling. It turned toward her, ignoring the two men that still fought, who took advantage of its inattention to rain fresh blows against massive legs. It fixed her with a murderous glare, and slowly walked across the distance, leaving a trail of blood behind it. It stopped before a fissure.

The girl blew the whistle louder. *I have your spirit in my little flute,* the song seemed to say. *Come to me.*

The beast took another step forward, its talons over the edge of the crack. *Come to me,* demanded the tune. The monster lifted its leg, and the damaged ice gave beneath its weight, splintering into thousands of shards. A geyser of water erupted, and it sank into the sea.

But so slowly, thought Kallaka. As darkness overwhelmed her, all she could envision were the eyes of the beast. Red, glowing orbs that flashed with betrayal as they disappeared into the sea.

Kallaka sat on a small chunk of ice at the edge of the water, and whittled at the piece of wood in her hand. Her brows drew together in concentration as she carved the horn of the Narwhal, careful not to break the thin shaft. But try as she might she couldn't stop the shaking in her fingers, and for the third time the wood broke. With a cry of frustration she threw the piece into the sea, and reached for another hollowed branch from her supply.

"May I?" asked an unfamiliar voice, and she looked up into the startling green eyes of the Traveler. She remembered them glittering with anger, but now they glowed with a soft intensity. Kallaka shrugged her shoulders and handed him her knife. He studied it for a moment and with a flash of white teeth gave it back to her, pulling his own knife from his belt. Her brows rose in surprise as he attacked the wood with apparent skill.

"You're a shape-maker?" asked the girl.

"As much as any man who's sat through a long blizzard."

Kallaka studied him as he worked. Large hands, but slender fingers. His clothes were made of the finest fur, the leather tanned to supple softness. That golden hair, a color that her people had never before seen the likes of, was pulled back with a thong. A small scar ran along the top of his square jaw and she wondered where he'd gotten it. For the first time she felt curious about this stranger. He'd arrived the day before the beast hunt, and since then she'd had little time for other than Alloc.

"Alloc, is he still asleep?" He'd lain unconscious since the hunt, and Kallaka feared he might never wake.

The man scowled and nicked his finger. "There's been no change since you left, Shaman."

Kallaka's black eyebrows rose in surprise. It was the first time she'd ever been addressed by that title. She hadn't completed the ceremony that would give her that right.

"You've come from far away, Traveler?"

The man grunted. "My name is Manuk."

"Why do you travel, Manuk? Are you running away from something?"

He turned and met her eyes, and the girl couldn't pull her own away. "You're the first person who's ever asked me that," he said. "You might say I'm running to something, or rather someone. I just don't know who it is yet."

Kallaka sat in puzzled silence, waiting for more.

"I was told," he continued, "to seek a Shaman. That only one of great power could answer my question. I've already asked Binuu, and his answer was the same as hundreds of others."

Kallaka tried to smother the feeling rising within her. The feeling of total confidence that her power

305

instilled, and the challenge this man offered to it. "And what is your question?"

Manuk looked away, out to the sea dotted with white icebergs on which walrus rested to soak up the distant sun. "I've met many Shaman, and none had the power to compare with yours, apprentice or no." He turned and met her eyes again. "Power that great can be a dangerous thing."

That feeling of confidence died within Kallaka, instead to be replaced by the feelings of her youth. Fear of what lay coiled within her, the loneliness her difference created. Her face reflected her emotions and Manuk flashed white teeth again, seemingly satisfied by what he saw.

"Kallaka," he whispered. "Who is my Kindred Spirit?"

She blinked, startled by the question. This man traveled to find his Kindred Spirit? This was a question no Shaman could answer! Either you were lucky enough to find one, or you waited for the next lifetime. You didn't spend your present life searching for what might never be found. What kind of man was this that his soul cried out so desperately for another?

Kallaka flicked back her hair. *I'm so lucky,* she thought, *to have found Alloc.* Her determination to help her beloved hardened into resolve. She reached for the carving in Manuk's hand and jumped to her feet.

"Perhaps I can help you find it after I deal with my own problems." She'd never admit that she hadn't an answer.

Kallaka looked at the flute in her palm and gasped. He'd finished it already, and it was so . . . real! Down to the spirals of the Narwhal's horn. Her carvings were crude imitations of the animals she Called, nothing like this sculpture she now held. He'd been overly modest in his appraisal of his skill. Kallaka wondered at how much stronger her Callings could be with whistles like this. Confidence flared inside her.

Without hesitation she brought the flute to her lips. She followed the same routine as she had with the beast. There need be no more calling ceremonies for her! With reckless abandon she summoned her power, letting it uncoil, taming it when necessary. The whistle began to play a watery tune that floated across the surface of the sea. And the great Narwhal came to her call. From beneath the depths he came, not a youngling, but a powerful male, the king of its domain.

Kallaka's song faltered for a moment when the mammoth surfaced, spraying a jet of water high into the air, the mist sprinkling back to earth with the shimmer of small diamonds. He was so huge that he couldn't come close without threat of being beached, so the girl softened her song. It became a gentle pulling, a background to her mindvoice.

"Grandfather of the sea, I seek your advice."

An old, warbling voice—yet not of human timber—answered her. "It's been many seasons since I've spoken to one of your kind." Hesitant. Noncommittal.

"There's one in my village who sleeps, whose spirit wanders and won't return. How do I get him back?"

Again the hesitation. Kallaka could feel her mind drifting, as though it floated on a warm sea.

"He's already in the Spirit World; his body only waits for death."

"No," screamed Kallaka. She could feel Manuk's hand grip her shoulder. "Can I go there, bring him back?"

Suddenly she felt lost, her mind adrift in a maze of

lights. *Remember this,* she thought. *This is the path to the Spirit World.* A crystal gate of ice stood before her, carved with intricate detail. Two beasts guarded the opening, protecting the souls within, and there seemed no way for her to get past them. "Not alone," whispered the Narwhal, "but with the help of another . . . one who carries a Spirit Sword."

Blackness enfolded her like a shroud, then she saw with different eyes. Silver fish swam before her vision, light flickered in filtered rays. Kallaka's identity slipped away. She fought to free her mind of the Narwhal, and she felt herself losing the battle.

"Shaman, come back! Kallaka, feel the sword in your hand."

Who troubled her? She drifted in a sea of calm, gentle currents nudging her this way and that.

Then a tugging at her soul, a Calling that wasn't of her own making. A face wavered before her, amber eyes glowed. No, they were green, the green of a blade of grass poking through the snow.

"Manuk?" The girl clutched at the sword in her hands, a Spirit Sword that had power in this world and beyond. She looked up into the handsome face of the Traveler. "I almost didn't make it back."

She trembled with fear, welcoming his arms around her. Only the warmth of his body assured her that she'd come home.

The villagers crowded into the Shaman's lodge, spread their furs around the fire, and looked with awe at the two mortals who dared to travel the Spirit World. Kallaka wiped sweat from her forehead and glanced at the still form of Alloc. The fear that threatened to overwhelm her subsided, and she straightened her spine.

Anything, she thought. *My life, the life of this man, even of all these people would I sacrifice for you.*

She bent over the fire, scooped the infusion of herbs into the ceremonial cup, and turned toward the man who'd agreed to make this journey with her. Kallaka brought the tea over to Manuk, and grinned when his mouth twisted at the bitter taste. She'd long since gotten used to it.

"You could still change your mind," she whispered.

He grinned, absently stroking the hair of the boy in his lap. "I want to make sure you come back, Kallaka. I still need the answer to my question."

The girl nodded and sat at his side, waiting for the mild drug to take effect. The boy Manuk held peeked around his shoulder, huge eyes in a small face blinked at her malevolently. She knew the boy, "Ommakia," the child who had no lodge. When his parents died none would claim him, so he begged at any fire, crawled into anyone's furs. He was supposed to be the entire village's responsibility.

When had he gotten so skinny? wondered Kallaka. *And why did he look at her with anger? Because she risked the life of this stranger?* She flicked her hair over her shoulder. She must remember to invite the Ommakia to her fire.

"The child should leave," said Kallaka. "If we disturb any evil spirits he might swallow one."

Manuk reluctantly pushed the boy away, and the child threw Kallaka a look that could burn.

"You have claimed him," mused the girl. "I wonder why."

The drug had already taken effect on Manuk, and he answered when he normally wouldn't have. "I was Ommakia. Still am."

"But Binuu said that the sword was a gift from your father, a great Shaman. Surely you wouldn't have gone unclaimed when he died."

"Mother, sister, father." Manuk slurred his words. "Gone to the Spirit World when I was five summers. I inherited no power, no great Gift but the sword. I was worth nothing to no one."

So that's why you travel, thought Kallaka. *To be a part of someone again.* She felt a familiar stirring in her heart. Not pity, but something akin to what she felt for Alloc. It disturbed her, and she felt relieved when the Shaman began his drumming. The beat began slowly, then increased in rhythm until the small room throbbed with its vibrations. Binuu pounded the whaleskin with a padded horn, threatening to crack the bone supports.

Kallaka's body swayed with the beat, and she felt Manuk move with her.

She began the mental disciplines, reached out to the Traveler and included him in the weaving. She went slowly, carefully, remembering the terror of being lost in the Narwhal's mind. She'd learned, the hard way, the purpose of these ceremonies. She wanted to return from this journey! The fire popped and sent a spray of sparks into the air. They danced above the flames, tiny pinpoints of light that swirled and formed—a path. The path to the Spirit World.

She parted silver mist. The gate of ice stood before her, the beasts still guarding it. They watched her with their red eyes, and when she took a step forward, they growled in unison. *Manuk,* thought Kallaka, *where is he?*

Suddenly he appeared, and the girl gasped. His body seemed almost transparent, only the sword at his side looked solid. Kallaka glanced down and stifled a cry of fear. They had the bodies of ghosts in this world.

The Traveler glanced at her briefly, then strode to the gate, waving his sword before him in a warding-off gesture. The beasts growled and charged, the puffy snow swirling around their legs. Manuk ducked between the two and spun, laughing at their surprise. "Now, Shaman!" he cried.

Kallaka ran, her fear only controlled by the thought of Manuk's laughter. He laughed. In the Spirit World, at not one, but two monsters. He was either incredibly brave, or terribly mad. Did he think that because their bodies were insubstantial, they couldn't be hurt here? She spun and screamed a warning. "They can steal your soul, Manuk!"

One of the beasts lunged, and Manuk swung at its leg, ducking low as the other one swiped extended talons at his golden head. He stabbed upward and pierced the monster's palm, let it scream while he turned again toward the other. Kallaka wondered how long he could keep up the fight, even with the power of the Spirit Sword. He could use her help.

She hesitated only a moment before turning away. Yes, she'd even sacrifice this brave man for her cowardly one. For if she was to succeed, she must hurry; the longer she stayed in the Spirit World, the more difficult it'd be to return to her own. Her soul wouldn't want to leave.

White, everywhere the whiteness. Kallaka ran through snow that was not-snow, stopped beneath a translucent glacier, then began to climb. The ice felt warm beneath her fingers. It pulsed as if blood flowed through crystalline veins. She grabbed at any cracks in the surface, trying not to sob with the effort of pulling herself up again. Ghost blood flowed from ghost fingers, leaving patches of sparkling red behind her. And she climbed on.

Lights again. Soft, swirling vapors of lavender. Kallaka stood at the top of the world, and gasped at the sight before her. Beneath the blanket of color hovered souls beyond counting, a sea of them floated before her. Alloc, Alloc. How to find his among all these others?

She studied the closest to her. They ranged from black to white with gray between. Fine threads were wrapped around many of them, some so covered that she could hardly see the soul beneath. Kallaka reached out, touched the thread of a black soul, and pulled back her hand as if burnt. Lifethreads. She'd instantly read one of the lives of that soul, and it was an evil, sad life. She wiped her hand on her tunic, trying to clean off the taint.

Beneath the threads she noticed that the souls formed different shapes, like pieces of broken pottery. Some were even joined, blending so that she could barely see the cracks. Made whole by joining with another. Could she see her own soul in this world? With shaking hands she reached into her chest and tried to remove it. She couldn't help but wonder at what color it'd be.

Kallaka felt a ripping sensation and cried out at the pain. What she held in her hands made her shiver. The girl never wanted to repeat this experience again. Quickly she looked down, before she lost the courage, and stared at the gray mass. Gray . . . neutral. Neither good nor evil.

She heard a soft gasp, and knew that Manuk had

somehow joined her. He always continued to astonish her.

And gave her an idea. Kallaka ignored him and studied her soul. It was shaped in a half-circle, as if a large part were missing, with an irregular notch at the break. Unlike those others her lifethread wasn't wrapped around it, instead the end disappeared into her body. She resisted touching the other threads, not sure if she had the time to read her past lives, not sure if she even wanted to. Hoping she might be right, Kallaka threw her soul as hard as she could into the whirling mass of them.

Alloc, she whispered. He was her Kindred Spirit; surely her soul would find his. She felt a gentle tugging at her lifethread, yet it continued to stretch itself out, until she could no longer see her soul. She turned away from the sight, wanting only to reel it back, afraid to lose it.

Manuk pawed at his own chest, and Kallaka's eyes widened when he drew his soul forth. Almost white, it shone like a beacon. Kallaka panted. The shape of it. How can that be?

Her lifethread trembled and slowed, began to melt back into her body. Her soul returned to her with reckless speed. It'd found what it sought and now wanted to be home. Kallaka screamed as it neared her, for she saw that Alloc's soul was with it. They fit perfectly together, except for the small notched piece, and they were both black as the darkest night.

"No!" Kallaka ripped them apart, and hers thankfully returned to its former gray color. She held on to the lifethread of Alloc's soul, still dangling, not completely wrapped around. She could still return it, but apart from her own. Yet the souls kept trying to fuse together, she had to fight to keep them apart. Until . . .

Manuk let go of his soul, and it flew to hers, battling Alloc's out of the way. They joined completely, even the notch at the end was filled. Kallaka's soul slowly turned an off-white, Manuk's glowed brilliant white, as if they needed each other to be the best that they could be.

"So, Shaman," sobbed Manuk. "You have answered my question at last."

"Leaving?" asked Kallaka. "What do you mean Manuk's leaving?"

The old man shook his head. "Why are things so obvious to me, yet no one else can see them?" The Shaman stood, bones snapping, and faced the girl across the lodge fire. "I know what happened in the Spirit World between you and Manuk, yet you've been avoiding each other for days. And now that Alloc's recovered, he's finally agreed to set aside his wife and bond with you. Yet you make no decision. How long did you expect him to wait?"

Kallaka cringed at the memory of To'nua's screams, the look on Alloc's face as he brushed by the woman to stand at Kallaka's side. This was what she'd wanted, wasn't it? Then why were so many people hurting?

"I haven't given Alloc my answer yet." Kallaka sullenly poked at a fur with her booted foot.

"Then you'd better make up your mind." Binuu slammed his staff against the floor, the scarlet feathers at the tip seemed to tremble with fear. "You've been given the gift of seeing another person's soul; now have the wisdom to use that knowledge."

"Wisdom has nothing to do with the heart, with the

shattering of one's dreams." Kallaka choked back a sob. "If Alloc's soul is so black, why does To'nua continue to love him? She also knows him for what he is. Besides, it's hard to let go of something I've wanted for so long."

Binuu grunted. "If To'nua chooses to stay with Alloc, who's to say that her soul may not whiten his? Some people can bring out the best in you, some the worst. The dreams of a child don't take that into consideration."

The Shaman turned his back on the girl. "Grow up, Kallaka."

The silky-haired camel danced with energy, its splayed hooves sending up puffs of snow. Kallaka squinted against the glare of the sun, and urged her mount forward. Manuk had turned around, looked back toward the village of frozen huts. Surely he'd seen her this time!

But he turned around again, the boy held tightly in his arms. As if that's all he had left to him. With an anger born of fear Kallaka bent over the neck of the camel and plunged recklessly ahead. Snowflakes stuck to her lashes and she blinked them away. "You're just going to leave me?" she screamed.

Manuk pulled his mount to a stop but didn't turn around.

"Kallaka?"

"Yes?" The wind swished in circles around her.

"What decided you?"

Kallaka rode around to face him. He watched her eyes with an intensity that made her squirm. Why *had* she decided to go with Manuk? Surely To'nua looked happy when she'd left, she knew Alloc would return to her with Kallaka gone. To'nua knew him for what he was, yet she wanted to stay with him.

She remembered how she'd fought to separate her and Alloc's soul in the Spirit World. And how after she'd returned they were still drawn to each other. So it wasn't the color that had decided her.

"Do you remember the notch in my soul? The small one at the edge of the break?"

"Yes."

She shrugged. "Alloc's soul didn't fill it."

Manuk sucked in his breath. "You decided by so little?"

Kallaka flicked her hair over her shoulder, and laid her hand against the arm that gripped the boy so tightly. "No. By so much."

CROW FEATHERS

by Lawrence Schimel

Lawrence Schimel, when I received an update of his biography, displayed one sign of being a true writer; his signature is almost as bad as that of some big-name professionals I will not name to protect the guilty.

My own signature is almost neurotically legible; maybe it's vanity, but if people are polite enough to ask for my autograph, why give them one where they can't tell whether it's me or my next door neighbor.

Lawrence is a writer of short stories. Lawrence, too, is one of my prized young writers. As he says, he has sold short stories nearly everywhere to more than eighty anthologies, mostly, and they count up fast when you don't write novels. His work has been translated into Dutch, Finnish, German, Japanese, Italian, Mandarin, and Polish. Recently he's been translating (another weird job) comic books into English from Spanish. He's living in Manhattan and writing full time now, except when he gets too stir-crazy from sitting in front of a computer, at which point he goes back to his day job, working part-time in a children's bookstore.

The fresh air almost made Ysabelle sneeze as she carried the heavy chamber pot out into the woods behind the inn. Spring was exploding all around her, flowers and buds and birdsong, and she was cooped up inside, dusting and working. It was her eleventh birthday, and she couldn't help thinking about how things would be different if her parents hadn't been killed in a raid last summer. The hostler and his wife had taken her in, it was true, and an extra mouth to feed, especially just before winter, was no light burden to shoulder, but they certainly worked her hard enough. She did far more work than either of their natural daughters, that was certain, and always the most unpleasant tasks. Ysabelle remembered when her parents were still alive: at this time of year they would go out into the woods and have picnics, picking herbs and berries and wild mushrooms . . .

"Ysabelle, you lazy wench, stop daydreaming and get back to work!"

Ysabelle started forward. She wondered what would happen if she just kept walking into the forest and never returned. A crow floated lazily to her left, and she stared enviously after it, longing for wings of her own that would carry her away from her unhappiness.

She dumped the smelly contents of her load under a bush and headed back to the inn. At the edge of the forest she turned around for one last look at the green, burgeoning life. It seemed alive with energy and vibrancy, whereas the inn she returned to seemed as dark and welcoming as a dank cave. She looked up for one last longing glimpse at the crow, and as she watched, it flew toward her. The bird flew in a tight circle above her head, once, twice, and on the third circuit dropped a feather down to her. Ysabelle let the pot fall to the ground as she reached to catch the ebon plume before it touched the ground. She smiled, and looked up at the bird, who flew off into the woods. She tucked the feather into her skirt, and hurried inside before Galen yelled at her again.

Ysabelle tied a string around the feather and wore it about her neck. It was a constant reminder for her of what life might be like elsewhere, and whenever she felt herself getting angry or frustrated she'd let her mind take flight, imagining herself flying over whatever had caused her disturbance, until she had calmed down.

Soon she began getting more feathers. Whenever she saw a crow, it would fly overhead, circle three times, and drop a feather to her. Ysabelle saved them all, although only that first feather was kept around her neck. The others she stored in a small bag, which she kept hidden from her foster family, who would have thrown out the feathers if they found them, not to mention teasing her mercilessly, if not beating her outright with the switch. It took very little to make them use the willow switch on her. Her bed was in a corner of the attic, and she stashed the bag of feathers outside her window, under the eaves, crawling out there each night to add the new feathers. Soon, Ysabelle had so many she began stringing them together, ten to a strand, to keep count.

One afternoon, Ysabelle crawled out onto the roof to add a new handful of feathers to her cache. She normally did this only under cover of darkness, but she had been gifted with so many feathers when she emptied the chamber pots that morning that she was afraid they would be discovered. The innkeeper's daughters made a point of regularly inspecting her sleeping area, and immediately reported any faults or unusual objects to their parents, which invariably meant the willow switch was brought out.

Ysabelle was so afraid of being discovered up on the roof, however, that she moved too quickly as she scampered back toward the open window, slipped, and fell off the roof.

Everything happened so quickly she hardly felt any fear of landing. Rather, she knew she was falling, and was more concerned that she would be in great trouble when she landed. She would make a terrible noise, she knew, and the whole family would be alerted and would come find her and she would be punished. The feather around her neck came out from under her shirt, and instead of plummeting, Ysabelle glided to the ground, landing on her feet a considerable distance from the inn. She glanced back at the building to make sure that no one had seen her brief flight. No one had.

She knew she must return quickly, before her absence was noticed, but it felt so wonderful to be out of the inn, to be outdoors, free. The call of a crow caught her wandering mind, and Ysabelle watched three of the large black birds flying in her direction. Ysabelle walked toward them, almost instinctively, yearning to be among them. They landed on a fallen tree, and as Ysabelle drew near she thought she recognized the middle crow as that first crow who had dropped the feather she wore about her neck. The one, she noticed now, with human eyes.

"Corax," she thought, though she had never before heard the word. She assumed it was the crow's name.

Girl and crows stared at each other for a long time, gazes locked, until at last Ysabelle looked away. Once the contact was broken, the three crows spread their wings. Ysabelle silently thanked Corax as they lifted into the air and flew back into the forest. She watched them until they disappeared over the horizon, then tucked the feather back under her dress and hurried back to the inn.

Ysabelle began to weave the strands of feathers together at night, working silently by the scant moonlight that came through her window while everyone else was asleep, and soon she had formed a cloak from the feathers.

As she grew older and came into her monthly courses, as her breasts began to develop and swell and hair to grow between her legs, Galen began looking for any excuse to tell her to lift her skirts and bend over to be switched. He never touched her, at least not often, when his hand "accidentally" hit her instead of the switch, but as the blow was much less painful than the willow she didn't mind. But Ysabelle knew she was switched often simply because Galen enjoyed looking at her naked and exposed. She felt unclean after every such incident, and thought often about running away; but where could she go? A young girl, alone, without family or means, she would be raped or worse if she left; at least here she was fed and clothed, if also overworked and beaten. It could be so much worse . . . .

It could be so much better, too, Ysabelle told herself.

One afternoon, after a particularly severe beating by Galen, she took the cloak of feathers she kept hidden under the eaves and walked out into the woods. She walked away from the inn, and as she walked, crows began to follow overhead, first one, then two, four, seven. By the time she could no longer see the inn at all, if she had looked back over her shoulder, which she did not, there were a cloud of nearly thirty crows circling over her head.

They followed her through the forest until the woods gave way to a cliff. Ysabelle sat on some rocks near the edge, overlooking the land below, green fields and a pool to her right, fed by a thin waterfall. The birds settled around her, and waited, uncommonly silent. At last, Ysabelle stood and untied the bundle. She flung the cloak around her shoulders and pulled the feather out from under her shirt.

She turned to face the birds. Again her gaze locked with a crow's human eyes. She heard the echo of a voice sounding within her head like her own thoughts, the same voice that had whispered "Corax" when she fell off the roof.

"Come," the voice said softly, moving like a gentle breeze across her mind. "Come with us. Fly with us."

"Teach me how," Ysabelle begged aloud, unaware how to answer with her mind.

"You are too heavy," a second voice echoed within her head.

Slowly, she stripped off all her clothes and left them folded atop the blanket. Naked, her wounds exposed to the light for any and all to see, she turned back to the crows, and thought, with as much strength as she could muster, "I am ready now."

"You are too heavy," the second voice repeated.

"Let yourself go," another crow said, hopping into the air to demonstrate.

Ysabelle jumped into the air in imitation of the crow, but fell back to the earth as she always had. "It's not working," she said out loud, forgetting in her frustration that they could hear her thoughts. Ysabelle met Corax's gaze, begging for help.

"Relax," said the crow's voice, echoing softly.

"Let your thoughts go."

"Let them drift among the clouds."

"Be free."

With a tiny corner of her mind, Ysabelle realized she was flying now, in the shape of a crow. She did not let herself worry about how she was flying, or why. She was too busy feeling the wind filling her wings and the sun on her back, soaring through the clouds and racing with the other crows.

When she had exhausted her first thrill of flight, the crows brought her back to the cliff where her clothes were. Ysabelle's human form returned to her as her thoughts ceased to soar and she remembered Galen and his family and the inn. The edges of the cloak swirled around her as she landed.

"You know how to fly now," Corax's voice echoed softly from within Ysabelle's mind as the flock dispersed.

She stared into the bird's human eyes and knew that he, too, had been human once, but had forever given up the form. Ysabelle considered, but she was not yet ready. She turned away from Corax and put on her human clothes, folding the cloak of feathers carefully. She would use it again, of that there was no doubt, but she was not yet free. She began walking back to the inn, of her own choice now, for there were matters left unsettled, and a leavetaking to be made properly, if not easily. Without that, she would never be free, and Ysabelle intended to be free. There was so much she had left to live, and she was determined now to leave this ill-suited nest at last, and begin to soar as high as her strength would take her.

JEWEL-BRIGHT

by Stephanie D. Shaver

Stephanie Shaver lives in our house; my own children are all gone and grown, and it's really nice to hear another teenager singing around the house, with a very sweet, true, untrained soprano. My own daughter is a highly talented soprano of operatic quality but seems to have chosen folk music; I doubt if I could tolerate a really untuneful or tone deaf singer.

Stephanie remains one of the youngest writers I have ever published, although by the time this story is in print she will probably be twenty-one. She is engaged to a nice young Italian man whom she tells me is also her fellow collaborator and idea-exchange person (or, at least, that's what her biography says).

She is now working on revising her book, *Shadowstrike* ("I could have sworn it was done—but I guess not!" she says.), which is set in the same universe as all her stories that have appeared in *Sword and Sorceress.* When she's not working for an online games company, she goes to school and works up in the office of my magazine. I'm not sure how she fits writing into that schedule, but judging from "Jewel-Bright," she manages somehow.

Of "Jewel-Bright" itself, she says the story evolved

from listening to too much Meg Davis, who she says
had a line in one of her songs that somehow touched
her in a way that she is certain Davis did not intend,
but that evolved into this story anyway.

*S*he had told him, when they first met, that she did
not want empty promises, could not live with them.
And he, who had promised her treasures untold, said
that he never took such things lightly, and would not
betray her.

*And this had brought her joy, which was more price-
less to him than anything else on heaven or earth.*

And so, once more, the cold touch of ice on the
cheek, and the slate of blue-gray sky above.

Once more, the endless expanse of winter—white as
a Queen's skin, cold as her heart—broken only by the
cracked Edge-of-Sword Mountains, which were gray
as slate, as stormy eyes.

Once more.

Once again.

Winter had the Northern Region of Eavris in a
clenched fist of chill; had kept it so for longer than
anyone could remember, though the reason was known
to all. Jewel-Bright. The elders whispered its name to
the children at night.

Many men and women had braved the diamond-
carved feathers of falling snow for the Jewel-Bright,
yet none had lived to tell of its fey beauty. The elders
whispered another name to the children at night:

Rei'son. The dragon. The ice-child and sole holder of the Jewel-Bright.

Rei'son, whose name meant the Bringer of Winter.

Time passed, and no heroes came to slay the dragon. Too much time passed, and the villagers began to worry that Rei'son would come down from the Slopes and eat them all. When no heroes came to feed the dragon, there was only one choice—a choice that had not been made in nearly fifty years. Someone of the village had to be chosen to feed it instead.

Wreyn—betrothed of Chauce, daughter of Eiva and Bjors, and barely fifteen—was picked out of all the others. She wept the night the elders came, grim and sober in their gray wool and white fur, lanterns in hand. They whispered her fate to her and then melted back into the blizzard outside, returning to their warm homes once again. Curled amidst her blankets, she wept, thus disobeying the first rule of the village as her tears froze on her cheeks. To her eyes, the future seemed bleak, hopeless.

And then dawn—or what one called dawn in the Northern Region—a pale lighting of the sky.

And then hope.

For a hero had come once more.

He looked back only once all throughout the trek north, and saw his own footprints set in a straight trail across the tundra. Empty tracks in the waste seemed to remind him of stars in the sky, said to be lights for the gods. He remembered, once, before he came to this gray, overcast land, gazing up at the pale lanterns burning through the velvet black, and thinking, *No wonder the gods are so blind.*

He was not very tall, and not very short, and some would have called him plain. Black hair, black beard, dark-tanned chapped skin, and gray eyes that burned with a coldness that made the North Region seem temperate. From where she stood in the doorway of her home she saw him enter, easily picked out amongst the blond, fur-swathed denizens of the village.

Sunlight glanced off the hilt of the sword that was strapped to his back as Wreyn stepped out of her home to walk toward the stranger. She stopped in front of him, taking in the sight of his coat and breeches—trimmed with a brown fur she had never seen before—and then waited.

His eyes focused on her, his gaze pinning itself on her eyes. Behind her, she could just hear the village priest beginning the daily prayers; a plea for an end to winter, for an end to the cold. Wreyn sometimes wondered if the villagers could even return to "the way things had been" now that "the way things were" had become routine.

But the man was speaking, and pulling her thoughts back to him, and away from the abstract.

"Hello," he said. "Is there a place I might get warm, and perhaps sleep?"

She nodded. "This way, sir."

The Ring of Stone Inn was the only thing in the way of accommodation that the village had to offer. It was fairly warm, built of strong stuff, and pleasant to stay in. Wreyn led him inside, and then went to fetch Siil, the owner.

Siil took care of the necessaries—money, what the man wanted to eat, whether he wanted anything special (like a bath, although Wreyn shuddered to think of it)—and then bustled off.

Wreyn lingered nearby, watching as the man stripped down to his firstcoat and warm underclothing, his pack now set against the table. She waited until Siil had brought food and drink, and then spoke.

"Are you ... have you come to ... ?"

He looked up at her, and she flinched under those eyes, suddenly feeling shallow. In her mind, she truly wished that he would die in her stead. But in her heart, she knew that wish to be wrong.

"Yes," he replied, and went back to his soup.

She swallowed. "You have come to slay Rei'son?"

He looked up again. "No. I have come for the Jewel-Bright. Rei'son will only die if it gets in my way."

She swallowed. "I see." Guilt twisted inside her. "What ... is your name?"

He took a bite of brown bread; a precious commodity. Wreyn wondered how much he'd paid for it, for Siil certainly did not give out his bread lightly. "Gaven. Yours?"

"Wreyn."

He nodded. "Will you show me where it is?"

Wreyn blinked at him. "The Jewel-Bright?"

He nodded again.

She swallowed, then nodded, "I can, but only so far."

He smiled with heartening bleakness. "I understand." He sipped his drink, from which steam was still curling. "Tomorrow, then?"

"I ... yes."

The smile faded, and he went back to his food. Wreyn departed, leaving him to his peace. He deserved that much.

He was a dead man, anyway.

The cup was rapidly getting cold in his hands. He looked up for a moment and sighed, trying to remember the last time he had been warm.

This land is cursed, Gaven thought. *This is not a normal chill. If the Archivist was correct, this place has been like this for over one hundred years. . . .*

Perhaps, if Rei'son gets in my way while getting the jewel, and, perhaps, if I kill the creature, I shall become a hero to these people . . . the death of the dragon would mean the death of the chill. I'm sure they would appreciate it.

He glanced out one frost-laced window and smiled slightly to himself. A hero. He reached for some sort of excitement, some sort of anticipation at the thought of that name added to his, but nothing came. Not that he was surprised. He hadn't felt anything in a long time.

And it won't change now.

Gaven went back to savoring the last of his drink's warmth.

Wreyn was torn by what she felt.

On the one hand, she would live.

On the other, another would die.

What right did she have to allow this?

He has chosen, she thought. *His choice. He came here of his own will, not another's.* She shivered. *His choice. Not your fault. You will live, he will die, and that is the Way of things. Let it go.*

It was so easy to say that, to repeat it in her mind. And yet.

And yet . . .

By midafternoon, everybody in the village knew

about the stranger, and why he had come. With this knowledge, by ones and twos, the quiet congratulations trickled toward her, the knowing glances and smiles. She felt, oddly, the way she had the first time she began to bleed, when she had been given smiles and winks by the women. It was as if she had gone through some strange Rite of Passage. Even Chauce once more found interest in her, melting back into her life with a smile.

A hero's feast was scraped together for the man Gaven. There was a fire, a goat slaughtered, and, on the whole, general joy and a great deal of relief. All done before dusk, of course. Nighttime was too cold for such celebrating.

It was while she was sitting in a corner of the Ring of Stone, watching people get drunk, that Chauce found her. Off to the side and secluded, she thought nobody could have detected her presence. And yet there he was. Drunk as a snow-cat on 'nip, his face rosy.

"Hello, Wreyn," he said, his words slurred, a drinking horn in his hand. "Why aren't you dancing?"

She shrugged. "Not feeling up to it," she replied, her knees up against her chest, her eyes on the wall behind Chauce.

He frowned, and wobbled himself into a kneeling position. Wreyn winced at the scent of his breath, and told herself that, when she became his wife, she would make sure that likker was not part of their stores.

"Is it That Time of Month?" he asked in a low, conspirator's voice, a silly grin on his face.

She smiled gently. "No, Chauce, I just want to be alone."

"Aw, c'mon," he said, reaching out to paw at her heavy woolen surcoat. "If you won't dance, maybe you and I can seal our vows tonight the old way."

She blanched. The "old way" was simply to have sex with the person you chose, thus sealing the agreement. That Chauce even proposed such a thing made her face burn.

"Chauce, you're drunk. Please, just leave me alone."

"Wreyn, you're being a prude," he complained, reaching toward the buttons. "C'mon, *everyone* does it—"

"No," she said more firmly, and began to push him away, realizing, on a rising wave of panic, that she was in a corner, secluded, and that Chauce was a *very* heavy, determined, and *strong* person.

"Wreeeeyn," he hissed.

"Sir."

Chauce whirled and stood so quickly he sloshed his horn. He shifted his attention to Gaven, who had come up behind them without Wreyn hearing or seeing a thing.

"Yeah?" Chauce said, eyeing Gaven.

"She told you to leave her alone. Perhaps you should listen."

Chauce opened his mouth to speak—

Wreyn felt a tingling over her skin, and, somewhere, the distant sound of bells. . . .

—closed his mouth, blinked once, and walked away.

Gaven looked down at her, his face expressionless.

"You should button yourself up before you leave," he said.

Wreyn blushed, aware that Chauce had managed to fumble a few of her coat's fastenings undone in the time he had been leaning over her. She quickly amended this, then looked up to thank Gaven.

But he was gone.

Gaven did not like using magic.

But he had been watching her, for she was the only thing he had yet met in this entire village that was worth watching or talking to. And, because he had been watching her, he had seen the sheep-in-wolf's-clothing approach her, and try to force himself upon her. Everyone else was either drunk or not paying attention. And she, despite determination, was small, and the one who had her cornered was not.

So he had fixed the situation, convincing the drunken sot to go away with a whispered spell and a wisp of magic.

And he had seen . . . recognition? in her eyes when he used that magic.

She felt it.

He had left, then, not wanting to answer questions, not willing to. He went to his room, and lay in his bed, and stared at the ceiling, and thought of the gods that were dead.

And, eventually, he slept.

She woke in the morning, wakened by cold. Always cold. She wondered if the rumor of warm lands to the south were even true. She wondered what warmth—natural warmth, not that made by fire—felt like. . . .

She was excused from her chores today, having told her parents of her plans to lead Gaven up toward the Slopes where Rei'son lived. They were worried, of course, but not so worried as they had been. Her mother told her to gather some withergreen when she came down from the Slopes and Wreyn had agreed.

She pulled on her warmest clothing, ate breakfast, and then slogged through the snow to the Ring of Stone. Gaven was waiting within the common room, his hands curled around a mug of something.

She looked down at him, dressed now in a gray coat, and saw the gleam of metal at his throat and the signs of a helm on his head. The heavy backpack was gone. He wore the sword on his hip now, and a shield was slung over his shoulder.

"Are you ready?" she asked.

He looked up at her. "One more cup of kafa," he replied, and went back to gazing at the walls, occasionally taking a sip from his mug.

She nodded, and sat down by the warm fireside, gazing into the flames, watching them dance. Dance. Dancing. Chauce . . .

The distant sound of bells . . .

"Would you like a cup?" he asked.

His voice startled her, and she became aware of how deep it was. She looked up at him and nodded. "But I have no money."

"I will pay."

She nodded again, and he signaled to Siil, who went off to obey Gaven's command.

"I have left all my other items in my room," he said when Siil had left. "If I do not return by dawn tomorrow, they are yours."

She swallowed. "Why me?"

"Because I think you will need them, when you leave here."

She looked up at him, startled. "Leave? Why would I be leaving? I am engaged to Chauce—"

"Ah." He took another drink of kafa. "Then perhaps I was mistaken. My apologies."

She paused, and then said, "I heard something last night, when you told Chauce to go away . . . what was it?"

"Magic," he replied, as if he were telling the day of the week to someone.

"Magic?" she repeated, her voice scarcely a whisper.

"Yes," he said. "You have a touch of it on your soul, no doubt. You could probably get it trained."

"Would you?" she asked, suddenly feeling tingly all over.

"I cannot," he replied.

"Why?" she asked, furrowing her brow.

"Promise to keep. I don't have the time."

She sighed, frustrated. "Who can, then?"

Gaven shrugged, and glanced at her from the corner of his eye. "To the south there is an Academy. . . ."

Siil arrived, ending the conversation, and she took the mug of bitter *kafa* gratefully, taking a long drink. It was very hot, and warmed her well. It was also expensive, because it had to be imported. Just like the bread.

"So that drunken sot was . . . Chauce," Gaven said after a time.

Wreyn blushed. "That . . . yes, it was."

"I see," he replied, and nothing more. And yet . . .

"Ready?"

She blinked tears—*where had tears come from?*—back and nodded, standing. She set the kafa mug—still half-full—on the table and walked over to the door. Behind her, Gaven followed.

* * *

The weight of the sword was reassuring, the shield across his back the same. It had been too long since the last fight. *She* would be waiting.

He looked up toward the sky as they left the Ring of Stone behind, and thought he saw *her* face, patient, as it had been when *she* . . .

When he had promised . . .

And a promise, in his book, must be fulfilled, whether it meant death or not.

Rei'son's cave was on the Slopes, just past a small grove of trees. When the young ones reached a certain age, the elders always led the children up to the very edge of those trees to show them Rei'son's home, to warn them, and point out the litter of bones that lay about the cave. And to tell them the story of Jiffen, who went up to play in the cave one day, and never came back.

Wreyn now doubted that Jiffen—whom she, as a child and as an adult, had nevereverever wanted to be—had even existed.

It was nearly a six-mile walk, and there was no talking as they forced their way—she panting slightly, he noiseless—through the thick snow. This area was untrod, even by the wildlife, for a mile all around. Rei'son's presence chilled the place so thoroughly that even the animals were reluctant to come here and the wings of birds froze still if they tried to fly through.

All too quickly for Wreyn they arrived and passed through the trees that signaled the parameters of Rei'son's lair. She pointed to the cave in wide-eyed fascination.

"There," she breathed, her words carried on a plume of white.

He nodded, and drew his sword. It was brighter, more real than she had ever thought possible. She stared at it silently, and wondered if it was as cold as the dragon's claws. The shield was the same way, burnished black, emblazoned with the device of a silver bird.

Wreyn blinked as, around her, snowflakes began to fall lightly. Gaven shed his coat, and now stood dressed only in helm, chain armor, and woolen undergarments. He looked at her with his cold, old eyes, and bowed slightly.

She began to bow back—

And burst into tears.

"You're gong to die!" she cried out. *"Don't you realize that?"*

He stared at her, and she thought she actually saw something enter his eyes, something like sadness. Or maybe it was the blur of her tears, distorting her vision.

Gently, he reached up and removed one of her tears, which had frozen on her cheek, and stared at it in his hand.

"Don't cry for me," was all he said, putting the tear into a pouch hanging from his waist, and left her.

He wore thin doeskin gloves, for to hold his soul—or, rather, his sword—without them would have probably frozen his fingers to the unwrapped handle. The blade was approximately three feet long, made of shining metal, plain as he. Strong enough to brave dragon's fire; or dragon's chill, in Rei'son's case.

He entered the cave silently, his eyes on the curled

mass of dragon, its head on its paws, its eyes tightly shut. He studied the creature and then tried to think of how best to go about the task, for the goal was to kill, not be killed.

And then he noticed something odd. Something . . . wrong.

The dragon was not breathing, the great bellows of its lungs unmoving.

And it was then that Gaven realized that, in the lull of time where no hero and no villager had visited the cave that, Rei'son, the Dragon of Winter—

Had died in its sleep.

You're just going to let him die in there, aren't you? a voice hissed in Wreyn's mind.

I can't do anything—what can I do? I'd only be in the way . . . , she argued back at herself as she peeled tears off her cheeks.

Find *something to do! Don't stand here . . . he's going to die. . . .*

So will I if I go in there!

You're already dead. You live here, remember?

The thought was numbing, and for a moment she was shocked by it.

Suddenly, she felt as if her whole life were *wrong.* As if marrying Chauce, having children, staying in this village—winter or no—was *wrong.*

Suddenly, she longed more than anything to run south, and never return. Her heart leaped—for warmth, for something other than this damnable cold. She felt it, like a bone-ache chill inside her—

I have to help him! she thought, and ran toward the cave.

* * *

Gaven stopped for a moment, taking in the six or seven bodies lying at the foot of the niche that held the Jewel-Bright. Preserved by the chill, they each had a certain look of horrific pain on their faces.

Odd . . . he thought, and reached for the jewel.

"Gaven!"

He stopped and turned, looking at Wreyn, who stood at the entrance to the lair, her face streaked with lines of frost.

"Wreyn," he said softly, "you should have gone home. . . ."

"I can't go home," she replied, her voice scarce a whisper. "Not ever again. The dragon . . ."

"Is dead."

"You killed it?" she asked, staring at the massive body, for all the world looking as if it were peacefully asleep.

"No. It was dead when I came here."

Silently, she reached out and touched the dragan's nose, her eyes large and focused raptly on the body. "But the winter . . . if the dragon is dead . . ." She looked up, confusion plain on her face. "I don't understand. How can it still be so cold with the dragon dead?"

He stared at her for a moment, contemplating the question he had not taken the time to ask himself, and then looked at the Jewel-Bright, sitting quietly in its niche. Silent.

And deadly.

He laughed then, laughed at himself and his own insanity, laughed at the villagers who had taken for granted that the dragan was the cause, and not the dragon's hoard, and then laughed at the true hero of the village, who would probably never be known by that name.

"The Jewel-Bright," he said softly, after the laughter had died. "The Jewel-Bright is the Bringer of Winter! Not the dragon."

She stared at him, her mouth forming a silent "o," then said, "How do you know?"

"Come over here," he said, and she did. She gasped as she rounded the dragon's tail and saw what he stood amidst.

"They're all dead," she whispered.

"From touching the gem, no doubt," he replied grimly. "Now, how to take the gem without dying myself . . ."

"Gloves?" she asked.

He pointed to one of the bodies, a woman with hands wrapped in strips of leather and fur. "She had the same idea, too, and look where it got her."

Wreyn nodded and seemed to think, then suddenly smiled. "Oh, it's simple," she said.

"Is it now?" he asked, raising a brow at her.

She nodded and smiled at him, and when she told him how, he laughed again.

The girl, he thought as he smiled down at her, *definitely has a future.*

She looked up at the sky, and wondered why it was blue.

She had never seen the sky so blue before. Patches of gray still existed, but they were thinning, allowing the sun to silently, quietly show its face.

For the first time she could remember, Wreyn felt the full force of the sun.

Behind her she heard the crunch of snow, and upon

turning saw Gaven emerge from the cave. He looked up once, took in a deep breath, and nodded.

"Now that the Jewel-Bright is covered," he said, "its power is dimmed. Your people can return to normal."

She nodded. *If they know how,* she added mentally. "But can you?"

She looked up at him, into his eyes, which were still quietly empty of emotion.

She swallowed, and shook her head "no." "I don't know . . . I don't think so."

"Leaving?"

Wreyn stared off through the trees, toward the south. "Maybe," she replied.

"My offer still stands on what's in my room."

She turned quickly, and stared at him. "But how will you . . . ?"

He shrugged. "Don't worry about me. You'll find most of the things there useless. Now that the cold is gone, the land will return to normal, and the coats and woolens are not needed. But the money, the knives, the gear . . . I think you shall find that useful."

Wreyn gaped a bit, and swallowed. "Are you . . . sure?"

He smiled. "Quite." He restrapped his shield to his back and then bowed to her. "I must go now," he said.

"Wait—" she said. "Let me go with you."

"No." He shook his head. "The places I go," he said, "I go alone."

"Gaven . . ."

"Good-bye, Wreyn."

"Good-bye," she said, and he turned his back to her, treading through the snow toward the south.

"Good luck," he added over his shoulder.

"As well to you," she replied. "Thank you."

"Thank *you*, Wreyn. May the gods watch over you and yours."

She made no answer, only watching him. Eventually, he vanished through the trees.

She returned to the village in a mild daze, answering questions as she went. Most didn't believe her, or didn't want to, despite the melting snow, despite the clear sky.

She went to the room Siil showed her to, and found the items Gaven had left her. The coats she left behind, the rest she carried with her.

She laid a pile of withergreen on the table of her parent's home, and, with a tinge of regret, left them behind. There was guilt, and sadness, and a good deal of something else she didn't wish to name just then, but she had made her choice, and, good or bad, she had to live with it.

That would be the hardest part, living with it.

And yet . . .

Her heart and her mind knew it to be right.

Gaven returned to where he had started a few months later, the untouched Jewel-Bright in his pouch. Along the way he had acquired a new backpack, and had filled it with necessities. The coat he had traded for food as the weather grew warmer and the air felt gentler on his skin. He entered his own land no worse for wear than when he had left.

Wrapped in a square of Rei'son's skin, the Jewel-Bright had been a constant weight inside the pouch at his hip. He arrived with it at the place where his lady

was resting, drew back the curtain of Power that surrounded the grave and kept others from approaching,
and knelt before her headstone as one would kneel before the altar of a goddess. Here also lay the Sword of
Crane, the Jade Iris, the Heart of Dawn-Rise. Here
grew wildflowers and twining rose. Here was beauty
that kings would give up their sons for.

All hers.

He laid the Jewel-Bright—safe in the only wrap-
pings that could ever safely contain it—on her grave,
and stroked the marble marker, and, after all those
months, finally let the tears fall.

Tears . . .

He opened the pouch that had held the wrapped
Jewel-Bright, and stared at Wreyn's tear, still there, un-
melted. He withdrew it and waited for it to turn to liquid, but it did no such thing. It sat in his palm like a
tiny star, and when he realized it would not now and
never would melt, he placed it next to the Jewel-
Bright.

Then he took some time to stare sadly at the gathering of gifts that he had promised to her in life, and
only succeeded in finding after her death.

After a moment he took a deep breath, closed his
eyes, and stood. When he opened his eyes again, his
face was once more set to expressionlessness.

"There is a pendant in the Black Witch's kingdom,"
he said to the gravestone. "I must bring it to you,
m'lady."

Once more, he stared down at the mound of dirt and
grass. Once more, he shouldered the backpack, and the
weight of the years, and caressed the handle of his
sword.

Once more, he began the journey.
Once again.

In another place and at nighttime, standing on a balcony and dressed in cool cotton, a young mage's apprentice stared up at stars that glittered like jewels, or frozen tears. She smiled to herself and prayed that the gods light their lanterns a bit brighter for one man's well-being. And then she opened her books of magery and returned to what she had been studying, her place marked by a scrap of ice-colored dragonskin.

THE COMFORTER
by Jean Marie Egger

Well, once again we come to the end of another *Sword and Sorceress*. I've always liked to end these things with something short and funny, and this year I have "The Comforter."

Jean Marie Egger says of herself, "I am a Franciscan Sister in Private Vows (which means I am no longer a formal member of a community) who follows the Franciscan Third Order Regular rule. In May 1996 I will complete a Masters in Pastoral Studies (with an emphasis on Feminist Theology). Born and raised in northeastern Minnesota, I moved to Kansas City, Missouri, in 1975 to go to college. For the past 7 years I've been working in Parish Ministry.

"I've known since high school that I had a gift for writing, but it's only been since my separation from traditional Community that I've had time and energy to devote to writing."

Jean Marie says that she would like to dedicate this story to Dusty, who was her pup and very dear friend and whose memory is now interwoven forever with these words.

"Gia! Gianna!! Lost in dreams?" a voice piped, calling Gia back to awareness. Gianna tore her gaze from the blond puppy sleeping in her lap and turned her eyes toward Karina. The sun caught their sparkling flecks of green, rousing in Karina the odd sensation of looking into a mirror, and confirming (as if she needed further confirmation) what she knew to be true. She turned her own green-flecked eyes to the road ahead and mused. Once or twice in a generation her people experienced the birth of a child with such eyes. Never three times . . . yet Gianna was the third. Never two from one family . . . yet Gia was her own younger sister. And now she was known to be a Comforter, like herself.

How could they have not known? How could Gia have lived to be a woman of near-legal age without her . . . their . . . family guessing? Of all people, why had she never noticed Gianna's eyes? The minute Gianna *Called*, Karina had intuitively known that there was a newly-wakened Comforter out there somewhere. But that wasn't until yesterday morning, barely at daybreak. The *Call* had been so wrenching that Karina had been jarred from sleep. She had spent all morning riding, changing horses in three villages, constantly refocusing her *Sight* to pinpoint the cause of the minor chaos that continued for hours after the *Call* sounded. The yelping and squalling and yapping that filled her head served as a beacon, leading her over the miles. Puppies. Lots of them! As far as Karina knew, no one had ever *Called* for puppies! Food, usually, or a blanket or toy—the kind of thing any small child would want.

Calling was the one-time event that indicated a

Comforter's gift was waking. Newly-wakened Comforters could always be found by the pull and tug of the space around them when they *Called*. Something suddenly appearing out of thin air always caused enough of a ripple that anyone with a smidgen of sensitivity could feel it. But no newly-wakened Comforter had ever *Called* so strongly before. That was indication enough that whoever had *Called* was not the usual toddler or child.

Their coach was not due to reach the Valley of the Holy Comforter for at least another hour. She might as well sort this out as best she could before they arrived at the Sanctuary. Shifting her position and looking into Gia's eyes once more, Karina took a deep breath and firmly grasped the Comforter's Ring which was hanging around her neck on a leather cord. Sending out a quick prayer to the Holy Comforter, she spoke, and the words came tumbling out.

"Gianna, my duties have kept me from home. I have not seen you for more than five years. You are nearly twenty summers now ... legal age to speak for yourself and decide your own future. You are only weeks away from the responsibilities and privileges of an adult! Yet here I am, carting you away like a child, expecting you to be willing to spend nearly ten years in training that usually begins in childhood—"

"—and you feel guilty, Kari. You think that it was through *your* negligence that my gift was not discovered sooner." Gianna stopped speaking and sent out subtle, but vibrant tendrils of comfort to her sister as she stroked the puppy.

Those tendrils ... Karina's gaze sought the window behind Gia as she felt them wash over her, and once more she tried to fit the pieces together. As far as she was aware, Gianna was the first Comforter to be wakened beyond the age of six or seven. Although Karina didn't remember her own *Call,* it had been described to her. She was three, and she had wanted more cake for dessert. Wanted it with quite a bit of determination, apparently, for as she clearly wailed out "Want mo' cake!" it had simply appeared before her. The pull and tug in the air around her left no doubt that the dessert had been *Called.*

Such a child was a blessing to any family. Her parents had eagerly arranged for the monthly lessons which preceded regular training at the Sanctuary. By the time she was twelve, and ready to set out for the Valley, she had already learned a great deal. But it wasn't until she was nearly a vowed Comforter . . . after eight years of intensive Sanctuary training . . . that she had mastered those same tendrils she'd just picked up from Gianna. And Gia had no training whatever.

"What have the last five years been like for you?" prodded Karina tentatively, fishing for another piece of the puzzle.

"Oh, really wonderful! Rufina was born just after your last visit. With my being the youngest, it was nice to have a baby around . . . she was like my own child! As she grew, I let her sleep with me. Such a nice warm presence in the bed. I'd been alone in the bedroom since Shella married Andri."

"Am I missing something?" asked Karina blankly. "I know I've been gone a while, but I had no idea Mother had another baby."

"Not Mother!" laughed Gia, rolling her eyes, "Rufina's mother was Frannie. She was killed in a hunting accident soon after Rufina was born. That's how I came to take care of her."

"Hmmm . . . I don't think I know Frannie; you can tell me about her later. Right now, why don't you tell me how you think your gift managed to remain undetected for so long. Your eyes, for instance . . . no one ever noticed?"

"I guess we miss things we're not looking for, Kari. You *Called* when I was a tiny baby, and I was eight when Mitchel *Called*. He was five. Summer festival was in our village that year, and his family had come with the crowd from the western towns. I remember some of the Council members saying that never again would this generation give us a Comforter. The way I look at it, Kari, they just weren't *expecting* a third Comforter, so no one gave my eyes a second thought."

"But what about your *Gift*? How is it the *Gift* wakened so late?" asked Karina.

"I suppose because I had all I needed or wanted. When a child wants for nothing, she *Calls* for nothing. There was love enough and food enough and warmth enough in our home. As a child, there was always Shella to take care of me if Mother was busy. I was never unbearably sad or lonely . . . especially after Rufina came along. And I never really grieved . . . until the other night, when Rufina was killed. Perhaps my own need for comfort awakened my *Gift*."

Gia's eyes welled up with tears and her voice broke as she continued, "Losing Rufi devastated me. I went to bed more depressed that I'd ever been in my life. I cried myself to sleep. I awoke the next morning still weeping. . . ."

Karina sent out a wave of comfort to Gia, and, after a moment, smiled slowly and continued, "That's when you *Called,* and suddenly there were puppies everywhere! I've never walked into such a chaotic mess,

Gia. I thought father was going to go mad trying to corral them all! I'm glad he let you bring one along, though there were certainly puppies to spare. There must have been a hundred of them!" Karina couldn't help giggling as she remembered. She would never forget the look of desperation on their father's face as he stood amid a sea of pouncing puppies. She knew his shock had begun to dissipate when he began calculating the amount of money dozens of spaniels would bring in. Good hunting dogs were in demand!

After a bit she reached over and stroked Gia's hair. Then, softly, she asked, "Do you have any idea how strong your *Gift* is, Gianna? Even without training, you project the most soothing tendrils I've ever experienced. You will make a strong Comforter, a great asset to people in need of compassion and strength. Can you tell me why your *Gift* might be so deeply rooted in you, so strong?"

Wiping her eyes, Gia smiled faintly and answered, "It was Rufina. She was such a comfort to me. I guess she taught me what it means to comfort others. When I was hurt, she kissed away my tears. She went everywhere with me. We ate together and played together. And Rufina loved the water. Any water . . . even mud puddles! Long walks always meant a bath afterward— for both of us! When I had a special treat for her, she would dance around my feet. And when . . ."

"Whoa! I think I get the point. You found someone who loved you with abandon. That kind of love will indeed teach compassion. Rufina had that gift. The ability to lend comfort, compassion and strength to those in need is not reserved only for those who are chosen to be vowed Comforters."

Satisfied that she had the pieces she was looking for,

and happy that Gianna seemed to be finally rejoicing in the memory of her friend, Karina said "You love Rufina very much. It was her dying that wakened your gift . . . our people will hold her in grateful memory. But I'm sorry you had to lose her, Gia. She must have been a very, very special child."

Gianna picked up the sleepy puppy and kissed her on the nose. A smile broke on her face, and she rolled her eyes once more at Karina as she said "Special, yes. But *child,* Kari? Whatever gave you that idea? Rufina was my *PUP!*"

MARION ZIMMER BRADLEY

THE DARKOVER NOVELS

EXILE'S SONG

A Novel of Darkover

by Marion Zimmer Bradley

Margaret Alton is the daughter of Lew Alton, Darkover's Senator to the Terran Federation, but her morose, uncommunicative father is secretive about the obscure planet of her birth. So when her university job sends her to Darkover, she has only fleeting, haunting memories of a tumultuous childhood. But once in the light of the Red Sun, as her veiled and mysterious heritage becomes manifest, she finds herself trapped by a destiny more terrifying than any nightmare!

- A direct sequel to *The Heritage of Hastur* and *Sharra's Exile*
- With cover art by Romas Kukalis
- ☐ **Hardcover Edition**   UE2705-$21.95
